BY YOUR SIDE

KARLA SORENSEN

For Rebekah,
My inspiration for all the best parts of Casey;
-her sense of style,
-her aversion to budgets,
-her OCD tendencies,
-her ability to justify anything.

But the most important trait that Casey takes from you is
your unwavering and unapologetic optimism.
You have the most incredible gift of positivity, no matter what life has
thrown at you.
For fourteen years, you have been one of the brightest friendships in
my life.
So, this is for you.

1

THERE WAS an oldies song that Casey Steadman's Mom loved to listen to. *Breakin' Up is Hard to Do* by Neal Sedaka. But Casey was going to change the lyrics, at least for this current phase of her life. Instead of *breakin' up*, it really should be *'growin' up* is hard to do'. And it didn't seem like it would be all that hard, right? People grow up and go to school. Maybe college, maybe not (not for Casey, wasn't for her). Married in mid-20's after some carefree years. Babies and a picket fence and a dog (also a no on that for Casey. Eww, hair.) by the time their thirties rolled around.

Only...she'd blown out the sparkly pink candle on her twenty-ninth birthday cupcake a few weeks ago, and what had previously seemed fun and joke-worthy because she was only in her twenties? Not quite as humorous anymore. The handful of entirely lukewarm relationships she'd had just felt sort of sad. Of course she wanted what her parents had, but short of posting a craigslist ad (specifically for non-psychos who were roughly four to five inches taller than her to accommodate her above average height and definitely above average heel collection), that wasn't happening yet either.

Casey wanted *more*.

Sure, she had a decent job. And working at a locally owned hardware and home design store kept her afloat, certainly, but her manager had this ridiculously annoying habit of overlooking every single attempt that she made to push forward. A steady paycheck at a job that she truly loved, and was good at, was one thing. One piece of the puzzle that she'd been completely sure she'd have figured out by now. And a couple years ago, she'd thought it really wasn't that big of a deal to sign a two year lease on a much cheaper apartment than she could actually afford. It's just a place to sleep. It doesn't have to be the fricken Taj Mahal. But ho boy, it only took a few months to realize just how idiotic she'd been. And while she'd had no problem shifting the cost savings from her rent over to her spending money, the three extra locks she'd added to her door and the pepper spray that was permanently lodged under her pillow took away just a teensy bit of the excitement that she got from shoving another shoe box into her hall closet.

Okay. In the hall, because the closet was totally full.

And suddenly, thirty was looming. No more stretching of the golden decade. It had officially snapped back and smacked her square in the face. And every single thing that her parents and four brothers had said to her about how 'ill-advised' it was to move in there, she just didn't listen. She'd be *fine*. It was *only* two years.

Ha. As she was nearing the last few days of the lease that would never end, she found herself playing off just how bad it was. There was absolutely no reason her brothers should actually hear that they were right. Technically, nothing had happened during her time there, so there was no reason for anyone to think otherwise.

Catching her creeptastic neighbor in 4B pulling her underwear from the dryer? Totally innocent. And if she repeated that to herself enough times, she just might actually believe that he hadn't been three seconds away from sniffing it.

So, here she sat...meticulously packing up her entire life because she was meeting with someone tomorrow about a new place to live. A place that she'd only looked at every single time she'd driven to her parents for the past eight years. And last week, she'd seen a 'for rent' sign perched in that huge stretch of emerald green grass. Breaking every speed limit on her drive home that day, Casey hadn't felt her heart settle down until she found the information online.

Three emails later, she had an appointment with the owner. One H.J Miller had asked some awfully specific questions (Yes, she could provide pay stubs for the past six months. No, she'd never changed a flat tire. What good is having four older brothers if not for mechanical issues?). She smiled thinking about it.

"Where did I go wrong?"

Casey looked around her bedroom, the stacks of moving boxes completely taking over the small space. Her Mom's voice came from somewhere behind the stack next to her door. She finally skirted around the edge, and shook her head at where Casey was seated in front of the closet.

"You've never made a wrong move in your life. And certainly not with me," Casey said, running a hand over a royal blue cashmere sweater before she placed it in the opened box next to her. "You know I'm your crowning jewel after having all those miserable boys."

Her mother's face softened. "You love your brothers. They were only miserable when you were little and they would hold you down and maim your Barbies in front of you. No, I must have failed somewhere along the path of motherhood because no daughter of mine would be packing up her entire apartment before she has a new place to live. What on earth are you going to do if this place you're seeing tomorrow doesn't work out?"

"Simple. It's the power of positive thinking at work. I'm packing it all up because I just know when I meet the landlord tomorrow, he or she will fall totally in love with me and let me

sign a lease on the spot. Now, be a good helper and get me
another box so I can pack up the last of my clothes. Then you
could help Rachel in the kitchen if you don't have anywhere else
to be at the moment," she said with her shoulders raised and her
eyes hopeful.

With a resigned expression, her Mom handed her another
box from outside the bedroom door and walked down the
hallway to the kitchen.

Casey sighed in relief at her Mom's easy acceptance of her
explanation. Her family never took her optimism flippantly.
They knew that once she had something in her head, she would
make it happen. Even if this entire endeavor was being driven
by sweat inducing panic, she could still apply the same
principle.

Hopefully. Maybe. Dear Lord, she needed to be able to.

As she folded the last of her sweaters into the box, she looked
around the tiny room she had called home for almost two years.
The walls were still covered in framed black and white candid
shots of her with her favorite people in the world: her four older
brothers, her five nephews, her parents, and her best friends
Rachel and Liz. The pictures were the first things she had
unpacked when she moved in, and they would be the last items
put into boxes when she moved out.

At the sound of jingling, she looked back towards the
doorway and saw Rachel leaning against the frame, twirling her
keys around one finger.

"Why does that look on your face make me nervous?"

"It shouldn't. Just savoring my last moments in this place,
remembering all the good times."

Casey snorted. "What good times? You hated coming here."

"Well, I can't decide between the time we listened at the wall
when your sex-crazed neighbors played 'naughty cabana boy',
which was highly entertaining, I admit. Or the time Liz and I seriously debated calling the cops because we thought there might

be a meth lab down the hall. It's truly difficult to decide what I'll miss most."

They both laughed, and then Rachel got a serious look on her face. "You realize this plan is insane, right? You could very well have packed up all this crap for nothing. And when I say you, I really mean your Mom and me."

Casey smiled a little, not trying too hard to put on a game face for Rachel, because her friend would probably see right through it anyway. "It'll all work out. Have some faith, my vertically challenged friend."

Rachel laughed through her nose, one short puff of air. "You got me there. If only I could take a few of your inches, and about half of your optimism, we'd equal each other out."

Instead of telling her that optimism was in short supply tonight, she just turned and started pulling frames off the wall, carefully wrapping them in towels.

"Seriously though, if anyone can make this work, it would be you, Casey Marie."

Casey turned with a smile, this one taking no effort at all. "That's so surprisingly mushy. I kinda want to hug you now."

"Don't even think about it. I gotta go. I told Marc I'd be home soon."

"Tell him I said hi, and that I am eternally grateful for his beautiful girlfriend's help in my insanely ill-advised packing plan."

Rachel saluted her and walked down the hallway. "Will do. Call me tomorrow if you're homeless."

She stuck her tongue out at Rachel as she left the room. Flipping her trusty sharpie through her fingers, Casey turned back to the boxes she had been labeling. *Short-sleeved tops (red through green), short sleeved tops (blue through white), warm boots, cute boots, flats, heels 1, heels 2, heels 3, sweaters (red through green), sweaters (blue through white)* and so on until she stood back to nod in approval at her progress. When she saw it all put together like this...everything in its place, colors blocked together, all her shoes in their original boxes with a Polaroid of each on the outside? Lordy, she felt good. Like extra-30%-off-the-sale-rack-at-DSW good.

Settling. That's what it was. Which, yeah, was a nice way to say she was completely OCD. It was almost as if the more things spun out of control in any area of her life, the more she needed to do this. Because this could make everything feel just a little less daunting. Whip out her label maker, organize her recipe box, clean out her Pinterest boards, or separate her clothes by sleeve length, then color, and then fabric within the color groups.

No place to live and all her earthly possessions in boxes? No problemo.

She'd just organize the shitake out of the rest of her life. And those boxes? Definitely the result of overcompensation about how fricken freaked out she was about this new place not working out.

Deciding that her bedroom was packed enough, she stood and stretched, releasing a groan that came from all the way down in her toes.

When she turned the corner to find her Mom packing away all of her kitchen utensils, she just stood and watched for a few seconds. Her Mom meticulously organized the contents of the box. Where she got her OCD tendencies? Yeah, no shocker there.

"So, I've been thinking," she started slowly, after she'd plopped onto the floor. "Tomorrow is pretty important."

"Yes, it is." Her Mom stopped what she was doing to look straight into Casey's eyes. The Mom look. That *I'm not screwing around right now* look. "Because if this landlord doesn't like you, you sure aren't bringing all these boxes to our house."

One side of Casey's mouth tipped up. "Oh, I wouldn't dream of it. And that's not what I meant. I'm thinking about the impression I have to give off tomorrow. Trustworthy, dependable, stable, those kinds of things. It's important they see me that way straight off the bat."

Her Mom didn't respond, just kept putting items in the box. After about thirty seconds, she stopped. And looked up at Casey again.

"No. You do not need a new outfit for this."

"Not what I was thinking." *Totally what she was thinking.* "Just recognizing the occasion for what it is."

She was already doing a mental cataloging of her wardrobe and finding it lacking. Plus, darn the luck, she'd packed almost everything she owned. No sense in unpacking it now. And it was *something* for her to do. Going through racks of clothes, crisp and pressed and soft, that she could do. Just center herself when she felt so, so...not centered.

Her fingers played with the frayed edge of her jeans while she studied her Mom. Watched her take in a deep breath and hold it for a few seconds before releasing it quickly, which was her tell-tale sign that she had something to say but didn't know how to say it.

"In all seriousness, Case, what are you going to do if you don't get the lease tomorrow?"

Casey tried not to, but she could feel the hairs on the back of her neck start to prickle like they always did when she felt like she had to justify herself. Cheeks? Flushed and hot. And what made it about a trillion times worse, is that she knew that some justification was completely called for right now.

"Why wouldn't I get it?" she said lightly, shrugging her shoulders. "I have a decent credit score, and I've never been late on rent at any of the places I've lived."

"I know, and I'm not asking as a reflection on you. I don't want you to get your hopes so high on this one place if it doesn't work out." She placed a hand on Casey's arm, totally doing that Mom thing where they thought it would somehow soften the blow of what they were saying. "We're so proud of you for how much you're trying at work, and I know that hasn't always been easy on you. On top of that, we see how you've been saving money knowing your lease is almost up here. Those are big, really great things you're doing. Your father and I just worry about you because we don't want you to be disappointed."

"It's okay Mom, I don't blame you for wondering," she said on an exhale. "But I do have a week left on my lease here. So if this landlord is a complete idiot and doesn't say yes, I have some time to look for another place."

"They *would* have to be an idiot. I'd rent to you," she said.

"You just told me I couldn't come back home if it doesn't work out."

"You can't. But if I owned rental property, I would have no problem taking your money."

Casey shook her head, but laughed all the same. She chewed her bottom lip for a few seconds while her Mom stretched the packing tape over the box she had just filled.

"We're pretty much done here. You can feel free to head home. I know Dad likes to see you before he heads to bed."

"Are you sure? I don't mind finishing up in here."

"Yeah, go ahead. I was thinking I should go to Macy's and pay my bill." She peeked at her Mom through her lashes. A sigh blew through her Mom's lips.

"Don't spend too much."

"I'm sure I have no idea what you're talking about."

2

"Dangnabbit."

The tip of Casey's mascara brush jabbed into the corner of her eye when she decided to give her lashes a quick second coat. With one watering eye open, she checked the time on her phone and then chucked the wand onto the counter with a huff.

In retrospect, she should have ditched the last makeup touch up, shouldn't have made a second cup of coffee and really, really shouldn't have taken the time to put a fresh coat of OPI *I'm not really a waitress* red on her nails. She flew down the stairs to the parking lot, careful to avoid the potholes in the parking lot that never seemed to get filled. When she side stepped a particularly dangerous one, she recited the ad for the duplex over and over in her head, like a good luck talisman.

2 BD/1 BATH duplex for rent, $900/month, utilities included. 850 sq. ft. Must be non-smoker, no pets allowed. Newly updated kitchen, appliances included, new carpet throughout, shared garage space.

She folded herself into her two-door Civic, the black color of her car sucking in every particle of hot air within a full city block.

The built-up heat in the car took her breath away. She cranked the A/C and her radio as high as they would go as soon as the engine turned over. The black pencil skirt she was wearing offered little to no air flow to her legs, but it screamed 'Responsible Tenant' and so it was looking like she'd just have to deal with some sweaty thighs.

She hit her cruising speed on the highway, a respectable ten over the speed limit, and drummed her fingers on the steering wheel along with the radio. The thought of finally getting out of her apartment caused a pulsing energy through her that seemed to match the beat of the song.

She felt the vibration of her phone from where she had it tucked next to her leg. *Favorite Brother* flashed across the glowing screen. She snorted, wondering when Dylan got a hold of her phone, and jabbed her thumb on the screen to answer the call.

"What's up, favorite brother?"

"See? I knew you'd automatically assume it was me. You always were a smart girl." She heard the clang of kitchen sounds in the background, telling her that he was at work.

"Oh, wait. Dylan? I guessed Michael. He did wash and wax my car last week, easily sliding him into my number one slot."

"Hey, I don't need to buy my sister's affections. Aren't you supposed to meeting with the landlord?"

"I'm running just a couple minutes late." She hooked into the right lane just before the exit she needed, earning a honk from the car behind her. "Wait. If you knew I was meeting with them, why are you calling me?"

"Because I knew you'd be late. Don't you think this should be the one day in your life that you show up when you're supposed to?"

She grimaced. "Yeah, yeah, story of my life, I know. I swear, I tried so hard today, and it's like my body rebels when I'm actually running on time. My limbs don't work right. I almost stabbed myself in the eye with my mascara because I was trying so hard to hurry." Casey waved apologetically at the disgruntled driver as they whipped past her. "So what's up?"

"Nothing, just wanted to wish you luck."

"Well, isn't that strangely generous of you. What do you want?"

"Don't read into it too much, I'm just sick of wearing kevlar every time I go visit you."

She rolled her eyes. "It is not that bad. But thanks anyway."

"You better hope it's a dude."

"Why's that?" She totally knew why.

"Because you might be forgiven for being late since you're not ugly."

"Gee thanks," she said dryly.

"You're very welcome." Casey yanked the phone away from her ear when Dylan hollered at one of the kitchen staff. "Ah, I gotta go. Good luck."

He hung up before she could answer, so she tossed her phone in her purse, shaking her head. He was right though. Casey had learned long ago the power of killer shoes at the end of a pair of long legs could help someone overlook her propensity for showing up late. It only worked with woman if their idea of fashionable footwear wasn't Birkenstocks. Ick. From a shoe standpoint, nothing was worse than chunky flat sandals that made a woman's feet look like beige bricks.

As she turned off the road and followed the slight curve of the driveway, she smiled at the fact that every single thing about the property looked as perfectly maintained as usual, and the flash of longing to live there was so white hot that she almost had to crank up the AC again.

The rain from the past three days hadn't done much to break the cloying humidity, but everything was thick and green because of it, so it was a fair trade. There were tall bushes of prairie grasses alongside the three garages that sat adjacent to each building, positioned in a large semi-circle at the end of the driveway. Along the front were red geraniums, over-sized hostas, and various bright shades of astilbe that spiked up against the river rock facade that propped up the bottom half of the houses.

The part of Casey that never really left work was impressed with the cooler tones of the rock that were picked up by the grayish blue siding and crisp white trim. The houses sat back off the street a ways, the driveway lined on one side with lilac bushes and covered on the other side with the boughs of two mature oak trees that towered over the front yard. The way the road curved back to the three buildings gave it privacy from surrounding neighbors.

Moving here would be a giant step towards whittling away at the list of "should have finished by thirty" that hovered right at the front of her mind. It was a beautiful place that she'd always admired. If the inside even remotely matched the outside, then it was worth every extra penny that she'd be paying in rent.

She found the correct number on the first of three buildings and saw a dark pickup truck parked in front of the unattached two stall garage. She did a little victory dance in her seat at the realization that the vehicle was decidedly male. One point for the killer heels, and another for the pencil skirt.

She smoothed a hand over her hair, pulling the low ponytail over her shoulder.

"Here we go Case, you got this." After pulling down her mirror for a final check, she gave her reflection a thumbs-up and then pulled herself up out of the car.

JAKE PACED in the living room, annoyance surging with every minute that passed. Nothing aggravated him more than people who were late. Which was borderline comical since the Army drilled precision in all things into every soldier, but then the majority of the time the 'hurry up and wait' mentality prevailed.

He was supposed to meet with a potential new tenant at two, and as the clock quickly approached ten after, he knew she would have to meet every single other criteria on his checklist. He'd already run a credit check with the information she gave him, and her score of 640 had given her a decent foundation in his eyes. Being late though? Knocked her down a peg.

The day that he'd signed the paperwork, purchasing the buildings from his Mom, he'd felt the pressing weight of familial responsibility back on his shoulders. And heavy though it might have been, he welcomed it. There was so much he hadn't been around for with her since he had joined the Army at eighteen, and being able to take this from her in the wake of her cancer diagnosis made him feel like he was finally doing right by his Mom. The upkeep was getting too expensive for her to hire out and, physically, she wasn't able to do it on her own.

She'd been ecstatic to see the immediate changes that Jake had brought to the exterior, telling him that maybe he'd be able to realize the potential she'd always seen in this place. And when she'd passed away six months later, he knew that this was still something he could do for her.

Something he had to do for her.

He could make these six units — five discounting the one he'd be living in for the time being — into everything she'd dreamed of. With mature, responsible renters who would respect everything he was trying to build.

The last person he'd met with had nearly given him a contact high from the marijuana fumes that wafted in with him, effectively ending their meeting. Jake had a put a lot of sweat and even more of his inheritance into the duplexes after he bought them last year, and wanted the renters to be worthy of his investment. He didn't expect perfection by any means, but because he shared the other half of this duplex, it was important that they could coexist.

At two o'eight, he heard a car pull into the driveway and

looked out the front window to see a dark colored Civic park behind his truck. He ran a hand over his short black hair and let out his breath in a short puff to clamp down his annoyance at her late arrival. He looked over at his two year old German Shepherd, Remy, who was pacing the living room beside him. It looked like tardiness stressed him out too. It might be a little underhanded to include his dog in these meetings, because most owners wouldn't. But Remy had free reign of the two and a quarter acres that surrounded the three buildings, and it was important for Jake to see how someone would react when they weren't expecting the dog. The first woman he'd met with had literally screamed and practically climbed up Jake's back like a howler monkey.

Jake gave him the hand signals to sit and stay, and walked through the dining area towards the door to greet Casey. She knocked a couple times, and he called for her to come in as he rounded the corner into the kitchen.

Long was his first impression. Long legs, long hair, and long lashes. She was tall, only a few inches shorter than his nearly six-foot-four frame. He had to ignore his instinctual male reaction to overlook her tardiness simply because she was a looker. Casey stretched pink lips over white teeth for a I-can't-even-fathom-not-getting-what-I-want smile and extended a hand toward Jake.

"You must be Mr. Miller, it's *such* a pleasure to meet you. I'm Casey Steadman." Her handshake was pleasantly firm, but his spine straightened at the lack of an apology for being late. He decided not to meet her smile with one of his own.

"Call me Jake." He pulled his hand back, crossed his arms over his chest and met her gaze straight on. "Did you have trouble finding the place, Ms. Steadman?"

Her smile wavered for just a fraction of a second, but he gave her credit for a quick recovery.

"Oh, not at all. My parents don't live that far from here, so I've admired this property for years. I just ran into that awful Friday afternoon traffic on 131, you know how that is."

He could swear he saw her eyelashes flutter for effect as she met his hard stare evenly. Seriously, women had it so easy. He kept his eyes locked on her for a few more seconds while trying to figure out how full of it she was.

"Uh huh." Very full of it, he decided, but at least she didn't come in on a cloud of recreational drugs. "Why don't I show you the rest of the place and we can talk about whether you'll be the right fit or not."

Without waiting for a response at that, he spread his hands. "As you can see, everything has been renovated recently. Cherry cabinets, floor and stainless steel appliances all were installed at the same time. Mosaic tile back splash is new as well as the counters."

He saw her eyes widen in appreciation of the room, and felt a swell of pride at his handiwork. It was the first kitchen he'd completely gutted and finished on his own, and was pleased at how it turned out.

"I love all of it," she gushed, not even trying to keep the excitement out of her voice. "You have no idea how long I've been cooking in a kitchen where appliances from the '70s went to die. The whole room was a pea green nightmare." She ran a hand across the front of the refrigerator as she passed through and hummed appreciatively. Something tightened low inside him at the sight of her red tipped nails drifting across the stainless steel. "You did all of this?"

He nodded. "I'm still working on the other units."

"Well, color me impressed. Is this laminate flooring, or real hardwood?"

"I went with the laminate. It's a lot more durable, and low maintenance."

She nodded, then looked back up at him when he didn't say anything else.

"Unless you have any specific questions about the kitchen, let me show you the rest of the place." One side of her lips tipped up, and she followed him as he turned the corner. Remy was just where Jake had commanded him to stay, eyeing Casey with interest. At the sight of the ninety pound dog framed under the window, Jake saw her freeze mid-step.

"Whoa, what's with Rin Tin Tin?" she asked, turning her big, ridiculously blue eyes towards him. "I thought no pets were allowed."

"Rin Tin Tin would be my dog, Remy." Jake searched her body language for any signs of fear and didn't see any. Just smooth stretches of skin, and curves under a skirt that should be illegal. He cleared his throat as if to erase the thought. "And no other pets are allowed, just him."

At that she arched one eyebrow in a silent question.

He signaled Remy to heel. The dog immediately came and sat next to Jake's right leg and looked up adoringly when his hand came to rest on Remy's head. "The perk of owning the place is that I get to make the rules. He rarely barks, isn't destructive, and does his business outside where dogs are supposed to. If I knew that any dog that came in here would be like him, then maybe I'd allowed it, but I don't know that so I don't allow it."

She hummed, pursing her lips and looked down towards Remy, but made no move to pet him. "Does he eat his own crap?"

"No," he snorted. "Why?"

She shrugged her shoulders, still giving Remy a long, considering look. "Just wondering. It's one of those things about animals I will just never understand. I guess he's cool with me."

Jake wanted to roll his eyes, he really, really did. Somehow he restrained himself and managed a short nod. "Wonderful. Let's move on."

After she made a slow circle through the living room, admiring the crown molding he'd decided to splurge on, he took her down the hallway that led to the two bedrooms and the full bathroom. Remy stayed glued to his side as they walked, and Jake thought he heard her say that the second bedroom would be a 'completely fabulous' closet room. He rubbed the back of his neck while she looked through the bathroom.

As he showed her the other two rooms, he discovered that she had a good job and had been with the same company for over ten years. She got points for that, and for the fact that she said she was carrying pepper spray in her purse. She had four older brothers — which probably explained why she knew to carry pepper spray — two of whom were married, and her parents lived about five minutes away. Having that much family seemed overwhelming to Jake.

As an only child of parents who had both passed away well before their time, he couldn't imagine it. He knew some guys in his unit thought he was a prick, but a certain level of detachment became as basic and necessary to him as breathing. Made it hard to comprehend someone like Casey, who had shared names and ages of her nephews in the first ten minutes of meeting him.

And none of it had he asked her about. Other than pointing out features of the duplex, he had to talk a blessedly small amount and found out quite a lot about Casey Steadman. She seemed nervous as one sentence ran right into the next, each dropping another small piece of information. To him, it felt like with each room they looked at, her nerves multiplied, piling up onto each other until she couldn't do anything else but talk. And yeah, he could have made more of an effort to put her at ease, but he decided to let this run its course in exchange for her running late.

Like he could see the 'dream renter' checklist laid out in his head, Jake took every sentence that spilled out of her rapidly moving mouth and checked it against the yes or no columns. And even though Casey was pretty heavily weighing down the yes side, something made him want to pull back. Was it idiotic to think about turning away his first decent shot at a tenant because she was smokin' hot? Possibly.

But she was just so...overwhelming. Her hair was. Her body

was. Her eyes? Yeah. Her smile was like a friggin spotlight, every-where she unleashed it.

They finished the tour, and she turned her bright aqua colored gaze right at him, completely unabashed in how hopeful she looked. It made him twitchy.

"I, uhh," he started and then cleared his throat. Why was this so hard? Credit score was there. Steady job was there. Her smile spread across her face, so naturally, he looked down at his hands where he'd parked them on his hips. "I'll have to think about it. I'll call you soon and let you know."

The look in her eyes shuttered first, and then her smile fell a second later. "You're saying no?"

Oh hell, he felt like he'd kicked a puppy. "I'm saying I need to think about it. This is a big deal to me, and I need to know I have the right person living here. I still have a lot of work to do on the other units, and I need someone who's going to be...the right fit."

For a moment, he thought she was going to say something, but she closed her mouth and just looked at him. And even though she nodded her head, the movement was so faint that it could hardly be considered an agreement. The air in the kitchen was so thick and heavy with her disappointment. At first, Jake thought she was going to leave without saying anything, but he was pleasantly surprised that she turned around and stuck her hand out to him.

"I really hope I hear from you soon, Jake. I love it here."

He took her hand, and nodded. "It was nice to meet you, Casey."

Yeah. She didn't like that response. With a sad looking smile, and a tiny wave over her shoulder, she walked through the door.

Remy pushed against Jake's leg, and Jake smiled down at him. "What? You disagree with my decision too?"

While he was scratching behind Remy's ear, he heard the very distinct sound of click-clacking heels against the driveway. Fast, determined sounding, click-clacking heels. Coming back toward the house.

And then a *rap rap rap* against the door. "Jake? It's me."

Warring between a grin and a sigh, Jake walked over to open the door again. And the Casey that was looking back at him did not wear a defeated smile. Oh no. This Casey looked combat ready.

3

WELL. He looked mildly amused, which was a good start. Because as soon as she'd grabbed the door handle on her car, the hot black metal feeling like it was burned into her skin, she knew there was no freaking way she was leaving this place without a twelve month lease, signed, sealed, delivered, notarized, whatever legal things could possibly be done to make it *hers*.

Just the thought of all those stacks and stacks of boxes in her apartment, and the looks of her family's faces when she had to tell them that she had to try again, oh no. No way. There was no way she could handle that. That place was hers. She knew it.

So she snapped her spine into place, threw back her shoulders, and marched back to the door that was firmly shut in her face.

Appropriate. Annoying, but very appropriate. And after a brisk, confident knock, she watched Jake open the door and then take her in. Yeah, he wasn't stupid. He could clearly recognize that she wasn't going to sulk off.

"Forget something?" he asked, not quite moving to let her back in. So, she did what any woman would do in that situation, she stepped right up into him, so that he had no choice but to back up. Unless he wanted to have a height measuring contest. Truthfully, with her heels, her mouth would probably land somewhere around his chin. He was tall. Really tall.

But so was she.

"Yup," she answered after she'd walked back to the kitchen counter. "I forgot to ask what I can do to change your mind. Jake, I have never been late with rent in my life. And I know you ran my credit score."

With two fingers, he scratched the side of his jaw. The rough, scrape of sound echoed through the still, quiet house, and she forced herself to let him think.

"It's not your credit score. That came in just fine."

"So, what is it then?"

"Do I have to give a reason?"

She furrowed her brow, chewing on the inside of her lip. "Technically, no. But you seem like a fair guy. I would be a great tenant, Jake. A *perfect* tenant."

He still just looked. Gah, she wanted to hide behind the counter at the way he narrowed his eyes at her.

"I swear, you won't even know I'm here."

The quirk of one eyebrow told her just what he thought of that statement. "Other than paying your rent on time, of course."

"Of course," she said with a furious nod. "So are you saying yes?"

He leaned back against the fridge, crossing his arms over his chest, the pop of muscles in his biceps momentarily drawing her eye. "Why does it mean so much to you?"

Casey blew a breath out of pursed lips, and shrugged her shoulders a little. "I've always loved this property, I told you that earlier. And yeah, it's closer to my family than I live now, but I just...it feels right. It feels *important* for me to be here. Does that make sense?"

Mentally crossing her fingers while he mulled that over, Casey really, really didn't want to explain to him that moving into this place made her feel like the rest of her list was just a little bit more attainable.

"So, in a couple months, am I going to have to remind you of your promise of perfection?"

She squealed and flung her arms around him. "Oh, thank you, thank you, *thank you!*"

When she realized that he'd completely frozen up, she dropped her arms and stepped back.

"Sorry," she said on a rush, digging through her purse for her checkbook. "I get a little carried away when I'm excited."

"Uh huh. I'd noticed."

"Tuck, do you think it's possible for you to carry a bit more than a couple fricken pillows?"

The voice behind her came from Dylan, who was struggling with her TV. When she was little, her Mom had told her about a town in Kentucky called Cayce, and in her eight year old mind she was completely convinced that the town was named after her. Her brothers had started calling her Kentucky, then Tuck shortly after. Twenty years later, they still used it on occasion.

It was two days after she had signed her lease, and her brothers and Dad were helping her move in. With an armful of colorful throw pillows, Casey followed Michael and her Dad as they carried her couch and strategized the best way to get it into the living room. She stopped in her tracks quickly enough that Dylan blew out an expletive but still managed to not run into her or drop her TV.

"Now why would I do that, dearest brother of mine? Don't men thrive on these types of displays of brute strength?" she said, laughing when he scowled. "And don't swear."

"So sorry. Now move your A-S-S before your TV dies a horrible death on the driveway. If you had a flat screen like everyone else in the world, I wouldn't have to worry about dropping it."

"Ass doesn't count as a swear word, Dylan. And that TV works just fine. If it bothers you so much, you go right ahead and buy me a new one." They were about to walk through the door when their Dad's voice came booming from the living room.

"Casey. Where do you want this couch?" After setting the pillows on the kitchen counter, she turned into the main living room. Her Dad took in the room around him while he waited for her to make up her mind.

There was a bright square of sun pulsing onto the off-white carpet coming through the large window that faced west. Most people would probably pull the shades and block the heat that would come along with it, but Casey didn't see herself ever doing that. She had suffered through almost thirty years of practically sunless Michigan winters, and she loved every second of the heat and sunshine that dominated the summers. Without having to think too much about it, she knew that window would be the centerpiece. Immediately she thought of a new fabric that had come into work that would make a killer valance.

"If you guys could put it along this wall that'd be great," she said, pointing to the wall to the right of the window. "I want to be able to see the TV from the kitchen, so I'll want the entertainment center opposite of the couch."

Dylan walked past her and set the TV down on the floor next to wall she had indicated, while Michael and her Dad moved the couch into place. Tate and Caleb came down the hallway from her bedroom, where they had just deposited the last of the boxes for that room.

"Looks good kiddo," her Dad said, clapping a hand on her shoulder.

She looked up and smiled. "Thanks Dad, I think so too. It'll look even better once I paint in here."

"I didn't think you could paint anything in a rental."

"A mere technicality. I know I can get him to say yes." She heard snickers coming from her brothers. She chose to ignore them.

Pulling her into his side, her Dad asked, "What are you thinking for this room?"

She squinted a bit, mentally running through paint chips in her head. Occupational hazard. But on the plus side, she rarely needed to look at a fan deck at work to find the right color.

"Maybe Roasted Pumpkin, or Georgian Brick. It would warm it up, and go well with the earth tones he picked when he redid the kitchen."

"'He' being your new landlord?"

"Yeah, Jake. I didn't see his truck in the garage, so he must not be home, but you should meet him the next time you're here. He seems a little serious for my taste, but nice enough."

And hot. She definitely did not say that part.

Her Dad's eyes hardened slightly, but enough that she noticed it. "And he lives in the other half of this building?"

Casey held up her hands as soon as she saw the spark of interest from all four brothers at that little tidbit.

"Seriously. Slow your roll. He's talking about my landlord."

The other three went about their business again, because they were sane. And rational. They were the nice brothers.

"Do you have deadbolts on all your doors?" Dylan asked, arms folded across his puffed up chest.

"Yes. Clearly. Since you checked them all already."

"What about an alarm system?"

Casey smiled sweetly, batting her eyelids because she knew it would piss him off. "Only if you're going to buy one for me."

Tate snorted from behind her. Dylan ignored it. "But it's just the two of you back here? Is that safe?"

Okay. At that moment, the attention from the brothers was back.

"How old is he, Casey?" Tate asked.

She met his gaze evenly, not looking at the others. "I'd guess around thirty."

Tate thought for a second, and then blinked slowly before asking another question. "Married?"

"Well gee Tate, we didn't get around to discussing his relationship status." She could feel every eye in the place burning into her. She would trade all four of them in for a houseful of cats. Hairy, shedding, hair ball hacking cats.

"But," she conceded, "he wasn't wearing a ring. And I told him I carry pepper spray in my purse, so I don't think he'll be assaulting me anytime soon."

At that she got a smile out of him. "Why'd you do that? Doesn't seem like typical first conversation material."

She wasn't about to tell her five trigger happy bodyguards it was because he made her so nervous that she had been babbling like an idiot. The whole time she'd been there, he hadn't come close to cracking a smile. She had felt something flash down her spine when he narrowed his eyes at her, and it made her go just a wee bit crazy. No way, she definitely couldn't tell them that. They'd be locked and loaded before she could say Manolo Blahnik.

"You boys taught me well. I deal with enough overly friendly contractors at work, I can spot 'em a mile away. Trust me, he's not a creeper." She looked around the room at them while they mulled that over, but it was her Dad who spoke first.

"Alright Case, we'll trust your judgment. Just be careful. I've only got one daughter, you know."

She turned back to her Dad and wrapped her arms around his waist. "I know, Dad. How about the next time I see him, I'll tell him I keep a loaded AR-15 under the bed." She winked up at him as he puffed out a laugh.

Dylan rolled his eyes and spoke slowly, as if she was a toddler. "Case, do you know what an AR-15 is?"

"I know that I heard Natalie telling Mom that if Tate bought one before they got married he'd be sleeping on the couch for six months," she said with a tight smile as Tate blushed and received a grin and an elbow in his side from Caleb. "So my guess is that it's big and expensive."

"That it is," her Dad replied.

"One pair of those stupid looboo whatever heels you drool over probably costs more than that gun," Dylan said in Tate's defense. "And I don't think you could defend yourself with them either."

"How about I kick you in the nuts with one of my stilettos and we see how they work as a weapon," Casey snapped. "And they're called Louboutins, moron."

"Okay kids, that's enough," her Dad said good-naturedly. Everyone in the family knew that Dylan and Casey's bickering didn't have any real bite behind it. "We've got more boxes, the entertainment center and that big dresser to bring in. Let's get moving, because your Mom will have my hide if I'm not home for dinner."

Two hours later, Casey was alone on the couch, chilled glass of moscato in hand, happily surveying the chaos surrounding her. Sweat made her shirt cling to her back, and her bare feet were propped up on the coffee table. Dishes and glasses were almost unpacked, TV was hooked up, DVD collection put away (alphabetically, of course), and she had a good head start on getting the bathroom organized. For the first time since moving out of her parent's house six years earlier, she felt like she was *home*. Contentment soaked into her bones as the wine relaxed her from the inside out.

Slowly, she stood up off the couch and winced at the sore muscles all over her body. She'd be moving like an eighty year old tomorrow, guaranteed. She walked down the hallway to her bedroom and stood in doorway looking over the photos that were already up on the wall, and the bed that was already made up. Casey smoothed a hand across her crisp white duvet, and straightened a couple of the purple and gray throw pillows that were heaped on top.

She set her wine glass on the dresser and flopped back onto the bed, pulling in a deep breath through her nose and letting it out slowly. Casey turned to her side and looked at the dresser. It would probably be better on the other wall, closer to the closet for picking out an outfit.

Jake's truck rumbled into the driveway, the headlights slicing bright yellow light through her room. She pushed herself off the bed and walked into the other bedroom across the hall from hers, its window looking towards the garage that she and Jake would share. She wasn't trying to spy on him...not really. She just wanted to see if she had remembered him correctly.

Maybe today he'd be short.

And ugly.

With a mullet.

Not short, definitely not ugly and no mullet in sight. He walked around the truck, slowly rolling his head back and forth as if to work out the same kind of kinks that she felt too, and opened the passenger door to let his dog out. Good grief, that animal was massive. Remy bounded out of the garage and into the yard behind the houses.

With the dusk settling around him, Jake stood at the edge of the driveway and watched his dog, giving her a perfect background of his profile. No one would confuse him for a pretty boy. No siree. This one was all male. He could probably snap one of the oak trees in the front yard with his bare hands. Definitely not her type. She was almost completely positive about it. Maybe.

Oh sure, he was a ten on a scale of one to Ryan Gosling. But dark and broody didn't typically rate high for her.

Dylan had told Casey after her breakup with Rick six months prior that she'd win a Nobel Peace Prize if she could figure out what her type was. When her brothers asked why she dumped him, they apparently needed more of an explanation than he was too *preppy chic* for her. Rachel and Liz totally got it.

Peering at Jake through the side of the blinds, she had to take a deep breath to try and squash the cracked out hummingbirds that had taken up residence in her stomach. He was grumpy and obviously incapable of smiling. And he had a dog. Hummingbirds needed to move along somewhere else, because nothing about Jake, other than the quite impressive height, made much sense for her.

With one last wistful glance at the broad shoulders and long legs, Casey sighed and turned around to walk back into her bedroom. And promptly tripped over a box that she forgot was behind her.

"Owwwwwwwwie." She rubbed her calf where the box had clipped her, knowing it would result in an ugly bruise in the next few days. She leaned back against the wall to compose herself and couldn't help the giggle that escaped her lips. "That's real smooth Steadman, the man has you falling all over yourself."

With a groan she pushed off the wall and walked back into her bedroom where she tossed back the rest of her wine and then started getting ready for bed.

4

THE DRESSER HAD TO MOVE. Casey had let it stay for two more days while she continued to get settled. She was pleased with all of the progress she had made, and knew it was worth the week of vacation she had taken at work. But her initial thought was right: the dresser had to be on the opposite side of her bedroom. After trying unsuccessfully to move it herself, Casey knew she should ask for help. She sent Dylan a text to see if he could come over and move it for her, but was promptly denied saying that it was her own fault for not thinking about it when she had all the men there. There were days where she seriously considered trading him in for a coat rack.

Earlier in the day she had heard the buzz of a power tool coming from one of the other buildings, and from the lack of any other cars coming in or out, she knew that Jake must still be doing work on it before taking on any other renters. After pinching her cheeks for a little natural color, she walked outside and crossed the driveway.

She reached the door where she heard the steady pound of a hammer, took a deep breath and rapped her knuckles lightly against the aluminum frame.

"Yeah, come in." Just the sound of his voice made her feel like someone lit a sparkler behind her belly button. It was low and rough and had just the slightest hint of annoyance behind it. And for the life of her, she could not figure out why that was so freaking hot.

"It's Casey, I hope you don't mind me interrupting." The hammering stopped, and she heard his heavy footsteps from the living room towards where she stood just inside the door in a kitchen layout identical to hers, without the upgrades. Light oak cabinets (which weren't bad depending on what they were paired with) but in here it was with a country blue and pink wallpaper border. Eww.

Jake stopped in the dining area and stared at her, his dark eyebrows knit together in confusion. "What are you doing here?"

Crap. He seemed annoyed and Casey noticed immediately that his eyes narrowed much in the same way that they did when she first met him.

"Well, I tried to move something in my room and it's too heavy for me, so I was wondering if you had a couple minutes to spare." One side of her mouth tipped up in a smile. He stood there for a few long heartbeats, regarding her with a slight wariness in his dark eyes, and it gave her a few seconds to study him again. A plain white t-shirt stretched just right across his chest, paired with worn jeans, and a tool belt slung low on his hips painted a pretty virile picture. And oh, the muscles. She'd never been particularly attracted to anyone this *big*, but for the life of her she couldn't remember why. She couldn't remember her own last name at the moment.

He nodded slowly, as if not confident of his own decision.

"Yeah, I can do that. Just let me finish in here a second." Still no smile, but at least he hadn't kicked her out. She exhaled a breath she didn't know she was holding while he turned to go back into the family room. Looking around as she wandered into the adjacent dining room, she was even more impressed with the transformation he had managed in her place, and she told him so while he methodically pounded the hammer in the other room. He grunted in response, but she couldn't really tell if it was good or bad.

"No, I mean it. You made it perfectly transitional. Not all men can think big picture when it comes to picking finishes."

"Transitional? Am I supposed to know what that means?"

"A decorating style that's between contemporary and traditional. Brown or tan would be the main accent colors, paired with mainly creams and whites. You know, it *transitions* easily between the two styles."

He stopped hammering, and peered over his shoulder at her. Mmm, good shoulders. "Are you an interior designer or something?"

Casey looked down at her sandals and clenched her jaw briefly. It was the biggest source of contention between her and her least favorite person in the *entire* world, her coworker, Melinda. That little pixie had a piece of paper from Michigan State that said she was an interior designer. Casey just had innately impeccable taste and superior customer service that had propelled her to manage the wallpaper department at Hearth and Home, where she'd worked for the past decade. Melinda never failed to flaunt her degree whenever she had a chance, especially in front of their manager Tom who was always panting at her heels, but Casey could take a small amount of pride that customers easily preferred her over the blond midget. They didn't care she didn't have a degree. No reason Jake needed to know that though.

She nodded, rather than tell him an outright lie. "Making West Michigan a more beautiful place, one room at a time." He turned back to what he was doing, and she continued her slow perusal of the unfinished rooms.

"So where did you go for all your supplies? I know I've never seen you at Hearth and Home."

"I usually go to Home Depot."

"Please don't use that word in front of me," she groaned. Again, he turned over his shoulder to stare at her. "Home Depot, that's a swear word at work. You should really support local business. We've been family-owned for seventy five years, all headquartered right here in town."

And as she said it, an idea occurred to her. She could see the proverbial light bulb appear over her head. It was all bright and shiny and brilliant. But it would need to be approached in just the right way with Jake. She quickly realized she couldn't skate by on her charms with this one. For whatever reason, he seemed to see right the heck through her. It was disconcerting. Hot, but disconcerting. As she turned that thought over in her head, she realized he had pulled himself up to his full height, geez, at least four inches taller than her, and was staring at her expectantly.

"Oh. Sorry, let's go."

He stayed a step behind her as they walked outside again, she imagined to discourage conversation. Like *that* would deter her.

"So, did all the units look like that when you bought them?" She swore she heard a sigh as she asked the question.

"Slight variances, but pretty much, yeah."

"Well, I approve of the changes. Shiny brass fixtures don't deserve to exist outside of 1992." She stole a glance sideways to see his reaction, and wasn't even mildly surprised to see it unchanged. *Here goes step one....*

"Did you ever think about getting a professional stager once you've finished renovating? They can work wonders, and you might even be able to get more rent if it's done properly."

At that, she saw his eyebrows rise fractionally as he looked over at her.

"Stager? It's like you're speaking a different language today."

She exhaled a soft laugh. "Someone who comes in and sets up the rooms in a way that makes them more appealing to buyers than an empty space would. Lays everything out so people can see themselves in the house easily and what it's capable of looking like. It's a pretty specific skill set and people will pay big bucks for someone to do it before an open house."

He actually looked interested until she said that. The eyebrows that had raised fractionally pushed back down over his dark eyes.

"Pay someone to move some couches and hang a picture? Yeah, right."

Bingo. Step two. She held her response as he reached past her to open the door, and stepped back to let enter first. Hot man plus chivalry? Yes please.

"Wow, it looks great in here. You've done a lot in three days."

Genuinely surprised at his compliment, it was her turn to look over her shoulder at him. "Thanks. I still have a few ideas, and some pieces stored at my parents that I couldn't use in my last apartment, but I'm really happy with it so far." She chewed the inside of her mouth as he followed her down the hall into her bedroom. *Patience, don't rush it.* She noticed how he took in the family room she was so happy with. Her ivory micro suede couch was a splurge last year after her Christmas bonus, and she loved how it looked with aqua, orange and brown throw pillows covering it. She had achieved just the right mix of patterns and solids. She paused inside the doorway to her bedroom and felt him stop just behind her. "So, I'd like to move this dresser across the room to the opposite wall, but I couldn't do it on my own."

When he passed by her, his bicep brushed up against her shoulder, sending a spear of heat through her arm. She tried to shake it out, as inconspicuously as possible, and moved to the side of the dresser opposite of him.

"I'll push, all I need you to do is help me steer it around your bed."

She held up a finger while he spoke and stepped away to kick off her flip flops, then took her place across from him again. "Okay, I'm ready."

Casey had to do very little as Jake made it look like he was pushing a matchbox car across the plush carpet instead of the solid mahogany dresser she had inherited from her Grandma Iris. When they maneuvered it into the right spot, she stood back with hands on her hips and grinned up at him. "Perfect. Thanks."

He gave her a quick nod and started out of her room.

"Hang on," she said before he hit the doorway. "I was wondering something, if you have a minute." He hitched an eyebrow in silent question when he turned, but didn't say anything. Geez, it was like pulling teeth with him. "Well, like I said earlier, I love the finishes you picked in here. But I know everything would just pop if there was a little color on the walls. Really make it homey."

"What do you mean when you say color? Like tan?"

"Umm, yeah. In that area, a nice warm earth tone." Roasted Pumpkin was an earth tone. Kind of. He thought for a second and looked like he was ready to say no, so Casey decided to plow ahead. "And if you're worried about when my lease is up, I'll cover it with a coat of primer if you don't like the color I picked. You'd have to repaint before a new tenant anyway, so I'm actually saving you work, if you think about it."

He folded his arms across his chest and leaned up against the door frame, giving her a look that made her want to twirl her hair or some other girly manifestation of nerves. "How does that save me time? I wouldn't have to prime the walls before repainting them, just put a fresh coat of the color that's already on here."

"True. But, if I'm priming, then I'll have already cleaned the walls and patched the nail holes. You'll have a perfect surface to start with."

It felt like an eternity before he spoke, when in reality it was only about five seconds. "You're good."

Casey felt her eyes go wide. He totally had her pegged.

"Excuse me?"

"You heard me. You probably don't usually have to work this

hard to get your way, do you?" His eyes weren't as hard as normal, almost friendly, but his mouth still hadn't budged from its firmly cemented line.

She felt a blush creep up her cheeks and averted her gaze. She figured with him, it was best to shoot straight. "No, I don't. I'm the youngest of five and the only girl in my family, I learned pretty early on that that'll get me my way if I really want it." He regarded her carefully, and she decided he'd appreciate her just coming out and saying it, so she lifted her chin and straightened her shoulders. "And since we're talking about me getting my way, which happens to be my favorite subject, I have a business proposition for you."

At this, he almost, *almost*, lifted one corner of lips. She was going to see this man smile if it was the death of her. "Do you now? I haven't even given you an answer to your paint question, what makes you think I'm open to your proposition?"

At the last word, he used his fingers to make air quotations. She tilted her head and gave him the same look she'd give to a customer if they asked a stupid question. It made it look like she was really concentrating on what they asked; when in reality she was imagining creative ways to cover their mouth with duct tape.

"Are you making fun of me Jake? Because I have four older brothers. It takes a lot more than that to intimidate me." Giving him a deceptively sweet smile, she felt the spark of challenge race through her.

"I'd be disappointed if it took that little to throw you off your game."

She smirked, hoping it came off as relaxed, very 'I could care less what you think of me' instead of 'my heart is pounding so hard it's about to explode through my bra'. She sat back onto the corner of her bed and slowly crossed her legs while she looked up at him.

"Okay, so my proposition is this: I'll stage the other duplexes when each one is ready for you to rent them out, and you knock a hundred and fifty dollars off my rent that month." Jake pushed off the door frame, his expression inscrutable as he regarded her. It took everything in her to not move backwards on the bed away from the sheer force of those eyes, dark and impossible to decipher. Instead, she casually kicked her foot to an imaginary beat. Back and forth, back and forth. Six more times until he finally spoke.

"If you can't afford the rent, you should have told me before you signed the lease."

Her eyes widened until they felt like they took up half her face. This was not the direction she had intended this conversation to go.

"Oh, I have enough money, I got a raise a couple months ago. I just thought we could help each other out. I could use furniture and supplies from work, if you'll let me put up a sign saying that's where they're from. I'll even help you paint if you like some of the colors I pick out. It's good advertising for Hearth and Home, it gives me extra money, you know...to put into savings, and you can ask for higher rent." As long as he didn't realize that her idea of savings was stockpiling spare change in her car to grab a diet coke from McDonald's without having to use her debit card, she'd be fine. "It's a win win, Jake."

Her foot swung like a pendulum, ticking away the seconds as he thought over her suggestion.

"I have a better idea."

JAKE HAD to dig his hands into his front pockets to keep himself from reaching out and stilling that foot she kept kicking around. As soon as she brought up her 'proposition', he knew where this was going. He wasn't stupid. He could see her closet holding the ridiculous stacks of shoe boxes, the hundreds of shirts hanging in color order. And he hadn't even looked into the second room that she planned on using as a closet. This chick had a spending problem. She wanted extra money to go shopping, and while he had to give her credit for her staging idea, there was no way he was giving her a hundred and fifty bucks a month off in rent for painting a couple walls and hanging some pictures.

She actually gave him the answer to a problem he'd been trying to figure out for the past few days. But since it was pretty obvious she didn't like dogs, he would have to make an offer she couldn't refuse. When his Mom had gotten her stage four diagnosis of lung cancer, he had arranged a transfer from his active duty service as an Army Ranger to the Michigan National Guard. He'd already put in his mandatory eight years with the Rangers, so the timing was perfect. Even when his Mom had been alive, she hadn't been physically able to take care of Remy, so on his last two deployments, and during his drill weekends once a month, he had left his dog with a friend of his Mom's, who lived forty minutes north of town. Unfortunately, the friend's husband had gotten a job in California and they moved last month.

"You don't like my staging idea?" Casey looked genuinely confused at the concept, and had mercifully stopped her foot from its rhythmic swinging.

"No, I like it," he said carefully. "And I'll agree to it on one condition." The look that flashed through Casey's expressive eyes told him that she thought she won this round. He couldn't wait to see what they looked like in about thirty seconds. "I'm out of town one weekend a month and I have something for you to do that I would be willing to knock two hundred a month off your rent if you agree, in addition to the staging of the other completed units." She crossed her arms across her chest as she sat up a little straighter on the bed and failed to keep the excitement out of her expression when he threw out the monetary amount.

"And that would be...?" she asked guardedly, drawing out the last word.

"You watch Remy for me."

She blinked once, then threw back her head and let out a laugh that came from deep within her belly. She fell backwards on the bed, throwing one arm over her eyes as the laughter continued. Okay, he knew she wouldn't be excited, but this was not exactly what he'd been expecting. Then as abruptly as it started, her amusement stopped. She lay there for another moment with her eyes still covered. He watched her ribcage rise and fall with each breath, not saying a word. Finally, she sat up. Her hands were folded in her lap and all that dark hair fell around her shoulders. Her expression was as solemn as he'd ever seen it.

"You're not joking?"

"Nope. I need someone to watch him. This weekend actually. I don't like leaving him at a kennel because it stresses him out, and it would be convenient for me since I won't have to bring him anywhere when I leave."

She started kicking that foot again, but it had a more determined swing to it so he figured it meant she was considering it. "How much of the weekend are we talking? Because I do have to work the occasional Saturday, this one included. I don't want to feel like I'm stuck at home because your dog needs a babysitter."

He couldn't have stopped the eye roll even if he wanted to. "Remy doesn't need a babysitter. You can do all your normal stuff, as long as you don't leave him home for longer than ten hours in one stretch, and you're home at night."

"I'm not really what you would call an animal person."

"You don't have to be. As long as you don't feed him antifreeze or anything. Do you plan on poisoning, abusing or generally neglecting him?"

She pushed her lips out in the universal sign of an annoyed female. "Not at the moment, no."

"Good. All you have to do is let him out a few times a day, make sure he has food and water, and you won't even know he's here."

She closed her eyes and pulled in a slow breath through her nose, holding it for a couple seconds before letting it out and looking back up at him. "You said two hundred?"

He knew that would get her. "I did."

She nodded thoughtfully, and he could practically see the visions of shoes running through her head. With any luck, she'd buy some boots. He always had a weakness for women wearing the ones that hit the knee. On second thought, hopefully she didn't buy any. That was the last thing he needed. As he tried unsuccessfully to rid the vision of Casey striding towards him wearing tall black boots that reached her thighs and all that thick dark hair brushing the small of her back, she stood off the bed and held out her hand to him.

"You've got yourself a deal."

5

THE NEXT DAY it was almost impossible for Casey to sit still as she waited for the clock to wind down to 6:30. It was her turn to host Ladies Night, and she was so jittery after her conversation with Jake that she felt like a kid with ADD who forgot their Ritalin. The house was spotless, her laundry was done, she had her famous sangria chilling in the fridge, and she'd almost started alphabetizing her pantry à la the creepy husband in *Sleeping with the Enemy*. Instead she decided to take her time straightening her hair, something she didn't normally do because of how long it took.

The squeal of brakes out in the driveway made Casey yank the power cord of her straightener out of the wall and let it clatter noisily to the counter before she started sprinting down the hallway. There were few times in her life where she felt it necessary to run. Rabid dog. Killer bees. Axe murderer. And the UPS truck.

Skidding around the corner of the kitchen, she heard the satisfying thump of the box hitting the pavement. Three days ago, she'd seen the shoes on bluefly.com and couldn't stop herself from clicking 'confirm purchase'. She leaned down to grab the box, and clutched it to her chest while she jumped up and down with unconcealed glee.

The door slammed behind her as she raced back into the kitchen and quickly found a pair of scissors. After carefully slicing through the tape holding together the cardboard box, she sifted through the packing peanuts and reverently lifted the slate gray box, tracing her fingers across the delicate silver letters printed across the top like a prayer. *Jimmy Choo.* She sank into a chair at her dining table and felt the smile spread across her face. Slowly, she lifted the lid of the box, and unfolded the white tissue paper surrounding the shoes.

"Hello beautiful," she breathed, carefully lifting one of the heels. It was a peep toe, with a delicate gold mesh overlay on a glittering silver base capping a four inch stiletto. They were sparkly and girly and amazing and she would love them forever and ever. She pulled the second shoe out and leaned down to slip it on her foot. Perfect.

She was already imagining them with a little black dress, or dark jeans with the white halter from H&M she had just bought. Stretching her leg out in front of her, she turned her foot to admire the shoe. At $250 they were a total bargain, especially since they were originally over $675. She was practically saving money, if she thought about how often she would wear them.

With a soft sigh of contentment, she pulled the shoe off and nestled it carefully alongside the other one. She closed the box and pushed it into the middle of the table. No point in putting them away since Rachel and Liz would want to see them when they got here in a couple hours for Ladies Night. Rachel would threaten to steal them, even though her feet were at least three sizes smaller than Casey's. Liz would shake her head and lecture her on the impracticality of the heels, saying that women shouldn't need torture devices like that to attract a man.

She and Rachel had long ago decided that it was their mission to get Liz in some killer shoes. She had all the tools to stop traffic, but refused to use any of them. From Casey's perspective, it was practically a crime that Liz had mile long legs, model slim frame and naturally blond hair that most women pay big bucks for and wouldn't sluttify herself occasionally.

The three women were so different, and probably wouldn't have stayed so close if they had met as adults. As it was, they were as much her family as the four brothers who shared parents with her. There was something about going through the inherent roller coaster of adolescence and then the uncertain ascent into adulthood with the same women by your side.

After graduating, Rachel and Liz had gone to college but thankfully not very far away, so the three had weathered the precarious 'post high school' transition of friendships with ease. It was a few years later that they had started their tradition of Ladies Night every other week.

Being an event planner, Rachel knew it would be easiest if they had some sort of structure to their time together. She said it discouraged anybody from being able to easily cancel. So she declared with her customary bossiness, or — as Rachel liked to think of it — her 'strong planning skills', that they would rotate whose night it was, not even asking Casey or Liz their opinion. Thankfully for her, they loved the idea. The person who was up that week would host the other two; pick the movie they would watch, and what the drink of choice would be for the evening.

Tonight was Casey's choice, hence the sangria, and one of her tried and true chick flicks was waiting to be cued up. It had been a toss-up between *Pretty Woman* and *Sleepless in Seattle*, with the latter winning out.

She laughed, thinking about an exchange they'd had the month before when it had been Rachel's turn.

Liz sighed from where she had been curled up in Rachel's recliner. "I really need to drink more on these nights."

"Woah, you got a problem with my choice tonight, Blondie?"

Liz had cocked one eyebrow. "No. No problem. All I wanted to do today was watch a shallow, materialistic narcissist sleep her way through Manhattan. And don't even get me started on Samantha."

Casey choked on a laugh, catching it before it came out of her mouth, and it had sounded like a strangled cough. Rachel leaned forward from her seat on the couch, narrowing her eyes. Casey shifted from her spot on the floor, hoping she wasn't going to have to break up some Jerry Springer style chick fight. She may have a good six inches on Rachel, but it was doubtful Casey could take her in a brawl.

"You know when Jane Austen wrote her books, she was kind of a rebel, right?"

"Yes," Liz had said warily. "Not just because she was a woman, but her social commentary could easily have been considered scandalous for that time. Not Bronte level scandalous, but shocking nonetheless."

Casey pinged her eyes back and forth between them, seeing where it was going way before Liz apparently. Oh, to have a camcorder at a moment like this.

"So, if Miss Jane was outrageous for telling stories like Pride and Prejudice, where a woman that's vastly beneath the hero ends up marrying him because they're actually in love, don't you think that she'd appreciate how female characters in books and movies have evolved to the point that it's commonplace for them to set their own happily ever afters? Where they no longer have to bow to social conventions to ensure their place in society. Carrie Bradshaw refuses to settle for anything less than an all-consuming love. I mean, shit, she's basically Elizabeth Bennett in better shoes."

Casey had finally laughed then, mainly because the look on Liz's face was incredible. Her jaw had dropped just a fraction, and she held up her hands in concession, settling back to watch Aiden and Carrie get back together. But when she'd looked back over at Rachel, Casey noticed the tiny tilt of her lips and a pleased look in her eyes.

And that was the kind of stuff that made her love them so ridiculously.

From her seat at the dining room table, she glanced at the clock on her stove and saw it was 5:45. Liz would be here right on time, as usual. Rachel would stroll in at least thirty minutes late, also as usual. Regardless of when the girls would show up, she couldn't even pretend that she was making a study of out of every clock in her house because of them.

Jake had told her the day before that he'd drop off Remy around six, before he headed up north. When she tried to ask where he would be going one weekend a month, he had very adeptly steered the conversation in a different direction. She had texted both Rachel and Liz that there would be an extra four-legged guest at Ladies Night, courtesy of Sexiness Personified (Rachel's nickname for him, not hers...though she could hardly argue with the accuracy).

Casey dumped some tortilla chips in a bowl and pulled out the ingredients to make guacamole when she heard a car door slam in the driveway. Not thinking anything of it, she continued scooping avocado into a bowl when the door into her kitchen slammed open. She jumped and dropped the slice of perfectly ripe green fruit onto the top of her foot.

"Did I miss him? Did I miss SP?" Rachel's eyes were the size of saucers.

Casey's jaw to dropped down to her chest. "What are you doing here? You're like an hour early."

"I thought you said six-thirty. I'm less than forty five minutes early."

"Right. Six-thirty, and you're always late. So in Rachel time...you're an hour early."

Rachel fisted her hands on her hip, cheeks still flushed pink from hustling inside. "That's an unfair accusation, which we'll deal with later. Did I miss him?"

"You're seriously here this early to see Jake?"

She blinked a couple times and gave Casey a 'duh' look. "No, Case, I just wanted to watch you mash up the guac with your big ol' feet."

Casey spit out a laugh and realized that the avocado that dropped onto her feet was indeed a mushy pulp on the floor. "I'm tall. If I had little feet I would tip over." She squatted down to wipe the mess off the floor and looked up at Rachel. "But to answer your question, no you didn't miss Jake. He should be here any minute actually. He and his giant, hairy dog. Didn't you get a good enough look at him the other day when you stopped over? Don't think I didn't see that excellent Linda Blair *Exorcist* impression you did. Your head whipped around so fast, I thought it was going to fall off."

Rachel barked a laugh. "That wasn't my most subtle moment, was it?"

"Umm, no. But I don't think he even noticed. Obviously your beloved wouldn't care that you ogled another man so shamelessly?"

"Hey. Just because I'm not single doesn't mean I can't appreciate a thing of beauty when I see it. And Jake is a thing of beauty," she said around the tortilla chip she was munching on.

"Hey, that's for later," Casey said when Rachel popped open her fridge and pulled out the pitcher of sangria.

"Oh puhlease." Rachel poured a generous amount into one of the glasses that were sitting out on the counter. "Liz never has more than two drinks and I had a rough day. Marc pissed me off, and everything that could possibly go wrong with the cancer research benefit did go wrong. I swear, you'd think a linen company would know the difference between ecru and eggshell tablecloths."

Casey nodded sympathetically since she had customers that

would agonize for hours over which off white would be better on their living room trim, she *did* know the difference.

"I didn't think that benefit was for another ten months. You have to pick tablecloths that early?"

"Not usually, but the head of the benefit is a hoity-toity country club princess who was born with her head permanently lodged up her own ass."

Casey shook her head, smiling as she watched Rachel take a generous gulp of the sangria. Yeah, there was a healthy kick of brandy hiding behind the fruit soaked wine. "Some people's kids, huh?"

Rachel nodded in agreement as much as she could with her head tipped back taking another swallow.

"Seriously Rach, did you come this early to see Jake? I mean, he's hot, but-"

"He's like 'I could make a hardcore lesbian hump my leg' hot." The look in Rachel's eyes dared Casey to argue.

Casey let out a loud sigh, and couldn't disagree. "Yeah, he's that hot. And somehow my brain got scrambled under hotness-induced duress and I said yes to watching his dog. Ugh. Why the H-E-double-fricken-hockey sticks did I say yes?"

"For the money. And because you want to have his babies. And you sound twelve when you say H-E-double hockey sticks," Rachel said without hesitation and in the same tone one would use when reciting a grocery list.

Casey snorted. "I don't want anyone's babies, Rach," she said. "At least, not yet. And you're right. It's totally the money. Does that make me a bad person?"

"Absolutely not. I'd worry about you if you turned it down. Two hundred bucks for two nights of watching a dog in your own home? That's good money. You may even realize you like having the dog here after a while." Casey gave her a *who do you think you're talking to right now* look. With a laugh, Rachel went back to her sangria. "Okay, that's a stretch. But you might not hate it as much as you think."

"Or I could hate it more. Seriously, just the thought of all that dog hair floating through here is enough to send me into a cleaning frenzy and he's not even here yet. What if he drools on my hot pink suede heels? I can't replace those. Ugh. This is why I hate dogs." And obviously the horrible thought of sharing her living space with a canine was enough to block out the sound of Jake lightly knocking before entering the kitchen.

"You must really need the money then."

Casey pinched her eyes shut and bit back a frustrated groan at the sound of his deep voice coming from behind her. Rachel slapped a hand over her mouth and unsuccessfully tried to hold in her laughter. Casey looked heavenward and took a deep breath before she slowly turned around to see Jake framed in the doorway, a large bag gripped in one hand, Remy sitting at his side. The dog looked at her with his head cocked, and Casey could swear he was judging her.

She let out a nervous laugh and somehow remembered to introduce Rachel to Jake, officially. While the two were shaking hands, it managed to penetrate her brain that he was wearing a uniform. Like a military-the only thing that could possibly make him hotter-uniform. In her mind, she was able to casually flip her hair over her shoulder before making a witty comment, but all that came out of her mouth was a strangled "uuuhhhmm" noise. Rachel looked over at her like she'd lost her mind, and thankfully asked Jake the question that had somehow stalled somewhere between her brain and her mouth.

"So, you're in the military?"

"Nah, I just like the outfit." He said it with such a straight face, that both women just stared, clearly not knowing what to say next. "Kidding. I'm in the Army National Guard. Infantry." Somehow the last statement jarred Casey back into her speaking capabilities.

"Holy crap, did you just make a joke?" Not exactly the smooth line she was planning.

Jake hitched an eyebrow and turned to face her fully. "You don't think I can make a joke?"

"All evidence to the contrary," she threw back, feeling her hackles rise at the challenge that was sparking from his eyes.

Rachel jabbed an elbow into her ribcage. "Casey, that's not being very neighborly to the nice man who's paying you to watch his dog and performs a great service to our country."

Casey dropped her eyes, rubbed the spot on her side and felt a slight warmth climb up her neck and stop behind her ears. She peeked back to Jake, hoping she looked as contrite as she felt. Her mother would skin her alive if she thought Casey was showing disrespect to a veteran. Her grandfather, who passed while she was just a baby, had served in WWII.

"She's right, I'm sorry. I guess I'm just nervous about the whole dog thing." His eyes said he wasn't actually upset at her, maybe that he even enjoyed her little outburst. Of course, it was quite possible she was projecting. At least that's what Liz said once when Casey thought the cop who had pulled her over at the time looked sorry for doing it.

Apparently Casey projected a lot.

"No harm done," he said as he walked forward, stopping just in front of her and hunkering down next to the dog. "Remy, this is Casey. Casey is a friend. Buono amico, Remy."

She stared. Maybe he was crazy. Which would go a long way in squelching her mini-crush. She may not know her exact type, but she was darn sure it wasn't someone who belonged in a padded cell because he spoke a different language to his dog.

Jake motioned for her hand, which she held out stiffly in front of Remy's nose. He leaned forward and sniffed around her palm and wrist. Then he plopped down on his haunches and lifted one paw until it landed smack in the middle of her hand. She couldn't stop the laugh, but managed to keep it quick and quiet while she decided to just go with it.

"Nice to meet you Remy," she said solemnly as she wrapped her fingers around the massive paw and shook slightly. "Do you have to categorize everyone Remy meets? Can't he decide who his own friends are?"

Again, one corner of his ridiculously perfect lips moved, but not enough to be considered a smile. "I told him you're a good friend in Italian, that way he doesn't get confused if I use 'friend' in conversation. And of course, there are some people he decides to like on his own. But I will only tell him two kinds of people so he knows how to treat them. Friend, buono amico, so he knows to obey and protect you, and the other one, which is a word I can't say because he'd probably rip your arm out of its socket."

Casey's jaw dropped in tandem with Rachel's, as if they were connected to an invisible string that someone just yanked towards the floor.

"Are you serious?" Rachel's voice held a tinge of awe.

"Are you freaking crazy?" Casey's, on the other hand, held a large dose of hysteria. "I don't want a killer dog here with me."

Jake stood slowly, dipping his head a bit so he could make solid eye contact. It was the first time she noticed how long his eyelashes were. Unfair. Men should never have longer eyelashes than women. "He won't hurt you now that I told him you're a friend." He started to raise his hand, like he was going to touch her arm. "I promise."

Without thinking twice, she stepped back, because she knew that if this hot man in an Army uniform laid a hand on her, she may climb him like a cat up a tree. He dropped his hand back to his side, and turned to get the bag of Remy's things he brought. She flinched once his back faced her. When Rachel mouthed, *What?* Casey only gave her a slight shake of her head and then pasted on a smile when Jake turned back around.

"Okay, so I have enough food for him until I get back Sunday afternoon. He gets four cups a day, you can just put it all in his bowl when you get up. There's a couple toys in here for him, just make sure he has them when you leave for work tomorrow so he doesn't get bored. He'll let you know when he needs to go outside. My guess is he'll sleep out in the living room; he likes to be where he can see the front door when he's in an unfamiliar place." He stopped and squinted his eyes like he was running over a mental list, making sure he covered everything. "I think that's it. Do you have any questions?"

Yes...can I change my mind about all this?

"Do I need to keep him on a leash when I take him outside?"

"Nope, just say 'go outside' when you open the door, and he'll know to do his business. Then just say 'heel' or 'come' when you're ready for him to come back to you."

Casey worried her bottom lip with her teeth, letting it slowly slide back out while she thought that over. His eyes flicked down to where her teeth had been, then quickly back up to her face before she could dwell on it too much.

"You're sure he'll listen to me?"

"Positive," Jake said, and he looked it. "You have my cell number in case you have any questions while I'm gone. I wrote down his vet's number too, if you can't get in touch with me. I may not be able to answer depending on what we're doing, but I'll get back to you as quickly as I can."

"So you're doing training this weekend?" Rachel asked, eyes slowly wandering the length of his uniform again. Casey thought it might look too obvious if she smacked the back of Rachel's head.

"We have drill one weekend a month when we're not deployed." She looked like she was going to ask another question when another tentative knock came from outside the kitchen door.

"C'mon in, Liz," Rachel called, much louder than was necessary considering the door wasn't that far away. Remy had turned at the sound, his ears pricked up and eyes alert.

"Stay Remy," Jake said before turning to Casey. "You know, you should check who's at the door before you tell them to come in. It could be anybody."

"True. But if it was a psycho killer, you could just say the magic word to Remy and he'd go all Kujo, right?"

"Something like that." His lips spread just a little bit wider this time. So close.

"Woah, am I late for the party?" Liz walked in as quietly as she did everything else, wide blue eyes taking in the crowd gathered in Casey's dining area.

"Ha, I actually beat ya this time, Blondie." Rachel grinned after Liz was introduced to Jake, then finished off the last of her sangria like it was the prize she won for getting there first.

"Yeah, Red, I noticed. How did that happen?" Liz leaned one slim hip against the kitchen counter, not at all fazed by Jake in all his uniformed glory. In fact, she'd barely given him a second look after they shook hands. What on *earth* was wrong with her? "You're never early."

"Priorities, my dear. Priorities," she said with a Cheshire Cat grin aimed directly at Jake. Lord have mercy. Jake didn't seem to notice the meaning behind what she said, but his gaze was volleying between Rachel and Liz as they spoke.

"Ladies," Jake interrupted. "It's been a pleasure meeting both of you, but I have to run." He leaned down and placed both hands on either side of Remy's face. "You be a good boy, listen to Casey." As his fingers dug in behind Remy's over-sized ears, the dog let out a contented groan and leaned towards the pressure. Oh great, now she was jealous of the dog. He looked back up to her, dark eyes looking serious. "Call me if you need anything, okay?"

Define anything.

"Will do." She pushed her hands into the back pockets of her jean skirt and rocked forward on the balls of her feet. "I'm sure we'll be just fine."

The three women and one dog seemed to hold their breath as Jake left the house to climb in his truck and back down the driveway.

"What did I get myself into?" Casey asked on an exhale and plopped into a chair. Liz bent down to greet Remy, who swiped an incredibly large pink tongue up the side of her face, causing a huge smile to stretch across her face.

"He's not so bad Case," Liz admonished. "He seems really sweet."

"Oh sure, until he eats you alive while covering all of your furniture with dog hair. I can't even decide which is worse." She leaned forward, balancing her elbows on her knees and buried her face in her hands.

Rachel got up to pour another glass of sangria, laughing at Casey's theatrics. As she took another sip, she narrowed her eyes speculatively. "You know, he reminds me of someone, and I can't think of who it is."

"Jake does?" Liz asked, pushing up off the floor and getting herself a drink.

"No, Remy," Rachel drawled. "Of course I meant Jake. Hmmm, who is it? It's someone super hot. Eh, it'll come to me later."

Casey rolled her eyes and laughed. Remy sniffed around the perimeter of the dining room, then made his way around her couch. All three women watched as he rubbed his snout, head and neck against the edge of the ivory fabric, leaving a noticeable trail of dark fur behind him when he straightened and shook himself out.

Casey ground her teeth. Rachel laughed.

"It'll be fine, Case," Liz said, sounding way too freaking amused.

Then Remy plopped down on his haunches, and dragged his butt right across her carpet.

6

THE NEXT MORNING, Casey yanked open the back door of the warehouse, not caring that it swung back with a fast *whoosh* and stopped mere inches before slamming into the passenger side fender of College Kid's piece of crap car. He had a name, of course. College Kid did, it was Jason. Normally she just called him that to tease him, as they had a new crop of them every summer. The part timers got increasingly worthless as the years went on. Lately, all they seemed to excel in was the ability to flick their Justin Bieber hair out of their eyes.

She liked Jason though, he worked hard and didn't complain when asked to do something new. She knew he had a little crush on her, as he was always the first to volunteer when she needed something from the warehouse. His cheeks would flame with twin spots of pink when she would so much as smile in his direction. He hadn't grown into his height yet, so his six foot five frame was reminiscent of one of the spindles on her parents' front porch. He was definitely her favorite.

But today, she didn't like anybody. She was so freaking tired, having gotten barely any sleep because that animal had paced and whined the majority of the night. When she finally stomped down the hallway and yelled at him to lay down and stay, he actually did it. She was so pissed at herself for not trying that hours earlier. But how was she supposed to know that was all he needed? The dog seemed to understand she was ticked because he steered clear of her while she got ready for work, only seeking her out when he needed to go outside. She had glared at him the whole time he did his business, and when she took one last look at him before slamming the door shut, it honestly looked like he was glaring right back.

So there she was, running late for work with bags the size of grapefruits under her eyes. Usually the smell that permeated the warehouse was comforting to her. The mix of dust, wet paint, and wallpaper paste tinged with paint thinner probably sounded horrible to anyone else. She'd bet that in seventy five years, that smell hadn't changed. Today though, she wanted to light a match to the whole place.

To say she didn't function well when tired was a monumental understatement.

After punching in at the computer in the warehouse, she made her way to the wallpaper department that had been her home away from home for the last ten years. The way she slammed her purse in the drawer at her desk had College Kid and another one of the little punks staring wide eyed in her direction. Thankfully, they were smart enough to keep their mouths shut.

The large counters formed a U-shape around her, and she flipped through the stack of orders that had been placed in the week she took off to move. Of course, no one called them in while she was gone. Heaven forbid Melinda do anything to earn her paycheck. She shook her head when she saw the paperwork for Mrs. Banks. That woman had redone her dining room at least a dozen times in the last four years. Casey was sure that the last attempt, a beautiful pale yellow toile was going to be the winner.

Guess not. Oh well, no skin off her nose if the lady wanted to order another six rolls of wallpaper.

From behind her, she heard her assistant manager Mike's heavy footsteps.

"Morning Casey," he bellowed, as he was completely incapable in speaking at a normal volume. His barrel chest and ham-sized fists always made her think of Popeye. "Have a good week off?"

"Hey, Mike. It was good." She looked back at her orders and feigned a casual tone. "So, who else is on today?"

She heard him snicker as he carried the cash trays to the registers in the front. Mike knew Melinda wasn't her favorite person, and clearly he knew she was only asking to see if that skank was working. Okay, she wasn't a skank...it just felt really good to call her names.

"It's the four of us and Melinda. She's back in the office brainstorming for next month's blog."

The blog that was Casey's idea. That their manager Tom had given to Melinda. She dragged her face into something that might resemble a smile in acknowledgment of Mike answering her question, but he was too busy at the registers to pay attention.

Casey busied herself with stacking wallpaper books that had been returned, putting them in order of where they went in the shelves that lined the whole back wall. She loved the routine that started her day. The brainless pattern of putting away books and seeing which paint chips needed to be restocked always helped her clear her head before dealing with customers. She loved all the different interactions her job gave her. It was a perfect mix of established routine and unpredictable circumstance. It kept her on her toes, and made her days fly by. Hearth and Home was only open six hours on Saturdays, which hopefully meant there wasn't enough time for Melinda to bother her.

Five and a half hours later, she realized just how wrong she was.

The click clacking of Melinda's heels got closer and closer to Casey until she couldn't ignore the fact that the midget was headed straight for her. She kept her head down and continued flipping through a new wallpaper book, pretending like she didn't see the pointy black toes of Melinda's shoes facing her when they stopped about three feet away from Casey's desk. One was tapping an impatient rhythm, and Casey could just about imagine her pint sized hands perched on her hips. The girl had the curves of a ten year old, basically non-existent. Her elfin features and piercing green eyes always made Casey think of Tinkerbell. Well, maybe Tinkerbell's evil twin, the one who leaves nothing but darkness, pain and abject misery in her wake.

"Eh-HEM," Melinda cleared her throat, in the way she always did when there was a customer she wanted to pawn off on Casey. To compensate for her tiny little voice that matched her tiny little body, Melinda had a never ending parade of power suits. She strutted around like she was in a Fortune 500 CEO runway show, and Casey figured it was the female equivalent of when a guy drove a truck jacked up to heaven with monstrous wheels to match. Everyone knew what *that* meant. "Casey, I was about to get started on the blog, would you mind helping Steve? He needs a color match for a job next week and thinks it's a Benjamin Moore color. I thought you could help him look through chips to see if it is."

Oh Lord have mercy, Casey clamped down on the groan before it escaped her mouth. Steve was one of her least favorite customers, and Melinda knew it. He was a painter who came in a few times a month, and he always asked for Casey. More often than not, she could smell marijuana wafting off of him, mixing not so pleasantly with the slightest tinge of body odor. Technically, he was never anything but polite to her, but there was something lurking just under the surface of his comments that made her want to hide under the wallpaper counter whenever he came in. The last time he stood hovering over her shoulder while she tried to match a color for him, she could have sworn he sniffed her hair. When she looked up she caught College Kid eyeing him the way that Dylan would if he had been there, like he wanted to kick the guy's teeth in.

At that moment, however, she was on her own. Jason was in the back mixing a thirty gallon paint order for Monday morning and didn't know Steve was there. After that last incident, he had given Steve the nickname 'Creepy Eye Guy', for obvious reasons. And dealing with creepy eyes was the last thing she wanted to do at the end her shift when she had started the day completely exhausted. She finally flicked her eyes up to Melinda and didn't even try to hide her annoyance.

"Are you sure you can't do it? I've got a lot to get caught up on from last week. Nobody seems to be able to manage to do these things when I'm not here." Casey wouldn't have been able to tell that the dig even affected Melinda, but her eyes narrowed slightly and gave her away as loudly as a bullhorn going off in church. "Besides, Mike told me the blog isn't due for another couple weeks, isn't that right?"

He hadn't told her that, but Casey knew it was the truth regardless. As Melinda was clenching her jaw trying to come up with another excuse, Steve sauntered up behind her. If Melinda was evil Tinkerbell, then Steve was a psycho version of Pigpen from Charlie Brown. The only thing he was missing was the cloud of dust. Even if he was more cleaned up than normal, he had this inherent dirtiness that surrounded him. It was partially the smell, partially the creepiness.

"C'mon Casey, you know you're my favorite," he said with a smile that didn't match the look in his eyes. The smile was polite, the eyes were definitely not. He scratched the side of his scruffy face with his blunt tipped fingers that always seemed to be tinged with some sort of dirt. "No offense, Melinda." He went to put his arm around Melinda's slight frame, and she easily side-stepped him, not immune to his ick factor.

"None taken, of course. I completely understand why you'd

want Casey. She's *just* your type," she said with a sickeningly
sweet smile. The insinuation went right over Steve's head as he
was too busy trying to look down Casey's shirt, but Casey
straightened so there was nothing to see. She slammed the book
shut, and pivoted towards the back wall to put it in its new place.

"Sorry, Steve," she called over her shoulder, and knowing full
well that he was checking out her rear in the denim pencil skirt
she slipped into this morning, she forced herself to walk at a
normal pace. "I have one last order I have to call in before we
close today. Waverly is always incredibly busy on Saturday after-
noons, and this can't wait until Monday. If Melinda can't help
you, I'm sure one of the guys at the counter will be available any
second."

Melinda let out a huff of air that sounded like a cat hacking
up a hair ball and spun to the office, her short legs carrying her
down the hall faster than seemed possible. Casey shrugged her
shoulders and forced a smile while Steve seemed to chew over
the sincerity of her excuse. She picked up Mrs. Banks' order that
she had actually called in three hours ago and picked up the
phone, hoping he was also too dumb to notice the giant red
stamp across the top of the order that said IN TRANSIT.

"Well," he drawled, eyes traveling her body from top to bottom
and back up to the top so slowly she had to force herself not to
squirm and back away. "I guess this can wait until next week, if
you're really busy. Are you working Monday?"

As she opened her mouth to respond, Mike came up behind
Steve and clapped him on the shoulder, causing the smaller man
to jump.

"Steve, let me give you a hand. Leave this lady to finish up her
work," he said with a small wink at Casey, and steered Steve
safely to the front of the store. He took one last look at her while
Mike practically dragged him away, narrowing his eyes in obvious
displeasure. She managed to keep a polite expression on her face
until he finally turned away, then she dropped her head back and

let out a lungful of air that had the weight of a linebacker behind it. Jason came around the corner from the warehouse, noticed Steve at the front counter and gave her a cautious smile. He was obviously still wary of her from her less than calm entrance this morning.

"Mike's helping him this time, huh?"

Casey felt her first genuine smile of the day stretch through her, a welcome relief after the encounter with Steve, still feeling a rush of creepy crawlies skitter across her skin thinking of the way he looked at her. "Yeah. Creepy Eye Guy strikes again. So," she said lightly, wanting to change the subject. "You have any big plans tonight, College Kid? Hot date maybe?"

She laughed when he couldn't dip his head fast enough to hide the flush that spread across his cheekbones.

"Naw, just hanging out with some of my friends. We might go catch a movie." He kept his head angled towards the floor, but lifted his eyes to her hesitantly. "What about you? Do you have a date?"

"Oh yeah. He's waiting for me at home actually. Slept over last night too."

Jason's head snapped up at Casey's answer, and she could have sworn he looked just a little crushed. Unable to torture him for too long, she leaned forward and gingerly touched his arm. She tried not to do that too much, thinking he might take it the wrong way, but he looked so sad when she said it. "I'm kidding. I'm watching my neighbor's dog, and the stupid thing kept me up all night. I'll probably go hang out at my parent's house just so I'm not this pathetic lady sitting home with a dog on a Saturday night."

Relief flowed over his features, and it made her want to hug him, but instead she slugged him in the shoulder as she walked to her desk. He dug his hands into the pockets of his khaki cargo pants and rocked forward on the balls of his feet, trying desperately to look nonchalant. He helped her put away a few remaining books and straighten the chairs around the large round tables scattered throughout the area.

"You ready to go?" Jason asked, watching the front where Mike was locking up the doors. "I'll walk out with you."

She looked up from where she was separating the day's orders, surprised at his offer. "I just need to finish straightening up, don't feel like you need to wait for me."

"No, it's fine. I'll help," he said in a rush. She shook her head, biting on the inside of her cheek to keep the smile in. Kid was kinda odd, but she'd miss him when he went back to school in the fall. They walked out the back door of the warehouse after punching out and Casey squinted into the sun. They reached her car, which was on the opposite side of the employee lot as his, and she let out a little laugh at the fact that he was still following her.

"I think I'm good from here, Jason," she said with a smile. A truck rumbled to life behind her, and she turned to look when Jason's forehead relaxed at the sound. Ick. Steve's truck was parked at the far end of the customer lot, and she caught the tail end swerving around the corner, tires giving a high-pitched screech as they bumped the side of the curb. She shook her head, finally putting it together. She shaded her eyes from the sun when she turned back to him. "You're as bad as my brothers, but, thank you. It's very sweet of you."

His lips rolled in and twin spots of bright red popped on his face. "No sweat. He just uh, freaks me out a little and I'm not even the one he's checking out all the time."

Laughing, she popped open her door and gagged from the heat that wafted out.

"So, umm, what kind of dog is it?"

"What? Oh, Remy. A German Shepherd. Apparently he's like wonder dog or something, trained up the wazoo. Shouldn't be too bad to have him for the weekend."

"Оннннннннн Holy mother of crap." Casey breathed when she walked in the door about thirty minutes later and spotted a few seemingly innocuous chunks of gray laying on the floor under the dining room table. "No. No no nonoNONONONO."

Innocuous, except for the fact that they were from the Jimmy Choo shoe box she had left on top of the table, the same box that as of 7:45 that morning still held the beautiful glittery-ness of her new shoes.

The same shoes that were nowhere to be seen.

Pinching her eyes shut for a moment, she focused on her breathing as she started walking around the corner into the living room. She slowly peeled open one eyelid and had her very first out of body experience. She heard the keening moan that apparently came from her own throat. Didn't remember making it. Then she floated, all weirdly separate and disconnected, onto the ceiling and saw herself sink to her knees in front of the pile in the middle of the room. Bits of silver sparkle mixed with gray, the whole top layer of one heel completely ripped off down to the stiletto. Which wasn't unscathed either, having German Shepherd sized teeth marks embedded in the entire length. The second shoe wasn't as completely mangled; he must have gotten bored with it after completely ripping the heel off of it.

"REMY!" she screeched, and her floating body self could see the veins popping out in her neck and her face turn an extremely unattractive shade of purple-ish red.

And oh, that mother-effing-about-to-be-skinned-alive dog. She heard him hit the floor in her bedroom with a suspiciously loud thud, meaning he had actually been up on her bed.

ON. HER. BED.

Clearly in no particular hurry, Remy came down the hallway and plopped into a sitting position at the entrance of the living room.

"You." She pointed a shaking finger at him as she pushed up onto her feet, not trusting herself to get any closer to him for fear that she would try and rip one on his ridiculously large ears off. "That shoe was worth more than your life. You are DEAD, dog."

Remy's ears twitched when she said 'dead' and he cocked his head slightly before slumping to the floor and twisting onto his back, where he remained for a few seconds before righting himself back onto his feet and looking at her expectantly.

Casey's jaw dropped. "What?! YOU ATE MY JIMMY CHOOS. You think you get a fricken dog treat?"

Remy's tail slowly wagged at 'treat', and then he dipped his snout before letting out a hoarse bark. Casey squinted so hard in his direction she could barely see him through the slits of her eyes. Her heart struck against her chest until she thought it would beat itself through the bones. Her lips rolled in while she pushed air through her nose.

"Dream on, mutt. If you make it until tomorrow night still breathing, you'll be lucky."

Count to ten, Casey...or maybe seven hundred and forty two.

She stomped back into the kitchen, not even able to pick up the mess on the floor without feeling like crying. Okay, so she could admit it was a tad dramatic to want to cry over ruined shoes. But she hadn't even worn them once. Why couldn't he pick one of her older pairs of shoes? Like her black Anne Klein boots? Replacing those were one of the first things she wanted to do with the money from Jake.

Ooooh, Jake. She was going to kill him right along with his dog. She started rooting through her purse until she found her phone.

Her thumbs flying over the keys, she didn't think twice about pressing 'send'.

FYI- I may have a new German Shepherd rug in my living room by the end of the day. If I'm not chaperoned until Jake gets back, I can't be held responsible for my actions.

Only about fifteen seconds later, her phone dinged in response.

Be there in 15. Don't kill him...please? And by him, I mean the dog.

Thank goodness for Liz. She could calm Casey down, make her realize that in the grand scheme of things, it was just a pair of shoes.

A really amazing, guaranteed to make your life prettier and shinier and happier pair of shoes. She whimpered just thinking about them, then took a deep breath and left the room to start counting. At this rate, she may never be able to stop.

425, 426, 427, 428, 429......nope, not working.

Jake eased his foot off the brake as he took the exit towards home on Sunday. The weekend had been a good one, with the guys in his platoon having one of their cleanest drill weekends that he could remember. The air was still muggy even though it had cooled since the afternoon, which was typical in August, but the damp air never bothered him, even though it seemed to cling to everything. It seemed to him that the humidity made everything more tangible, especially when the skies in the west were promising a pink tinged sunset. It felt like he'd be able to reach out and grab it if he wanted to. It was the only time he missed living on the water. This kind of sky reminded him of the summers before his Dad had died. Every night the sky glowed like it surely would tonight, Jake and his Dad used to go perch on the edge of the dock that stretched out over the lake they had lived on. Jake's legs had hovered frustratingly far away from the surface of the water, and he used to stretch his toes down to see if they could reach as far as his Dad's did.

His Dad never pointed it out, even though Jake knew he noticed what he had been trying to do, he would simply scoot back on the dock until their feet hung at the same level. Then they would talk. About the weather, or baseball, or his Dad's work, or Great Aunt Mattie's horrible meatloaf. It didn't matter what the topic had been, he just remembered the feeling that used to give him.

It had been as real as the water below them, shimmering and sliding around inside him.

His Dad had made him feel like an equal, like a man. Like he couldn't imagine anything better than sitting and talking to his ten year old son while watching the sun set. On a night like this, over twenty years later, all he wanted to do was take his dog to the beach and stare into the horizon until the orange faded into blue.

He had thought a lot about Remy and Casey over the weekend, wondering how they were getting along. He couldn't quite explain the feeling he had as he had driven away a few nights ago. This morning, when he rolled over in his bunk it hit him.

He wanted Casey to have a good weekend with his dog.

Which was strange, if he was being perfectly honest. He hadn't genuinely cared what a woman thought in years. And now, this girl he had only seen a couple times — who smelled like oranges and something else sweet he couldn't name — was making him lie awake at night. Friday afternoon he felt something band around his chest when she smiled at Remy shaking her hand. It was a real smile, not one she had used on him to get her way, and he liked it. Really liked it.

Not that the other smile had sucked. But this one was softer, unplanned.

Then she'd bit into that lower lip and he wasn't entirely certain he wouldn't back her into the wall and try tasting it himself. The image had flashed through his brain for a split second, in blazing, vivid Technicolor glory. One hand was braced on the wall next to her head. The other was anchored on the small of her back, wanting to be underneath that simple white tank she had been wearing. And that night, finally, her hair wasn't in another damn ponytail. In the vision, he imagined how it would brush along the top of his hand on her back. She was arched into him, and her slim hands were gripping the back of his head, pulling him down to meet her lips. Then he blinked and it was gone. Thankfully, ten years in the military had trained him to keep his emotions in check and his physical responses at bay.

He was so taken aback by what had flooded into his head in that moment, because he hadn't been truly attracted to anyone in so long. He knew she was smoking hot, but he'd seen lots of beautiful women over the years, and none of them had affected him the way she had Friday night. Casey had the physical attributes any man with a working set of eyes would appreciate, but normally he liked a sweet, girl next door personality to go with it. Not a feisty, slightly pushy shopaholic who didn't like dogs. Hopefully the last two days had changed the last part.

Not that it mattered anyway. Getting involved with a tenant was always a bad idea.

He pulled his truck into the driveway, feeling a seldom-practiced grin tug on his lips when he saw Remy bound out the garage, Casey walking slowly behind him. Remy tossed his head back, letting out a few high pitched barks while he circled the slow moving vehicle. It was then Jake noticed Casey's face.

Instead of the warm, welcome home smile he expected to see, her lips were twisted up tight under her nose and her eyes were definitely not projecting warmth. In fact, she looked like she was ready to do battle. He took his time grabbing his duffel from the passenger seat and tucking his keys into his front pocket. When she slipped her arms together in front of her chest and cocked a hip out to the side, he knew he couldn't stay in there any longer.

Remy's paws hit the middle of his stomach the second he stepped out of the truck, and it pushed him back a step.

"Hey boy, I missed you too," he said as he quickly thumped the dog's heaving sides. Remy dropped his paws back down to the driveway when Jake shifted to face Casey, who was now tapping one foot in the same staccato tempo that his Mom had used when Jake would take too long getting ready for school.

"How did the weekend go?"

"How did it go?" She repeated slowly, and a little too calmly. Her jaw clenched briefly, and she pulled in a huge breath before she dropped her hands back to her sides. This couldn't be good. "Your...*animal*...ate my brand new Jimmy Choos while I was at work yesterday."

"What are Jimmy Choos?"

"They're shoes, Jake." The way she said his name had some force behind it, so he knew he was treading on pretty thin ice. Probably not going to have any up-against-the-wall visions during this conversation. "They're really high end, really beautiful shoes that I never got to wear."

"And he ate them. As in..."

"As in destroyed, maimed, ruined for all *eternity*, ate them."

"Did you leave his toys out for him when you left?"

Her eyebrows shot up on her forehead and her voice took on a screeching quality. "Are you implying this is my fault?"

"No," he answered slowly and set his duffel on the ground, realizing beyond a shadow of a doubt that this wasn't going to be the quick greeting and recap he had envisioned. "I'm just surprised, and trying to figure out what happened, because Remy has never destroyed any of my stuff."

"Well, isn't that nice for you. Now you owe me a new pair of shoes. Those were on clearance on bluefly, so I won't be able to get the same pair."

He really wanted to argue, but knew it would be like kicking a skunk. A skunk that just walked past you without spraying you. Never a good idea. So he literally bit down on his tongue to keep quiet. "How about I just knock some more off your rent this month? I don't think you want to leave any shoe buying up to me."

"Fine. But I swear, if he does this next time...you need to figure something else out. I don't care how much you pay me."

"Fair enough. So, what are you thinking, another fifty bucks off your rent?"

She threw her head back and let out that incredibly loud, somehow still attractive belly laugh. It was the kind of laugh that told him she didn't worry about what people thought about her. It was also confusing as hell at that exact moment.

"How *cute*," she said, even though her face belied the fact that she didn't actually think it was cute. Then she took a couple steps towards him until she was an arm's length away. She leaned in and he caught another trace of fresh oranges coming from her. Her sudden closeness threw him off more than the laughter, and he figured he looked like a fourth grader who was just thrown into a calculus class. Completely lost and really fricken clueless. "If you think I'm this upset about a fifty dollar pair of shoes, then you have a lot to learn about me."

As quickly as she had tilted towards him, she spun on her heel and marched back to the door to her kitchen. Right before she walked inside, she looked back over her shoulder.

"I'll send you my bill, Jake. This'll be the most expensive two day kennel you've ever used."

7

"Mom, I *did* get over it. I told him that a hundred and fifty would be enough to cover the shoes when they were a hundred more than that. How much more over it can I be?" Casey wedged the phone in between her ear and her shoulder while she loaded dirty dishes into the dishwasher. She had only spoken to Jake once in the last two weeks, when he came by the day after he returned to get a few things of Remy's that had been left at her place. He apologized again for the shoes as he took the slobbery tennis balls from her through the screen door. She'd seen him come and go from the other unit he was still working on, but she always waited until he was back inside if she had to leave. She knew it was ridiculous to avoid him, but she felt a little embarrassed about the incident in the driveway.

And it wasn't even because of how upset she had been. Oh, he deserved her wrath after the murder of her shoes. It was because she was projecting again, and she didn't need Liz to tell her that she was. She had been so twisted up inside over his hotness that she could have sworn he looked at her differently on Sunday night when she got in his face. He didn't look like a man who was annoyed with her, or couldn't stand her, or thought she was crazy for getting that upset over a pair of shoes. He looked...puzzled. Like he didn't know what to think about her getting up in his face.

And she had been. In his face. And she had to pull from every thread of her righteous indignation to not notice what a good face it was, and how close it had been to her own.

"I'm glad you told him that was a sufficient amount, because anything more than that on shoes is ridiculous, Casey Marie. He's not only your landlord, but you'll be watching his dog again in two weeks. Don't you think you two should kiss and make up?"

Hmm, kissing and making up stirred up all sorts of yummy things. Casey slammed the dishwasher shut to sweep the image out of her head, knowing *that* would never happen. Even if she wasn't ticked about her shoes, it was pretty clear he didn't want to be around her any more than she wanted to be around him at the moment.

"Mom, you're acting like Jake and I are in a fight. We aren't friends or anything, I wouldn't be talking to him any more than this under normal circumstances. Most people only deal with their landlords when a pipe is leaking or they're late on their rent. I don't have either issue at the moment."

"I hope I can meet him the next time I come visit. Rachel said he was...oh what word did she use again?"

This ought to be good.

"Delicious. That's it. She said he was delicious," her Mom continued, clearly choosing to ignore Casey's rationale for avoiding Jake. 'Avoiding' sounded worlds better than 'hiding'. "What do you know about him? Where's he from? Does he have family nearby?"

"Geez Mom, you're worse than the boys. Honestly, I don't know a whole lot about him, other than he's in the military and has incredibly unfortunate taste in pets." And he's really, incredibly hot and I probably ruined any chance with him by acting like

an insane person the last time I saw him. Probably best to leave
that out.

"Rachel told me about the military part."

"What, do you two have gossip hour on a daily basis now?"
Casey flopped back on the couch and arched her feet, still feeling
the tingling effects of a nine hour shift in heels. Totally worth it
though, because she'd searched long and hard for those kelly
green peep toes.

"Quit being snarky just because your friends tell me more
about your life than you do. I had to call her about the research
benefit. Poor Rachel has been getting the brunt of Emily's wrath.
I wanted to apologize for the rant she went on today at our planning meeting over the centerpiece choices Rachel brought for her
to look at. They were so lovely, and that old biddy went out of her
way to make Rachel look incompetent."

"I thought Emily was in her thirties."

"She is. Why?"

Casey rolled her eyes. "You called her an 'old biddy', Mom."

"Well, biddy was the nicest 'b' word I could think of at the
moment. And it still applies. She does everything in her power to
knock everyone around her down a peg or two. And Rachel's boss
walks around like Emily walks on water. She's lucky her family
gives so much money for the benefit, otherwise I'd try to kick her
scrawny ass right off that chair she treats like a throne."

Casey laughed, imagining all five foot two inches of her Mom
starting a chick fight.

"No starting fights Mom, you always told me violence never
solved anyone's problems."

"I told you that?"

"Umm, yeah. All the time." Casey and her brothers used to
hear that at least once a week growing up. It was usually after one
of the boys had fashioned a weapon from whatever they found
lying around the house and then ran after the nearest sibling
with it.

"Oh. I probably just said that to keep your brothers from killing each other. I never had to worry about you fighting, dear, you were too worried about getting your dress dirty to show any violent tendencies."

"Well, then they've been brewing inside of me for twenty nine years, because it was like Mount Vesuvius when I saw that pile of silver glitter on the floor. Mom, I swear I wanted to shove that dog through a wood chipper."

"Casey. That's an awful thing to say."

"I didn't say I was *going* to do it, I said I wanted to."

Casey swung her feet down so she could sit up on the couch, then reached up to pull a few bobby pins out from where they were digging into her scalp. She dropped them next to her and noticed yet another Remy hair embedded in the cushion. A few choice words tumbled through her head and she pulled out three more. She had already vacuumed the couch twice since he'd been here. "Mom, I gotta go. I need to run a couple books back to the library before they close, and Liz is already hassling me about the fines I haven't paid on the last two I brought back late."

She said her goodbyes to her Mom, and right before her thumb pressed the end call button, she swore she could hear her Mom say something about Jake.

She and Rachel really needed to get a life. Standing in front of her closet, trying to decide if she should make the effort to strip out of her outfit from work for a quick run to the library, Casey dragged her fingers across hangers without really seeing anything in front of her. One side of her mouth pulled up thinking about Liz sitting at her behemoth desk, piles of books and papers scattered all around her, hair probably slicked back in a bun.

Liz was always suggesting books for Casey to try out, sometimes she liked them, and sometimes she wondered how she was friends with someone who would intentionally read books so depressing. When Casey finished reading *Wuthering Heights*, she told Liz she would excommunicate her if she ever suggested something like that again. Like her movies, Casey liked books with a happy ending that left her with a smile on her face. And oddly enough, in the last couple weeks, she'd been gravitating towards books with a military hero. And if pressed about it, she would swear under oath that it was a total coincidence only two weeks after seeing Jake in camo.

Total. Coincidence.

Deciding that the effort of changing just wasn't worth it, she scooped up the books that were laying on the small table next to her door, and made the monumental mistake of not looking in the driveway before she swung the back door open.

"Oh, hey Casey. You got a minute?" Jake's voice came from the two stall garage that they shared. He was standing by the bed of his black truck holding what looked like tile squares in varying sizes.

Crap. Double crap.

She pulled her keys from her purse and pasted her *I'm really busy but I suppose I spare you a moment* face that she had perfected at work.

"What's up?"

Jake shifted the tile in his arms and it made his annoyingly large biceps bulge. "So does this mean you're talking to me again?"

She swallowed loudly. Triple crap.

"Why wouldn't I be talking to you?" She kept her face carefully blank even though she was sure at any moment a cartoon tongue was going to roll out of her mouth and slowly uncurl down to her belly button at the sight of him all sweaty and gorgeous. And if she wasn't mistaken, his face said he was really enjoying this.

"Oh, I don't know. I'm afraid if I bring it up again I'll have to watch you do a really good job of avoiding me for another two weeks." One of his eyebrows arched up as if daring her to disagree, but there was humor making his deep brown eyes light up from within.

But he was baiting her, and if there was anything she learned from having four older brothers, it was learning when not to take the bait.

"Listen, I have to run to the library to return some books, is there something you needed to ask me?"

"Yeah, I was wondering if you could help me decide on some of the finishes for this unit I'm working on. I know I could go with the same ones I put in yours, but I figured I might as well get my money's worth from the interior designer I have on payroll."

"Oh." Casey pulled on her bottom lip with her teeth. This she could do. Be a professional, treat him like a customer at work and not imagine what it would be like to lick his abs. "Sure. How long do you think it'll take? The library closes in an hour and I really need to get these back."

"Shouldn't take too long." He slipped past her and nodded at the door to the bed of his truck. "Can you pop that open a sec? This tile is digging into my hands."

"Yeah, sure." Casey reached past his arm and flipped the handle so the door could drop down. He set the pile down with a grunt, and then walked back to the passenger door where he reached inside to grab a thick black binder. Papers bulged from the edges in various colors and thicknesses, and Casey recognized some paint chips about to fall from one of the inner pockets. She moved to the side as he came to stand next to her at the open tailgate. He spread out the tiles, and then started flipping through the binder. After thumbing through a pile of paint chips, he pulled out four of them and laid them above the tile.

Her first thought was that he had surprisingly good taste. Okay, her actual first thought was that he smelled really, really good. But she gave that thought a quick, violent shove out of her head and focused on the task at hand. All of his tile choices were warm while maintaining a contemporary edge.

"I like this one," she said, pointing at a subway tile that had more cream tones in it than the other options. "And if you paired it one of these darker beige tones, it would make the lighter tile really pop."

She held it upright and set the paint chip she liked best up against it. "Plus, the subway style makes it look more modern. But we should really look at it inside the kitchen, paint will look completely different in there than it does here in the outside light."

He nodded and brushed his pointer finger across his lips in an absentminded gesture. She squirmed a little bit and felt a tightening well below her belly button. "You don't think that color is too dark?" He glanced sideways when he said it, but didn't take that diabolical finger off his full lips.

She tilted her head to the side and pretended to think about it while looking at his other paint chips. She was about to paint her living room Roasted Pumpkin, so no...she didn't think this medium beige was too dark.

"No, it probably seems too dark right now because you're looking at it in comparison to the two lighter shades on the strip. Once you get it on the wall, with the cherry cabinets, I think you'll be surprised. Trust me."

"Uh huh."

"What?"

"'Trust me,' she says. This coming from the woman who was ready to kill me and my dog over a pair of shoes." His lips twitched as he said it, but he kept looking down at the tile, so she couldn't tell if he was actually going to smile. Because if he was...she needed full frontal for this.

Okay. Not *full frontal* full frontal.

"Yeah, yeah," she said on a sigh. "Make fun of the girl with the ruined shoes. C'mon, let's go look at these inside so I can head to the library."

Over the next ten minutes, she looked at samples and gave

suggestions for the space. He took everything in and made notes in his binder. She was pleasantly surprised that he ended up picking everything she liked for the finishes, even though he brought up that the paint color might be too dark twice more while they talked. She just rolled her eyes didn't acknowledge it either time.

"So," she started slowly, perching her hip against the counter after turning to face him fully. "How'd you end up in this gig?"

Staring down at the closed binder for a few long seconds, he drummed his fingers in a rapid rhythm before meeting her stare with an intense look that made her want to back out of the door.

"It wasn't a trick question," she said as lightly as possible.

"I know," he replied, not breaking eye contact. "I bought these units a little over a year ago, thought they'd be a good investment."

"I don't remember seeing for sale signs."

He shook his head and then rubbed the back of his neck with one hand. "I bought them from my Mom."

"Oh," Casey said with surprise, dropping her hands down to her sides. "She didn't want the responsibility anymore? I can imagine this would be a lot of work."

Jake cleared his throat and picked up the binder, then gestured towards the door behind her. "Don't you have to get to the library?"

"Seriously? That's it?"

He kept his arm held out, but took a resigned breath. "She died shortly after I bought them from her."

Casey slapped a hand over her mouth, wishing she had room to shove her foot in there. "Jake, I'm so sorry. I wouldn't have pushed it if I had known."

He laughed in a way that was short on, but not devoid of humor. "Yeah, you probably would have. But it's okay. You didn't know."

In a bit of a daze, she walked out in the driveway and let him walk past her so she could get her bearings. She felt like such a jerk. Not that there was any way she could have known, she pushed air into her cheeks, puffing them out while she turned to follow him. But the air quickly escaped her lips when she saw the walking Levi's ad in front of her. The sun was dropping in the sky, perched directly above his head, creating a diffused light that made everything around him glow. The smell of the lilac bushes that lined one side of the driveway rambled through the thick air and surrounded both of them with their heady, sweet fragrance. Casey felt like she was on sensory overload. It was all too much, so she stopped mid-stride and stared at him walking ahead of her.

Jake was *more*. More than what she'd originally thought.

Every time she was around him, another little piece of the Jake puzzle fell into place. There was no way she could live here and not fall, just a little bit, for him.

He kept moving but turned his head over his shoulder to look at her, after noticing she wasn't following anymore. "Smells good, doesn't it?"

"Does what smell good?" Was he talking about himself? Or the lilac bushes? Because either way, yes. It smelled good.

Jake stopped and turned to face her where she was standing and probably looking like a complete moron as she had her 'aha' moment. He shifted the binder and the tiles in his hands and screwed his eyebrows together in confusion. "The lilacs. They were my Mom's favorite flower, which is why she planted so many of them when she had these built. Are you okay? You don't look so good."

Which is just what every woman wants to hear. But it was enough to snap her out of her haze.

She shook her head, closing and opening her mouth a couple times before deciding to lie through her front teeth.

"I'm fine, I saw a bee and didn't want to move until it flew away."

"Yeah, they're attracted to the flowers, only downside to having so many of them." He stopped by his truck as she finally got her feet back in motion and headed to her car. "Thanks for your help tonight, I really appreciate it."

She mumbled something that sounded like agreement before scrambling into her car. She drove to the library not really sure what had just happened. When she pulled into a parking spot in front of the stately brick building, she dropped her forehead onto her steering wheel with a groan.

She was so incredibly screwed.

8

JAKE YANKED the choke of the lawn mower and gripped the handle, relishing the vibration that resonated through his arms up to his shoulders before pushing forward into the grass. As he walked in straight lines behind the machine, he reached up to wipe the sweat off his forehead before it dripped into his eyes. Coupled with the sharp lines crisscrossing the emerald colored grass, everything about the landscaping in pristine condition, the result of hours of his hard work. He could spend all day out in the yard and never have anything to complain about. After multiple tours in Iraq and Afghanistan over the past ten years, he had learned to enjoy the sultry humidity of Michigan in the summer.

The smell of freshly cut grass ranked right up there for Jake. Along with any home cooked meal he didn't have to make himself, and most recently, the smell of oranges was rounding out the list. For the last ten years he started his day with a large glass of orange juice, but ever since Casey lodged herself on endless loop at the back of his brain, he never enjoyed the smell of it so much. Maybe he should stop drinking the juice, because there was no way he could go there.

Just the thought of dating made him jittery because it had

been so long. Lisa had been over four years ago. Her and her 'Dear John' letter, coming after over a year of dating, six months of that being thousands of miles apart. The stress of worrying about him, which was the constant, unyielding companion of anyone in a relationship with a soldier quickly became too much for her. So yeah, under normal circumstances it seemed like a bad idea to attempt that again. But dating a tenant? Forget it.

One day last week, he was coming home from a run with Remy and looked up towards her car just in time to see the door to her Civic open up and one bright red stiletto clad foot reach to the floor of the garage.

Those shoes, and the tan, bare legs attached to them, had fueled his fantasies for days afterward. Thankfully she had been on the phone when she fully exited the car, so she didn't notice him gawking. Because he had been.

Over the rumbling of the lawn mower and the shuffling of his thoughts, he heard Remy bark out a greeting, so Jake turned to look to where the he was sitting by the entrance of the garage. His tail was slowly wagging, and his ears were relaxed, so Jake figured it was someone he knew, which narrowed down the list considerably.

He killed the engine on the mower when he reached the edge of the yard, and in the gape of silence that followed he heard a woman speaking in friendly tones. At the front of a black GMC Envoy stood a petite, dark haired woman leaning forward and scratching behind Remy's ears, the dog leaning into her attentions. She straightened as he approached and he saw the gray hairs threading through her hair, but when she smiled widely, familiarity swept through him. It was Casey's smile.

"Well, you must be Jake," she said as she held out a tiny hand to grip his. "I'm Marie Steadman, Casey's mother."

"It's a pleasure to meet you, ma'am." Jake released her hand and picked up the tail end of his t-shirt to mop sweat off his forehead. "I see you've met Remy before. He certainly seems to know you."

"Oh, this handsome boy? We met a couple weeks ago while Casey was watching him. She may have needed some supervision that last day," she said with a wink at Jake, turning back to Remy and patting him on the head.

Jake folded his arms and let out a soft laugh. "Yeah, I bet she did."

Marie pulled herself to her full height, which couldn't have been more than a couple inches over five feet, and put her hands on her hips, pinning Jake with a look that he imagined she had used a time or two on her kids. It was a look that said she was going to get her way. "So, Jake, tell me about yourself. I want to know a little bit more about the man putting a roof over my daughter's head."

Jake had faced company commanders that were less daunting than this little woman asking him questions. Questions led to the pitying look that people inevitably gave him when he admitted both his parents were dead, and then Jake always felt like he had to comfort them.

"Not much to tell, ma'am. Been in the Army for ten years, eight with the Rangers, and the last two with the National Guard. Other than that, I'm just a man who hangs out with his dog a lot."

"What about your family?" she asked with a faint smile and a tilt of her chin, and he knew he couldn't get off that easily. "Are they from around here?"

"My mother was originally. She met my father in Colorado where they got married, he was stationed at the air force base in Colorado Springs, and we stayed there until my father passed away when I was eleven. Then she moved us back here."

She regarded him for a long moment, but didn't have the look in her eye that he usually got at this point in the conversation. "I'm sorry to hear that. I lost my father when I was sixteen, and I miss him to this day. Casey told me your mother passed away recently."

Ah, she'd been prepped for this conversation. He couldn't even be annoyed that Casey had told her mother, because the look on her face after Jake had told her about his mother passing, it was pretty obvious she wanted to shove one of her high heeled feet as far into her sexy mouth as it could go.

"Yes ma'am, she did. About a year ago from lung cancer."

"That's a shame. It's a terrible disease."

"Yes ma'am."

"Any brothers or sisters?"

"No ma'am. I was a single child."

"Okay, if you keep calling me ma'am, my gray hairs are going to double in number. Please call me Marie, or Mom, or just 'hey you'. Not Mrs. Steadman though, that's my mother in law, and she'd whip you before she'd let you give me her title of honor."

"Marie sounds good to me." Her eyes smiled as much as her mouth did, and he realized it was another thing that reminded him of Casey. The color was off though, as her mother had eyes as dark brown as the hair that she shared with her daughter. "I'm pretty sure Casey's home."

"Oh, I know she is," she said as she waved her hand absent-mindedly towards Casey's door. "I came here to see you."

He pulled his brows together and was about to respond when he heard the screen door swing open behind him. Maybe he was imagining it, but Jake could swear he could smell Casey about ten feet before she actually reached them. She quickly smiled at him as she came next to her Mom, and he had to clench his fists together to stop himself from pushing aside a piece of hair that slipped across her face. Thankfully, she tucked it behind her ear before turning a confused look to her Mom.

"Hey Mom, I didn't know you were stopping over." Casey grabbed her Mom by the elbow and started steering her towards her house, not really waiting for a response. "I'm sure Jake needs to finish mowing the lawn, so we'll just let him get back to it."

Marie pulled her arm out of Casey's grip and planted her feet on the driveway. "Now, I was right in the middle of a conversation, honey. Jake was telling me all about himself, and you know I need to report back to your father and brothers. They're practically foaming at the mouth to know more about him."

"Ah," Jake said as he rubbed his chin. "So you're doing the recon for the men in the family. I can respect that."

Casey snorted. "Please, they're worse than old ladies. And no offense Jake, it has nothing to do with you. I could rent from Mother Teresa and they'd want a full background check."

"Casey Marie. Of all the things to joke about." Her Mom gave her the *I've raised you better than that* look. Jake used to get that one a lot in high school. But in all fairness to his mother, he deserved it every single time it was sent his way. "It's true, those boys are awfully protective of Casey. But it certainly doesn't help matters that you're a strapping young man. Makes them feel threatened if you ask me."

Jake chuckled under his breath when Casey groaned, "Mom," and slapped a hand over her eyes. He decided he liked embarrassed Casey, the pink tinge on her cheekbones pleasing him more than it ought to. It made him want to know what else would make her blush. He cleared his throat, getting annoyed at the direction of his own thoughts.

Ignoring her daughter's plea to stop the conversation, Marie winked at Jake again. "What my boys need is to get to know you themselves."

"Mom-" Casey's voice was low and full of warning as she pulled her hand away from her face, her turquoise colored eyes narrowing in a way that told Jake she knew exactly where her Mom was going with this.

"So," Marie continued, "I was wondering if you'd like to come to our annual Labor Day barbecue. We have the whole family over for a big meal, the men go off and shoot guns while the women sit and gossip, and then we set off some fireworks after dark. What do you say?"

Jake's eyebrows raised in surprise at the same time that Casey's jaw dropped. She turned to look at him with eyes as big as he'd ever seen. Obviously she hadn't known where her Mom was going with it.

"I-I'm sure Jake has plans already, we wouldn't want to subject him to the craziness of the whole family." She looked at her Mom in an almost pleading way, and it was just enough to cement Jake's decision. She could only be so adamant about him not coming for two reasons; either she hated him and couldn't stand the thought of him being around her family, or she wasn't as indifferent to him as she'd been acting the last couple weeks. His gut told him it was the latter given some of their earliest interactions.

"I'd love to come," he said firmly just as the words 'This is a REALLY bad idea' flashed in neon through his head. Bright red flashing neon. Well, it looked like he was all in.

"You would?" they said at the same time. Marie beamed and Casey gawked.

"Absolutely. You can't beat food and guns in the same day."

"Well," Marie said with a pleased smile on her face. "You certainly will get along with my boys if that's the way you feel. They'll be thrilled you're going to join us."

"Or they'll try to murder him." Casey looked perfectly serious even though Marie laughed in response. "Mom, you're going to give them firearms and send Jake off with them? Are you sure this is a good idea?"

"Hopefully my five deployments have adequately prepared me to handle your overprotective brothers. If they fight anything like insurgents, then I should survive the afternoon."

She gave him a withering glance while Marie laughed.

Marie gave him all the details for the gathering, which was

next weekend, before she briefly hugged Casey and walked back to her car. Casey remained silent, but he could feel her peeking sideways at him through her lashes. They stood side by side while Marie turned the car around and made her way down the driveway. Jake pulled in a deep breath, briefly closing his eyes at how incredible she smelled. *Walk away*, he told himself. *Walk away right now before you make this worse for yourself.*

"So," he started. "Your Mom seems great."

She just nodded, and then turned to face him, face more serious than he was expecting. "Do you really want to come next weekend?"

No. But, kind of, yes. And that was the crux of it, wasn't it? He obviously had no idea what he wanted. And it was a feeling as foreign to him as he could remember.

"You think I don't?" Deflection. Always easier than the truth.

She thought about that for a second, looking down at the driveway and wiggling her hot pink painted toes against the warm concrete before looking back and scrutinizing his face. "I think I'm surprised you said yes. I just want to make sure you're doing it for the right reasons."

Jake pulled up his shirt to wipe his forehead again, still sweating. He didn't miss the way she zeroed straight in on where his stomach was bared and then rolled her lips in while a blush lightly stained her cheeks. She definitely wasn't immune, and it made him want to high five, and then immediately punch himself.

"I know you don't know me that well yet, Casey. But if I really didn't want to go, I wouldn't have said yes. I promise."

Her smile was slow to spread, the kind that doesn't show any teeth, but he knew was just as genuine.

"Okay. I believe you then."

"Good."

She turned to go, and then hesitated before looking back at him with a question in her eyes.

"You're not bringing Remy, are you?"

He looked down at his dog, snoozing at his feet, and then back at Casey.

"You really don't like him, do you?"

"If he hadn't eaten my shoes, I'm sure we'd just be best friends, but as it is...we're on a break until the next time I watch him."

"Fair enough. He stays then."

"Just like that?" She looked surprised.

"Just like that." Remy was actually terrified of fireworks, but he figured it wouldn't hurt to let her think he was doing it just for her. Shit, he was digging his own grave here. But he'd give himself this little bit of banter, and then vow to leave her alone.

"Thanks Jake," she tucked hair behind her ear again, this time in a nervous way, walking backwards towards her door as she spoke. "I'll let you get back to work."

She turned and practically fled into her place, and Jake couldn't stop the smile that spread across his face.

And then he moaned. "Shit. What is wrong with me?"

Remy heaved out a deep breath, sounding pretty much exactly the way that Jake felt.

9

"YOU SURE you remember what you're doing?"

"Of course," Casey scoffed while trying to steady herself. That was harder than it looked, due to the fact that the four inch wedge on her sandals didn't give the most stable platform on the sand beneath her feet. She pulled in a deep breath, shifted her weight to her front foot and narrowed her eyes to bring her target into focus at the end of the shotgun barrel. In her mind, she was totally Angelina Jolie, all hot and kick ass and ready to shoot stuff up.

As she was releasing her breath, and about to squeeze the trigger, Dylan's slap-worthy smug laugh came from behind her.

"Casey?"

She took her finger off the trigger and lowered the gun until it pointed to the ground, and even though she'd die before admitting it in front of Jake, or her brothers, she could feel the muscles in her arms shaking from holding it up to her shoulder even that long. She turned slowly to see six sets of annoyingly amused male eyes directed at her.

She pulled the noise canceling headphones to the side. "Is there a problem?"

"The safety?"

Darn it. She tossed her hair and threw off what she hoped was a casual smile.

"I was just about to do that. I like to get all set first."

Dylan rolled his eyes. "So when you were about the pull the trigger just now, you were what? Doing a dress rehearsal?"

Jake was studying the dirt around his shoes as if it held the secrets of the world, thankfully not joining her other three brothers as they hooted with laughter. Her Dad smiled and shook his head, walking up to her and laying a hand on her shoulder.

"Alright, bring it back up to your shoulder, press the butt of the gun nice and tight next to you."

She took a deep breath and glared at Dylan before turning back towards the target, entertaining brief visions of shooting at the ground in front of his feet to see how quickly he could move.

"C'mon, Casey," her Dad said in a soothing tone that could only be reserved for a Dad talking to his daughter while she was holding a loaded weapon and feeling upset with her brothers. "They'll be fine once you get started. You blow up that water-melon down there, and they won't be laughing anymore."

She hoisted the gun up to her shoulder again, thinking she might need to start working out to strengthen her arms. Why did that have to happen in front of Jake? She always did stupid stuff in front of her brothers, their laughter didn't even faze her after twenty nine years of hearing it ringing through her ears at every misstep. Up until that moment things had been going smoothly all day. The weather was as if her mother had custom ordered it. Eighty degrees, relatively low humidity, and enough of a breeze that Casey was glad she had put her hair in a fishtail braid hanging over her shoulder. And yes, she had put a bit more care into her appearance for this family get together than she normally would. She wore the aqua tank top that her Mom told her made her eyes glow, and it floated away from her body enough that it wouldn't seem like she was trying too hard. Couldn't be looking skanky in front of her nephews.

And she may or may not have put an extra dab of her Ralph Lauren perfume behind her ears. When she had taken a final turn in front of her mirror at home, she felt the same nervous swishing inside her stomach that was typically only reserved for a first date. Somewhere in the time after her Mom had invited him, Casey found herself in an unusual situation.

She wanted Jake. Really, really wanted him.

And Jake? Well, Jake did not seem to want her.

He seemed to do everything in his power to avoid her. A couple times when she *happened* to run into him outside over the last week, he rarely did more than nod in response to her greeting and go back to whatever he was doing like she wasn't even there. It made her wonder if she'd hallucinated the entire scene with her Mom. Maybe he'd been regretting saying yes, but whatever the reason, it jacked up her own tension about the whole thing. As the days wore on, she became increasingly nervous about him meeting her family. She had known her two sisters-in-law would be as nice to him as her Mom had been. They had eyes. It was hard to be rude to a man who looked like Jake.

Oh sure, there had been plenty of overly firm, statement making handshakes and steely eyed looks from her Dad and brothers. As soon as they had started talking about the Army, the renovations on the other duplexes, and the guns they all loved so much, the men seemed to fall into an easy pattern.

It was almost annoying. She figured there would be at least one of her brothers that would make him uncomfortable.

Equally annoying was that she hadn't been able to keep her eyes off of him the whole afternoon. Helping her five year old nephew Preston get food, she had accidentally filled half his plate with potato salad while trying to listen to what Jake was saying to her Dad about his last deployment and some of the differences between transferring from active duty to Guard. She wasn't used to him stringing together multiple words, let alone full sentences, so she was trying to gather as much as she could about him.

Even on the drive over to her parents, her eyes had stayed locked on her rear view mirror longer than was probably safe, watching his dark, immaculately clean truck follow her to her parents' house. When they had pulled up the long drive that ended at the house she grew up in, she couldn't help but watch as he took in the stately, red brick two-story house with flawless landscaping and a lawn that rivaled most golf courses. Both of her parents enjoyed spending time outside, and it showed. With the way Jake kept up his own property, she knew he'd appreciate it.

Large hedges of impatiens lined the sidewalk winding from the driveway to the front door, the pink, purple and white blooms so tall and full that she'd often accused her Mom of feeding them steroids. Hanging baskets overflowing with deep purple ivy geraniums framed within the white columns of the front porch, serving as a striking adornment to the stalks of daisies that were below them. Each side of the house was flanked by towering maple trees that had been sentinels guarding the house as long as it had been in place, and in the fall turned vibrant, flaming shades of red and orange.

She loved everything about her parents' house. Typical Jake, all he'd said was, "nice place" with a quick nod, and then followed her into the back yard where her Mom had enough food to feed fifty people.

A couple times after the meal, she caught him looking back at her, but it was hard to tell if it was a good look or a *she's fricken weird* look from behind his aviators. Yes. Aviator sunglasses that added about the same level of hotness that his Army fatigues did. It was like every Tom Cruise from Top Gun fantasy she'd ever had. Except Jake was tall, and not couch jumping crazy. He just stood there, arms folded across his chest, wearing the khaki cargo shorts and white polo shirt like he was doing them a favor.

Who was she kidding? He *was* doing them a favor.

The first time she saw him blatantly stare in her direction, she was playing airplane with Mason. It was his favorite game, and something she'd done with all five of her nephews at one time or another, but now Mason was the only one small enough for her to do it with. Clearly, he didn't recognize that she was not wearing the correct shoes for this, so when he ran up to her with arms raised above his head screaming, "Apwane Tasey, Apwane!" there was no way she could say no. When she'd stopped twirling and put Mason back on the ground, she stood back and laughed at the unsteady circles he ran around her. She looked up to where Jake was standing next to her brother Michael, but he was looking back at her. She didn't need to see his eyes to know it. She could feel it as if he was actually touching her, dragging one calloused fingertip along her facial features.

She stared back, holding the smile and feeling a slow kindling of heat tickle the base of her spine, but then Michael said something that had Jake turning back to the conversation, effectively breaking the moment. Michael's wife Jen had walked up next to her, digging an elbow into Casey's side, dragging a very inconspicuous "OW" out of her.

"He's hot, Case," Jen said a bit louder than she had been comfortable with. "Imagine the babies you two would make."

Casey tried to laugh but it came out sounding like she was choking on her own spit. "I don't want to have his babies."

"Why don't you try saying that again, except this time tone down the raging desire in your eyes at the thought of procreating with him. Knowing you, you've probably already started a secret Pinterest board with wedding ideas."

Pfft. There was absolutely nothing wrong with bookmarking a few things here and there. Just because she knew she wanted hydrangeas as her bouquet, and that Jake, with his coloring, would look better in a soft gray suit versus a black tuxedo was completely beside the point.

She glanced down at her sister-in-law, not daring to look back at Jake. "It's not that bad, is it?"

Jen scoffed before taking a sip of her lemonade. The dixie cup shaded her cheekbones an unnatural shade of red when she held it up to her mouth. "You put perfume on for an outdoor picnic during the height of mosquito season. It's bad."

"Do you think I'm stupid?"

"Because he's your landlord, with all the complications that go along with that, or because he's the ultimate unattainable bad boy alpha male who's destined to break your heart?"

"Umm." She thought about that for a second, and found both labels equally depressing. "Either?"

She put an arm around Casey's waist, probably because she was too short to reach her shoulders. "Not stupid."

Casey leaned into Jen's slight frame. "Thanks, I knew-"

"I'd say you're blind as shit."

Casey turned stiffly, Jen's arm falling back to her side. "Excuse me?"

"Liam!" Jen bellowed, causing Casey to flinch. "If you put that worm in your brother's ear, you *will* live to regret it." She held the scary Mom glare on Liam for about five seconds, then turned back to Casey, facial features smoothing instantly. "I swear that kid will be the death of me. Now...what was I saying?"

"I'm blind, apparently."

"Ah, yes. You honestly don't see it?"

Casey held her hands up as if an answer would drop down into them, trying not to look as desperate as she felt. "Clearly not. What don't I see?"

"Jake is avoiding you."

"Uh huh. What's your point?"

"He's making it very clear that he doesn't want to stand by you, talk to you, or be caught looking at you."

"Aren't you supposed to be making me feel better?"

At that moment, Michael must have said something funny

because an unfamiliar burst of deep laughter caught Casey's attention before Jen could answer.

It was Jake.

Laughing.

Jake, with head tipped back, hands on his hips with a full grin across his face. Oh sweet baby Gucci, it felt like someone had dropped a bowling ball on her lungs. He had perfect, straight white teeth...and dimples. Two deep rivets on either side of his lips that were surely created simply to torture her. She wanted to dip her tongue into them.

Beside her, she heard Jen whisper something that sounded a lot like, "Holy shit, that's not fair."

Casey swiped her suddenly dry lips with her suddenly dry tongue and turned to her sister-in-law, begging her for a distraction with her eyes. One more second of watching that and she didn't think she'd be held accountable for her actions. "So, you were saying?"

"Oh, yeah...I was," she started unconvincingly. Casey snapped her fingers in front of Jen's eyes, and she drew her focus back instantly. "Yeah. So, I was saying that Jake wants you."

A hysterical giggle started somewhere at the bottom of her stomach, and even though she tried to shove it down, it erupted from her throat, unbidden and definitely unwanted. Jen was not as amused, looking at her like she'd lost her dang mind.

"Why are you laughing?"

"Because I've been thinking all week that he hates me and was probably regretting that he came here and that the fact that I'm even trying is probably a complete waste of time," she said, taking deep breaths to calm her suddenly racing heart. "You really think he does?"

Jen rolled her grass green eyes. "Yeah. If he hated you he never would have come here, no matter how persuasive your Mom is. And if he liked you as a friend, he'd actually talk to you for five seconds. He's doing an incredible job of pretending you don't exist...which only means one thing in guy language."

"What?" Casey asked breathlessly, everything clicking into place in her head.

"He's terrified of you, girl. In the very best way," she said with a glint in her eye. "You just need to show him he's got nothing to be afraid of."

The food got cleaned up, and Casey let Jen's words sink in. The men started gathering all the supplies to go shooting in the back acreage of her parents' property.

Every ill-advised plan of hers started someplace like this. With a taunt. Or a dare. A challenge that she just could not resist. And one innocent comment from Jake after Dylan had asked her to come shooting with the guys was the catalyst.

"C'mon Tuck, are you gonna come with us this time? Or are you still too afraid of the big loud noises?"

"I just don't want to show you up Dylan, you should be grateful."

He grinned, knowing just exactly how full of baloney she was. Hitting the broad side of a barn would be a great victory for Casey, especially with some of the smaller guns her Dad owned.

"I should probably be thanking you too," Jake said, addressing her for one of the first times all day.

"Why's that?" Dylan asked, before Casey could.

"Well, with her aim, and the loss of her dearly beloved shoes still fresh in her memory, she'd probably shoot my legs off."

Casey narrowed her eyes while Dylan bent over laughing. "You don't think I can shoot a gun?"

"Shooting one and hitting the target are two pretty different things."

"Dad?" Casey yelled, not taking her eyes off Jake.

"Yeah?"

"Are you taking your shotgun out?"

"Of course."

"Great. I get first up with it. And could you grab those big black ear protectors I like?"

"You got it."

Jake rubbed a hand across his jaw, regarding her. Dylan's eyebrows were almost hitting his hairline.

"Hey, you asked for it, boys. I hope you saved some room after lunch."

"Why?" Dylan asked, clearly very pleased with her little performance.

"Because you *will* be eating your words."

So for the first time in years, she found herself taking another deep breath before squinting at the heart of the watermelon that sat twenty feet away from her. When the last bit of air left her lungs, she gently squeezed the trigger and caught the sight of pink and green exploding at the same time that the kick from the shotgun knocked her back a step. Instead of whimpering and rubbing at her shoulder like she wanted to, she clicked the safety back on and calmly turned towards the sounds of triumphant whooping behind her. Even Jake was smiling. Her Dad clapped her on the back, then took the gun from her while she pulled off the headphones.

"Nice work, Tuck." Caleb wrapped his arms around her and lifted her off the ground in a bone crushing hug.

"Okay, you can put me down," she said on a laugh.

Dylan shoved her sore shoulder and gave her a smirk, knowing exactly what he was doing. "That hurt yet?"

She grinned and bit down on her tongue so she wouldn't wince at the pain radiating down her arm. "Of course not. It's not like I've never shot a gun before."

"Yeah, but it's been how many years since you have?"

"Probably not as long as you think," she replied. It had been six, but no way was she admitting that.

He leaned in so his mouth was right next to ear. "Jake can't hear you." She looked behind her, and noticed that he was about fifteen feet away from them, looking at the some of the other guns her Dad had brought along to the sand pits on their property where the family went shooting. "I give you shit about your aim all the time. You want to tell me why it suddenly spurred the tough girl routine?"

"It's not a routine. And I can ignore you because I've done it for years," she said as she smoothed back some strands of hair that had escaped her braid over the course of the day. "I can't let him think I'm inept, now can I? It was either that or do dishes with Mom, Jen and Marissa."

He made a face of disgust at that, because he knew it was true. "One of these days, Mom is going to pitch a feminist revolt and make us do it. I'm just waiting for it. She only let you out of it because she wants to adopt Jake."

Casey snorted, and couldn't disagree. "Speaking of routines, what's with the 'nice brother' one? I've never seen any of you be so welcoming to someone of the male species that isn't part of our family."

He shrugged his shoulders, his gaze flitting over to where Jake was still talking to their Dad. "He seems like a good guy."

"I don't buy it. Since when has that mattered to you? When I brought Rick home the first time you told him that you would shove a tire iron up his ass if he looked at me in a way you didn't like."

He barked out a laugh and looked completely unapologetic. "I forgot about that. Rick was a douche, Casey. He wore penny loafers with shorts. With actual pennies in them."

"And that justifies violent threats?"

"No, not by itself. But that and the obvious fact that all he wanted was a trophy wife did."

She couldn't disagree with that either. "Okay, fine, he wasn't the guy for me. But that still doesn't explain the warm welcome for Jake. You know I like him, I'm not even gonna pretend with you that I don't."

He looked at her for a second before answering. "I know you do. But no offense, the fact that he doesn't seem to reciprocate means I can be nice to him. My God given right as a brother is to think he's an idiot for not liking you, but then threaten his life if he ever decides that he does." He rolled his head back and forth, causing his neck to pop a few times. "And don't pretend that you don't like having protective brothers. You know we're awesome."

"Yeah," she said dryly. "And if I ever forget, you have no problem reminding me."

"So true," he said on a sigh, slinging an arm around her shoulders and walking them over to where the rest of the men were congregated.

Jake looked over at them and moved aside so that they could stand in the circle. "Nice shootin', Tex," he said with a slight curve to one side of his lips. "I guess you showed me."

"Thanks. Now aren't you glad I didn't have one of those on hand when I found Remy with my shoes?"

The other side of his lips rose forming a small, but definite smile, and she felt her heart stumble a bit on the next few beats. "I suppose I should be. How about we agree that you stay unarmed the weekends you have him."

She shrugged one shoulder lightly, struggling to look completely unaffected by the fact that the smell of his soap was burning a path through her. She was about two seconds away from dragging him into the trees, tying him to one and taking advantage of him. She wanted to eat him alive. "I guess that's fine."

"Careful Jake," Dylan warned. "You have no idea how creative Casey can get. She can make a weapon out of just about anything if she feels like her shoe collection is threatened. A few years ago, I pretended I was going to start a bonfire with some ugly ass sandals she had bought, and she tried to strangle me with a curling iron cord. Just consider your dog warned."

Jake looked over at her, narrowing his eyes a bit like he was trying to figure something out. "A curling iron cord?"

She smiled and ducked her chin down. It hadn't been her finest moment. "What can I say? It was either use the materials at hand, or let my Prada sandals die a fiery death."

Her Dad shook his head and chuckled. "Okay, let's head back to the house. Your Mom will want to dish up the ice cream before we get the fireworks set up. Besides, if you keep telling these stories, Jake will never dare leave his dog with you."

"It takes more than that to scare me, sir." Jake gave a slight nod in Casey's direction. Tate nudged her in the back while the rest of her brothers laughed. "I guess Remy and I will just have to be on our guard around her."

"Dude," Dylan said gravely. "You have no idea how right you are."

10

CASEY TAPPED the end of her pencil against the binding of the wallpaper book she was flipping through, not really seeing the designs in front of her. She flicked her eyes from the subtle stripes over to the phone sitting silent next to her. Back and forth until she thought she would scream if she didn't get a return call soon. For the last two months, she'd been doing research for an idea that she wanted to present to Tom. She'd worked at Hearth and Home since she was eighteen, and in the ever growing market of big box retail stores, she wanted to do everything in her power to see it stay around for a very long time. Ever since Melinda commandeered the blog that was her idea, she was determined to one up that little snot.

Okay, if she was capable of thinking about the situation rationally, she could admit that Tom was the one that had given Melinda responsibility for the blog...but she just *knew* that the pixie tyrant had manipulated the situation to piss her off. With a sigh, she flipped the book shut and shoved it aside. Glancing around quickly to make sure Melinda wasn't within sight, she pulled the blue folder that she kept wedged between color sample books that nobody used except her. As she fingered through some of her notes, the shrill ring of the telephone actually made her jump. She took a deep breath and pressed a hand on her stomach before lifting the receiver, knowing no one else would get the phone before her. The guys had an uncanny talent of ignoring calls while she was working.

"Thank you for calling Hearth and Home, this is Casey," she said in her most professional 'work voice'.

"Casey, this is Kevin Jackson from White Pine Real Estate returning your call."

She snapped up as if her spine had suddenly been turned into a concrete beam. "Mr. Jackson, thank you so much for getting back to me. Do you have a few minutes? I'd love it if we could go over the idea for a partnership opportunity that I mentioned in my voicemail."

When he agreed, she quickly placed the call on hold so she could switch to the phone in Mike's office. No way was she chancing Melinda lurking around a corner and hearing her conversation. Fifteen minutes later, she walked back to the desk as calmly as she could physically manage. She shoved the folder back in its hiding place and allowed herself a small victory dance. She was about to transition from a few excited jumps to a full out hip swing when she heard College Kid's distinctive shuffle come up behind her.

"Uhh, Casey? There's a customer asking for you."

She cleared her throat and tried to pretend like she was fixing something in her shoe before turning around with a polite smile firmly in place, only to find Jake standing a few feet behind Jason, arms crossed and doing that thing where he managed to smirk at her without moving his lips from their normal, frozen position.

"Of course," Jake said slowly, without losing the expression on his face. "I wouldn't want to interrupt anything too important."

Casey did a mental run down of her appearance right after she gave herself a firm mental bitch slap for being caught doing something so stupid at all, let alone in front of the man who made her ovaries stand up and sing the Hallelujah Chorus. Fitted black capri pants, white button down pin-tuck blouse with cap sleeves, wide red patent leather belt at her waist, and her beloved Jessica Simpson red patent peep toe slingbacks. That woman may not be a scholar, but she made some cute freakin' shoes. The four inch boost they gave her in height always made her feel powerful, and now that Jake had obviously caught her little shimmy, she needed every shove into the 'I'm a sexy and interesting yet somehow attainable goddess' category that she could get.

"Nope," she said as casually as she could manage, turning up the wattage on her smile just a bit. "A customer is never an interruption. Especially one who puts a roof over my head."

College Kid's eyes widened and snapped over, no doubt taking in the impressive width of Jake's shoulders and the biceps that didn't particularly want to be contained within the confines of his plain gray t-shirt. Poor Jason, even though he was easily the same height as Jake, it looked like you could take three of him and take up the same amount of space.

"You guys," he started, voice cracking slightly before he cleared his throat. "You guys live together?"

Jake raised an eyebrow at Jason before looking back to Casey with a slight curving of his lips.

"College Kid, meet Jake," Casey gestured slightly between the two, wanting to put Jason out of his all too apparent misery. "He's my landlord and next door neighbor."

Jake held out his hand, which Jason shook quickly and firmly before he heard Mike bellow his name from the other end of the store. Casey couldn't help but chuckle at how quickly he high-tailed it away from the two of them.

"College Kid?" Jake asked, with a trace of humor in his voice, even if it still didn't show on his face.

"Yeah, that's just a joke. His name is Jason, he's a good kid." Casey wasn't sure what to do with her hands besides ripping his shirt off, which she didn't think he'd appreciate. Instead, she busied herself with stacking the books in front her into a pile. "So what I can help you with, Jake? I'm sure you didn't come here just to visit."

Dear Lord, please let him have come just to visit.

Maybe with a 1.5 carat emerald cut diamond ring in his pocket and a declaration of undying love. I promise I'll be nice to my brothers for the rest of my life. Amen.

"I was wondering if you would be willing to put together some ideas for the unit I'm working on now. Obviously you already picked the tile and paint for the kitchen, and it uhh, it actually looks really good. So I was wondering if you had any other ideas for the rest of the rooms."

She laughed as she led him to one of the large round tables in front of the long rows of wallpaper books.

"I love how you say that like you're surprised." She pulled a few books while he sat down, already spinning ideas through her mind that could work in the space. She walked down the row of shelves while he sat at the table and pulled four books out.

"No, no," he said quickly. "I can tell you know what you're talking about. What I meant was that you did good, and it made me think that I might have played it too safe in your unit."

She turned and set the books down in front of him on the table, and didn't try to hide her amusement.

"Why, Jake," she said as she slid into a chair next him and pulled the first book in front of her. "If I didn't know any better I could have *sworn* you just admitted I was right."

He shook his head, then grabbed another one of the books, effectively ignoring her statement, which only made her laugh again. She liked this kind of interaction with him. It made her a little lightheaded and warm inside, like she drank a glass of wine too fast.

Such a lovely feeling.

"So what are we looking for in these books?"

Flipping through a few pages, she landed on a neutral-colored grass cloth and tilted it towards him.

"Something like that. You could put it on the wall next to the front door in that unit, and add some wall hooks for coats and hats and stuff. It'll give a sense of an entryway without actually having a separate space."

"It looks weird. Do you have something that doesn't have that crap woven through it?"

"Ouch. And here I thought you trusted me," she said lightly, not really surprised at his reaction. Men had absolutely no vision when it came to texture on the walls. "Alright, you flip through those three books and put a piece of paper in any page you like, or at least ones that you don't hate completely. Look for something in this color tone though. I have two orders that I need to call in real quick and then I'll check back with you. Unless you want to check out the books and do this at home?"

He looked at the paper she had chosen for a few seconds, then his dark eyes met hers and just...held. His face was completely blank, but his eyes were strangely intense. She swallowed thickly, not able to look away.

"I'll stay." His voice was so deep, it reached down inside her and pulled any feelings she had towards him straight up her throat. She felt like there was no possible way he couldn't see right through her.

Without another word, she pivoted quickly and walked back to her desk, taking a shaky breath while she pulled the phone off the cradle. Ever since the day at her parents, her increasing feelings for Jake swirled through alongside the knowledge that it was probably monumentally stupid to get involved with her landlord. Before that day, she was able to brush aside how she felt because she didn't think there was a snowballs chance in Hades that he was interested in her. But the observation from Jen had the same effect as the cartoon anvil smashing into her skull. Except instead of little birdies flying in circles around her head, it was miniature versions of Jake in camo. Mmmmmm.

He still did such a good job of staying away from her that she refused to let herself get too carried away.

Until today.

It *had* to mean something that he came here today and didn't feel the need to rush out.

Realizing that she was still sitting there with the phone in her hand, the dial tone long since changed to a bleating pulse, she shook her head and pulled out the paperwork that she needed.

WHAT THE HELL am I doing here?

Jake sank his head into his hands, barely stifling the urge to drop his forehead to the table and beat a steady rhythm on the cold, hard surface. When he left the house this morning, he had absolutely no intention of coming to Hearth and Home, and all he could do was blame it on the simple fact that he had barely seen Casey since Labor Day at her parents. He hated, totally and completely loathed, that he felt like his skin was getting itchy at the fact that he had only run into her once in seven long days.

It probably didn't help that today was the anniversary of his Mom's passing. Normally, he wasn't one of those people that paid close attention to those kinds of things, but for some reason when he woke this morning, all he could do was lay and stare at the white ceiling above him and think about how it felt to watch his Mom's breathing slow and change. It was so different than the type of death he'd seen in war.

The hospice nurse had told him what to expect, that his Mom would probably refuse food and drink in the days leading up to her death, that her extremities would start turning cold, and that at the very end, her breathing would simply start slowing down until she just wouldn't take another one. They'd said their goodbyes, she'd said how much she loved him, how proud she was of him, and apologized for the fact that he'd be alone once she was gone. He assured her that he was fine, and that she didn't need to worry about him. He could tell she had been at peace, and just like the nurse said, she simply slipped away while he sat there holding her hand.

He didn't cry, just kissed her cold fingers, and started implementing the funeral plans they had talked about the week before. He hadn't thought about that day again until now. And for a reason he didn't want to look into too much, as he drove in the general area of Hearth and Home, he found his truck pulling in the parking lot without making a conscious decision to do so.

Every single night since seeing her around her family he actually felt haunted by the image of her swinging her nephew around. The sheer joy on her face from something so simple as a laughing child running clumsily around her legs was a picture that seemed to be tattooed on the back of his eyelids. As sexy as she looked that day, especially holding that shotgun up to her shoulder, that wasn't what his brain conjured when he thought of her now. He'd seen her smile before of course, but in that moment, with her mouth stretched so wide, he didn't know if he'd ever seen anything so beautiful. Then she'd looked up and caught him staring. Her smile had softened into something different than it had been seconds before, but her expression was still so...open that something had cracked in his chest.

Even outside of Casey, it had been so damn long since he felt anything close to what he had experienced that day at the Steadman house. If he thought really hard, he didn't know if he'd ever felt it.

It was loud, and chaotic, and messy, and so full of people who loved and accepted each other it almost made him uncomfortable. As an only child, he'd never fully understood the dynamic of large families, even if there were many years growing up that he would have killed to be a part of one. As he got older, he didn't long for it anymore, partially because being part of the Army gave him as much a family as he figured he'd ever get. He was so used to it just being him and his Mom, that even after she passed away, he'd missed her, of course, but it wasn't the way you miss someone that's been a part of your day to day life.

It was more like a dull ache when he would recall memories of growing up with her, a vague sadness at how painful it had been for her the last eighteen years of her life. She'd done her best as an unexpected widow and single mother to an angry and confused eleven year old boy, but it quickly made her weary. The exhaustion was written deeply in the lines of her face, and Jake felt like she must have been slightly relieved when he joined the Army after high school.

While he enjoyed the camaraderie of his brothers in arms the first few years, enjoying the close bonds forged among the constantly humming state of tension that came with war, it only took a couple flag draped caskets for him to realize that maintaining a certain distance from the men around him was preferable to the visceral feelings that ripped through him whenever one of their lives was cut too short. His failed attempt at forever with Lisa had only served to cement his belief. Maybe after so many years of holding himself at arms-length had finally caused something inside to weaken to the point that he was vulnerable. Maybe that's why Casey, with her wide smiles and eyes that practically glowed, was actually affecting him.

Well shit, listen to Dr. Phil here.

He stared down at the wallpaper book in front of him blankly, thankful that Casey was still on the phone with her back facing him. Putting an immediate halt on the girly-ass mental ramblings, he took the rare opportunity to simply sit back and study her. He couldn't help but smile when he thought of how she had been dancing in place behind the counter. Left up to him, he probably wouldn't have announced his presence, just watched the swing and sway of her body. She looked immaculate, a friggin *vision*, walking that fine line between classy and sexy, not straying too closely to either side. The only thing that would make her even better in Jake's eyes was if all that hair was loose around her shoulders. He flexed his fingers on the table at the thought of what it would be like to push his hands through all those dark waves. He liked that her hair wasn't either curly or straight. Somewhere perfectly in the middle of two extremes.

Just like her, it was effortless.

Dude, you are waxing poetic about her hair. Why can't you just check out her ass and call it a day like a normal guy?

He flipped through a couple pages, knowing that Casey would notice immediately if he was on the same page as when she left the table. It only took about a page and a half to realize that ugly wallpaper served as a pretty great distraction from the thoughts that had no place in his head. Yeah, she might deal with decorating trends every day, but there was no way in hell he would put this stuff up on any walls that would possibly be seen by another human being. He looked over to Casey, where she was laughing and talking with a customer who had walked over to her desk. She had an ease in dealing with people, something he'd never had.

He could see how much she was in her element here, with the long wall of shelves filled with wallpaper books, each tall, slim binding different than the one next to it. Hanging racks along another wall holding large swaths of fabric, another shelving unit filled to the brim with coordinating pillows. Framed display boards were perched attractively throughout the area, and even though most of the pattern and color combinations would have given Jake a headache on a daily basis, he could clearly see her mark.

Colorful and vibrant and elegant without an ounce of pretension.

It was exactly how he would define Casey. He gave a cynical laugh, because despite her talents so obviously on display in this area, it couldn't save the god-awful options she gave him to look at for the unit he was working on. With a shake of his head, he closed the book and gave it a not so gentle shove towards the others she had pulled out, having absolutely no intention of looking at them.

"Well, that's not the reaction I was looking for."

Jake glanced up to where Casey was standing across the table from him, hands propped on the back of a chair, looking too damn appealing for her own good. He met her gaze as evenly as he could, given where his mind had been traveling while she was on the phone. He knew his eyes would give nothing away, a talent he'd honed early on in his time in the Army. One of the other platoon leaders summed it up perfectly: it was 'The LT Miller guaranteed-to-make a-PFC-shit-in-his-pants look of soul-less disdain'. A little wordy for his tastes, but it held more than a kernel of truth and had served him well on many occasions. Granted, he certainly didn't want Casey to be afraid of him, but there was no way he was going to let her see just how much she affected him.

"What can I say?" he said easily, leaning back in the chair and stretching his arms over his head, not missing the way her eyes flicked from his biceps and then back to his face. "I guess I don't go for wallpaper that looks like it's been ripped from the floor of a tiki hut."

Her head tipped back with one throaty burst of laughter, and oh hell, that sound had him shifting slightly in his chair. Somehow, she managed to garner the same reaction with a laugh that was normally reserved for a fleeting glimpse of cleavage or a flash of smooth contoured skin that should be covered.

She moved around the table and stood behind his chair, reaching past his shoulder to grab one of the books he didn't open. He could feel the warmth radiating off her skin even though they hadn't actually touched, but her scent was wrapped around him as if they had. That clean tang of citrus seemed to pulse through him as she reclaimed her chair from earlier. Jake couldn't promise himself that he'd be able to keep his hands off her if he sat here too much longer, seeing the long line of her neck slope down to where it met the white collar of her shirt as she perused through the pages in front of her, a spot that he could easily say he'd never noticed before on a woman.

With a start he realized she had been talking, and was looking over at him expectantly while he ogled her neck like a vampire-ey creeper.

"Jake?" she asked with an arch of one dark brow and a smile lightly touching her lips. "Where'd you go?"

Purgatory. That's what he felt like saying. He was trapped in a Casey filled purgatory, relegated to stare at her hair and her neck and her ridiculously long legs in sexy heels and smell nothing but the sweet orange scent that followed her and not be able to do a thing about it. Shit, he didn't even know who he was right now.

"Sorry, what did you say?" His voice sounded a little bit like he had been chewing on gravel, but hopefully she wouldn't notice.

"I was telling you about a customer that I just helped who picked one of these and her room turned out amazingly. I know it's a lot to ask, but would you trust me to do something in that front family room while you're gone next weekend?"

Okay. That snapped him out of his neck fantasies. He narrowed his eyes, not liking the hopeful, puppy dog expression that had taken over her face.

"Define 'something'. That's a tad too broad for my liking."

"If I tell you what I have planned, you'll say no."

"Is that your best argument?" He crossed his arms in front of him, noticing that when she was feeling stubborn her eyes looked slightly more green than blue. "Because you might want to revisit your strategy."

"Have I led you astray yet? Weren't you the one who said I was right about the kitchen choices? And if I'm choosing stuff for these units to advertise Hearth and Home, why would I choose anything that looks bad?"

"You really want me to answer those questions?"

She tilted her head and looked less than amused for a split second before setting her face back into persuasive mode. It wasn't that he didn't trust her taste. He did. But man, when she looked at him like that? All feisty and riled up. He liked it. A whole helluva lot. And what was even more unnerving, was that the determined glint in her eye was working. It was actually working on him.

They held in that stalemate for a few more long, charged seconds. He could practically feel her force of will spitting and flaring between them.

"Fine," he said grudgingly, trying to ignore the triumphant smile that lifted her cheeks and showed more teeth than he thought he had in his entire mouth. "But if I hate it-"

"You won't," she interrupted quickly. "But if you do, I'll take it down."

He stood from table while she struggled to keep her face impassive. This woman wore her emotions like one of her accessories, but he had to admire that about her.

"So when I walk outta here, are you gonna do your little 'I got my way' dance again?"

Her jaw dropped and a flush crept up her neck before staining her face. He couldn't help his quick grin after her eyes dropped to the table where her fingers were picking at the side of one of the books.

"I don't know what you're talking about, Jake." Her voice was prim, and she straightened her shoulders before finally looking up at him. Her eyes were wide and unblinking, not showing him anything for the first time since he'd gotten to the store. He decided he liked it much better when she was worked up, but he figured that was easy enough to do.

"If you say so." He picked up his binder off the table, tucking it under his arm and walking towards the entrance of the store. He only made it a few steps before turning back to where she was still sitting and watching him. Against his better judgment, but not being able to resist the opportunity to throw her off balance, he gave her a slow, deliberate grin. "Whatever it was, I didn't hate it."

Her eyes widened, and her perfect lips formed a perfect 'O' shape.

Bingo.

He gave her a little wink and then strode out of the store without a backwards glance.

11

CASEY SQUINTED AT HER PHONE, reading the text from Rachel one more time. Maybe it would change if she looked at it again.

Change of plans for Ladies Night. Be ready in your driveway in 15 minutes. Dress slutty.

She looked down at the skinny jeans, basic white tank and brightly patterned scarf she had planned on wearing over to Rachel's house.

Fashionable? Sure.

Slutty? Not so much.

She wasn't quite sure what had happened or why Rachel was obviously planning on going out. The couple times it had happened, it was usually triggered by something fairly big. She had talked to Rachel yesterday, and everything had seemed normal.

Hmmmm.

The last time this happened was over a year ago when Casey had dumped Rick, and she had felt the overwhelming need for shots and the desire to dance to a sweaty, thumping bass line to negate the disaster of that relationship. Probably because Rick would have rather had bamboo splints shoved under his finger-nails before he chose to go to a bar where people actually had *fun*.

Not wanting to waste any of her precious fifteen minutes of prep time, she quickly skipped down the hallway, whipping off her black ballet flats and the scarf, bracing her hand on the wall as she went to keep her balance. She walked into the second bedroom, finding the section of shoe boxes that held all her three inch or higher heels. Nothing could sufficiently sluttify an outfit quicker than a pair of stilettos. Slowly dragging her finger down the line of boxes, Casey stopped every once in a while to try on different options, finally settling for her cheetah print platform pumps.

Quickly swiping a tan cowl neck tank off a nearby hanger and pulling it over her head, she stood back to look in the full length mirror in the corner. She pulled the elastic band out of her hair, digging her fingers into her scalp at an attempt at volume. She tipped her head to the side, and decided it wasn't too shabby for...ten minutes.

Once she added a little more makeup, she couldn't help but wish that she would accidentally-on-purpose run into Jake. She hadn't seen him in almost a week, since the day he stopped in at Hearth and Home. When he had been sitting at the large round table, she knew she wasn't imagining that he had looked at her with, oh, what was the word?

Hunger. He had looked hungry. For her.

When she had walked back over to him, sitting there being all grumpy and broody and delicious about the wallpaper she wanted him to pick from, he had looked up at her and she could see it. She'd miraculously kept her composure, even though her long neglected lady parts were screaming at her to *do something*. She didn't want to play hard to get with him, but she also knew just enough of him to know that, at best, he would probably be the type to proceed with caution. At worst, he could be a total commitment-phobe who would treat a relationship with her like most people would treat a mailbox full of anthrax. Just because he was attracted to her, at least if Jen was right, didn't mean he would ever do anything about it.

But then, as she had watched him walk away from the table, unabashedly admiring a rear view that was easily as attractive as the front view, it had happened.

The flirty comment. The wink. And she had about swallowed her tongue.

There were moments in life where a woman was capable of reacting gracefully and coolly when the object of her so far unrequited desire finally gives her something in return. Unfortunately for her, it had not been one of them. In the three hundred and forty two times that she had replayed that teeny point in time, Casey had come up with about three hundred and forty one reactions that were better than the one she'd actually had in that moment. Her favorite was the one where she had stood up slowly from the table, not saying a word as she walked purposefully towards him, grabbed a fistful of his shirt, dragged his mouth down to hers and promptly shoved her tongue in his mouth.

Even thinking about it now made her get all throbby and tingly where she hadn't been *throbbed* or *tingled* in a really, really long time. Three short bursts of a car horn pulled her from the fantasy. She clearly heard the pulsing music from Rachel's car before she even yanked the door shut behind her.

"Hurry up, bitch, let's get this show on the road," Rachel bellowed over the rhythm of Justin Timberlake.

Casey laughed and arched an eyebrow as she folded herself into her friend's low-slung 1970 Camaro. It had been Rachel's 'baby' since high school, and was still in the same immaculate condition that it had been in since the day her parents had presented it to her with a red bow on the gleaming black hood. Casey wasn't a car person, but had always appreciated the growl of the engine as Rachel would expertly shift gears, and could almost understand why men strayed to cars during a mid-life crisis.

She glanced towards the driver's seat, turning the music down slightly while taking in her friend's demeanor. At the moment, it was reading just a little, or a lot, aggressive. Rachel punched the car into reverse, not waiting for Casey to click her seatbelt before peeling backwards.

"Wow," she said thoughtfully. "What did Marc do? It must be bad if you're willing to drop your transmission in my driveway."

"I need at least three shots before I get into this." Rachel finally looked at Casey, her eyes flashing. Yup, Rachel was pissed. And also clearly taking her dress code mandate to heart. Black leather short shorts, a Bridgette Bardot inspired hairstyle, and a cleavage baring fuchsia top. Most redheads wouldn't be able to pull off the bright color, but Rachel with her enviable hourglass figure, just looked daring and confident. And mildly slutty.

"No problem", Casey said easily. She let the music fill the car for a few moments. "So you're wearing leather shorts. That's new."

Rachel didn't say anything at first, just stamped one nude heeled shoe down on the clutch as she shifted gears. "Three shots, Casey. Don't push your luck."

She knew better, knowing that Rachel in this kind of mood could easily tip into irrational. When they got to Liz's house, Casey gave the blonde a warning glance before letting her into the seat behind her. Reading the non-verbal cues exactly the way she was supposed to, Liz wisely said nothing on the rest of the drive, not even when Rachel yelled at her for her boot cut jeans and decidedly non slutty black turtleneck top. The tires squealed in protest as Rachel cranked the car into a parking space in front of a rundown looking bar. She marched in through the doors, not waiting for the two very confused friends trailing in her wake.

After deciding that they didn't have much choice but to

follow, Casey and Liz pushed through the heavy wooden door and found Rachel already perched at a slightly dirty high top table, placing a drink order.

An hour, and an impressive five lemon drop shots later, a sufficiently drunk Rachel finally started talking.

"Marc cheated on me." She said it in a deceptively quiet voice, belying the violence that sparked through her hazel eyes.

After the appropriate gasping, screeching and vilifying, Casey and Liz listened in horrified silence as Rachel slurred her way through her story. She had come home early from work to the house she shared with Marc, only to find her handsome, caring, generous, devoted boyfriend of three years handcuffed to their four poster, wrought iron bed, thoroughly enjoying the ministrations of a whip thin brunette wearing a black leather bustier and crotchless underwear.

"And you know what pisses me off more than anything?" Rachel bellowed, slamming one fist onto the table and making the empty shot glasses tremble, and not particularly caring that everyone within ear shot could hear the entire sordid tale. The good thing about her ear-splitting volume was that the waitress had brought them another round of shots on the house, mumbling something about assholes and then patting Rachel on the shoulder. Even Liz had taken the shot without an argument. "They were using the handcuffs that I bought six months ago. The ones that he said were a 'little outside his comfort zone'. Well, apparently they're in his mother effing comfort zone as long as it's not *me* putting them on him."

Her voice wavered for just a moment at the end, betraying her alcohol fueled bravado. Heart aching for her friend, Casey moved her hand across the cluttered table, knowing that Rachel would hate to show too much weakness. She wrapped a hand around one of Rachel's, where it gripped an empty shot glass so tightly that her already fair skin was practically translucent. Rachel pulled her hand out, not in a rude way, because Casey knew her

friend well enough that a simple touch could easily be the difference between staying inside the protective cocoon of anger or
losing the tenuous grip that was holding a hurricane of emotions
inside.

Liz cleared her throat, and brushed a trembling finger underneath one eye, attempting to conceal the wetness that threatened
to spill from her blue eyes. Casey could only imagine how the
unwavering romantic inside Liz was grieving. Thankfully Rachel
didn't notice, because she was too busy flagging down their
server.

"I don't care what kind, but three more shots, please."

"Sure thing, sweetie," the waitress said and spun around back
to the bar.

"So, what are you two gonna drink?" Rachel's face was
completely serious, brooking no argument that either of them
would be partaking in that *that* particular order.

Liz blinked a few times, while Casey laughed through her
nose, taking a sip of the water in front of her.

The harried looking server came back, placing three small
glasses on the table. The lines woven around her mouth and eyes
said that she could probably sit and tell some tales that would
easily rival Rachel's.

"What are those called?" Casey asked, gesturing at the shots.
Only then did her thin, pinched lips curve into a smile.

"Those little gems are called 'Brunettes are sluts too'." Liz
gaped at the waitress, Rachel threw her head back and roared
while Casey sputtered into her water glass. "No offense, honey."
Her eyes flicked to Casey's dark hair with a smirk before turning
and disappearing into the rapidly growing crowd milling through
the bar.

"Mmmmm, deeeeeeeelicious." Rachel sloppily licked her lips
after tossing back all three shots in rapid succession.

As the evening stretched on, their waitress Nancy, as her
named turned out to be, decided to cut Rachel off and was only

bringing them water. Liz stayed glued to her chair whenever Casey and Rachel would head out to the informally staged dance floor, casting apprehensive looks around her as if someone would pounce on her just because she was sitting there alone. Casey plopped down next to her when her poor feet needed a break, fanning her face with one hand and taking three long pulls from her water.

"Casey, how are we going to get home? Neither of us can drive a stick shift, and there is no way Rachel can get behind the wheel right now. I already took her keys out of her purse in case she would try." Her soft voice was liberally threaded with unease, and the truth of what Liz was saying was just enough to sober Casey up.

Well, a little bit. She still felt like she had a wonderfully hazy curtain draped over head, a product of the magic little glasses that Nancy had been bringing them. The obnoxious name notwithstanding, those shots were quite tasty. When she looked around the bar, she didn't notice the dark paneled walls that were in need a good painting, the dingy carpet or the brass plated light fixtures that had seen better days. She pretty much saw the funnest place she'd been in a while.

Funnest? Funniest? Most fun? Whatever. She never wanted to go anywhere else.

"Hmmm," Casey said, snapping back to the conversation with Liz and feeling like the sound of her voice was coming from someone else's mouth. "Oh yeah. I would say we could call Dylan, but I know he's working tonight."

"What about Tate?" Liz already looked more at ease, knowing she would have some reinforcements in getting the three of them home safely. "He doesn't live that far from here, does he? Do you think Natalie would mind if he helped us out?"

Both Liz and Rachel knew Natalie was...easily inconvenienced when it came to sharing Tate. And that was on a good day. Casey had to have a serious talk with Tate about marrying that girl, she just never knew how to bring it up considering that Natalie was typically harnessed to his hip.

"Ugh. Who cares what she thinks," Casey sniped, and tapped out a quick text to Tate on her phone, saying they needed a ride and the address of the bar, but not going into any other details. Almost immediately, her phone flashed.

I'll be there in five. Don't go anywhere. And don't drink anything else unless it's water.

I mean it, Casey. WATER ONLY.

She rolled her eyes and slipped her phone back into her purse.

With a wave at Nancy, Casey signaled for the check when their waitress couldn't make her way through the crowd right away, knowing that they might have a fight on their hands in trying to peel Rachel from the dance floor. She was feisty enough when sober, but add some hard liquor to her stereotypical redheaded temper? Yeesh. She'd just let Tate deal with getting her out of here. That's what nice, gentle, strong and sober brothers were for.

Liz looked over Casey's shoulder to where Rachel was swiveling her hips to an 80's hair-band song. Her languid, shot-loosened movements had attracted a small contingent of admirers from nearby tables. Liz gave a small smile before shaking her head.

"What are we going to do with her? And I don't just mean tonight. She was planning on *marrying* him, Casey."

Oh Lord have mercy, Liz was about to get into her serious fixey mode, and it was all Casey could do to not sway where she sat in her chair.

"No clue." She answered succinctly and honestly, not capable of anything else given the amount of alcohol prancing happily through her veins. "I'm guessing she'll have to move out since it was his place first, which violates the natural order of things if you ask me."

"The natural order?" Liz only looked at Casey briefly before locking her bright blue gaze back on Rachel, as if looking away for too long would be the catalyst for something terrible to happen on the crowded dance floor.

"Yeah, he's the one who cheated. He should be the one moving out. Why should he get the house *and* the skinny brunette with a sex fetish?"

"Ix-nay on the brunette talk, she's coming back."

Casey turned around in time to see Rachel attempt to navigate through the loud, shifting crowds of people on the dance floor. She managed to make it most of the way unscathed, then lurched into one incredibly large man who gave her a dirty look until he noticed the bountiful cleavage threatening to spill from her top. His demeanor slowly shifted until he looked like a kid who just woke up on Christmas morning to find his favorite present waiting for him, wrapped up in a shiny, drunk package.

"Ohhhhhhh boy," Casey breathed, praying he decided to be smart and keep his hands to himself. Dude did not know what he would be getting into with Rachel in a mood like she was in tonight. Casey looked over towards the entrance, hoping to see Tate's dark blond head weaving towards them. No such luck. She wasn't even looking so he could step in and protect Rachel. She figured he might be necessary to pull Rachel away from an all-out brawl.

Liz was wringing her hands together on the table. "Casey," she started to say, voice wavering with undiluted nerves.

Well, Big Dude was not smart.

He was incredibly stupid.

Placing one of his big paws around Rachel's shoulders, he leaned down and said something in her ear. Thirty seconds before, she hadn't been capable of walking a straight line, but now she became eerily still, facial features carved from stone as she looked over at his hand on her skin.

One perfect eyebrow arched, Rachel calmly reached up to

place her hand atop of where his was currently playing with the strap of her tank top. She peered up into his face, which held a lecherous grin, and returned his look with a deceptively sweet smile. Casey and Liz groaned in unison, imagining what was going to come next, but knowing there was absolutely nothing they could do to stop it.

Big Dude's facial features twisted in a comical meld of pain and surprise when Rachel suddenly twisted his pinky finger backwards at a completely unnatural angle. When he jerked backwards, attempting to pull his hand out of her grip, she rammed one stiletto clad foot directly on his shin bone, causing him to roar out a very naughty word. Liz looked sufficiently horrified, and Casey couldn't help but grin. Amongst the general clamor of the bar, only a handful of people surrounding them were even aware of what happened, so Rachel dropped his hand before it became a scene, shoved at his husky arm and threw a few choice words over her shoulder as she turned and headed back to their table. She attempted a curtsy when Casey applauded her arrival.

"Stupid, piece of crap Neanderthal," she muttered as she plopped indelicately into her chair.

"Do I want to know what he whispered in your ear?" Liz asked, looking completely miserable at the turn of events.

"Nope. It would make your saintly, virginal ears go up in flames." Rachel beamed, still riding the high of her encounter with Big Dude, who had limped off the dance floor looking quite deflated. "Geez Louise, I am *wasted*."

"That you are, my friend." Casey readily agreed, glad that Rachel knew it. "Nancy-pants should have our check here soon. How about we head home and you can shack up with me for the night?"

"A sleepover? Maybe we could invite Jakey-poo!" Rachel exclaimed, clapping her hands and only missed making the connection a couple times. Her eyelids fluttered a few times, like she was contemplating sleep when they suddenly popped wide open.

"Eeeeek. LOOK." She flung one arm in a wide arc and gestured wildly towards the bar, clipping Casey in the back of the head. "It's Jason Statham. Jaaaaasooon."

"Ow." Rubbing at the spot on the back of her skull, Casey craned her neck trying to see what her friend was seeing. Definitely a bald guy at the bar, but he was easily into his sixties, and not even remotely attractive. Liz tucked her credit card into the black folder containing their bill from Nancy, who had just shoved it at them before delivering an overloaded tray of shots to the table full of frat boys next to them.

"Honey, I really don't think that's Jason Statham."

"Ohhhh, it's *so* him. I see his beautiful bald little head." She squinted her slightly unfocused eyes, leaning so far over in her chair to get a better look that the legs tipped sideways from the sudden weight shift, dumping her unceremoniously onto the dingy carpet.

Casey clutched her sides, trying to contain the giggles spilling out of her throat. Even Liz was having trouble, slim shoulders shaking in silent laughter after dropping her forehead to the table.

"Are you okay down there, Red?" Liz's voice was slightly muffled by her napkin.

Rachel's head popped up above the tabletop, like that whack-a-mole carnival game, except drunk. Her cheeks were flushed from equal parts alcohol and the tumble to the floor. "Thanks for nothin', bitches. Don't help the drunk girl off the floor."

Casey lost the battle containing her laughter, tears clouding her vision as she watched Rachel attempt to push herself up off the floor using her chair. She was about halfway up, trying to get her feet steady beneath her when her face split into a blinding smile focused somewhere behind Casey.

"Taaaaaaate." She practically sang. "You're at Ladies Night."

Casey swiped under her eyes, and then lost her composure all over again when she saw Tate standing behind her, jaw hanging open and a completely horrified look in his dark eyes as he took in the combined state of the three of them.

"Oh my," he said quietly, shoving his hands on his hips, assuming the 'annoyed older brother' position. He spoke so low, Casey only knew what he said because she knew Tate. He gave his head a slight shake, leaning down and easily pulling Rachel up from floor, trying unsuccessfully to help her sit back in her chair, which she was currently trying to stand on in order to look over Tate's head.

"Move it or lose it, Steadman. Well, other Steadman. Steadman two. Steadman boy. Whatever. I don't know why you're here, but I'm trying to find Jason. I need to ask him to have my babies."

Casey choked down another laugh when Tate clamped his eyes shut, and then actually looked irritated when he opened them again and looked over at her. Yikes, that did not bode well. It looked like calling the calm brother might not have been the best course of action. Rachel hooked one arm around the back of Tate's head, trying to use his shoulders to leverage herself up onto the chair. God bless him, he didn't even sneak a peek at the abundance of cleavage that smashed into his arm as she tried to climb over him. After saying her name a couple times with no response, he gently grabbed her chin and pulled her face towards him.

"Rachel, if you do me a favor and sit for a minute, I will help you find Jason before we get you ladies safely home. Okay?"

She blinked up at him a few times, then gave a small nod before slumping down into her chair. He pulled in a huge breath, and slowly released it before turning to Casey and Liz.

"What. Happened?" Despite it being an inquiry into their sad state of affairs, there was no question present in his tone. Liz gave Tate a very abbreviated version of why they were there, and his broad shoulders collapsed on an exhale. He pinched the bridge of his nose, and visibly shored up his emotions before crouching down in front of Rachel - who was focusing all her energy on getting the straw from her water glass into her mouth. She leaned forward to try again, only to stab the side of her mouth with the end of the red and white plastic. Tate's mouth softened just a smidge, but enough that Casey knew he'd go easy on them.

"Rach?" He spoke in a soft, firm voice. Casey changed her mind again, Tate was the perfect one to call. He would be able to bring her back down to a level emotional state.

"Hmmm?"

"Marc is an asshole, and he obviously doesn't deserve you. I'm so sorry."

"Yeah," she said matter-of-factly, not looking him in the eye. "You want to hear something else that's crazy?"

"What's that?"

"The ho-bag that was with him totally reminded me of your bitch of a fiancee. You know, long dark hair and no ass to speak of? You sure Natalie was accounted for tonight? Because I certainly wouldn't mind a reason to kick *her* scrawny ass."

Or maybe not.

Casey dropped her head in her hands and groaned. And Tate, saint that he is, just sighed and helped Rachel stand up, wrapping an arm around her waist to keep her steady as their sad little group moved towards the exit.

"Okay Mike Tyson, let's go." He turned to Casey and spoke out the side of his mouth. "You? I will deal with you later."

Excellent. Hopefully she'd be able to have about four more drinks before *that* happened.

12

CASEY STOOD over the utility tub in the garage, sucking air through clenched teeth trying to withstand the scalding water she was using to clean out her paint brush. The rapidly diluted orange color swirled down the drain making her practically giddy. It signaled her victory of getting paint color on her living room walls before Jake could stop her. Thinking back to that conversation now, after getting to know him better, made it that much sweeter.

He was going to crap a brick when he saw it. But goodness, it looked amazing so far, and it wasn't even completely dry yet.

Shaking out the excess water from the smooth bristles once she got all the paint out, she turned her thoughts to the wallpaper project in the other duplex. In the days since Jake agreed to give her carte blanche, she had decided on a plan that offered a slight compromise between both of their tastes and placed a rush order. She may or may not have flirted a teensy bit with Blaine, her Thibaut rep, in order to get another ten percent off the order. Probably not a smart move because he had already asked her out three times. Ick. Just thinking about his slicked back ponytail and clammy, pale little hands gave her a full body shudder.

But she had to give the guy props, because even though she was at least five inches taller and ten years younger than him, he just kept persisting. Actually, the first time he asked her out, she laughed, because up until then she had thought he was completely and totally flaming gay. He wore patterns and colors that would make Clinton Kelly weep with happiness. In fact, that afternoon he had been wearing a navy cardigan with a crisp, pink polka dotted shirt underneath, and pants that had a subtle gray plaid to them.

Gay, right? Apparently not.

In fact, it was immediately after she had complimented him on his shirt, he reached across the counter and stroked the back of her hand, asked if she wanted to go out for drinks after her shift and then see him out of said shirt. She laughed, thinking how cute it was that the gay wallpaper rep was teasing her. Because hello, he's a sales rep for a *wallpaper company*. If that wasn't the proverbial cherry on top of that glittery homosexual sundae, she didn't know what was.

He didn't think it was funny, and then she had to try and fix the horrified expression on her face into something a tad more graceful. She politely declined, saying that she was seeing someone, but the guy was irritatingly steadfast in his pursuit. This last attempt he had told her that they were a match made in fashion heaven, considering her taste in shoes. But, she was again able to put him off saying that her boyfriend probably wouldn't appreciate her going out with someone else. Thankfully he hadn't asked for too many specifics on her fictional beau. Knowing the current state her fantasies lived in, she'd be giving out Jake's stats, including address and medical history just to keep Blaine at bay.

After cleaning up the rest of her paint mess, she pulled out sizing, paste and rolls of wallpaper in order to get started. She had a little over six hours until Jake was due home, which would give her plenty of time to finish up. She wanted him to walk in, take in the glory and majesty of her work, fall to his knees in gratitude and awe, and then swiftly follow up with a date invitation. Shifting the wallpaper supplies in her arms, she gave a little laugh. At this point, she'd be more than happy with the gratitude portion.

Yesterday, she had painted the wainscoting and chair rail a crisp white to match the trim he had already finished. All she had to do today was hang the paper she picked on the upper half of the wall, then use Jake's nail gun to install the wainscot and chair rail. Bonus knowledge that she gained from her job? An absolute kickass mastery of most basic power tools. Once the wallpaper was up, she had gotten a beautiful mahogany wall plaque with six double hooks that would give the entryway feel she was looking for. But she knew that in order to get him on board, it would have to be totally done so he could see the finished awesomeness. Because man, she did not want to have to take it all down.

As she was about to walk out to the other unit, she looked back at Remy where he was sprawled out on her kitchen floor. He perked his head up at her hesitation, thumping his tail optimistically on the dark laminate floor, probably thinking that she would allow him to come with.

She snorted. "No way, dog. You may not have committed any murder-worthy offenses this weekend, but I am *not* risking you messing up my masterpiece. You're gonna have to stay right where you are."

With a discontented groan, he flopped back into his original position. So freaky how he seemed to understand her. It actually hadn't been a terrible weekend with Remy, though it didn't take much to be an improvement over the first attempt. He stayed away from her shoes, and in turn, she hadn't had to threaten his life. Friday night, after Jake had dropped him off (which unfortunately, had only taken roughly three minutes and included no flirty banter or French kissing), Tate had stopped over on his way home from work.

The night before, when he drove her and the girls home, he

told her he would come back when he had "sufficient time to discuss what had happened." She was going to try and schedule a dentist's appointment (sans Novocain) for that exact time, if she could manage it. Unfortunately for Casey, Natalie had gone to Chicago to see her parents for the night, so Tate had called to see if she'd be around. As much as she didn't want to hear his ahem, thoughts, on their night, she couldn't pass up uninterrupted time with him.

Natalie was so rarely gracious enough to get the heck out of town, so Casey said yes and started mentally preparing for the lecture that was about to head her way. Pulling out fresh mozzarella, tomatoes and basil leaves to make a caprese salad, she thought about whether she should say something to Tate about his relationship with Natalie.

No one, and she knew *no one* in the Steadman family was excited about having Natalie in their lives forever. Whenever she thought about it, she pictured Squints from *The Sandlot*, the part where the camera zooms in on his little boy lips over-enunciating the word. White, pearly teeth pulling the bottom lip in, dragging out that 'f' sound like a curse word. FOR-EV-ER. That's how she felt, forever sounding like the worst possible curse word in regards to Natalie.

They'd dated for so long, and while she hadn't been so bad at the beginning, she had started with whiny, and then gradually moved to clingy, ending up at jealous and outright manipulative. Even jealous of the time he spent with his own family. She figured Tate stayed with her because he felt like had to take care of her. Natalie was such a fragile-looking thing, with a soft quiet voice and big doe brown eyes and, as Rachel had so aptly put it, no ass to speak of. She would inspire the white knight syndrome in a lot of men, but with a Steadman?

Forget about it. Hook, line, and sinker.

She had snagged a true, dyed in the wool rescuer. The difficult part came in explaining to Tate that underneath her dove-like, cooing voice, there was a whole lot of cunning. That whole 'I'm scared to be alone at the house' routine just hid a possessive and intolerant nature. Any woman worth her salt could see through those tricks. But sometimes men need a little guidance, and no one in the family had made it past a cursory attempt at talking to Tate about it. He always calmly explained that he knew her better than they did, that he knew what he was doing and not to worry. After six loooooong years of dating, Tate had finally put a ring on it.

Thanks for nothing, Beyonce. Worst advice ever.

As the baby sister, Casey didn't have many opportunities to stand up and protect her brothers the way they had always done with her, but this was one of those times that she could. Tate deserved far, far better than Natalie, bottom line. She had actually felt nervous waiting for him, because she was not the one to start confrontations, not real ones at least. She and Dylan bickered constantly, but it always had an undercurrent of affection. This was an entirely different animal. Tate was so...so...Tate-ish. He was deliberate in everything, always annoyingly level-headed. He didn't react emotionally like she and Dylan did.

They had small talk when he first arrived, mainly about Remy, who wasn't entirely sure about a new male entering the domain. He'd cautiously sniffed around Tate before deciding he must be good people, because after about thirty seconds, he'd laid back down in the living room, back resting up against the couch. Though Casey noticed that his golden eyes never strayed from where she was.

Freaky, freaky dog.

"Tuck, you're a grown woman, I shouldn't need to tell you that what you three did last night was not only irresponsible but borderline dangerous."

"Don't you think you're overreacting just a bit?"

He slowly chewed the bite of salad in his mouth, eyes never wavering from hers. "No," he said after swallowing. "I don't think

I'm overreacting. You, my baby sister, were in a dive bar, completely intoxicated. Rachel couldn't even get into her chair by herself, for crying out loud. And no offense to Liz, while I know she was sober, she's not exactly going to be much help if you ran into trouble with some random guy at a place like that. She'd more than likely hide under the table."

Her eyes narrowed and she drew a breath to speak, but he held up a hand.

"Don't go all Casey on me, you know I love both of your friends. I'm not saying that to be cruel, but it's the truth. Now Rachel can clearly hold her own, I've seen the girl in action more than once." He actually smiled then, rubbing a hand across his jaw. Probably thinking about the time they had all gone out a few months ago and Rachel had decked a guy for slapping her rear when she walked past. It was a customary mistake for extremely stupid men who had too much alcohol in their system. Clearly, there's something about a short, stacked redhead that makes them lose any sense of personal boundaries. "But, she was *past* drunk, Casey. And worse than that, she was vulnerable because of what happened with Marc."

She gave a huff of laughter. "C'mon, Tate. Rachel and vulnerable in the same sentence? She was pissed more than anything. And I'll give you the drunk thing. Obviously she was. But I wasn't."

He tilted his head and raised one eyebrow. Jiminy Cricket, it was remarkable how much judgment he could pack into moving one teensy body part.

"I wasn't," she said indignantly, and maybe a tad defensively. "I was buzzed, yes. And if I thought we were in any real danger, don't you think I would have called one of you sooner?"

He nodded slowly. "Yeah. I do. You would have called Dylan for sure."

She lightly shrugged one shoulder, not denying she usually

went to him first in those situations. Old habits and all that. "He was working."

"He would have left work if he thought you were in trouble. He's a bar manager, not a brain surgeon. It's not like they couldn't function without him. And if they hassled him, he probably would have just quit."

She grinned down at her food, dragging a slice of tomato through the drizzle of balsamic glaze adorning the plate. Tate was right.

"And Mom would have been so thrilled he left that job, she might not even badger him about not being married yet."

He drew his brows together. "Does she hassle you about it? I've never heard her do that."

"Oh, you wouldn't. She's pretty stealthy. And honestly, she knows that I at least *want* to be married, so it's not as bad for me. Dylan has never given her any reason to hope. Plus, she's careful how she brings it up. Never any witnesses so that she has, what do you lawyers call it? Plausible deniability?"

He tipped his chin up, an impressed smile covering his handsome face, so much like their Dad. "So you do pay attention to me once in a while. That sounds like her. Although, she's never done that with me, must be because I've been with Natalie for so long."

"Yeah," Casey drawled, patting the corners of her mouth with the black linen napkins they were using. "Speaking of Natalie..."

And just like that, perfectly framed in the moment of silence after she spoke, his phone vibrated next to where it was perched next to his almost empty plate.

"Oh, hang on, it's her."

"Of course it is," she said under her breath. He cut her a less than amused look as he picked up the call.

"Hey, honey. Did you make it to your parents alright?"

Casey stood up from the table to refill her water glass, rolling her eyes at Natalie's eerie sense of timing. She probably had Tate's phone bugged so that any time he said her name in conversation she would know to call for some asinine reason. Thank goodness she was out of town and couldn't try any of her usual 'Natalie sabotages sibling time' techniques, NSST as Dylan referred to it. She and Dylan had started tracking NSST about two years ago, and Natalie currently held an impressive seventy five percent success rate of getting Tate to leave when she wanted him to.

"Are you sure? Uh huh. No, probably not. Where are you now?" He pursed his lips while he listened. "That's about two hours for me, Nat."

Casey froze, hand reaching in the fridge.

No. Freaking. Way.

"Did you try calling your Dad?" A little pinch at the bridge of his nose, and she knew. "Uh huh. Right."

Yes, freaking way.

Casey slammed the fridge shut, and this time the look he sent her was more nervous than anything. Schooling her features while she poured water into her glass, she walked back to the table and slipped into her chair, tucking one leg underneath her while Tate wrapped up the call.

"Just hold tight. I'll be there as soon as I can."

Another uneasy look at Casey. "Yeah, I'm sure she'll understand and of course, she says hi back."

"No, I don't. And no. I don't," she said loudly enough that Tate tried to quickly cover the bottom of his phone.

"Love you too, honey." He ended the call and slowly pushed his chair back. "I'm so sorry, Casey, but I've got to go. Natalie has a flat tire, and her Dad isn't answering his phone so she needs me to come pick her up. I'll probably just stay out at her parents tonight with her." Oh, she just brought NSST to whole new level. Keeping Tate from hanging out with her *and* still scoring an evening with her parents in one fell swoop.

"Hmm, where is she exactly?"

"In one of the southern suburbs, she thought she was close to

Tinley Park. Thankfully it's a nicer area and she noticed the low tire pressure light and was able to get off the highway before it blew completely."

"Lucky for her." She swung her foot back and forth a few times, watching Tate gather his things. "Tate, you're almost done with your salad, just finish it real quick before you hit the road."

He looked back at where she sat, chagrin etching a few lines on his forehead. She could tell he didn't want to leave. "I really should go Casey, she's going to have wait there for a couple hours as it is."

"Exactly. So what's another five minutes? This will be your only chance at dinner, at least until you get to her parents, and isn't that on the north side of Chicago? At least forty five minutes from where she is now." *Plus, this is my only chance to say this, and really, Natalie could not have handed me a better opportunity to say it. Chick probably jammed the nail in her tire herself.*

"Okay, yeah. You're probably right. She said she was just going read at the Starbucks until I got there."

"Man, imagine if she'd had the tire go out just fifteen or twenty minutes later. She could have been in some rough areas of town. Certainly no Starbucks right off the highway to hang out at."

Tate slowly chewed a bite of salad, giving her an even look, clearly not missing the sarcasm in her voice.

"If you have something to say, just say it."

"Well, her timing couldn't have been more perfect than if I had planned it myself, because actually, I did want to talk to you about Natalie."

Tate heaved a tired sigh. "Case, c'mon. You know I can't do this right now."

"Can't do what? I haven't even said anything yet."

"I know where this is going."

"Do you?" she challenged. "Go ahead and tell me what I was gonna say then."

He moved his dinner plate aside, and set his clasped hands in front of him on the table. Looking down at them for a moment, Casey wasn't sure he was going to answer. "I've heard all of this before. From Mom and Dad. And Dylan. And Michael. And then Dylan again. You don't like her. And you don't think I should marry her."

"You're right," she conceded. "But it's more than that."

She stood from the table, taking her empty plate and moving towards the kitchen. Here was her golden opportunity. She slowly rinsed the dish, aware that he stayed seated and was watching her. Okay, she was being a teensy bit overly dramatic in stretching this out. But this was Tate, she wanted to say everything right. He'd never really hear her otherwise. Leaving the dish in the sink, she pulled her dish towel off the oven handle to dry her hands and turned back to him.

"What if it were me?" she asked, knowing he was probably expecting the opposite.

He instantly looked confused. "What do you mean?"

Ah, for such a smart boy...

"Just imagine for a second that I've been with someone for years. He's perfectly polite to our family, you've never heard him speak a cross word in my direction, but there's something about him that doesn't seem to click, either with me or with the rest of us. Something you might not even be able to define if you had to. Right from the beginning you feel it, just hovering under your skin. But you don't say anything because of how much you love me. The rest of the family brings it up occasionally over the years, but I claim over and over that none of you know this guy the way I do. But every time, every single time I'm spending time with someone other than him, some crisis comes up, some reason that I need to leave and go back to him. Imagine how much you would hate that, how much it would worry you. And then he asks me to marry him, and I say yes. Imagine how much that would kill you inside."

Tate pulled a hand down his face, suddenly looking very tired. "Casey-"

"Please," she said simply, hanging the towel back, precisely folded just the way she liked it. "I've never talked about this with you. And as your sister, I'm asking you to respect me enough to hear me out right now."

His jaw hardened for moment, but his eyes showed just enough resignation that Casey knew she might actually have him. Duh. How had she not realized all along that in order to get through to Tate, she needed to act like him?

He nodded slightly, gesturing for her to continue without meeting her eyes. She walked back to the table, rolling her lips inward while she mulled over her words. Trying to convince a lawyer out of a belief they'd been committed to for years was like trying to jam your foot into a shoe that was a size too small. Difficult, uncomfortable, but not completely impossible.

"You know how Dad always goes straight to Mom when he comes home? She is the first thing he looks for when he walks into any room. And how Mom curls into him every time he gives her a kiss? How she can go from ripping one of us a new one to completely melting thirty seconds later when he rubs her hands the way she likes? How he runs a bath for her every night because he knows she needs it? How she always lets him go hunting in the fall, even though she hates the thought of him shooting Bambi, because she knows it makes him happy. How he would never, ever speak a single negative word about her in public, not because she doesn't drive him crazy sometimes, but because he respects her so much. You've noticed that stuff, we all have. It was normal for us growing up. And all of us know now that it's hardly typical. I know they're not perfect, but we have been able to witness a fricken miracle our entire lives. That was our example."

His pointer finger traced along the wood grain of her dark table, wisely guessing she wasn't finished yet.

"Do you wish that for me, Tate?"

His dark eyes snapped up to her then. "Of course," he said incredulously.

"Why?" Goodness gracious, he can pass the fricken bar exam, but he was still one step behind her here.

He stared at her for another beat, then she saw his face harden just enough that she thought she might truly fighting a losing battle. All those Steadman men, so stubborn. Good thing she escaped that particular trait.

"Because you're my sister, and you deserve the best."

"And you don't?"

"Natalie loves me. I have never doubted that," he said resolutely. "Look, I know she has her insecurities-"

"Insecurities?" Casey repeated, her voice rising along with her hackles. Okay, she tried it Tate's way. "She's a stage five clinger, Tate. You practically have to wear an ankle monitor every time you leave the house."

"That's enough, Casey."

She speared one hand into her hair, shaking her head in disbelief. "Look at tonight, Tate. You and I haven't spent time together in months. *Months.* And again, something comes up where you have to go running off to rescue her. It's really too bad there's not some service that could, oh I don't know, change a flat tire for her. And last time, what was it? Oh yeah, you finally come out with the rest of us, and she got a cold and needed you to go get her cough drops because she didn't have the *right kind* at home. Seriously? Cough. Drops. You have been with her for so long, how can you not see the things we see?"

"Casey-" His face held a clear warning, but no way could she stop now. Oh no, this baby had been brewing for way too long.

"Tate," she mimicked his stern tone. Ooh, Rachel would be proud. "I have kept my mouth shut for over six years, and I can't do it anymore. That woman is not good enough for you. Not even close. She is a manipulative, controlling psycho and I-"

"That's *enough*." He slammed one hand down on the table,

remorse covering over the anger in his eyes almost immediately. As shock reverberated through her, Casey became aware of a strange sound coming from behind her, so she looked over her shoulder.

Remy. Growling.

He was still laying by the couch, but his head was up, ears pricked forward and his eyes bored directly into Tate. No shiny, white teeth were showing, but the sound was no less ominous for it, sending a stark warning across the room.

"Please tell me he's not gonna eat me."

Casey floundered for a moment, since Jake had never really told her what to do if Remy went all guard dog on her.

"Umm, it's okay, Remy," she said in a soothing tone and reached across the table to pat Tate's hand. She had a feeling that Tate needed it as much as the dog did right then. "See? I'm fine. He's okay, he's good."

Remy's ears relaxed slightly, and he laid his head back down, but his eyes never left the table.

Tate blew out a short breath and turned his hand over to grip hers. "I can't believe I just snapped at you like that. I'm so sorry, Casey."

"It's okay. And I'm sorry too, I probably shouldn't have called her names." *At least not to your face. I will later when I recap this conversation to the girls.*

He smiled then, more subdued than usual, but it was something. "I'm not used to this with you. Usually I just get to sit back and watch the fireworks between you and Dylan. It's a lot more fun when he's the one pissing you off."

"Eh, he doesn't scare me anymore. Your yelling actually has the ability to shut me up. Just don't tell him that, he'll be insanely jealous."

They had both laughed, and he pulled her into a hug before he left.

"I love you, Case." He spoke into her hair, squeezing her so tightly that she struggled to breathe for a moment. But she figured losing some oxygen was a small price to pay, since he probably still felt awful about losing his temper. "But I have to ask you not to bring this up again. I heard you out, now I need you to trust me that I know what I'm doing. Okay?"

She pressed her face into his blue oxford shirt, feeling that prickly tightening she always got when she was about to cry. She blinked a few times to make sure her eyes were dry, then looked up at him and nodded. And she meant it. Dang it.

Even now, two days later, it just made her want to bawl her eyes out, watch some mind-numbingly sad movies and eat a pint or two of Ben & Jerry's. The rhythmic push and pull of her wallpaper brush smoothing the paper down along the wall was soothing to her, but it still couldn't make her stop dreading the day she'd have to stand in a church and watch Tate pledge his life to Natalie. And flickering right behind that dread was anger.

Anger at Tate for not listening, and being so stubborn.

Anger at herself for not doing a good enough job when she had the chance to make a difference.

And of course, anger at Natalie, pretty much just for being herself.

Tate would marry her and stay devoted to her forever. FOR-E-VER.

She stepped off the silver ladder that Jake had graciously left in the living room for her, and went to her makeshift work table a few feet away, the long piece of plywood stretched across two sawhorses was a bit wobbly, but she only had one piece of paper left to hang. Once that was done, it wouldn't take her long at all to put up the wainscoting and chair rail with his nail gun. She smiled thinking how she'd love to see Jake use it, knowing full well that a woman had it bad when the thought of a man's power tools were a turn on. As opposed to his, ya know, *power tools*, which were probably pretty spectacular too.

Gah. Focus. No dirty thoughts while hanging wallpaper.

It looked like once she finished that wall, all he'd have to do in there was put in the carpet. The paper she picked was a bit of a splurge, as she'd chosen a deep brown that gave the illusion of a texture. It was subtle, and not too masculine despite the color. It was unpasted, which was kind of a pain, but she knew Jake would be happy that it wasn't 'something that looked like it was ripped from a tiki hut'. As she pulled on the roll until she hit the desired length, she heard a car door in the driveway.

A quick glance at her phone showed about four hours before Jake was supposed to be home, so she thought maybe her Mom or Dylan were stopping by to check on her progress. After she rolled the cut length into her water bucket, she pulled it out and up onto towel draped plywood. She started scooping paste onto the back of the paper and spreading it into a uniform coat, stopping a safe distance from the edge of the paper. Brow furrowed in concentration, it took her a minute to realize that no one had come inside since she heard the car door.

Hmmm. Jake would've texted if he was going to be home that early, right?

Just as she was thinking about going outside to check, she heard his voice from the kitchen screen door. Yup. Apparently he would come home four hours early without letting her know. *Crap.*

"Casey, you in here?"

"Stop!" she shrieked, trying to spread the paste as quickly as possible without screwing it up. "You can't come in here."

"Why? What's wrong? Are you okay?"

Great. It was like waving a red flag in front of a ramped up bull. Of course he wouldn't stay out now.

He charged around the corner, a look of concern stamped across his features. If she wasn't so ticked that he was seeing the wall before it was finished, she might have thought he looked quite adorable.

"Noooooo," she wailed, head falling back. "I wanted to be done with this before you saw it. Shoo. Go away."

Concern was quickly replaced with amusement. And Holy Dimples, Batman...he was smiling. Right. At. Her.

And what pissed her off even more was that she couldn't even fully appreciate the heavy zing it sent through her stomach at the sight, because she had to be stupid and buy an unpasted paper that couldn't be ignored now that she started working with it.

"Afraid I'm not going to like it and I'll be less likely to make you take it down if you're done with it?"

"Pretty much," she admitted, folding the large piece in half to spread the paste on the bottom part of the paper. "Now, *go away.*"

He leaned up against the wall, clearly quite pleased with himself. Cheese and rice, he looked so good her hands shook, almost dropping the paper where she was still trying to get the edges lined up. He still had his ACU's on, but had taken off the jacket and was just wearing the tan t-shirt neatly tucked into the camouflage pants. Probably inappropriate to ask him to do a slow turn so she could see all angles.

"What does it matter now?"

"It just does," she practically spit the words out. Thinking about stupid Natalie had made her work slower. This was all *her* fault. Plus, if she'd had the rest of the day to finish, she would have had time to shower and change before he came home. As it was, she was wearing her 'paint outfit'. The cut off denim shorts had paint splatters on them from about ten different projects, the edges tattered and frayed beyond what she would wear in public. The gray wife-beater tank top had seen even more activity than that, stripes and globs of reds and whites and oranges and blues from different things she had painted over the years. She was barefoot, always hating the feel of shoes on her feet when she was painting or papering a room for some odd reason. Worst of all? Not a stitch of makeup on her face. Heck, she probably had orange paint across her forehead and wallpaper paste across her chin or something. Flippin' perfect.

The ladder shuddered as she stomped up three rungs, gripping the folded strip of paper in one hand and balancing herself with the other. Maybe if she ignored him, he would leave.

He cleared his throat behind her. "You do realize that the pieces you put up don't reach all the way down the wall, right?"

Her hand paused right as she was going to let the bottom half fall from where it was folded up. She tilted her head up towards the ceiling, saying a short concise prayer asking for patience.

"Because," he continued, oblivious to her simmering, "that will be a problem for me."

She let the paper unfurl and lined the edges up the piece next to it, making sure everything was even before she started smoothing it out.

"Casey?"

"Hmmm?"

"Aren't you going to answer my question?"

She worked in short, quick strokes starting from the middle of the paper, making sure there weren't air bubbles. "Wasn't planning on it."

"Well then, you might as well stop with that piece. Because I don't like it."

Her hand froze, and she turned to look at him, where he was still leaning against the wall. No smile anymore, which was good, because she may actually want to smack it off his face right now. She narrowed her eyes, and stepped down one rung before turning slightly towards him.

"This is why I didn't want you to see it," she said, struggling to keep her tone even. Struggling and failing, based on the expression on his face. He narrowed his eyes right back, though in a mocking way, and he pushed off the wall, taking one step towards her.

"Casey?"

"What?" she snapped, feeling like everything around her was crackling with the force of her annoyance.

"Your wallpaper is falling."

She spun around on the ladder with a gasp, trying to catch the piece as it began its slow slide off the wall. With a yelp, she realized barefoot was not the way to go because she couldn't get enough traction to step back up to her original position while both hands were splayed against the paper, well above her head.

"Need some help?" Ugh, he was smiling again, she could hear it threading through his deep voice.

"What do you think?"

He chuckled, and she practically growled. "I am going to murder you for this. I swear."

And then she felt one incredibly large, incredibly warm hand curve around her waist at the same time that he stepped on the ladder behind her. And she stopped breathing altogether. Which seemed odd, because if she wasn't breathing, how was it physically possible for her heart to triple its cadence in her chest? There was no way he couldn't hear that. Because it felt like the sound of it bounced off of every surface around the room.

His chest wasn't actually touching her back, but the heat pouring off of him seemed like a physical, tangible presence. One hand still on her waist, steadying her, he brought the other one above hers onto the wall, his added height affording him a better reach to hold the paper up. She felt her arms start to shake with the effort of keeping them still on the wall, so she slowly brought them down to grip the top of the ladder. They still weren't touching other than that one small point of contact at her waist, but it seared into her skin.

She didn't dare speak, not wanting to break this moment and the sweet pulse that was coursing through her, each one chasing another until her fingertips started tingling with the need to touch him. It was then that she realized he was just as silent as she was, the only sound in the room was their breathing, a little heavier than it should have been. She turned her head enough to look at him, but kept the rest of her body exactly where it was.

No laughing or smiling in his face now. His eyes were so, so dark as he stared back at her and his broad chest heaved with one large inhalation, bringing it within a millimeter of touching her back. Without much more than a passing conscious thought, she slowly wet her lower lip and a muscle ticked in his jaw. She dropped her gaze down to his mouth, but he still didn't move. Then the hand on her waist tightened, not quite pulling on her, but definitely not pushing her away. But instead of holding her up as before, it now gripped her into place.

She brought her eyes up from his lips, and this time when their gazes locked, she could feel the tether snap.

Their mouths met in the middle and crashed, it was the only way she could describe it. He pushed the length of his body against hers on the ladder and the cold bite of metal at her side told her she wasn't imagining this, not this time. It was better than what her mind had conjured, harder and hotter in all the best possible ways. Wedged in between the press of his body and the equally unyielding ladder, she managed to turned against the solid wall of heat and stability he provided to twine her arms around his neck and grip the back of his head. He tasted sweet, which surprised her, like chocolate and mint. All she could feel was the heat from his mouth as it meshed with hers, and she opened her lips, whimpering, wanting more. Just that tiny sound on an exhale seemed to propel him even farther.

He gave her more, a hot slide of his tongue against her own that let her know that he had thought about this just as much as she had. This wasn't a slow, sweet kiss where they took their time. This held a frantic, almost panicked edge, like if they didn't taste each other now, they never would. Jake slid his hand from her side around her and pushed it in an upward motion underneath her tank that made her aware of every bump of her spine that he encountered along the way.

She pulled back to catch her breath, noticing for the first time that he had taken them off the ladder and back onto the floor. Impressive, that man was. She thought he might pull away then, but he didn't, and everything boiled up inside of her again when he dragged the tip of his nose down along the line of her neck, pulling in her scent along the way.

"Jake," she said shakily when he placed one tiny kiss above her collarbone. Her knees literally shook and she tightened her hands where they still gripped his head. Then everything about him stilled, his mouth where it hovered over her neck, his hands, one on the small of her back and one anchored at the base of her skull.

He lifted his head and, for a suspended moment, they just stared at each other.

BAM. They both jerked in surprise, and then the hoarse bark outside the kitchen door made Casey practically groan. Her earlier statement about Remy not committing any murder-worthy offenses was officially retracted. Jake's hold on her loosened and he stepped backwards, so she had no choice but to drop her arms back down to her side. Seemed a little desperate at that point to dig her nails in and try to wrap her legs around his waist.

"Uh, I guess he realized I was home." It was comforting that his voice was rough, uneven.

BAM. BAM.

Remy's paws pounded on the door again, broadcasting his displeasure at being kept from Jake. Casey pressed a hand into her stomach, and turned back to the incredibly sad looking piece of wallpaper still stubbornly clinging to the wall in one small spot. Fixable, thank goodness, but it wouldn't be fun. This moment with Jake? Probably not quite as fixable, and definitely, definitely not going to be fun considering he was probably planning his "I'm so sorry, that was mistake" speech. No way she could handle hearing that right now, not when she could still taste him, still feel the thrumming in her veins that no man had ever been able to produce before.

From one kiss, it was so much more than she'd ever felt.

"I should try to fix this. Don't want the paste to dry anymore." She didn't dare meet his eyes when she said it, but she could feel his eyes boring into her. "Plus, Remy might take the door off the hinges if you make him wait any longer."

"Yeah," he said slowly, his voice back to normal now. "You're probably right."

He was regarding her intently, looking like he was going to say more, so she threw him as much of a smile as she could manage, and in the end he simply turned and left the room without another word. She staggered back until her back met the wall, and she sank down to the floor, lightly touching her still wonderfully tingly lips. They curved into a slow smile, completely without her giving them permission to.

"Jake Miller, you may not realize it yet, but there's no way we're not doing that again."

13

THE NEXT DAY had started Casey's official *avoid Jake until I can convince him we're soul mates* operation. She knew it was risky, that he might think she didn't want anything more from him. And she did, oh Lord have mercy, she really did. She almost snapped the stem of a wine glass just replaying that kiss the other night while doing dishes. As rough and hot as the kiss had been, his hands had been the opposite. And not in the limp-wristed wussy boy way that Rick's had been, but tender, moving up her back in a way that seemed almost reverent. The kiss along her collarbone, softer and sweeter than she thought possible from him, now screamed out to her. Thinking about it afterwards, that small little gesture took on a weighted significance that it hadn't in the moment.

Because a man who spent time lingering around necks and collarbones, well, let's just say they weren't a dime a dozen. That was the kind of thing that you do when you've thought a lot about your first kiss with someone. What they'll feel like, smell like, taste like. Casey knew now that the close cut of Jake's hair felt surprisingly soft against her hands. Sort of prickly, but not in an unpleasant way. She knew now that his lips were smooth, but not in the way where he used chapstick regularly, just natural. Those were the things she had wondered about, and now could say she knew about him. Maybe he had laid in his bed thinking about what it would be like to take his time breathing in the scent of the skin from just under her ear down to where her shoulder curved. Maybe Jake had wondered what that small spot of skin tasted like just above the line of her collarbone. He knew those things about her now.

And it was that small press of lips that gave her hope. And why she was darn near hiding out from him now. Rachel told her she was either a genius or completely demented in her logic, but if she had to put money on it, she would lean towards the latter.

In Casey's mind, it was quite simple. Even if Jake had spent hours thinking about her in the same way she had about him, he would be wary to start any sort of relationship. He was someone who had to think through the logistics of any situation before he entered it, thanks to all his years in the Army. He would let the landlord thing be the number one reason they couldn't be together. She could almost hear his little speech, that rumbling voice explaining to her that he liked her, was attracted to her, but he wouldn't want to make things awkward for her if they broke up, blah blah blah. Better to let him think on it for a few days. Hopefully he was doing the same thing she was, recounting every detail of what happened. Letting it weigh on him until he thought he might go crazy with wanting to do it again. Then he'd be so amped up that by the time they finally saw each other again, his whole let's be friends speech would go out the flippin' window.

If that wasn't the work of a genius, then she didn't know what was.

Operation Avoid Jake had been going really well. He had sent her one text the evening of the kiss, saying that he liked the wall now that it was finished, and she could leave everything up. A victory, to be sure, especially since neither one of them would ever be able to look at that wallpaper again without thinking about what had happened. And other than that text, she had only seen him once in three days.

She was backing her car out of the garage, on her way to work just that morning, when she saw him walk out his place, wearing the blessed tool belt. Mmm, it just hung there, emphasizing the slimness of hips compared to how broad his chest and shoulders were and framing everything that could possibly need to be framed quite nicely. When she almost knocked off her driver side mirror on the side of the garage because she lost focus, she figured that was not the time to break down his appearance piece by sexy piece. She just gave a casual little wave when he tipped up his chin in greeting, and went on her merry way to work, car thankfully unscathed.

She should have known that everything would go downhill from there.

The first thing she saw when she rounded the corner by her desk was Melinda, looking all sorts of evil in red. Head to toe red. Fitted blazer, wide legged pants, pointy toed heels, hoop earrings, and shiny lipstick, all in the same astonishingly bright shade. All she was missing were the teeny little horns sticking out of her pixie haircut and a long tail twitching out behind her. And goodness, as much as Casey wanted to say she looked washed out and horrid in that color, she actually didn't. The matching earrings were definitely overkill, but other than that, Melinda just looked annoyingly put together, the shade of red making her pale complexion look translucent and actually kind of radiant. Dang it.

Radiant and currently pawing through papers on Casey's desk. Her fingers curled into her purse strap with the overwhelming urge to punch Melinda in the throat.

"Something I can help you with, Melinda?"

She didn't even flinch, just cut her eyes over to Casey. Probably because she was demonic and had eyes in the back of her head. "Well good morning to you too. Just checking on an order for a customer on the phone. You're late, by the way."

Casey pulled in a slow, steady breath. It was on the tip of her tongue to justify why she was, in fact, five minutes late but she reined that in knowing that it wouldn't make a lick of difference. Over the past couple years of working with Melinda, Casey had learned that responding to any of her snide little comments just made it worse. And one would think that since Casey was about a foot taller than Melinda that she could just stand over her and intimidate her.

Not so much.

The one and only time Casey had tried that, Melinda had told her to move her 'big-boned, sasquatch ass' out of her way. She had been so shocked that all she'd managed was a decidedly un-intimidating squeak of outrage while Melinda stomped past her. The devil himself probably wouldn't scare Melinda. So it was fitting that she looked like Satan's offspring today.

Apparently Melinda found the paperwork she wanted, yanking it out of middle of the stack, sending the rest of the papers flying.

"Oh darn," she said, not making a move to pick anything up. "You really should keep your desk more organized, Casey. It reflects so poorly on your work ethic when you can't find the things you might need."

Casey pushed her tongue into the side of her cheek, literally choking on the things that she wanted to say. Lots of words that included b's and f's and were totally not appropriate for the workplace.

"Are you done here, Melinda? I've got things to do."

She gave a simpering smile, a slick red curve of her thin lips, and went gliding past.

Casey threw herself into work in order to keep Melinda from getting under her skin, reorganizing her desk, helping a few customers with picking colors and papers, and answering phone calls. It wasn't until she heard an angry grumble come from the vicinity of her stomach that she realized it was after twelve and she could take her lunch. She found Mike, made sure he was okay with her leaving, and she darted down the hallway and back through the warehouse before she could chance another run in with Melinda.

Normally she read in the break room, or went to the mall for her lunch, but it was such a perfectly gorgeous early fall day that she had to take advantage and eat outside. Along the side of the building were a couple rarely used picnic tables in a narrow strip of lawn, but tall, waving prairie grass and a few large spruce trees kept it private from neighboring businesses. Casey sat with her back leaning up against the table and stretched her legs out in front of her, groaning at the sore muscles from being on her feet all morning. She bit into the apple she had taken from home, tipping her head back so her face could soak in the warmth of the sun.

The weather hadn't quite made up its mind as to whether it was summer or fall yet, and it was that perfect time of year where the temperature hovered in the high sixties and low seventies, but the humidity was blessedly gone. A few trees had started their change for the year, trying valiantly to usher in the crisp scent of fall along with their color tipped leaves in orange, yellow and red.

Just as she was thinking about how a day like this could erase even Melinda's crimson colored blight on her morning, she heard a familiar sounding truck pull into the parking lot around the corner from where she sat. Familiar because when she heard it at home she was already feeling an involuntary tug somewhere in the area of her womb when it pulled into the driveway.

Couldn't be. Rising from the table to peek around the side of the building, she had herself almost convinced that she had conjured the sound. Probably just some contractor whose truck sounded similar to Jake's. As she walked, she dragged her hand against the brick of the warehouse, the sun warmed surface pricking her palm. Operation Avoid Jake just got a lot harder, seeing as he was striding across the parking lot, long legs covering ground quickly and purposefully. Casey let out a disappointed sigh that the tool belt was gone, and that her lunch break was now over. Because there was no way she could let Melinda, in all her red robed glory, sink her talons into Jake.

She tossed the core of her apple into the trash bin next to the back door and headed back in. She smiled at a few customers browsing through the aisles as she walked through the retail floor, looking around for the broad shoulders and dark head of hair that she'd been so actively avoiding the last four days. Walking around the corner from paint and stain into the area for tile and flooring, she finally saw him. He was looking at different carpet options, and while he knelt down to look at some of the samples on the lower racks, she saw red. Literally.

Melinda was about ten feet from Jake, looking sort of like a starved junkyard dog that just found a big juicy steak laying on the floor. Then her gaze flicked from Jake crouched in front of the display up to Casey, and she gave the look. That universal look, the one that every female above the age of twelve could instinctively recognize. The *bring it on honey, this one is mine* look. Casey just smirked and kept up her pace, which thankfully was about twice as fast as Melinda's due to the extra length in her legs. They stopped on either side of Jake at the same time, but he looked up at Melinda first. At her *I'm so helpful and competent* smile, he gave a brief nod, then did a double take when he realized Casey was on the other side of him.

"Hey Jake," she said smoothly, absolutely loving the poisonous look that entered Melinda's eyes when she realized Casey knew him.

He slowly straightened, his face not giving anything away. "Casey."

"Aren't you going to introduce me to your friend?" Melinda asked in a deceptively sweet tone.

Casey couldn't hold back a smile at that, knowing 'friend' might be a stretch. Renter, dog babysitter, one time make-out partner and general pain in his ass would probably be a more apt description, at least if Jake was the one handing out labels.

"Melinda, this is Jake, he owns the building I live in." He gave her another short nod. "Jake, my coworker Melinda."

She held out one dainty claw, err, hand and instead of going for a handshake like a normal person would, she laid it on one of his muscled forearms. He quirked an eyebrow, but didn't move his arm.

"So nice to meet you, Jake," Melinda practically purred. "Is there anything I can help you with? Casey was on her lunch break, but I'm available."

Casey clenched her jaw so tight, it was a miracle that the sound of cracking teeth didn't echo around the store. Even Jake looked slightly uncomfortable with Melinda's blatant flirting. He shifted his shoulders, which moved his arm away from Melinda, and then cleared his throat a couple of times.

"Actually, I was just on my way back in," Casey started, when a page came over the intercom saying there was a phone call for her. She ran her tongue over the front of her teeth, and gave a smile of apology to Jake before excusing herself. Trying to refrain from stomping over to the phone like she wanted to, as a childish temper tantrum would probably not help her cause, she picked up an extension by the front sales register. Unfortunately, the customer's questions were not quick ones, so she wasn't able to get back over to help Jake. She tried not to stare over at him with Melinda, she really did.

Next to Jake's towering height and broad shoulders, Melinda looked even more petite than usual. Cute. Delicate. Her blond hair and fair skin stood in striking contrast to his dark head and golden skin. An unusual feeling sank into her gut, stretching and pulling over her whole body until she felt it raise the little hairs on the back of her neck.

Jealousy. Green eyed monster was straight up slapping her across the face.

She just stood there, watching Melinda smile and talk and give little touches and laughs to Jake. She had never felt this way with any man she'd dated. She must be losing her mind, feeling like this after one measly kiss. Okay, one toe curling, insanely passionate, made her heart feel like it was going to explode kiss. But it was still only one kiss. What would she be like if they actually went on a date and had a relationship? Oh geez, maybe she would end up like Natalie. Soon she'd be calling Jake home for cough drops with chewy centers because the ones at home weren't good enough and driving nails into her tires to stage a fake rescue and making him check in with text messages everywhere he went and picking out matching outfits so people knew they were together. Yeah, that had been a low point for Natalie. The outfits hadn't even been good.

Casey shook her head, snapping back to the conversation with the customer on the phone that she'd be drifting from. No, she'd never be like Natalie. She just felt like this because it was Melinda. Watching them now, she could see the stiffness in Jake's body language when Melinda would lean in a little closer than necessary. He kept shifting away during their conversation, and she kept inching closer, obviously not reading his signals. Casey stifled a laugh and finished up with her phone call. After she hung up, she rang up a contractor who was waiting for College Kid #4 to mix an order, smiling at him when he gave her his standing offer to whisk her away on a beach vacation to Tahiti. He had to be in his late eighties, happily married for sixty plus years to the sweetest woman in the world and asked Casey to run away with him every time he came in the store.

"You know I can't, Max. Ruby would hunt me down, and she absolutely terrifies me."

His burst of throaty laughter made his entire bony frame

shake. "You're a good one, Miss Casey. I'll make sure to tell Tom to give you a raise."

It was another thing he said every time he came in. She squeezed his hand over the counter, winked at him and turned to go back towards Jake, not quite ready to concede this time to Melinda. She only made it about three steps when Tom intercepted her.

"Do you have a minute Casey?"

Flicking her gaze towards Jake and Melinda, who were still looking over carpet books, she nodded at her manager.

"Of course. What's up?"

He clapped his hands together, which was what he did when he was really excited about something.

"Well, I'm gonna need you to help us out with something, a really great new project that could provide a boost for us."

"Sure, you know I'll do whatever I can."

"Great!" he exclaimed, loud enough to draw the attention of both Jake and Melinda. Jake's look not much more than glance, giving nothing away. But it was Melinda's that immediately made her feel apprehensive. She looked triumphant.

And then she noticed what was tucked under Tom's arm. It was her blue folder.

In slow motion, he pulled it out and started flipping through pages. Some of the pages were foreign to her, but enough of them were the exact ones that she had typed up that she knew.

Roaring white noise filled her ears and only snippets of what Tom was saying broke through in between the heavy beating of her heart.

"Phenomenal idea for a joint venture...presented to management last week...would increase community visibility and increase sales...will need Melinda to focus her energies here...you to step up back at the store with design responsibilities."

When she opened her mouth and nothing came out. Absolutely nothing. She licked her suddenly bone dry lips and tried to speak again.

Still nothing.

"Casey? Are you okay?" Tom's bushy red eyebrows pulled together in understandable confusion, since she was just standing there staring, not able to speak past the growing lump in her throat. It was sitting like a rock, trapping her vocal chords from any movement.

That. Little. Witch.

She risked a quick look over at Melinda, and the grin that passed across her tiny little face was the definition of gloating. Mind racing, she realized that she must not have hidden her folder well enough when she pulled it out the week before. She squeezed her eyes shut for just a moment, trying to rein in the heart that was threatening to beat straight through her chest and then looked back at Tom.

This wasn't the time for a meltdown or a throat punch or *any* of the things she wanted to do.

"You know you can count on me, Tom. For whatever you need."

The words literally felt like chunks of glass crawling up her throat. So did the tears that were pushing at the back of her eyes. He clapped her on the shoulder and then went back towards his office. She reached out to place one hand on the counter, feeling lightheaded. All of her research, the proposal she'd been working on for months, everything. Gone.

And now, it would be Melinda's.

From the corner of her eye, she saw Jake making some notes in his large black binder and start heading towards her. She couldn't handle this right now. If she got even the slightest bit of kindness from him, she'd end up a blubbering mess all over his black t-shirt and big, muscled, amazing smelling chest. And there was no way she would be giving Melinda that satisfaction. No freaking way. Even if she really, really wanted to be a blubbering mess on Jake's t-shirt.

She quickly picked up the extension she'd been on earlier, almost dropping the receiver in her haste. He slowed as he reached her, and she gave him a small smile and gestured to the phone at her ear. He nodded in understanding, gave her a wave and kept walking. Risking a quick glance over her shoulder, she waited until he was clear of the automatic sliding doors, everything inside of her dropped. Her head dropped down, her shoulders following suit, and her hands dropped to brace herself on the counter, as if knowing she would crumple straight to the ground without their support.

Her nose burned, the tears pressing up into her throat with how badly they wanted to escape. This, this had been the thing that was going to push her through whatever barrier had been propped against her for the last couple years at work. She pulled three deep, cleansing breaths, absolutely refusing to lose it when Melinda was anywhere near her.

"Wow, you look like you're having a rough day. Want me to make it all better?"

Oh, and wasn't that just fricken' perfect. Creepy Eye Guy's creepy little voice slithered through her and it took every shred of discipline not to shudder at the sound. She raised her head and then snapped back a step at how close he was standing to her.

She laughed nervously. "Steve, I didn't see you there. I can go grab one of the guys to help you, I'm in the middle of something."

He smiled and licked his lips and, ew, it made her want to retch. Especially because when he smiled, he was looking straight at her chest. She cleared her throat and crossed her arms, making his eyes finally flick back up to her face.

"No need. You're more than equipped to give me what I need."

And the need to retch immediately fled, replaced by a healthy twinge of unease. College Kid #4 was close by, but not paying even a smidge of attention. Because they were all utterly useless.

Except Jason, of course, but he was off today. Her professionalism was difficult to find at the moment, because as much as she didn't like Steve on a normal basis, this was different, this was the most blatant he'd ever been. And she really, really didn't like it. But she took a deep breath and gave him a perfectly polite smile.

"If you need to place a paint order I can write it up for you, but I do have something else that I need to be doing right now."

He shifted on his feet and flipped his car keys around on one finger. The jangling of the keys reflected her nerves; loud and discordant. "I don't need paint. I came to ask you out on a date. We've been dancing around each other for a while, I figured it was time to do something about it."

Her jaw dropped before she could stop it. "We've been *what*?"

"You know, the sexual tension thing." He shrugged. "I thought you might make a move first, but obviously you like the guy to do all the work. So here I am."

The verbal filter that was usually firmly in place at work? Gone. Completely deserted her. She pressed a hand to her forehead, struggling to put in back in place. "Steve, I have not been waiting for you to ask me out. I think you've misread me."

"You've gotta be shittin' me. You flirt all the time. I'm good at reading this kinda stuff."

Oh yeah, she just bet he could. Like a first grader picking up *War and Peace*. It was quite obvious that he was genuinely surprised at her reaction. But the surprise was quickly giving way to annoyance when she didn't answer right away.

"So, you're saying no?" His face was turning pink, and it just served to highlight the receding hairline above his shiny forehead.

"I'm sorry Steve, but I am saying no. I don't think it's a good idea to date a customer." Sure, it was possibly the flimsiest excuse she could have come up with. But the day had sucked enough already, she clearly wasn't firing on all cylinders. "I really need to get to work."

She turned to walk past him, giving him a wide berth. He muttered something under his breath that sounded suspiciously close to 'stupid bitch' and stormed out.

Focusing on counting each heartbeat until she felt herself calm down, she barely made it four feet before Melinda approached with a customer in tow.

"Oh, Casey. Would you be a peach and ring up Mrs. Carter's order? I really need to get cracking on my new project. I saw Tom mention it to you earlier, and I'm *sure* you understand just how much work it'll be."

The expression on Melinda's face was perfectly pleasant with only the exultant gleam in her green eyes betraying what she really meant by that statement. Casey swallowed roughly and then gave a polite smile to the customer, determined not to crumble until she could leave the building. That much she could keep from Melinda.

"Of course. I can take you right over here, Mrs. Carter."

With that, she turned her back and did what she did best for the next four and a half hours, keeping a smile on her face and making customers happy. Until her car left the parking lot at 5:32, when she promptly burst into tears.

14

WAITING to turn left at the light around the corner from home, Casey took a quick look in the rear view mirror to gauge the cry damage to her face. She wasn't a horrifically ugly crier, but the first five minutes in the car after leaving work had definitely been the kind of emotional outburst that left her skin feeling like someone had repeatedly slapped her with a damp rag, leaving a blotchy film that would only go away after a hot shower and maybe a microderm abrasion treatment. She wiped away the remnants of mascara and was surprised that she didn't look more like she felt. Because she felt like she had been run over by a train. A few trains even.

She felt such a range of emotions on the drive home, it was hard to fixate on one for more than a few seconds. Most of them were aimed towards Melinda, obviously. She knew they didn't click, but this level of malice and deceit was honestly surprising to Casey. She had no idea that Melinda was capable of something like this. But she was ticked at herself too. To assume that she had hidden her research well enough was a ridiculous oversight. It was embarrassing to imagine what Melinda might have felt when she stumbled upon that little gem.

The quick burst of a horn came from car sitting behind her, making Casey realize that she had a more than a clear opening to turn. She lifted her hand in apology and pushed down the accelerator. Nearing the turn off for her driveway, she clicked her blinker on and slowed. The car behind her obviously wasn't over the left turn incident, because they zoomed around her, giving her the finger as they passed. She scoffed and tried really, really hard to pretend that even that didn't make her want to cry again.

What did people *want* from her today? Geez. It was kinda starting to feel like the universe was just sitting back, sending a slow, arrogant chuckle directed right at her every time she got a new little poke throughout the day.

Then she looked down the end of the driveway and whimpered in total and utter defeat. Now the universe, that little prick, was laughing uncontrollably. Any other day she would groan in ecstasy at the sight of a shirtless Jake doing yard work, but today, it just felt like one more thing that would send her over the edge. And by send, she meant give her a violent, unforgiving shove. Given the day she just had, there was no way she could be held accountable for her actions if faced with all that smooth, hot, golden skin. She managed to pull her car in the garage without whacking it against the side, thinking about how ironic it was that for the second time today, Jake almost caused her to decapitate her side mirror.

She stepped out of the car as the sound of the lawn mower rumbled to a stop just on the other side of the garage.

"Casey, do you have a minute? There's something I wanted to talk to you about." He sounded slightly out of breath and just that sound, even without the visual, twisted something up inside her. In a really good way that made her want to un-twist it. Stat.

After she carefully closed her car door, Casey took a fortifying breath to shore up her mental defenses, not sure she was at all prepared to turn around and see him.

Nope. Because he was pretty perfect.

Solid and big and muscular, not the freakishly hairless gym worshipper that tended to turn her off. Heavens, he was just such a *man*. She chewed the inside of her cheek to try and focus her eyes on his face, which was perfectly nice, but sweet baby Gucci, she really just wanted to stare at the beautiful dip of his obliques that cut down into the waistband of his black gym shorts. Vaguely aware that she hadn't answered him, she managed some sort of sound that he must have taken as agreement because he gestured for her to sit down on the open tailgate of his truck.

The heat radiating off of his skin was a comforting, solid weight pressing into her as she took a seat on the hard plastic next to him. After her day, just sitting there next to him was warming her up from the inside out. It felt so good it almost hurt and she couldn't bring herself to look over at him. Geez, when had she turned into such a complete and total wuss?

"Sorry I didn't get a chance to talk to you earlier."

"It's okay, it was a busy afternoon." She hated how small her voice sounded. Another thing she could blame Melinda for.

"Seemed like it." He absently stroked the top of Remy's head. "So. We kissed the other day."

She let out a small laugh, somewhat surprised that he would start out so bluntly. "Yeah, we did."

"I feel like I should apologize." He shifted and his bicep brushed along her shoulder, causing her to roll her lips inward, the pressure of her teeth against the sensitive skin helping to keep her emotions inside. And her hands to herself. When she opened her mouth, she had every intention of saying one of the many clever and witty things she had practiced when she thought of when having this conversation with him.

Instead, what came out was, "Jake, could you please put a shirt on?"

∾

JAKE'S HEAD whipped over to see Casey slap a hand over mouth and her eyes widen in complete horror.

"Sure," he said slowly as he reached behind him to find his t-shirt from earlier. He pulled it over his head, trying to keep the confusion from his face. Seriously though, what the hell?

From behind the hand still at her mouth, she let out a muffled giggle, one that held a more than a tinge of hysteria. Maybe she was drunk. Her eyes looked tired, and a little red. Had she been crying? Lord, the one thing that might send him into a state of abject terror was if he had to see this woman cry.

"I'm so sorry," she stammered. "I can't believe I just said that. It's just, you're sitting there all shirtless, and I think I know what you're about to say, and my day was so, so, so crappy that clearly I can't handle you saying what you're about to say while sitting next to me looking like that."

Okay, this was a Casey he was not prepared for. He couldn't help the small grin that crept across his face, because he couldn't deny that he liked seeing her so flustered. If he was completely honest with himself, he just plain *liked* Casey. Almost every inter-action they'd had, she managed to surprise him in some way. Especially last Sunday.

Seeing her get so mouthy and feisty about him seeing that stupid wall had weakened him. Still, he would have been perfectly capable of staying in control, even after stepping up onto that ladder behind her. Putting his hand around her waist had been stupid, amazing but stupid. And it wasn't even the thing that made him give in.

It was the look in her eyes when she looked back at him. It had been so heavy with need that he felt like he'd been unleashed. No other word for it. Normally, he would be disgusted in himself for not having better control of his own body. But the way she had felt pressed up against him, he couldn't regret what had happened.

And the way he'd felt in that moment, it was like he was being split down the middle, the devil on one side whispering to keep taking and touching and tasting and the other little devil screaming at him that she would just be one more thing ripped from him.

Yeah, long ago he recognized that he had a devil on each shoulder, rather than one angel to balance things out. Those white robed suckers were reserved for the glass half full type of people. Though, he imagine that if he did have one, it would agree...Casey was probably better off not getting involved with him like that. All week he had struggled with finding the right time and the right words to say to her, because after a few days of very conspicuous avoidance on her part, he knew it would be up to him to initiate this talk. He had to admit he was surprised she didn't try the usual chick stuff afterward. Just one more thing he could add to the list of things he couldn't quite figure out about her. Right before her asking him to put a shirt on.

She had seemed off when he'd seen her earlier in the day, and still a bit pale and drawn when she'd gotten out of the car. But now she looked absolutely miserable. Time to make a quick decision about whether to take pity on her or not. She was studiously avoiding direct eye contact, hands still perched in front of the mouth that he know knew should be considered a national treasure. Yeah, better go easy on her.

"What was so bad about your day?"

She looked over, dropping her hands down into her lap. "Huh?"

"You said your day was bad. What happened?"

"You really want to know?"

He paused, like he was considering her question. "Nah, just don't feel like mowing the lawn."

A small smile touched her lips, even if it didn't quite reach her eyes. But she still didn't answer.

"Was it that Melinda chick?"

"Yeah," she said, drawing out the word. "Well, she was definitely the worst part of it. How did you know?"

He shrugged. "I'm pretty good at reading people. Sensed a little tension there."

"Ha, understatement of the century. Long story short, I had a project that I've been working on for the last few months, something that could be really good for business, and before I had a chance to show it to my manager, she found my research and presented it as hers."

"What a bitch," he muttered, fighting against every single urge to wrap an arm around her shoulders and pull her in. Would not help his current 'we can't be romantically involved' platform.

"Pretty much." She slowly kicked one foot back and forth, and watching the smooth movement was oddly soothing to him. It made him think about the first time he noticed her do that same thing, sitting on her bed when she had agreed to watch Remy. Back then, he hadn't known her at all. At the moment, he didn't know how much closer he was to that end, but one thing he knew was that he hated seeing this defeated look that was draped over her.

"So what are you going to do about it?"

"I don't really know yet. It would be my word against hers, and if I was going to say something, it probably should have been right away when my manager brought it up. I mean, why would he believe me now?"

"That's a good point." When he said it, she nodded, still looking down at her lap. "It's also total bullshit."

Her face whipped up so fast that Remy sat up next to him, wondering what was going on. "Excuse me?"

There was a chill to her voice now, and she narrowed her eyes in a way that shouldn't have been sexy, but it was.

"You heard me. One thing I never pegged you for was a coward, but this girl clearly does."

She scoffed and crossed her arms in front of her chest, but didn't argue.

"Just tell me one thing, Casey. Why did you do all the work in the first place?"

Her jaw twitched back and forth, matching the rhythm of her still moving foot. "I love my job, and I love where I work. I want to know I've done everything I can to make it successful. And I know I can be doing more than I am, this gives me a chance to prove that." She kicked one foot sideways then, knocking into one of his. "And you don't have to Jedi mind trick me, but I appreciate what you're trying to do."

"No trick. Just telling you what I see." He loved that she was calling him on it though, meant she was snapping out of it. "People like Melinda don't deserve to win, and so often they do. I know those types of people, they're bullies, and they get off on it. And if you don't fight back on this, she'll never stop pushing you around. And I don't think you're the kind of girl who lets herself get pushed around."

She turned slightly, facing him more fully, those blue green eyes looking at him like she was trying figure something out. Trying to figure him out.

"What?" he asked, fidgeting a little under her close scrutiny.

"I just," she started, then closed her mouth. She weighed her words, still watching him. "I guess I wasn't expecting you to be the pep talk type. Most men suck at it, but that was surprisingly non-sucky."

Jake smiled, not missing the fact that she stared at his mouth every time he did. Which brought him back to the original purpose of the conversation. Only now he wasn't sure how to turn it back that direction without making it awkward.

She looked away, taking a deep breath. "You're right though. I need to do something, I worked too hard on that to just let it go now." She readjusted the strap of her purse on her shoulder after sliding off the tailgate. Before she walked away, she hesitated, like she knew he hadn't said what he meant to when they sat down. The opening was there, she was giving it to him. And all of a sudden, every word he had practiced shriveled up in his throat. Which was a damn shame, because as speeches went, it had been a pretty good one.

"Thanks, Jake," she said.

"Anytime. That's, uh, that's what friends do, right?"

He. Was. A. Chickenshit.

"Yeah," she replied slowly, head cocked to the side. "Is that what we are?"

Remy groaned in his sleep next to him in the bed of the truck, and Jake absently ran a hand along his side, glad for the momentary interruption. Because his whole speech was shot to hell anyway, he figured he might as well go with honesty.

"I hope so. But if I suck at it, you'll have to tell me, because I don't have too many friends." Saying it out loud was easier than he thought, and the way her whole face softened, he knew it was worth it. Thankfully, her gaze held no pity. She looked resolute.

"Then you're in luck. Because as a friend, I pretty much rock." She smiled widely, and he couldn't help shake his head. She turned to go inside, and before she got to the door, he called out to her again.

"So, do I get to ask why I had to put my shirt on, now that we're buddies and all."

She ducked her head, but he could tell she was grinning. The bluish-gray of the siding behind her made her hair seem darker and her eyes seem lighter when she looked back up.

"Well *friend,* just imagine if I'd wanted to have that talk with you, but I was wearing my bikini."

Then she winked and walked inside, the door slamming behind her. He swallowed roughly.

Yup. Point taken.

15

CASEY LEANED across the counter to turn the dial on her iPod where it was perched in the docking station. She flipped the circle around until she hit the volume she wanted, knowing that Jake wasn't home and wouldn't march over demanding that Pink be turned down to a more acceptable level. She turned back to chopping up the red, green and yellow peppers on the butcher block in front of her, then dropped them into skillet, causing a satisfying sizzle to spit back at her.

She wiped her hands on the legs of her jeans and checked the clock, then pulled the tortillas out of the fridge. She'd warm those up as soon as Rachel got there, which considering she was supposed to be here ten minutes ago meant that she'd be walking in anytime. She was stirring the peppers and onions in the skillet when JLo came on. It was like hips and butts everywhere couldn't stay still when that woman was singing, as if they recognized that she had singlehandedly made it okay to be curvy. Soon enough she was swinging and rolling through the kitchen and singing into the bamboo spatula. Casey loved dancing and singing, though she could easily admit she wasn't particularly gifted at either. But one of the beautiful things about living alone was that you could unleash your inner fly girl and no one was around to judge you.

She heard a small rap at the door and hollered over the music for Rachel to come in.

"Perfect timing Rach, you can tell me if this song makes my butt look big." She was about to execute the slow grind of her hips that Rachel had perfected, and Casey only seemed capable of doing when she was completely liquored up.

"Not from where I'm standing. Friend." Jake's low voice rumbled behind her.

Casey shrieked and jumped backwards, slamming one hip into the counter.

"Holy *crap*, Jake." She rubbed at her hip bone, knowing she'd have a bruise from where the edge caught her. Seriously, did he have an app on his phone that alerted him every time she was doing something that could remotely embarrass her? She laughed nervously, trying to cover it with a cough, then reached over to lower the volume on the music. Turning down the heat on the burner below her vegetables, now hissing angrily, she looked over at where he stood leaning in the door frame. "I, uhh, thought you were Rachel."

"Clearly." He had the *I'm mildly entertained by you but can't be bothered to move my facial muscles enough to show you just how much* look on his face. It made her want to slap him and then lick him, maybe somewhere in the pectoral region...because after the shirtless glory she saw, she knew that it was a really, really good region on him. "So, dare I ask what that question was about?"

"Ha," she said, then cleared her throat when she realized she was still brandishing the spatula like a weapon. "It's silly."

One eyebrow quirked on his handsome face, telling her there was no way she was getting out of this so easily. Taking a deep breath, she turned back to the skillet.

"Well, a few years ago, Rachel was dancing to a really popular song at the time, and said that the way she danced to it probably made her ass look huge. So, it just kinda became a thing. 'Does this song make my butt look big?' Which is code for 'I'm probably dancing like a streetwalker.'" Casey faltered a little when he just kept staring at her. "So. That's it. See? It's silly."

Jake lifted one side of his lips in a pseudo-smile, but still didn't answer. Seriously, this man drove her *insane*. It was like he *wanted* her to babble incessantly.

"Anyway," she continued, "what's up? I wasn't expecting to see you."

"I pulled up and heard the music, thought I could maybe grab your rent check."

Well frick. The bag from Macy's sitting inside her bedroom may or may not have been holding an incredible pair of black leather, over the knee boots by Guess that, though they were fifteen percent off, would still bring her checking account balance just low enough that a rent check may or may not clear before payday.

Jake may or may not murder her.

Gah, she could feel it, rising up. Surely something in her house needed to be organized. Why? *Why* did she do this to herself?

"Oh. Sure. Let me, umm, let me see if I can find my check-book. Come on in while you wait, grab a beer from the fridge."

He raised his eyebrows in surprise, but said thanks as he opened up the fridge to grab one of the Coronas she kept in case Dylan was over.

Solid plan, offering booze to distract him from your inability to pay rent. Way to go Casey. Next up? Offer him a lap dance while wearing the boots. She pretended to root through her purse where she had dumped it on the floor by the couch, even though she knew exactly where the checkbook was, tucked in the kitchen drawer with the bills she couldn't pay online.

"Hey, can you just turn that burner off for me? I don't want the veggies to burn before Rachel gets here. It might take me a minute to find this, I just never use my checkbook anymore...you know how it is, everything is debit card these days." She heard the click of the handle being turned in the off position, but he was completely quiet other than that. After shuffling around for another minute, she walked back into the kitchen, humming like she was thinking about something. "I'm so sorry Jake, I'm not quite sure where it is. Do you want me to just drop a check off for you later after I have more time to look for it?"

He watched her over the top of his beer as he took a sip, then licked across his bottom lip when he swallowed.

Do not swoon. Do not swoon.

She could tell by the warmth in his dark eyes that he was in a fairly good mood, and could probably see right through her crap but couldn't decide whether to call her out on it. He opened his mouth to say something when Rachel barged through the door without knocking, her phone wedged in between her cheek and shoulder.

"So then I said, listen chica, if anyone deserves gift baskets with a thank you note from me today it will be Mom and Dad Hemsworth. And she actually looked at me and goes, who are they? Did they donate or something? So then I go, ummmm yeah, they *donated* two of the most beautiful men on the planet."

Casey smothered a laugh at the look on Rachel's face when she realized Jake was in the kitchen. He, of course, merely stared in tempered amusement.

"Yeah, I gotta go, I'm at Casey's and her landlord, whom as you know I refer to as Sexiness Personified, is staring at me like I've got two heads." Jake shook his head at her audacity, but a slight flush tinged his cheekbones. And wasn't that pretty fascinating? Casey had not pegged him as someone who embarrassed easily. At all.

"Nice entrance, Rachel, as always," Casey said on a sigh.

"It's a gift," she stated, dropping her phone in her purse. "Jake, what a lovely surprise. I didn't expect you'd be joining us for dinner. I can't blame you though, few can resist Casey's...*fajitas*." She managed to make the last word sound dirty, and Casey gave her a pointed *you are so not funny* look from where she stood behind Jake, knowing he couldn't see her. Rachel just returned the look with a beatific smile, not phased in the least.

"Oh." Jake rubbed at the back of his neck with the hand not holding his beer. "I'm not staying for dinner, just stopped to grab her rent check."

"Don't be silly. Knowing Casey, there's plenty of food, plus it will give you and me a chance to chat a bit. You may not know this, but my asshat ex-boyfriend was recently discovered cheating on me, so I'm in a fragile state of mind. Who knows what I'll do if you refuse."

"Oh my word, Rachel." Casey walked around Jake to warm up the tortillas, then had to laugh at the look of complete bewilderment on his face. "You cannot shame him into staying for dinner. Jake, just ignore her, it's the easiest path to take, trust me."

Rachel pouted, then grabbed a beer and made her way to the dining room. Jake looked between the two of them, then with a decisive nod, went to join Rachel at the table.

"I'd hate to be added to your male hit list, so count me in. Plus, all I have waiting for me at home is-" He stopped mid-sentence, gaping into the family room. His sudden silence, coupled with the look of abject horror on his face had all the puzzle pieces clicking into place for Casey. Painted walls in the family room. Roasted Pumpkin painted walls that he hadn't seen yet. Walls that he thought were going to be tan.

"What's his deal?" Rachel mumbled around a mouthful of tortilla chip. Jake clenched his jaw, then turned towards Casey with decidedly less humor in his eyes than before. She shrugged her shoulders and offered what she hoped was a winning smile.

"An *earth tone*, Casey. You said you were going to paint an earth tone, a tan, which is why I agreed."

"Ohhh," Rachel drawled, taking a large drink of her beer.

"That's his deal. Yeah, you need to be specific with Casey when you're talking paint colors. Girl does not have boring in her vocabulary."

"I distinctly remember that I hadn't chosen the color yet, and you're the one who assumed tan. I never said what color."

"It's orange."

"It's terra cotta. And it *is* an earth tone. Are you seriously going to try to tell me what constitutes an earth tone and what doesn't?"

"Don't do it, Jake," Rachel interjected, watching the two of them with unconcealed fascination. "Or do, and let me enjoy the fireworks."

He took a deep breath, shaking his head. "How many arguments do you win simply because you steamroll over the other person?"

She smiled sweetly. "Every single one. Ask my brothers."

Shortly after that, the three of them sat down to have dinner. Rachel kept them both entertained with stories from work, and musings from her breakup with Marc that even had Jake chuckling from time to time. Casey couldn't help but notice that he stayed quiet unless specifically asked a question, but somehow still managed to seem engaged in the conversations around him. He seemed to particularly enjoy watching the banter between her and Rachel, but maybe it was because he wasn't used to being around people who knew each other so well. And, oh holy crap, maybe she was supposed to be in his life just to give him friendship. Well, if that was the case, she'd be the best dang friend he'd ever had. And just secretly want to rip his clothes off and marry him and have his babies and because she couldn't do those things would inevitably pine away for him for the rest of her natural born life. Hey, she could admit she was nothing if not a tad overly dramatic.

But sitting at her dining room table, listening to Rachel tell a story about an event she planned last year, making huge gestures with her hands and then seeing the way that Jake's eyes crinkled when he looked down and grinned, clearly fighting laughter, she figured it was worth it. He was eating a home cooked meal, laughing and smiling, instead of sitting home alone again.

"So, Jake, Casey tells me that you gave her quite the motivational speech about her little work sitch."

He shrugged noncommittally. "Just gave her my honest opinion, for whatever it was worth."

"I think it was worth a lot. She didn't like my advice all too much, I think yours was more in line with her moral code."

He looked over at Casey. "What'd she tell you to do?"

Rachel snickered while she gathered up another bite of chicken, and Casey just gestured for her to go ahead and share. Rachel finished her bite and carefully laid her fork down next to the plate.

"Well, I told her that if it were me, and I had found out in the most humiliating and humbling way possible that my arch enemy had just stolen months of my hard work and passed it off as her own, I would cut her. Not hypothetically like 'oh I'm going to cut her down to size and let her know she was wrong'. No, I would *cut her*. Physically. Just thinking it about makes me want to straight up shank her. You know, prison style."

"Right," Jake said slowly. "You are completely terrifying."

Chin resting in one hand, Casey just grinned.

"Thank you," Rachel said sincerely. A slow, bright smile spread across her face, and the small dimple hiding in her right cheek winked out. "That's the nicest thing you've said to me so far. So. Jake. Any relationship horror stories you've got that can come close to rivaling the one that I just experienced?" Then she inconspicuously winked over at Casey. Casey kicked at her under the table, then choked on a chip when Rachel's foot kicked her right back.

Of course he didn't answer right away, because that would be completely out of character. Finishing the bite that was in his mouth, he kept his gaze on Casey, like he *knew* that Rachel was asking this for Casey's sake. Freaking Rachel. Who'd invited her anyway?

"I wouldn't call it a horror story. No cheating or anything." Then he stopped and cocked his head. "At least not that I know of."

"So," Casey said as casually as possible, even though she was really, incredibly interested in this particular story, "what happened?"

Another kick at her shin under the table, and Casey glared at Rachel. Thankfully, Jake was oblivious.

"Nothing that doesn't happen to a lot of military relationships. I dated Lisa for about a year, this was almost five years ago now. It takes a special woman to be able to handle dating a soldier. It's tough as hell. And it took her about six months of me being deployed to figure out she wasn't one of them. So I got the letter telling me that."

"What a bitch," Rachel said under her breath, leaning back in her chair. And yeah, Casey kept her mouth shut but she was definitely thinking along those lines. About *Lisa*. She'd never loved that name anyway.

But Jake just shook his head. "No, she wasn't. It was just too hard for her. And I can't blame her. It's pretty stressful, waiting for phone calls and emails, just getting scraps of time here and there. And when she'd get ticked at me for not getting in touch with her more often, I wasn't very understanding of what she was going through."

"You haven't had many people there for you, have you?" Casey spoke without thinking. It just popped right out of her aching heart and straight out of her mouth. The look of surprise on Jake's face mirrored what she felt.

"No," he said simply. And what made her even more sad was that he didn't look upset by it. "But, Lisa did us both a favor. We were doomed from that first date, when she thought it was really exciting to date a soldier. And it's not. Stress is constant in this life. It's unyielding and uncompromising. And most people can't handle it."

"Well, this is depressing as all get out," Rachel stated and stood up.

"You're ditching me?" Casey said, trying to snap herself out of the cloud that was smothering her heart at listening to Jake talk. "I thought we were going try and convince Liz to swing over after she's done working."

"I know, but I was already beat from work, and the couple beers just made me all sleepy. Plus, you know Liz doesn't do spontaneity too well. It's like beating your head against a brick wall to get her to deviate from her schedule. I'm still not sure how we're able to stay friends with someone that's so stubborn."

Jake made a quiet choking noise as he tried to swallow his beer.

"Yeah," Casey said dryly. "You'll just have to show her the ropes on how to be more agreeable and cooperative."

"I know, right?" Rachel replied.

Jake pushed his chair back from the table and stood. "I should head out, too."

"Don't leave on my account, Jake," Rachel said as she walked to the door. She gave Casey a tiny wink and a thumbs up, mouthing SO HOT as she passed. "I mean, I know I'm the life of the party and all, but I bet you two could find something to do when I leave."

"Subtle, Rachel," Casey hissed quietly enough that she doubted Jake could hear. Rachel completely ignored her. Typical.

"No, I really should get some work done at my place," he said. "If you don't think you can find your checkbook tonight, I can get rent from you tomorrow."

"Didn't I see you throw your checkbook in that top drawer next to the fridge when I helped you unpack?" Rachel added, clearly trying to be helpful. Casey pursed her lips and glared at

Rachel. Understanding dawned in Rachel's hazel eyes, her mouth forming an 'O'. "Or...umm...never mind, maybe I'm thinking of Liz. You know, I gotta go. You two have a wonderful evening."

And, damage done, she was gone in a swirl of red hair and the roar of a car engine. Casey rubbed her forehead and took a deep breath before turning around. Come to think of it, she did that a lot around Jake. It was like she needed physical manifestation of expelling the nerves that seemed to bubble and swell inside her whenever she was around him. Didn't help that she seemed to do some spectacularly stupid things when he was around, like pretend she didn't know where her checkbook was.

Before she turned, she made a decision, feeling his weighted silence like a concrete wall behind her. She took the three steps to the kitchen drawer in question and quickly pulled it open, grabbed the checkbook out and dropped it on the counter, then turned to face him. He was still behind the table, but was leaning back against the wall, arms folded across his chest. He raised one brow very, very slowly, asking a silent question. She felt herself deflate.

"So," she started out slowly. "You're probably wondering why I lied to you about that."

"It's entirely possible." Yeah. He sounded pissed.

"Well, it's kind of a funny story."

"Funny like *my landlord thinks I'm painting my walls tan but I'm really painting them orange* funny?"

She winced. She wasn't scoring many points tonight. "No?"

"Then what kind of funny is it?" His voice was quiet. Even. Calm. And for some reason that made her even more nervous.

"Funny as in, I saw this really amazing pair of boots on sale at Macy's," she started in rush, and seeing his expression instantly turn incredulous, she just plowed on. "They're Guess, which I know doesn't mean much to you, but they were the kind of thing that just never goes on sale, and they're black leather with a three inch stiletto and a buckle around the top."

A muscle in his jaw clenched and she just kept on rollin'. "*Real* leather, did I mention that? And they're over the knee just high enough that they're fashionable, but I won't look like a hooker, and I kinda forgot about rent being due today, so if you could just wait to deposit my check until Friday, I would really appreciate it. And I thought if I pretended I didn't know where my checkbook was I could hold you off the two days until I got paid, and you'd never know. Umm, that kind of funny...I guess." Her voice was faint by the time she finished, and she felt like she needed to gulp in the oxygen that she sacrificed to get that all out.

He didn't move. Didn't even blink. Just stared. Finally he closed his eyes for a few seconds and took a deep breath. "Casey."

"I know," she said. And she did. It sank like a brick in her gut. "I don't know why I did it. It was so stupid."

"And irresponsible."

She hung her head, feeling the hot bite of tears at the back of her eyes. "Yes. It was."

When he let out a hard breath, she dared to look up at him. He shook his head a little, and gave her a stern look. "I'll wait until Friday to deposit it, but don't ever do it again. I'm not going to wait next time."

"I won't, oh you have no idea how much I won't do this again."

"Good."

"Thank you so much Jake."

He held up a hand to stop her. "I know. But never again, Casey. I'm serious."

She nodded quickly and whipped around the fill out the check before he could change his mind. She heard him mutter "had to be black boots", but she ignored it and scrawled out her signature, then handed him the check after he walked around the table into the kitchen.

He took it, then looked at her for a long moment. "Anybody ever tell you they don't know what to do with you?"

Standing next to him in her kitchen, she looked up into his

hard, handsome face and actually felt small. It felt really good. And she wanted to cup his face so bad, but she pushed her hand into the back pocket of her jeans. She gave him a wry grin and answered with complete honesty. "Only my entire life."

He made a hard exhale through his nose that could have been a laugh, then he shook his head a few times.

"Thank you for dinner, by the way. Don't tell Remy, but you and Rachel are much more entertaining dinner companions than he is."

"Are you kidding me?" She made a dismissive gesture with her hand and wrinkled her nose. "You think I talk to your dog?"

He assessed her face, then actually gave a flash of a boyish grin that made everything inside of her tighten up quite deliciously. "Yeah, I actually do."

He tapped her rent check on the counter, tipped his chin up in farewell, and was out the door leaving Casey slumped against the counter. Sure, the evening had ended on a positive note. But she still felt a little queasy. What had she been thinking?

He'd taken a chance on her, one that she'd had to convince him of when she moved in. And one of the first chances she got, she pulled *this*.

"No more," she said firmly and started putting away dirty dishes.

No more. But now she just had to figure out how to make it up to him.

16

JAKE PUSHED against the heavy wooden door that led into the brewery where Chris Stockton had suggested they meet. The substantial weight set the stage for the rest of the dark toned wood along the interior of the building. Everything was masculine and old-fashioned, from the gleaming varnished floors to the upper level filled high top tables that sat framed in behind a railing of aged brass. It was the kind of place where the food was inconsequential, because patrons pretty much came for the beer. Considering Jake rarely found his way into downtown Grand Rapids, it would be this type of place that would draw him in. There wasn't an inch that was fussy, overdone or pretentious. He liked it.

He grabbed a seat at the empty stretch of bar, tapping his finger on the surface along with the sounds of Creedence Clearwater Revival that was being piped through the building. He smiled at the song, *Proud Mary*, because it had been one of his Mom's favorites. Whenever she played it or it came on the radio, it was one of the few times he could remember after his Dad died that she would dance around the house, singing in the off-key voice she was always self-conscious about. She really couldn't sing for crap, but something about that song just made her not care. Funny how as an adult, he recognized something in her response to that particular song that he didn't see the significance of as a teenager. Back then he would usually just roll his eyes and think about how nerdy his Mom was. Now he understood how powerful those couple minutes of music were in helping her maintain her sanity. More than a few times during his years in the sandbox, he found himself laying on his bed and pulling up a little Creedence on his iPod, giving him an escape from the scratchy wool of Army issued blankets underneath him and sound of mortar fire all around him, a few minutes when the constant, draining state of awareness could take a backseat. It must have been how she felt when she would dance around the living room, reverting momentarily to a place where she wasn't a young widow with a moody teen and a world of unplanned responsibility hanging around her thin shoulders.

And thinking of off-key singing, the visual of Casey dancing through her kitchen was one that had made him grin for days after witnessing it. Her rhythm was just slightly off, her hips trying desperately to keep up with the beat of the song that was blaring through the speakers. It had been difficult for him to imagine yet another thing to make her even more appealing to him than she already was, but that had done it. In a short amount of time, he'd found her to be funny, usually in a completely unintentional way, sexy without being obvious about it, a little demanding when it came to her work, loving and loyal to her family and friends, and definitely feisty. She had moments of being flighty, her being late on the rent definitely annoyed him, but that feeling had only surfaced after he had pushed, shoved and practically burned his brain to rid himself of the vision of her long legs encased in those black boots. She hadn't lied to him in the end though, and he gave her credit for that. But it was seeing her in those unstaged moments, that imperfection that she obviously tried to hide, that made it even more difficult to stay away.

He really had stopped for the rent check, that much was true. But he'd stayed because there was just something about her that drew him in like the cliched moth to a flame. He should take a lesson from that, really. The moth would always lose to the flame, be sucked in and scorched by the heat. But he couldn't even care anymore. It seemed all but impossible to him now to completely shut her out.

He'd wager a guess that she drew people in no matter where she went. She was taking their agreement to be friends seriously, and it just made him respect her as much as he already liked her. It was pretty apparent that she was attracted to him, but the moment he had said they were friends, she'd put it aside. And just like that, he'd found the idea of going home alone...again...completely unappealing. He'd done it for so long, pushed people away, and until Casey he didn't realize just how exhausting it was. But he knew well enough that to let her shoulder the responsibility of being his only friend wasn't fair. She didn't even realize all of his reasons, so he couldn't expect her be the only person to take on that yoke. Oh, she'd do it, of that he had no doubt. Because she took care of people, she had that kind of personality. Wanting to feed everyone, clean up after them, keep them comfortable and feeling welcome in her home, it was the kind of thing that you couldn't fake.

And that part of her personality is precisely why Jake found himself sitting there sipping a pale ale, waiting for Stockton to show up. He was another platoon leader in the same company, and he'd tried on numerous occasions to reach out to Jake. They'd only done one deployment together, but since being home, Jake had rebuffed his few invitations to come over to his place for dinner or to watch a game, or like tonight, just to meet up for a beer. Stockton was a good guy, lanky as a damn bean pole, with a crooked grin and sharp cheekbones. Jake figured that if Casey could make the effort for him, then he could make an effort with one of the few guys who was still doing the same. In the mirror stretched across the wall behind the bartender, the only way Jake really felt comfortable keeping his back to the entrance, he saw the door swing open and Stockton walk in and do the same slow scan of the room the Jake had done himself. He motioned to the hostess when he saw Jake sitting at the bar.

"Shit, Miller, you actually came," he said, clapping Jake on the shoulder as he slid into a barstool next to him.

"You thought I wouldn't?"

"Figured it was a toss-up. Either way, I get a night out of the house to drink some good beer. I swear, Vanessa is trying to drive me out of my mind." He signaled the bartender for one of what Jake was drinking, and then turned in his seat to face him fully. "So you want to tell me why you made me work so damn hard to get you to come out?"

Jake smirked, taking a long sip of his beer. "Didn't want you to think I was easy," he said.

"Easy? No, that you're not. I think Ness was getting jealous. She told me if I bitched one more time about you not hanging out with me she was gonna revoke my man card."

Jake knew he hadn't really answered the question, and that Stockton was smart enough to realize it. But he ignored it for the moment, and the two made easy conversation about the Tigers game, the last drill weekend, trading stories about their company commander. Stockton spoke a little bit more about Vanessa, and Jake could easily see that beneath his griping was a man who was completely and happily whipped.

"Alright man, we're three beers in, which means shit's about to get real. This is where I start making you talk about your *feelings.*" Stockton had an easy smile across his face, but his eyes very clearly said he wasn't joking.

"In that case, I might need another one," Jake muttered.

"Seriously, dude. You're not a prick or anything, so what's up with the ice queen act? I can't figure it out."

Jake watched the bartender pull a beer from the handles

lining the end of the bar, then met Stockton's eyes in the mirror. "Is there a compliment buried somewhere in there?"

"A half assed one. You still didn't answer the question."

He sighed and rolled his pint glass between his hands. "Maybe I just don't like people."

"Maybe. I don't get that feeling though."

"You're really not gonna drop this, are you?"

"Not a chance. Guys respect you, that much is obvious, and you do a pretty stellar job of puttin' the fear of God into 'em. But it's hard to go over there with a group of guys as often as you have and not have any friends. That's no accident, Miller. Watching you over there for eleven months, shit, made me feel like someone kicked my puppy every day. You're depressing."

Jake couldn't help the chuckle. "So if I talk to you about it, do we have to man hug and then watch The Notebook or something?"

Stockton groaned. "Don't joke about that. Ness makes me watch that every single time it comes on tv. I told her my next deployment she needs to watch a chick flick every day so that by the time I come home it's completely out of her system. If I have to hear one more time about how Noah Calhoun is her movie husband and how come I don't do romantic shit like he does, I will rip my own ears off." Then he tipped his beer glass at Jake. "And don't deflect again."

"There's no big mystery. Only child, Mom and Dad both died, so I'm a loner by nature. Had really shit deployments my first couple trips over there, lost too many good guys." He shrugged, different faces filtering through his thoughts, not sure what else to say. "Guess it felt easier to keep myself separate."

And as soon as he said it, he realized that he wasn't doing that anymore.

At all.

A family picnic at Labor Day, dinner with Casey and Rachel, just sitting and talking to her on the tailgate of his truck, seeking her out at work and now beers with Stockton. It stunned him, so he was glad he could hide his face into his pint glass momentarily, to let that feeling roll slowly through him.

Stockton was quiet, sipping his beer. The fact that he didn't rush to speak went a long way with Jake, made him feel more comfortable for sharing, even though some people would probably have the opposite reaction.

"Makes sense," Stockton said when he finally spoke. He drained the rest of his glass, checked the time on his phone and pulled some cash out of his wallet. "We'll take baby steps then."

"Baby steps?"

"Yeah. Towards our epic bromance." He grinned at Jake, showing the slightly crooked front tooth that the guys always gave him crap about. Jake shook his head, but smiled. Strangely, he didn't feel like Stockton's joking detracted from his honest answer. "Look man, I've gotta head home or my wife will withhold sex for the rest of the week and I can't have that."

"Smart woman."

"Works every time, I haven't been out past curfew since we got married. Hey, a group of people are going camping the weekend after our next drill, last hurrah before it gets too cold out. You should come."

"Yeah? I know anyone else going?" Jake loved to camp, but hadn't gone in years.

"You'd know a couple people. VanderWall and his wife, I think he's bringing a cousin or something. A couple of my wife's friends, but they're cool, you'd like 'em. We're gonna head up to Silver Lake Friday afternoon, camp a few miles away so we can still ride the dunes during the day on Saturday. Probably head back Sunday afternoon."

Jake nodded, knowing he didn't have anything going that weekend, but not quite ready to say yes. "I'll think about it, let you know."

Stockton smacked him on the shoulder again and left. Jake

blew out a breath, feeling almost ridiculously relieved at how that had gone. He looked over his bill while he finished his beer, then felt his phone vibrate where it was sitting on the bar. His eyebrows rose when he realized it was a text from Casey. They'd exchanged numbers for the weekends she had Remy, but up until now, they'd only communicated face to face. He pulled his wallet out of his back pocket, thumbing through the bills and laying down enough to cover the bill and a generous tip. He always tipped high when the wait staff was practically invisible unless he needed something.

Walking through the doors, he squinted into the late afternoon sun and walked down the few blocks to where he'd parked his truck. After starting the engine and slipping on his sunglasses, he finally swiped his finger across the screen of his phone to read the text message.

Hey, it's Casey. Made dinner to bring over to my parents and have way too much. I left a covered plate for you on your workbench in the garage. Consider it part of my thank you for understanding about the rent check. :)

He dropped his head back on the headrest. Yup, she couldn't help herself. He smiled and typed out a response.

No thanks necessary. Besides, what if I already ate?

His phone vibrated almost immediately.

I've seen how much you eat, you can manage some more. But if you can't, and you feed that to your dog, I swear, you BETTER lie to me and say it was amazing.

FRIENDS DON'T LIE to each other Casey. Plus, Remy has excellent taste, I'm sure he'd enjoy anything you made.

YEAH, I know he has 'excellent taste', those shoes were sheer

perfection. I still have nightmares of the rubble he left behind to taunt me. Just eat the food, it'll make me feel better, k?

He considered messing with her a little more, but was already struggling with how easy it would be to take a text out of context and have it sound like he was flirting. Couldn't have that. Though with three beers creating a relaxed feeling he didn't often have, he was struggling to remember why that was exactly. He saw it again, her dancing in her kitchen, and his chest pinched in a weird way. He rubbed at his sternum, like it would somehow make the feeling subside. He stared out the windshield, watching the ebb and flow of cars down the narrow brick paved street outside of the brewery. No...no flirting. It was better this way.

Okay. Thanks, we're even.

He tossed the phone into the passenger seat and pulled into traffic, heading home with a vague feeling that edged towards disappointment at the knowledge he wouldn't see her tonight.

17

THE SCREAMING and yelling would never stop. She could already tell that her ears would probably be ringing for hours and hours after this was done. Maybe days...weeks even.

"Okay boys," she hollered over the cacophony of three boys running down her hallway, all of them competing to be heard over the other. "Time to play outside."

She flattened herself against the kitchen counter as they whipped past her to go running out into the yard.

"Holy. Freaking. Crap," she whispered as a blissful silence swelled through the space in their absence. She had told Caleb and Marissa that she would *gladly* watch their three boys, ages eight, six and three, so they could go out for their tenth anniversary. Now she would gladly tip back an entire bottle of wine. She'd only had the boys for four hours. She figured she had about two more hours to go. Marissa had just sent her a text that the musical they had gone to see was done, and they were heading to the restaurant...making sure that everyone was still alive and accounted for.

In the most literal sense, yes. All the boys were alive, though not for a lack of trying on Isaiah's part. Casey had walked in on him holding Tyler down with a pillow over his face, Tyler's skinny arms trying to find purchase against his big brothers wiry frame. Isaiah, of course, claimed he was just trying to show his brother how good her pillows smelled. She gazed wistfully at the bottle of chardonnay sitting unopened on top of her fridge, wondering how on earth Marissa and Jen did this every single day without becoming alcoholics. Every room in her house looked like a hurricane had ripped a path through it.

Peeking out the slider in her dining room to make sure all three were playing in the yard and not murdering each other, she absently thought about the fact that if she had Remy right now, she wouldn't have to bend all the way over to pick up the remains of the dinner that Mason had chucked onto the floor. Chicken nugget pieces littered the carpet in a perfect semi-circle around the chair that he had sat in. Seriously, what kid doesn't like chicken nuggets? Mason, apparently, who said it tasted like seaweed. Because she wasn't even entirely sure how to respond to that, she decided not to battle it and let him fill up on crackers and cheese.

With a grin, she thought about wrapping up a plate of dinosaur shaped nuggets and leaving it for Jake, just to see what his reaction would be. She had gone with an impulse in leaving him a plate of food the other night. Her Mom hadn't been feeling well, and she knew that if left up to her Dad, they'd be having cereal for dinner, so she decided to whip something up and bring it over to their house. Once she realized that she had made enough for a full grown family of six, she had thrown some under foil, drawn a smiley face on top with a sharpie and sent off the text before she could chicken out. Casey had a feeling that Jake didn't often get to eat a meal of homemade pepper jack chicken enchiladas. She knew that doing things like that could easily veer out of the friend category and slip right into the 'I sort of want to marry you' category.

It was nuts, and she was totally aware of that. If she stepped back and thought about it, she didn't know that much about Jake, not the small details that came along with anything other than time spent with each other. But from the first day, something about him drew her. She wasn't quite ready to define it, definitely couldn't say that it was love yet, but she knew enough about herself that she knew it would be so, so easy for her to end up there. She'd known it the day he told her about his Mom, and she could still remember the way she felt when that knowledge had filtered through her brain and trickled down into her heart. It was the same thing that made her know that she'd be able to move out of her apartment, that this duplex had been *the* place for her. She knew it as a truth, not something that was up for debate or open to discussion. There was something there alright, but for now she'd have to live with the big ol' question mark that was hovering over what exactly that thing was.

"Auntie Casey, Isaiah keeps throwing the soccer ball at my head." Poor Tyler. She could hear enough tremble in his voice to know that he was probably using every shred of his being not to cry. He was such a tender heart, he took after Marissa that way. While she was making dinner earlier, she had seen him rub a tightly clenched fist roughly over his eyes, and when she peeked around the corner, she saw one of those Sarah McLaughlin sad puppy commercials flickering on the TV screen. She just smiled and ducked quietly back into the kitchen, loving him so much in that moment she had to swallow back a thick lump in her throat, but she didn't want to draw attention to him because she knew that Isaiah would tease him mercilessly.

When she stepped outside to referee, she pulled her cardigan tighter around her, feeling how much the wind had kicked up since earlier in the day. Today was the first day that it smelled like fall. She pulled in a huge breath, holding that scent in her lungs, wishing she could bottle it. She walked in between the edge of her house and the side of the garage, where it opened into a spacious yard that stretched behind the three buildings. She figured the entire plot of land must be close to two acres, considering how far they were set off the road.

The three boys had started an impromptu soccer game, which really consisted of the two younger ones chasing after the much quicker Isaiah, with little success. She pulled a blanket from the backseat of her car and spread it on the grass so she could sit comfortably. She watched them for the next hour or so, reigning in Isaiah when his playing got a bit too enthusiastic for his brothers, laughing when Mason tripped over his own feet and simply popped back up, pumping his short little legs and arms furiously to catch up with his brothers.

That kid was going to conquer the world by sheer force of will. Every time she was around her nephews, she always thought about sending her mother a thank you card, for the fact that they had the balls to try one more time, after four boys in such a short amount of time. Lord knows, whenever she had kids, she would have definitely capped things after that many males.

She turned her head at the sound of Remy's hoarse bark, heart tripping over a few beats knowing that Jake would be just behind. Remy came tearing around the corner of the house and flew right past her, tail wagging and ears perked to attention at the sight of the boys. The three let out a chorus of enthusiastic whooping and hollering at addition of the dog, who immediately nosed the ball away from Isaiah, making her laugh. She heard the heavy tread of Jake's work boots stop at the edge of the grass, and she bit the inside of her cheek to keep herself to turning to look at him.

"You got something to tell me, Casey?"

She smiled. "I inherited three children. That's not going to increase my rent, is it?"

"Nah. Might as well kiss your damage deposit goodbye though."

Casey turned around, eyebrows raised. "Did I pay a damage deposit?"

"Nope. But with those three living with you, I'd probably have to charge you one."

She laughed, looking back at tangle of limbs and fur that was currently tussling over the soccer ball. Looks like Isaiah had finally found someone to keep up with him in Remy. "So, Wonderdog can play soccer too? There anything he can't do?"

"Can't hang wallpaper worth a damn. But it's quite a skill, or so I've heard."

She gave him a long look over her shoulder, but savored the warmth that slithered through her thinking about the last time she'd done exactly that. He met her look with one of his own, like he was silently daring her to bring it up. This was a decidedly non-friend stare down happening, but she would not be the first one to crack. At least, she wasn't going to until Mason chose that moment to fling himself onto the blanket next to her, snapping her attention away from Jake. He was breathing hard from all the running, his round cheeks flushed from exertion. She pushed a few of the sweat drenched blonde strands off his forehead, smiling down at him.

"Need a break, buddy? You can sit by me and watch for awhile if you're tired."

"I not tired," he said very seriously, sneaking a peek over at Jake. "You hab my water bottle, Auntie Tasey? I soooo sirsty."

She stood, telling him to stay put by Jake while she went inside to get water for all the boys. After she had found and refilled the drinking cups that Marissa had sent along with the boys, she walked back out the door and almost tripped over the step at her door at what she saw by the blanket. Jake had all three boys standing in a line in front of him, Remy sitting dutifully by his side.

She caught the door from slamming shut, not wanting to interrupt. Okay, she wanted to be nosy and see what the heck he was doing with her nephews. A lot could be said about what kind of father a man could be in situations like this. Not that she often

imagined Jake as a father...with three little dark haired children...two boys and a girl...

Dang it. Bad Casey. She shook the vision out of head in time
to hear him give a few instructions.

"Arms behind your back, hands together. Yup, just like that
Tyler. Now, spread your feet a little bit wider, Isaiah. Good.
Mason, stick your chest out more, like you have big superman
muscles."

Casey swallowed a laugh at how far the three year old puffed
out his tiny little chest, like he was holding all the air in his lungs
in order to do what Jake was telling him.

"Great job, soldiers. This is how you stand when your
commanding officer says 'at ease', it means you can relax and just
listen."

"Doesn't feel relaxed. Kinda feels weird," Isaiah said.

"Yeah, at first it doesn't feel too natural. But, after the other
stuff you have to be able to do in basic training, it starts to feel
pretty good to just stand there like that." He said it with a small
smile, and her fingers itched to pull out her phone and take a
picture. All three boys were staring at him like he was some GI
Joe/Iron Man/Captain America come to life, wide eyed and
soaking in everything he was saying. He slowly and patiently
went through how to salute, spending extra time showing Mason
how to hold his arm at just the right angle.

This was bad. So very, very bad.

A piece of hair blew across her face, and the movement of her
hand sweeping it out of her eyes must have caught Jake's attention, because he almost looked shy as he stood back from where
he was helping Mason, not quite meeting her gaze.

"All right boys," she said brightly. "Say thanks to Mr. Miller for
the soldier lessons and for letting you play with his dog. Come
drink some water after all that running around."

She passed out the bottles, and could only shake her head
when Tyler went down on one knee to pour water into one

cupped hand for Remy to share. He beamed up at Jake's heartfelt thanks, and Casey fell just a little bit further. Jake said his good-byes, letting each boy get a 'pawshake' from Remy before walking over to one of the empty units.

Casey and the boys filed inside, and she was surprised at how much time had passed while they had been outside when only a few minutes later she saw Caleb and Marissa's maroon SUV pull into the driveway. The boys all ran out to the driveway, talking over each other to tell their parents about the things Jake had taught them. Never mind the carefully planned out craft Casey had found on pinterest or the game of hot lava they had played in the family room, oh no, all the stories were about Remy playing soccer and Jake teaching them 'Army stuff'.

When the boys were secure in the car, and Casey had given Caleb the bag of all their stuff, she couldn't help but laugh when Marissa pulled her aside before getting in the car.

"So," her sister in law's brown eyes sparkled. "He helped you babysit?"

Casey snorted. "Hardly. The Jake portion of the evening was about fifteen minutes total, he just had a bigger impact than I did. No story here, sorry."

"Mmm hmm. Well, story or not, he gets my vote. Anyone who can get all three of my offspring to agree on the right way to do something deserves a freaking medal. Plus, that man," she sighed, "he is quite good looking."

"Yeah, that seems to be the general consensus." Caleb laid on the horn, causing both of them to jump.

Marissa leveled a dirty look at her husband where he sat chuckling behind the wheel. "You'd think he'd want to get laid on his anniversary. That is *not* the way to go about it."

"Ew," Casey moaned. "Still my brother, sex talk is off limits."

Marissa laughed and gave her a tight hug, thanking her again for taking the boys. Casey stood in the driveway watching until the car turned out of the driveway and disappeared out of sight.

She took a deep breath and let it out slowly, thinking about how much she did not want to go inside and clean up the mess that was left behind. For now, she was perfectly fine with sitting out here, smelling the fall smell and pretending like the disaster inside her house didn't exist.

A day like that could probably convince her that only having one child was perfectly acceptable. After a few more quiet moments, she decided that denial of the state of her house would do her no good. She bent and started folding the blanket she had used during the boys soccer game when she heard Jake quietly talking.

To himself, apparently.

"Don't do it. Don't do it, man. It would be monumentally stupid. Do *not* do it."

She shifted the blanket over her arm, waiting for him to walk past the garage and come into view, cocking her head to the side. Nope, he wasn't on the phone, and even though Remy was at his side like usual, he wasn't talking to the dog. His dark brows were drawn together, and his hands were gripping his hips like they were the only keeping him tied to the ground, tension clear in the way he walked. Biting her lip in an attempt to keep her laugh at bay, Casey basked in the knowledge that she was finally, *finally* catching him in an unguarded moment.

"I think you should totally do it," she said lightly, savoring the look of the surprise on his face, and slight jolt at her presence. "But then again, I'm a *live in the moment* girl."

"You don't even know what I'm talking about." He had recovered quickly, she noticed, the impassive mask back over his face. Not even a slight trace of a smile.

She shrugged lightly at his response. "No, I don't. But I typically find that if I want to do something bad enough that I have to start talking myself out of it, it might actually be worth doing. If someone else tries to talk me out of it? I might actually listen."

He took a few steps closer to her, those melted chocolate eyes flicking over her face. "Not sure that's the best line of logic I've ever heard."

She laughed. "No one has ever accused me of having the most sound logic, that's true, but as long as it makes sense in my own head, I'm good with it. So, what's the dilemma? I happen to be the go-to person for justification."

"That a fact?" He still looked so serious, it reminded her the first few interactions they had, before she saw the hairline crack in his bad-ass-ness.

"Oh yeah. Michael's wife once called me from a dressing room in Chicago, and I helped her justify buying a pair of two hundred dollar cropped jeans."

"I don't think I even want to hear this," he said dryly, but his lips had softened a little bit, still not quite smiling.

"You don't," she agreed. "My point is, what are you trying to talking yourself into? I can totally help."

His eyes darkened a bit, and everything tightened south of her belly button when they quickly dropped to stare at her mouth. "Actually, I was trying to talk myself out of something. Not into it."

"Same difference," she said, proud of the fact that her voice came out even, despite the fact that she felt quite tremble-y inside.

"Not really." He took another step closer, bringing him within arms reach now. She tightened her grip on the soft flannel of the blanket, glad she had something to hold onto, because she was feeling a little dizzy from the effort of not reaching out to touch him. "I was trying to talk myself out of going to knock on your door, to see if you were home."

Her eyes flew up to meet his, and she could practically feel her eyebrows hit her hairline they flew up so fast. "Really?"

He nodded slowly, a muscle ticking in his jaw. How did guys do that? It wasn't fair, really. And it was always the ones with the ridiculous cut-from-granite square jaw, they could somehow make some minute muscle jump out, increasing their sex appeal about a hundred fold. She felt like she should take a step back, there was so much crackling between them, but she stood perfectly still instead, soaking it in.

"Wh-what's wrong with coming to see if I'm home? That's a friendly thing to do."

This time, he shook his head, eyes never wavering. They speared into her, and oh, she could feel it slide deliciously all the way down her spine, coiling and wrapping around itself. She blinked rapidly, trying to decide if this whole thing was a figment of her imagination, because Jake looking at her like he wanted to devour her whole was definitely something she had shoved out of the realm of immediate possibility.

"No? It's not friendly?" Her voice was just above a whisper, like she was afraid to break the moment. Actually, no 'like' about it. She was afraid to break the moment. Afraid she'd make one wrong move and he'd vanish like the proverbial mirage in the desert.

He shook his head again, stepping into her, but still not touching her. The blanket hanging over her arm separated them now, just a few layers of blue plaid flannel.

"The purpose of my visit was not to be friendly," he said in a low, scraping voice.

"Oh," she breathed, and struggled to swallow as every single drop of moisture in her mouth had disappeared.

"Can you still help me justify that?"

She lifted her lids, which seemed to weigh about eight hundred pounds, and met his gaze. "Definitely."

The second the word left her lips, one of his large hands cupped the side of her neck, his thumb putting just enough pressure under jaw so that she had to tilt her chin up. He stamped his mouth over hers, angling his head to the side so that there was no question as to who was controlling this kiss. He ripped the blanket out of her hands, flinging it to the ground next to them. She hated that blanket anyways.

He walked them backwards until her back hit the hard siding of the garage, each piece of siding digging into her in a way that wasn't entirely unpleasant. She literally felt like she might die at the way his tongue swept into her mouth, the way his arms gripped tightly around her. Fisting her hands into the soft cotton of his t-shirt where it covered his chest, Casey relished in the hard thrumming of his heart. No man had ever, ever made her feel this out of control. This explosive. It was like every part of her that was fierce and fiery and savage was detonated just by him placing his lips on hers.

He pulled back from her, both of them breathing heavily. But he didn't pull away, and at that realization, she slipped one hand up his shoulder and cupped the side of his face. When he leaned into her touch, she smiled softly at how much that small movement warmed her inside.

"See?" she said contentedly, lightly licking her lips and enjoying that she could still taste him. "I told you I had the best ideas."

His eyes softened, but he didn't laugh or smile. It didn't bother her anymore. "Yeah. Though, it was actually my idea."

"Eh, tomato, tomahto."

"I think you should let me take you out."

"Huh?" The grin spread slowly across her face, even though she wanted to rewind about fifteen seconds and retract that reaction with something a little wittier. Obviously it didn't bother him too much as the hands around her waist tightened. They couldn't draw her any closer, because there really wasn't any space to be had between them.

"I said," he began slowly, "I think you should let me take you out."

She smacked his shoulder, and he chuckled. "I heard you. I'm just a little surprised."

"Me too," he said, sincerity echoing through his low voice. He brought a hand up to push some stray hair off her face. "But, I'm not good at pretending."

Everything inside of her raced. Her mind. Her heart. Heck, her ovaries were sprinting over hurdles like gold medalists. Not wanting to scare him off by jumping up and down while screaming *Yes. Yes. Yes.* she simply nodded and grinned up at him. "Okay. We'll figure something out when you come home from drill on Sunday."

"Deal."

A little bummed about the fact that he was leaving the next day, Casey looked over and saw Remy sprawled out in the grass, watching the two of them with only passing interest.

"I'm not gonna lie, it's completely weird to me that your dog just watched us make out."

He smiled this time, and while his hands stayed on her waist and his eyes never left her face, he took a step backwards. It was ridiculous, how much she missed the press of him up against her.

"So, he can't come on our date with us?" Jake tilted his head a little. "That might be a deal breaker for me."

She narrowed her eyes at him in a glare, softening only when he tapped the end of her nose with his index finger and chuckled under his breath. The warmth from his body dissipated when he pulled away from her and started walking away. After a few steps, he turned back to look at her. She was still leaning up against the siding, exactly where he'd left her. Considering she didn't think her legs would work just yet, she stayed put. It just would not do to crumple in a heap in front of him.

He shook his head, muscle ticking away in his jaw. She wanted to *lick* the fricken thing. "Still don't know what I'm gonna do about you, Casey."

18

CASEY ROLLED OVER IN BED, reveling in the feeling of waking up without an alarm. She stretched her arms up over her head, sighing as she arched her back up off the mattress. The answering huff of air that came from the general direction of her floor caused her to wrench her eyes open and cautiously peek over the side of the bed. Remy was stretched on his side, head propped up, quite comfortably, on one of her pillows that must have fallen during the night. She rolled her eyes and flopped back onto the bed. Then, mind catching up through the fog of sleep, she reached back down and yanked the pillow out from underneath the dog's head. He sat up at the sudden movement, stretching his jaw in an exaggerated yawn.

"My pillow, Remy. Mine. You and I still have work to do on our personal boundaries."

Looking completely uninterested in her sharing issues, he stood, then stretched forward until his back legs dragged behind him on the floor. Punching the pillow in between her knees where it was supposed to be, she watched him circle the room and come back to plop right in her face. His golden brown eyes stared pleadingly at her, and a low whine came from the back of his throat.

"Ugh," she groaned halfheartedly, pulling herself up into a sitting position. "You're so needy in the morning. Haven't you learned how to open the door on your own yet? You somehow managed to escape when I was finally having an awesome make-out session." He cocked his head to side, seemed to realize that he was winning this round, and took off down the hallway to the front door. Still trying to fully wake up, it dawned on her that this was the first night Remy had slept in her room.

Typically, he was in the living room, with his back along the length of the couch, or as the forever embedded hairs suggested, up on the couch. As much as he bugged her, and he still completely did, she could admit that she slept pretty darn good knowing he was under her roof. It was like the two of them had settled into an uneasy truce ever since he had growled at Tate. Not that she had actually needed it in that moment, but it was kinda nice to know that even though she had plotted his death on numerous occasions, Remy would still protect her if necessary. And that was a fact she wouldn't ever admit out loud, couldn't have the dogs ego stroked.

It was bad enough that last night, during an impromptu Ladies Night, Rachel had caught her dropping a piece of popcorn on the floor for him when she thought neither of the girls were looking.

"Oooooweee." Rachel had crowed. "You've got it so bad, Case."

Cheeks burning, she chucked a kernel over Liz's head and across the room at Rachel. "I accidentally dropped it. Just keep watching the movie."

"What happened?" Liz flicked her eyes in between the two of them, absentmindedly reaching down to scratch Remy's head. He pressed into her legs, eyes rolling back in pleasure.

"Nothing," Casey said firmly. "Rachel thinks the fact that I accidentally dropped a piece of popcorn on the floor somehow means I'm softening towards the dog."

Before Rachel could respond, Liz opened her mouth first, not pulling her attention from where the movie. "You are."

"I am not," Casey huffed.

"It's probably subconscious on your part," Liz continued as if she hadn't even spoken, smiling as Remy carefully took a kernel of popcorn from her fingers. "You have feelings for Jake, and we know he reciprocates them now. Plus, Remy is important to him. If you begin a relationship with Jake, then Remy is part of the deal. You're accepting Remy because deep down you know that if you don't, it could cause friction with Jake if you continue calling him things like couch-ruining, shoe-eating, shaggy-haired spawn of Satan."

"Plus," Rachel interjected, "that's the longest, most awkward nickname for an animal I've ever heard. I get tired just hearing you say it over and over."

Casey blew a breath out of pursed lips, hating it when they were always so right. "Great, so I'm stuck with Remy forever. How long do these kinds of dogs live again?"

While Liz lectured her on making those kinds of comments anymore, Casey really thought about what she had said and it planted a teeny, tiny seed in her head. Remy *was* part of the deal.

She clicked off the tv, ignoring the grumbles from Rachel about not being able to stare at James Marsden anymore, and laid out her idea.

Liz sighed, grinning the entire time, and even Rachel, still firmly entrenched in her 'I hate all men' mode, admitted it was pretty genius. The three quickly went into full planning mode, Liz making itemized lists while Casey trolled the internet for ideas, Rachel heading to her closet and pulling out clothing options. By the end of the night, they had polished off two more bottles of wine, made three more bags of popcorn (one of which was consumed almost entirely by Remy), and had the soon-to-be-epic first date planned out.

When Liz had been about to walk out the door, she turned back to Casey, her blue eyes soft and speculative. "I've never seen you like this, Casey, with anyone. It's really different with him, isn't it?"

"Yeah, it is."

Liz smiled. "I can tell. It's going to be such a great story to tell someday, how this all started."

Then with a tight hug, she had left. Casey had stood by the door, watching their cars leave her driveway. Remy had stayed by the door long after she'd moved to clean up, an occasional growl lifting from his throat. She hadn't seen anything when she looked out into the backyard from her kitchen window, so it didn't worry her too much. After about a half an hour, he had finally walked away and settled in the living room.

Letting Remy back in the door when he returned from doing his business, Casey glanced at her to-do list for the day and felt the slow smile spread across her face. Her first date with Jake. Intentional, uninterrupted time together with a romantic purpose. The notion did magically delicious things to her insides. She squatted down until she was eye level with Remy.

"I'm making an honest to goodness effort here, dog, so you need to try and not sabotage me tonight. Do we have a deal?" She held out her hand, Remy immediately plopping his heavy paw in it. "Great. Now let's get to work, shall we?"

JAKE ROLLED his head over tight shoulders, trying to relieve some of the tension lodged back there. Didn't work. He repeated it over and over in his head, *this is part of the job, this is what he signed up for*, but that wasn't working either. It was his own stupid fault for letting himself get sucked in by Casey, caving into those tugs and urges that had been brewing since she walked in the door the first damn time. Now he knew why he should have just kept his eyes facing forward and his hands off of her.

Another deployment.

He would be leaving in a little over six months, back to Afghanistan. The absolute last thing he had wanted was to get involved, and he let his guard down piece by piece until he felt like he'd go postal if he didn't kiss her again, touch her again, shit, even just say something to see that wide, beautiful smile. So, now what was he supposed to do?

Hey Casey, I know I asked you out three days ago, but I'm heading back overseas for probably close to a year, so can I take it back? Or how about we date for a while and make it completely awkward if we break up, that way if something happens to me, you can feel guilty for the rest of your life because of how we fought or things we said to each other? Or worse, let's give it a try and you can go through twelve months of constant worry and stress that will more than likely cause you to dump me anyway.

He clenched his jaw so tightly he felt like the tendons in his neck would pop. He would just have to tell her the truth when he got home, and looking at the highway mile marker, it would be about another hour yet. He snorted a humorless laugh. Tell her the truth? Sure.

Hey Casey, I think you're gorgeous and kind of amazing and something about you has made me become less of an asshole loner and I know I kissed you like I would die if I didn't and then asked you out and you tried so hard not to look too excited about it that it almost took me to my knees, but I need you to forget all of that and we have to go back to just being renter and landlord because it makes my life easier. Because, as always with you, I'm a giant chicken shit.

Those thoughts rolled through his head so quickly, he could barely even dwell on the magnitude of what they meant. It was...big.

Important.

Terrifying.

The vibration of his phone in the cup holder yanked him from his thoughts. He tried to never look at his phone when he drove, so he pulled off the next exit to grab a coffee and fill up his truck. While he waited for his gas tank to fill, he saw he had a text message waiting from Casey.

I know you'll probably be home soon...I have something that I need to show you. But in order to do that, I need you to run home first to shower and change. Remy and I will be waiting at my place. :)

He rubbed a hand over his head, hating that his first reaction to her words was curiosity, second was ridiculously unbridled excitement at seeing her, and a distant third was the nagging thought that this was probably a bad idea given what he had to tell her when he got home.

Maybe he'd get lucky and she'd just be showing him that she painted her room hot pink or something without his permission. Either way, there was no point in speculating what it was, he already knew he would do as she asked. He drove home keeping all thoughts about broken first dates and upcoming deployments out of his head, focusing instead on the road in front of the truck and the white lines flickering next to him.

With no sign of either Casey or Remy upon his arrival at home, he let himself into his back door, took a cold shower, briskly soaping up, drying off and then grabbing a pair of clean jeans and a black long sleeve thermal shirt that was hanging over the chair by his desk. He looked at his reflection in his bedroom mirror, feeling like a complete idiot for contemplating whether or not he should use a spray of cologne. No, he decided and set his jaw. Keep it casual, it would make it easier. Probably should have thought of before he showered and changed upon command like a whipped puppy.

He walked out the door ten minutes after he went in it, and stopped short when Remy bounded up to him.

"Hey boy, did ya miss me?" He took a few moments to greet his dog, relishing how Remy was just as excited to see him after a weekend away as he was if Jake had simply stepped outside for five minutes. One of the reasons dogs were usually preferable company to humans, in his mind at least. He straightened, pulled in a deep breath and promptly lost it when he saw Casey leaning against the back of his truck.

Everything about how she looked was incredible and perfect, waiting there for him with a soft smile on her face. And God help him, those forever long legs were encased in skin tight jeans tucked into knee high brown boots. There was a sweater, maybe some jewelry, a lot of hair, but those really didn't register very much. His mouth completely dried up as he walked towards her.

"Welcome home," she said simply. No one had said that to him in a very, very long time. Hearing her say it, knowing that she would actually mean it, sent a pang of longing so deep through him that he had to break eye contact. It was then that he noticed that there were two large baskets in the bed of his truck.

"Thanks," he said gruffly. "What are those?"

"Well, that's what I need to show you. But before you can see what's inside, we have to go for a little drive." He looked at her again, noticing that she was working very hard not to fidget with the edge of her cream sweater. She was nervous.

"Is there something wrong?" He tried to keep confusion out of his tone, but he couldn't figure out what she would need to show him that would make her nervous.

"No." she said quickly, tucking a piece of hair behind her ears. "Nothing wrong, I promise. Can you just...trust me?"

"Pretty sure the last time you said that to me, you talked me into letting you have your orange walls." He crossed his arms, grinning at the spark that immediately fired in her eyes, making that bluish green seem like it was lit from within. She quickly reigned it in, and he got even more suspicious. No argument that it was actually orange? Yeah. Something was up. She tilted her head, apparently waiting for him to make up his mind, a tiny quirk in her lips. He sighed. "Fine. From the additions to bed of my truck, I take it I'm driving?"

She nodded, trying valiantly to keep the wide, triumphant grin off her face. "Of course. Remy and I have made our progress, but my car is still a hair free zone, and I'd like to keep it that way for at least a little bit longer."

"Remy is coming too?"

"Yup."

He narrowed his eyes. "What are you up to?"

"Nothing," she said innocently, giving those long black lashes a few flutters for effect. Girl was too dangerous for her own good, because hell if he didn't actually feel himself weakening when she did it.

The three of them piled into his truck, Remy taking his usual spot in the bench of the extended cab. Other than giving him directions of where to turn, comfortable silence took up its own space between them. After only a few minutes of driving, she had him turn into the parking lot of the local branch of the district library, which was set close to the road but situated in front of a huge county park.

There were no other cars around, as the library was closed on Sundays. She directed him to park towards the back of the lot where there was a small paved pathway leading into the vibrantly colored clusters of trees and lush, thick grass of the park. Knowing she wouldn't explain until she was darn well ready to, he didn't ask what was going on, but simply picked up the baskets out of the back and truck and fell into step beside her. He gave a mock groan as he shifted the baskets in his arms, drawing a soft laugh from her.

"What, you have a couple bodies you need to bury and needed me to do your dirty work?"

She elbowed him in the side, smiling quickly. "You did tell me to stand up for myself against Melinda. Should have been more specific on how to do it."

He laughed. "She's definitely small enough to fit in one of these baskets..."

Her mouth opened to say something, but she just stared.

"What?"

The shake she gave her head was quick and dismissive. "Nothing, I've just...oh, never mind. It's stupid."

When he was about to push for an explanation, she gestured that they walk up a slight hill to her right. They crested over the top, Remy running ahead of them, his snout glued to the ground, tail wagging furiously. Jake squinted, then felt a few bricks of understanding drop into place somewhere in the vicinity of his stomach. The same navy plaid blanket she had been sitting on while watching her nephews play soccer was spread on the ground, a few large pillows facing each other. A small red cooler anchored down one side, a old fashioned lantern sitting next to it emitting a warm glow, giving the small square a cozy feel despite the wide open setting. Everything was framed by two large maple trees that were blazing with oranges and reds. He struggled to swallow, words jumbling through his head, but nothing finding its way to his lips.

Mistaking his silence for confusion, Casey looked up at him with wide, hopeful eyes. "I hope it's okay that I did this, but I thought maybe this could be our first date." She rushed ahead, taking the top basket out of his hands, and opened it while he tried to figure what the heck just happened.

Typically, Jake prided himself on being able to read situations almost before they happened. Following gut instinct in a war situation could mean the difference between life and death. His had never let him down before. But Casey had just frickin blindsided him.

"What," he started, still not sure what he was going to say, he was so tilted off his axis. "Wait, are those tennis balls?"

She nodded up at him, setting aside an unopened sleeve of the bright yellow balls. Then he noticed the long orange plastic arm that was sitting behind the cooler. He'd seen them at the pet store, knowing that they were used to launch a ball much further than a person could throw it, and with a lot less arm strain. He'd almost bought one once, since it took a lot to fully exert Remy's energy.

Casey had bought a toy. For Remy.

"How else are we going to keep Remy out of our hair while we eat? I did bring some doggy snacks for him, but he'll get those once he's tired out."

He noticed that he was still standing there, hovering over where she was kneeling on the blanket, holding the second basket like a new recruit who didn't know to piss without someone telling him to do it. She had prepared a picnic for their first date, arranged it so his dog could come along with them after he'd made a joke, a bad joke at that, about him coming with. And the entire drive home, while she was putting the finishing touches on a more than likely homemade meal, he was planning on how tell her they shouldn't go out. If he hadn't fully realized before that she deserved better than him, he sure as hell did now.

He slowly lowered next to her, placing the basket down carefully on the blanket. Knowing that the longer he stayed quiet, the bigger of an ass he would seem like, he cleared his throat and stole a sideways glance at her. She didn't return his gaze, and her hand shook slightly as she pulled the plates and napkins out of the basket.

He reached over and laid a hand on her back, smoothing it up underneath all of that thick, curling dark hair. He closed his eyes briefly at how good it felt against his hand. She still didn't look back.

"Casey, look at me. Please?"

She leaned back on one hip, tucking her legs under her before she finally met his eyes. Instead of looking like she had when they'd arrived, she looked embarrassed. And it made him want to kick himself in the balls.

Repeatedly.

"Too much?" she asked quietly. "I've been known to get a little carried away when I get an idea in my head."

"It's not that. It *is* a lot to take in, I'll be honest." Her cheeks pinked slightly at that, eyes darting down to where her hands knit together in her lap. "But mainly because no one has ever done anything like this for me. And if you hadn't noticed, my social interaction skills can leave a lot to be desired. So, if it's okay with you, can we back up like four minutes so I can have a mulligan?"

"If I knew what a mulligan was, I might say yes."

There. Just seeing her say that with a tiny smirk on her lips made him take in a relieved breath.

"A golf term for a do-over."

"Oh. Then yes, you can *absolutely* have a mulligan."

He sat back on his heels, resting his hands on his thighs and facing her straight on. "It looks like you put a lot of work and thought into this, I wasn't expecting it, but I do appreciate it. I'll overlook the fact that you've threatened my dog's life on more than one occasion, and consider this your official apology to Remy for overreacting about him chewing up your ridiculously overpriced shoes."

She narrowed her eyes and scoffed, looking all kinds of sexy while she did it, then shoved at one of his shoulders. "Your mulligan kinda sucks."

He caught her wrist when she tried to yank her hand back, clearly annoyed that his shoulder hadn't budged in the slightest. Her pulse fluttered and skipped underneath where his fingers circled her wrist. "Want me to try again?"

"I don't know," she said. "If you backslide any more, I'll have to feed your sandwich to all the little fishies in the pond back there."

He fought a smile and pulled lightly on her arm, forcing her to lean towards him. Her eyes widened, then warmed in understanding. She braced her free hand next to his legs when she needed the balance, and he stopped when her face was just a few inches from his. There was that scent again, that sweet citrusy one that he decided would very well make him lose his mind at some point. They both held there, neither ready to move that last little bit. She let out a tiny, frustrated huff of air and he felt it on his lips, causing them to curl into the smile that he held back earlier.

As was rapidly becoming standard whenever she was involved, he found himself caving. He didn't want to not have this date with her. He didn't want to ruin whatever this was with talk of a deployment or thoughts of it not working out before they had even gotten started. He pretty much just wanted her.

So he moved forward, brushing his lips lightly across hers. Once, and then twice. They hadn't had any sweetness before this, and even though he felt a little rusty administering it, he knew it was warranted right now. The hand that he still held onto curled into his shirt, and when she tried to deepen the kiss, he pulled back, not wanting to get too caught up just yet. "Thank you, Casey. I would like nothing more than to have a picnic with you, my dog, and those most incredible boots you're wearing for our first date."

She tipped her head to the side and laughed, still looking a little dazed from the kiss, and he loved that.

They talked, her about growing up under the shadow of four brothers, him about transferring to the National Guard, and finally a few memories of his parents after a ridiculous amount of pleading from Casey. She opened a thermos of cider for them to share, and they ate the most incredible sandwich he'd ever had in his life. She beamed when he told her that, and she lit up talking about the combination of roasted chicken, arugula (he had no clue what that was), avocado, parmesan ranch dressing and sharp white cheddar (which he didn't know came in any other color than orange).

After they finished eating, Jake picked up the plastic arm and heaved one of the tennis balls across the open field to an ecstatic Remy. After a few turns, he signaled that Casey should try. Jake fell back on the blanket laughing when ball bounced on the ground only about five feet in front of her because she wasn't holding it correctly. She whirled around and whacked him in the stomach with it, effectively ending his laughter, and he snatched it out of her hands to show her how to use it.

The air started to cool as the light faded, making him check his phone. They'd been out there for almost two hours. Other than a few people who had wandered through the paths, they'd had the park to themselves the entire time. Remy was flopped next to the blanket, chest heaving after the workout they'd given him, and Jake thought it might have been one of the best two hours he'd spent in an incredibly long time. Maybe ever. They hadn't kissed again, just subtle brushes against each other throughout the meal, hands lingering if they'd happened to touch, and eyes holding a few moments longer than usual. It made him feel like there was a prickling, twitching live wire feeding an electric current under his skin. He loved and hated it in equal measure.

And truthfully, he didn't really hate it. It was just...unfamiliar.

Without talking about it, they started picking up the blanket, collecting all the items she'd packed.

"So, do I get to ask how you pulled this off? Any helpers?"

She pursed her lips and studied him as if she was thinking really hard. "You're asking me to give up my secrets? C'mon Jake, that's like asking a woman what she weighs or how old she is."

"Wait, those are bad things?"

She snickered and walked around him to go dump their trash. She stretched her arms above her head on her way back to where he was folding up the blanket and groaned. He almost did the same, as the motion made her back arch in such a way that her hair brushed below the small of her back. It wasn't fair, women had weapons that men were completely powerless against.

She looked over at him while he contemplated just how full her arsenal was, and it was obvious by the way she stared back that the little minx knew exactly what he was thinking. He looked away, feeling like a complete pansy at how transparent he was being. Maybe a tattoo on the forehead would be more subtle, big cursive letters saying "Yes, I *do* think you're gorgeous.".

Wordlessly, they picked up the baskets, blankets and cooler, and started the walk back to his truck. Thoughts of what could, might, should or shouldn't happen when they got home hurtled through his head. Considering how much forethought she had put into this evening, he decided he was going to follow her lead. She wouldn't beat around the bush with her expectations of how the night would end. The sudden vision of her wrapped in his navy sheets had him tightening his hands on the steering wheel, knuckles turning white.

They still hadn't spoken a word on the ride home, and it made him think that she was feeling exactly what he was. That some spell might be broken if they tried to have casual conversation. Nothing about this felt casual, and while it caused a slight swell of panic to roll through him, he shoved that down quick.

If he was only going to allow himself these few stolen hours with Casey, before snapping back to the reality that he knew awaited them both, then he was going to give himself permission to completely shut off his brain. He knew enough to know that nights like tonight could serve as tiny pinpricks of sanity holding you to the ground once a deployment started. This night, this date, was something he could give himself, even if it ended with her walking out of the truck and going straight home without him.

He pulled in the garage, sliding the gear shift into park, and then turned to her.

"Any other tricks up your sleeve?"

She glanced back at a sound asleep Remy in the backseat, then stared back at the front end of the truck. Her wheels were turning up there, he could sense it, but he didn't say a word. After a few more seconds of quiet, she shifted in her seat so she was sitting sideways facing him.

"No tricks."

Disappointment, dull and uncomfortable, scraped through him. He nodded twice, reminding himself that it was for the best that way.

Then she shrugged lightly, watching his face carefully. "But, I do have an apple crisp that I baked this afternoon. Figured we would probably want to wait a bit for dessert. If you're interested, that is. I know you've had a long weekend, so I'd understand if you just want to go home."

She'd understand, and probably wouldn't even hold it against him. He believed her when she said that. But he knew she'd feel that same disappointment that he had just felt. It was enough to firm his decision.

"I happen to love apple crisp. I'll bring Remy back to my place and then come over, unless he gets to be part of the dessert portion of the date too."

Her smile was brilliant, almost blinding, and his heart made a ridiculous stutter when she did it. "I think he'll be fine by himself for a while."

Five minutes later and one dog lighter, he stood outside her door trying to decide if he should knock or just go in when she swung the door open and gestured for him to come in. Unlike on the ride home, they struck up conversation easily again. He updated her on the next unit that he was almost finished with, and they planned out what she would set up in a few rooms before he showed it to renters. He still doubted she could get him more rent money than he charged for her unit, but she just gave a smug little grin and told him to wait and see.

"Mmm," he moaned around a bite of the dessert. "Casey, this is amazing. I'm feeling a little lazy after everything you put together today."

She waved it off. "I love cooking. And my brothers will enjoy the leftovers. Dylan has a sixth sense when I make any sort of dessert, I expect he'll show up tomorrow with a fork in hand before I've even had my coffee."

"I can manage a few decent meals, but nothing like this. And I certainly have never loved doing it. I'm always impressed with people who do."

"There's something fulfilling to me when people enjoy a meal that I've made. I love the feeling it gives me. It's kind of like my job. When someone comes back in and tells me how much they love the wallpaper I helped them pick out, or the new paint color in their dining room that I convinced them to use, and they want my help with another room...I don't know...they look at those walls every day. Their lives happen within that space, and I like knowing that I had a tiny part in making it a place they really love." She propped her head in her hands, blushing a little. "That probably sounds so stupid."

"No," he said sincerely, thinking that if someone put a gun to his head right now, he wouldn't be able to take his eyes off of her. "Not stupid at all."

It was clear that she was still embarrassed when she stood to clear their dishes. He moved his plate out of the way before she could grab it. "Oh no, I'll clean up. You've done enough work today. Go put your feet up, I'll be in there in a minute."

"What? And miss the opportunity to watch my hot date stand over the sink doing dirty dishes? No way. A girl's gotta get her kicks where she can."

He gave her a long look as he put the plates and forks in the dishwasher.

"Oh yeah, this is totally working for me." She looked a little too pleased. "It's like I'm the bored, rich housewife who hires man candy to do work around the house."

He lifted an eyebrow as he closed the dishwasher. "So, you're saying you're objectifying me right now?"

"Totally."

"Just what every guy wants to hear at the end of a date."

She stood and walked towards him, stopping just out of his reach. Not that *that* would stop him. He could move pretty quickly when he needed to, and he had a feeling she wouldn't give much chase if it came down to it. Not the way she was looking at him right now.

"Is it the end of the date?"

He regarded her for another second, knowing what he was seeing in those eyes, but wanting to make sure before he spoke again. "Not if you don't want it to be."

She swallowed, looking suddenly nervous, like she had at the beginning. "Remember earlier when you asked me what I was thinking about, and I told you it was nothing? It was before you joked about Melinda fitting in the basket."

Thrown by her shift in topic, he thought back, and remembered how quickly her face had changed. "Yeah. Why?"

"Well, that was the first time I actually made you laugh. I was thinking that if nothing else happened tonight, I would still be happy when I came home because of that moment." She took in a big breath, looking at him with such directness that he felt naked. "But, if you're asking me if I want this to be the end of our night, I don't."

CASEY HELD the air in her lungs while he stared back at her. The seconds stretched, feeling like hours, probably because she couldn't believe she had basically just told Jake she didn't want him to leave tonight. She never did stuff like this. Never, ever did stuff like this and could already hear Rachel calling her a shameless hussy when she heard about it. But she literally felt like she might explode through her skin if he didn't touch her again, kiss her again.

"Good," he said on an exhale that felt like it was drawn straight from her own lungs. They seemed to reach for each other at the same time, mouths melding in a way that wasn't the softness he had given her earlier, and not the frantic movements of their first two kisses. The way he tasted her mouth, and the way his arms folded around her, the way his hands gripped her hair had just enough edge to let her know that he was teetering on the same cliff that she had been all afternoon. And with a rough exhale, she gladly toppled over it, opening up to him in way that wrenched a groan from deep within his broad chest. The sound rumbled through her breastbone, making her fingers dig through the cotton of his shirt in order to feel the shifting muscles of his back.

He turned, hoisting her up onto the counter, and her legs wrapped instinctively around his hips, drawing him as close to her as she could. They might have stayed that way for hours, twined around each other, if not for the pesky need for oxygen. He pulled away from her lips, leaving them swollen and throbbing and gasping. He rested his forehead against hers for just a brief moment, then buried his nose into her hair, placing a few lingering kisses behind her ear and down her throat. Oh, she could barely breathe when he did that. With one hand still wrapped around her back, he drew the other one through her hair, pushing it behind her shoulder.

"Casey, I don't want you to think that I expected-" She placed her hand over his mouth to stop him, enjoying the feel of his lips. He nipped at her pointer finger when she traced the outline of his mouth lightly.

"I know you wouldn't, Jake. I didn't have any expectations for tonight either. I mean, I made sure not to wear granny panties just in case-"

He dropped his head onto her shoulder and groaned. "Not helping my honorable intentions, Casey."

She laughed and placed her hands on either side of his face, loving how his stubble felt against her palms.

He *was* honorable; a truly good person down to his very core, something that was more than his training. And she knew she had to do right by this relationship. They would have other nights, she knew that now. "Would you at least stay over tonight?"

He searched her face, taking his time over each of her features. "On two conditions."

"Conditions?" she asked warily. He nodded, dark eyes holding hers.

"First is a big one. If you agree to that, then number two will be a piece of cake."

"Okay. Hit me with it."

"Go camping with me next weekend."

"Huh?" Mind blank, she suddenly had horrifying visions of bugs and dirt and sleeping on cold, hard ground.

"Is that going to be your response every time I ask you out?"

She swatted his arm, loving that he was inviting her somewhere, but ugh, camping?

"Umm," she said slowly, trying to figure out how to play this without sounding like a total girly girl wuss. "How do you know I'd be a good camper? I've never gone before and I'm not exactly what you call 'outdoorsy'."

"You don't say," he said dryly. And as soon as it left his mouth, he boosted her up so she was hanging over his shoulder fireman style and he started strolling down the hallway, calm as can be.

"Hey. Do you mind?" She felt ridiculous, and kind of awesomely feminine, that he had just flipped her up over his shoulder like that. She smacked at him, not one to pass up an opportunity to grab his butt a little. Yup, it was a good one. "Could you please put me down?"

"Sure thing, boss."

She squealed when he flung her down into the center of her bed. "If you wanted me in bed, you could have just asked."

He sank down on top of her, grinning, then pressed a kiss where her pulse fluttered at the base of her throat.

"You still haven't answered me. And remember, if you want me to stay here," another kiss under her jaw, "like this." One under her ear. "You have to agree to both conditions."

"That's so not fair," she said weakly when he lightly bit down on her earlobe. She pushed against his chest, and struggled to sit up. Looking back at where he was laying on his side, she reached down to pull the hem of her sweater over her head. He ran a finger up her arm, then over the thin strap of her brown tank top that only showed hints of her hot pink bra strap underneath.

"Speaking of not playing fair," he mumbled, then pushed on her shoulder until she was laying down next to him again. She wrapped both arms around his neck, not able to resist pulling him for another kiss. His mouth tasted like apples, and heavens, it made her hungrier and hungrier the longer their lips pushed and pulled at each other. She broke off, giving him another narrow eyed look.

"I can't believe I'm saying this, but yes, I'll go camping with you." Geez, Dylan was never going to let her hear the end of this one. They'd been trying to get her to go camping for oh, twenty eight of her twenty nine years. Thankfully for her, her Mom hated it, so they'd always had an excuse for a girl's weekend when her Dad and the boys went.

He smiled widely, those elusive dimples winking on either side of his mouth. When she dipped a finger into one, Casey had to work really hard to hold back the dreamy sigh that she wanted to let loose.

"Don't gloat, it's not attractive." *Uh huh. Liar liar, pants are so on fire.* "What's number two?"

"Ah yes, number two," he said as he sat up and then moved so his back was propped against her headboard. He motioned for her to stand up. She looked at him suspiciously, not leaving the edge of the bed.

"What is number two exactly?"

"Oh. You just have to model those new black boots you bought, you know, the ones that caused an unfortunate delay in your rent."

"That's it?"

"Uh huh."

She stood, looking back at him and feeling wary of the self-satisfied expression on his face. "What's the catch?"

"No catch. Just model the boots. Paired only with those non-granny panties you're wearing." His raised both eyebrows once, then grinned again. She grabbed a pillow from the floor and whipped it at his head, making her way back onto the bed and curling up into his side. He scooted down from the headboard, and wrapped an arm around her shoulders. Pressing her nose into his chest, she breathed in his scent, clean and spicy, and knew she was exactly where she was supposed to be. Forever.

Now just to get him to agree.

19

"So, how are we not going to freeze to death again?"

"Casey, it's only going to dip into the high forties tonight." She looked slightly mollified, but was still knitting her fingers together where they sat on restless legs that had been bouncing up and down ever since they left. "Besides, why do you think I invited you? It was purely for the warmth factor. Remy sucks at sharing sleeping bags."

She smacked him in the thigh, but still didn't smile. Seriously, she was nervous about a *camping trip*. If he didn't think it would end with him bruised in some way, he'd laugh out loud. It boggled his mind that she'd made it her entire life with four outdoor-loving brothers and had never gone camping.

Oh, she'd tried to explain it to him more than once, but he knew it was just another perk of being the youngest and the only girl in the family...he'd seen enough in the last four months that he knew her entire family adored her. And clearly he was as big of a sap as the rest of them when it came to her.

Waking that morning after their date with her wrapped around him, and taking up the majority of the bed, he'd taken a moment to steady himself where he lay. From his spot, practically crammed up against the wall, the faces of her loved ones smiling down from dozens of photos, he wouldn't have been able to pinpoint his feelings even if he'd wanted to. She had laid down after nailing him with that pillow, burrowing into his chest as if trying to draw every bit of warmth from his skin, and then promptly fell asleep.

Granted, he wasn't sure what was going to happen that night, but he sure as hell hadn't expected that. After listening to the sound of her breathing even out, dragging his fingers up and down one smooth arm just to see if it would be enough to wake her. It wasn't.

It had been almost laughably innocent, considering the chemistry sparking from them whenever they got within touching distance. As he'd drifted off that night, the only thought that ran through his head was *I'll tell her tomorrow. Tomorrow would be better.* He'd repeated it to himself every time he pulled his finger up the side of her arm that was wrapped around his waist, every inch of that remarkably soft skin serving as a teasing glimpse of what he'd miss while he was gone.

Tomorrow, I'll tell her tomorrow.

Might as well brand 'chump' straight over his heart, because there he was seven days later reassuring her about a camping trip she only agreed to so he wouldn't leave that first night.

"C'mon, it was a joke. Both of the bags I brought are rated down to twenty degrees. And we'll have the air mattress that will keep us off the ground."

She nodded absently. "They're really pretty."

"What are?"

"The sleeping bags," she said like it was obvious. "I like the gray with the spring green, it's really trendy right now."

He scratched his jaw and bit the inside of his cheek to hold in his chuckle. This woman had made him laugh more in the last seven days than he probably had in the last two years combined. It had felt rusty the first few times, like his vocal chords hadn't quite remembered how to vibrate in the right way to produce the sound.

"Yeah. That's why I picked 'em."

She sighed out a quiet laugh. "Don't make fun. I'm trying not to have a mental breakdown over here."

"It'll be good for you, prove that you can do it, stretch your personal boundaries a bit."

"Hey, I'm plenty stretchy."

"Is that a fact?" he muttered, enjoying the cloud of visuals that swept through his mind.

"Oh, get your mind out of the gutter."

He reached over and squeezed her thigh, trying to make her smile as he'd found out after the first night how ticklish she was there, then left his hand there when she curled her arm through his. Easy affection. It was another thing he'd forgotten how to do.

Relaxing a bit at his touch, she turned to stare out the truck window at the blur of trees as they headed north with the directions that Stockton had texted him a couple days ago. He was excited Jake had agreed to go, and of course, he couldn't resist a poke at him about how nice it was that Jake would be bringing the missus along.

As great as the past week with Casey had been, hearing that had sent a mild shiver of panic through him, making him shift in his seat even as he thought about it now. He had to tamp down the guilt he felt about not having a more serious conversation with Casey about where this relationship stood in his mind. He'd corrected Stockton saying that they were just seeing each other casually, she wasn't his girlfriend. And yet just typing those words out on the screen of his phone made him feel guilty.

She hadn't said anything about the future, but he knew she thought about it. She'd had one of those golden, glowing upbringings that most people only dreamed about. Parents who still adored each other after decades together. Siblings who loved and supported each other.

It wouldn't make sense for someone like Casey to not expect her own future to be more of the same. The kind of future that didn't come from a guy who was part property owner but still all soldier, leaving his family behind more often than not on Uncle Sam's command.

"Okay," she said firmly, snapping him out of his thoughts. "I need a distraction. Let's play the question game."

"How do you play?"

"Seriously? You ask each other questions. Duh."

"So how do you win?"

She rolled her eyes, smiling over at him. "You are such a guy. It's not about winning, it's about getting to know people. Creating conversation."

"I don't know, I usually only play games with the objective of beating the other person."

"Fine." She pursed her lips, making a little humming noise that he knew meant she was plotting. Always a scary thought. "Okay, we'll alternate asking each other questions, and you can only pass on two. The first person who passes twice loses."

He grunted in agreement, as 'creating conversation' and 'getting to know people better' were fairly high on his list of things to avoid the past few years. She smiled and turned to face him more fully, eyes fairly glittering at the prospect of him willingly answering questions.

"Hmmm, I guess I'll start easy. What's your full name? When you emailed me, your handle said HJ Miller. I've always been curious."

Shit. He couldn't pass on the first one, but the thought of telling her his real name made him growl. Literally.

She cracked up. "Oh, this is gonna be way too easy. Are you passing, Jake?"

"I was named after my two grandfathers. Jacob is my middle name."

"Doesn't cut it. So you concede the point?" She looked positively gleeful.

He ran his tongue over his top teeth, then cleared his throat. "Herschel. Herschel Jacob Miller."

She blinked, jaw slowly dropping. "No way. You're lying."

"Why on earth would I make up *that* name?" He checked the mirrors, then went to pass an older model Camry that was putzing along in the right lane. He flicked his eyes over to where she was clearly trying to process something that he'd had thirty years to try and get used to. He might have to pay her off so she didn't mention it this weekend. Oh, the hell he'd go through if Stockton heard about that.

"Well," she said slowly, carefully. "I can understand why you go by Jake." Then she looked over at him and choked on the laugh that was bubbling up in her throat. She slapped a hand over her mouth when she couldn't quite contain it, then looked at him apologetically.

He sighed. "All right, moving on. When you were young, what did you want to be when you grew up?"

"Ha, everything. I had a ballerina phase for like three years until I discovered that they're all tiny, skinny things and I would have towered over every one of them. And I can't dance. I wanted to be a Broadway star when I was in middle school, but I can't really sing. There were fleeting thoughts of being a teacher, then a maybe a doctor, until I realized how long I'd have to go to college. I kinda stumbled into the job I'm in now, and I love it, so I've stuck with it. I guess I just always pictured myself as being a wife and a mother, and the job that I did outside of those things didn't matter as much to me."

"I can see that about you. Your turn."

"What's something you're afraid of?"

You. The thought popped into his head so quickly that he went mute with shock. He rolled his neck from side to side, thinking of something a little more appropriate to say. Though she'd probably love it if he said that, there was no way he could go down that road right now.

"Lady Gaga."

She burst out laughing, the sound throaty and full, and tilted her head back into the seat. "You're not taking this game seriously."

"Says who? She is completely terrifying. Most days, I'd choose to be locked in a room with armed terrorists over her. At least I know how to handle them."

"Fair enough. I wouldn't go so far as *terrifying*, but it's your answer."

"My turn. What's with all the shoes?"

She arched one eyebrow. "Like, why do I have so many?"

"Pretty much. I don't understand. I see all those boxes and I just think you probably could have bought a brand new car with all of that."

"They just...I don't know...make me happy." She laughed softly and then thought for a few seconds. "They're like a mood ring, at least for me. It's like, if I'm not sure how I feel, I just figure out what shoes I feel like wearing that day. My cheetah print platform pumps? I want to party. My nude heels? Sedate, classy, but still wanting to be on my game. Flats? I'm feeling mellow, just needing a chill night. My hot pink or red heels? Watch out, because I'm in full out man-eater mode. That probably sounds stupid to a guy. I just like how they make me feel. And a well-made shoe? Mmmm. Gives me something to save my pennies for."

"Besides little things like paying your rent." She scrunched her nose but laughed again, leaning forward and turning up the volume on the radio he had set to a country station. "What ones are you saving for now that you obtained the perfect black boot? Not that I'm complaining about those anymore, believe me."

He'd gotten his wish the other night, with her strutting into his place wearing those boots, a fierce smile on her face and a small enough dress covering her curves to be ridiculous given the weather. The only rational response to that was for her to end up straddling him on the couch where they stayed until his head had been swimming with need, his hands shaking from the effort of letting her walk back home that night. She flushed, clearly thinking about the same thing he was, and it reminded him that the same flood of color spread across her chest when his hands and mouth had finally made her explode.

"If that's a serious question, I have a serious answer. I know exactly what my dream pair is."

"I probably shouldn't hear this-"

"The New Declic heels from Christian Louboutin. They are the *perfect* shoe, they would never go out of style and I would love them forever." She said it so sincerely, her eyes taking on a disturbing dreamy quality. A man had to only hope he could make a woman look like that, and Jake wasn't positive he'd ever put that look on her face the past week. He was close on the couch, but she was looking like a whole other level of satisfied right now.

"So what's the grand total of the perfect shoe?"

"Last I checked, around seven fifty."

He gaped. "Seven hundred and fifty *dollars*?

"Yeah, and that's cheap for a pair of those. I mean, the Camilla, which is my dream wedding shoe, costs over three thousand."

He had to pull at every thread of training over the last ten years to keep his face blank. This was the Mars/Venus thing, it had to be. Because no way in hell could he fathom paying three thousand for anything other than a house, a car, or something that spit out a lot of bullets.

"Please tell me you wouldn't seriously consider spending that much on a pair of *heels*."

"No, but if I ever did," she sighed, now looking a little forlorn, "I would wear the shit out of those shoes."

He shook his head, not sure how he ended up having this

conversation, but could not help but smile. Life was strange, he thought, him sitting in his truck, taking a woman camping who'd never gone in her life and would spend thousands of dollars on a pair of shoes just to wear them under a wedding dress. And looking over at her rooting through the giant ass purse sitting on the floor next to her feet, he still wouldn't give back the past week for anything. He was a selfish prick like that.

An hour later, neither of them had passed on a single question, and he was surprised at how insightful some of hers were. She didn't just ask the surface level stuff, though there was some of that, like favorite foods and movies and childhood tv shows. He almost passed on a question about his Dad, when she quietly asked how he died. But after that initial ache passed, he simply opened his mouth and told her about his heart attack at work.

He told her about how neither he nor his Mom got to say their goodbyes to him, because he was gone by the time they got the hospital. How, at eleven, he'd felt the weight of trying to comfort his mother who wasn't with her husband when he died. A weight that had seemed insurmountable to carry at the time, since he could barely process his own grief.

But he didn't go into how, when he wasn't home for his Mom when she received her diagnosis, he'd felt it pressing on him again, and even with the broader, stronger shoulders of adulthood, he never felt like he was enough to help her through it. Using money that had sat untouched since his father's death, he'd done what he could by buying the property from her. He didn't want to burden Casey with that. She looked too beautiful with a smile on her face, he didn't want to drag the mood down by going into any of that.

He started seeing landmarks that Stockton had described, so they called the game a draw, which chafed at his competitive nature, but he needed pay attention to where he was driving. When he saw the turnoff marked by a rusted mailbox on a large white post that desperately needed a new coat of paint, he was surprised. He assumed they were going to a campground, but this looked more like private property.

The dirt road was narrow, but covered in gravel, making it well defined and even to drive on. It stretched back through the tunnel of trees, casting an eerie gold-ish tint to the inside of the truck. The road curved slightly, then opened up to a massive clearing, where he could see a couple tents already set up, and one pop up camper to the side. A large, glossy white and gray fifth wheel trailer was stretched along the left of the pop up and drew his eye to a smaller clearing in between two large groupings of pine trees. Through the pine trees, Jake could see winks of light against the surface of smooth water. Sitting in the middle of the whole set up, was a massive bonfire pit, already roaring in welcome.

Stockton stood next to a petite, lean woman outside of the pop up, and he waved one arm at the sight of Jake's truck pulling up. Jake rolled down the window, introducing Casey and Remy when Stockton leaned against the driver's side door.

"Ma'am," he said, flashing his crooked grin. "I can already tell you're too good for this chump."

Casey laughed, and Jake scowled, knocking Stockton's arm from where it rested inside the window.

"Man, quit flirting and just tell me where to park and where we should set up our tent."

Stockton chuckled and pointed to where they could set up, saying that they were only waiting on VanderWall and his cousin, whose Mom actually owned the property they were using. Jake parked the truck and Casey pouted a little bit about why they couldn't sleep in a nice big trailer, but when he looked over and gave her a long look, she smiled and then leaned across the console to nip him along his jaw. His damn breath caught in his throat before he could give it permission not to.

"I know, I know," she said quietly, her breath warm on his neck. "I'm stretching, I get it."

He turned his head to catch her eyes, and while he could still see apprehension in them, he also saw humor.

"It's not gonna work, Casey." Her eyes widened, and considering how close their faces were, he could see every variation in those bright irises. "You can work that talented little mouth all you want, you still have to help me set up the tent."

He caught her lips with his before she could plop back into her seat, and she softened, opening up and reaching her tongue out to meet his long enough that he knew he had won the round, but then she shoved back at his chest, separating them.

"Maybe I just wanted to bite you."

"I appreciate it, trust me, but you still have to help with the tent."

She turned to open up the truck door and slide out, but she wasn't quick enough to mask the 'dang it' mumbled under breath. He chuckled and yanked the keys out of the ignition, opening the door for Remy to jump out in front of him.

Casey stepped back, wiping her hands on her jeans, after straightening the corner of the two sleeping bags that were opened up and zipped back together to form a large enough bag for two people. The tent was surprisingly spacious, and with the lantern hanging from the center rod, a blanket folded in the corner for Remy, it was possibly the cutest little setup she'd ever seen.

She smirked, knowing she could never admit that to Jake because he would probably feel like she'd sucked all the manliness from the tent just by saying it. But it was true, he had a couple coolers of food for them, and all this fun equipment that she'd never paid attention to when her brothers got ready to go. Camping wasn't so bad.

She picked up a large red plastic thing with knobs and a large black handle, turning it over in her hand trying to figure out what it did. The zipper behind her clicked open, Remy coming in the opening before Jake.

"What the heck does this thingie do?"

Jake came to stand right behind her, which was not difficult to do in the space, but she happily leaned backwards to close the few inches he had left in between their bodies. He reached around her to pluck it out of her hand.

"It's a portable electronics charger. I pretty much just use it for my phone, but you can charge other things too."

"No kiddin'. That's pretty fancy."

"Mmmmhmmm." His face was right next to hers and the vibration from the sound made her squirm just a teensy little bit. When he wrapped his other arm around her waist, she bit her lip to keep the smile back. Just in the last couple days, even after they'd, ahem, slept together, he'd become much more hands-on with her. And oh, those hands. She loved the way his callouses felt against her arms and legs, or her face when he pulled her in for a kiss. They felt manly and rough and all sorts of delicious. "My lifelong goal is to be the fanciest camper around. You've got me pegged again."

She turned at the teasing tone in his voice, it was as rare as his laughter, and they both still managed to leave her feel a little stunned when he used them. She spread a hand over where his heart thrummed, deep and steady, then leaned up to meet his mouth in a quick, sweet kiss. He gave a small hum when she gave a tiny lick to his bottom lip as she pulled back.

"Well, if you ever want me to go camping with you again, you better have some fancy toys. This is about as far as I'll go towards roughing it."

He stepped back quickly, almost making her lose her balance. He set the charger back down on the floor next to the air mattress, and then gestured towards the opening of the tent. She opened to her mouth to ask him if he was okay, then closed it again. One week in was not the time to start pressing for his feelings.

To be nice, she'd give at least a month. Or three weeks.

She could hear the steady thumping of the music someone had turned on, peppered with laughs and loud conversation. She'd briefly met a couple of the girls who were in the tent closest to them, friends of Stockton's wife: Candace and Taylor. Taylor, the one who had flipped long blonde hair over her shoulder, had done just a little bit more gawking at Jake than was typical for a first introduction. The vivid streak of jealousy that she'd felt when Jake was talking to Melinda at work wasn't there this time. She knew who'd be curled up with him in those good-looking sleeping bags tonight. And it wasn't Taylor.

Realistically, it would probably be her *and* Remy. Ew.

They stepped out of the tent, and Casey breathed in the thick, heavy aroma of smoking charcoals from the grills over by the bonfire. If she *had* to camp, this set up was probably one of the most beautiful ways to do it. A private lake, amazing fall colors as their backdrop, and Jake to keep her warm at night. And a portable phone charger, apparently.

Not too shabby.

A deep rumble from an incoming truck cut through the noise around the campsite. She knew that shamelessly, ridiculously loud roar without turning around. Every time she heard it pull into the parking lot at work it gave her that creepy crawly feeling, that uninhibited urge to run, look busy, hide under her desk, or some impossible combination of all three.

Please be wrong, please be wrong, *please* be wrong.

Jake was talking to Stockton about how many burgers they should grill for dinner, his back to her and her impending mental freak-out, so Casey steeled her stomach and turned just enough to see the jacked-up maroon truck with the Steelers vanity plate rusted on the front.

Not wrong. What the ever-loving heck was Steve doing here?

She couldn't hold back the groan, and it had Jake turning back to her, forehead creasing when he noticed she was covering her mouth with a clenched fist.

"You okay?"

NO, she thought, wanting to scream. *I want to leave. I want you to kick his ass because he completely and totally freaks me out. I want to have a fabulously wonderful time camping with you where you realize that you're head over heels in love with me and instead now I have to sleep within twenty feet of Creepy Eye Guy.*

She swallowed, lowering her hand back to her side. Pulling a few breaths while she could hear the grating sound of his voice greeting people behind her, she decided that she could do it. She could suck it up for a day and a half. She was here with Jake, and that thought went far in flooding her limbs with some relief. Jake's presence would make Steve back off. But she didn't want everyone else to be uncomfortable.

"Yeah. Just felt a little lightheaded for a second, but I'm okay." She pushed a smile across her face. Jake's eyes flicked down to where her hands fiddled with the edge of the black, red and white plaid shirt she'd bought yesterday when she concluded that her wardrobe was woefully lacking in camping appropriate attire.

"You sure?"

She nodded and walked over to him, slipping one arm through his, drawing a strength that felt tangible.

"Casey. Did I win the lottery or somethin'? To what do we owe the honor of your presence this weekend?" Steve said in a booming, snide voice.

"Oh, hey Steve," she said, proud that she kept her tone even. She felt Jake look down at her as they both turned to where Steve stood, arms folded across his soft belly. "Jake invited me, and he was invited by Stockton. Jake, this is Steve, I know him from work. He's umm, he's a customer."

Noise bounced everywhere, but to Casey it felt like there was a silent bubble that pushed up from the ground, coming up around the three of them. Steve eyed Jake, then puffed out his chest and stuck out an unsurprisingly dirty hand. Jake slowly reached forward, still not saying anything.

In their little bubble, where no one outside seemed to notice anything going on, Casey felt Remy make a subtle shift, easing forward a few inches so that he sat slightly in front of her left leg. The two men clasping hands broke whatever tightly-stretched charge was in the atmosphere, and Casey nearly flinched from the sudden shift. Linkin Park screamed from a set of speakers, the grill hissed where the burgers cooked and Taylor let out a nasally giggle at something Stockton was doing.

"Casey, you want to help me unload the last of our stuff?"

She looked up at Jake, knowing the truck bed was emptied. Face blank, Jake pulled his arm from her grip, where her fingernails had ended up practically embedded in his skin. So much for playing it off. He placed his hand at the small of her back, turning her towards his truck with enough gentle pressure that she wanted to bury herself in his side and not leave. Ever.

"Nice to meet you, Steve," Jake said over his shoulder as they walked away.

Steve huffed out a breath. When they reached the far side of the truck, Jake dropped his arm from her back and stared. Casey chewed on her lip, looking over at the uninterrupted glossiness of the lake.

"What?" she asked when the quiet finally got to her. Geez, this man could out-silence an entire monastery.

"Who's the douche? And don't say he's just a customer, because you practically drew blood on my arm when he came over."

The breath she blew out was slow and steady. "He really is a customer. He just, I don't know, weirds me out a little."

"I hadn't noticed."

She smacked the back of her hand against his hard stomach. "Nobody likes a smart ass, Jake."

"You don't seem to mind too much," he said, brushing a piece of hair behind her ear. "You promise that's all it is?"

She nodded. "There are enough people here, I can avoid him pretty easily. Plus, I have my built-in bodyguard, so I should be just fine."

Jake smiled at where Remy lay by their feet, ears pricked and eyes alert on the group of people by the fire. Casey reached up to grip Jake's chin, forcing him to look at her. "I meant you."

The way he moved his gaze over her face was familiar now, and she felt it down to her toes. The skin on the back of his neck was warm when she reached to pull his head down towards her. She kept her eyes open, loving how he smiled just before their lips met.

She slanted her mouth into the kiss when his hands smoothed down her ribs, finally settling on her hips. Even though she sighed when he pulled back, she relished the feel of his thickly muscled biceps under her hands. It felt silly that she even worried about Steve with Jake around and she felt a real smile spread.

"That's better," he murmured in her ear. "Even if you're only smiling because you just licked my tonsils in front of Taylor over there."

When she slapped his stomach again, he laughed, and together they headed over to join the group.

EVERY ONCE IN A WHILE, Jake saw Casey flick her gaze over to where Steve was reclined in a camping chair across the fire, legs crossed in front of him and hands resting behind his greasy brown hair. She was still nervous, even though it was much less obvious than when the guy had first gotten there. Steve watched the group with heavy-lidded eyes, but they stopped on Casey much more than anyone else.

It wasn't that Jake blamed him for looking at an attractive woman; most men with a set of eyes probably looked twice at Casey, but Steve's looks in her direction seemed like more than that. Jake slid his hand up her back, drawing her closer in case she was cold now that the sun had gone down, and to remind her that he was there. The fire dwindled, and the whole group seemed fuzzy and slow-moving from the food and beer. Jake hadn't had anything to drink and neither had Casey, but they were definitely the only ones.

Stockton's wife Vanessa nudged Casey from where she sat on the other side of her. It hadn't taken long for Jake to figure out that Stockton hadn't been joking about how tough his wife was. She cursed like a weather worn sailor, peppering her sentences with enough f-bombs to make any infantrymen blush. But she'd immediately included Casey in all the women's conversations, making sure she felt comfortable, even though she was the only unknown to the group, except him of course.

"Casey, girl, you've gotta come out with us when the boys go back over. I can introduce you to the rest of the group. They'll be a good source of information for ya."

Shit.

Casey tipped her head to the side. "Go back over?"

Somehow, Jake held in the groan that wanted to rip up his throat. And the way he so badly wanted to smack himself for being so incredibly, horribly stupid.

Ness tipped back her can of Miller Lite, scrunching up her face and tossing it over her shoulder when she realized it was empty. "Yeah. When they leave for Afghanistan in April. It's good to get to know some of the other wives and girlfriends, you know, support each other so we don't all lose our damn minds for eleven months."

She went completely still under his hand, muscles locking and tension seeping back into her frame. In her buzzed state, Ness had no clue what she'd just done. Casey's chin dropped into her chest for just a moment, and she pulled in a deep breath.

"That sounds good, Ness. Umm, I'm pretty beat. I think I'm gonna go get ready for bed." Hesitating another moment, she turned and looked at Jake, eyes wide and confused, searching his. He felt like the world's biggest ass. Yet again. He ran a hand down her arm, relieved that she didn't pull back when he took her hand.

"I'll come with you," he said, eyes never straying from hers. Everyone except Steve said their goodnights, with Stockton throwing out a few lewd comments as they walked in silence to their tent. Jake held in a breath after letting Casey and Remy go in before him, then slowly let it out as he closed the zipper. Casey sank down on the air mattress, staring up at him in a way that made him want to strip his flesh off. The confusion was bad enough, but the hurt in her face made him feel so, so much worse.

"Why didn't you *tell me*?"

"I don't-"

"Don't you dare say you don't know, Jake. There is no way this was accidental. Did you think I wouldn't want to be with you if I knew?"

The lantern hanging from the peak of the tent swung back and forth from the movement of the tent walls, and Jake let the unnatural greenish light suck him in. He shook his head, then moved to lay down on the mattress next to her, making the mattress sway under his added weight.

Casey had no choice but to rearrange herself, the natural movement making them sink towards each other in the middle. She stretched out beside him, tucking one hand underneath her face. He could already see the worry clouding her eyes, dulling them, and he hated it.

Hated it so much that it made him want to claw his eyes out so that he didn't have to see it.

"I didn't know what to say." He shrugged his shoulders and then let out a humorless laugh at how lame that sounded. "I wanted to tell you, I thought about it every day, felt like a jerk for not being able to. You just...you have to understand, I haven't had to answer to anyone outside of Uncle Sam for a very long time. No one wondering when I'll be home or waiting to hear from me."

She was quiet for so long, but he forced himself to just wait. He'd had weeks to process this, and she was just thrown at it without any warning. When he finally couldn't take it anymore, he looked over at her and she looked sad.

Finally, she hummed in acknowledgment at what he'd admitted, propping up on her elbow and leaning over him. He didn't know how, but she still smelled like oranges after sitting around a bonfire.

"No one to worry about you," she said, laying three soft kisses across his forehead.

"That too."

"Or miss you." More soft, small kisses down the side of his face, then on the edge of his lips, and he found himself turning to inhale her sweet breath.

"Yeah." He wasn't even sure why he was agreeing. His mind swarmed with effort to resist capturing her mouth, where it hovered so closely to his. But like every other time with Casey, he couldn't resist.

He didn't want to.

He straight up ignored every part of him that screamed and raged at the idea of Casey sitting home waiting and worrying. Of that worry sinking her every single day, of bitterness tightening her smiling face, of frustration spilling over into the handful of conversations they would be able to have.

Of her left alone when she deserved someone who could be with her every day.

Instead of letting those thoughts consume him again, he sank into the kiss, gripping her tightly and feeling how much she was pouring into him, filling him with a disquieting sensation.

Helplessness.

He felt so vulnerable against what she was giving to him. He let it flow through him, knowing that at some point he would have to get that under control. But for right now, he didn't fight it. For right now, he willingly gave into it.

Soft hands gripped the edge of his shirt, tugging until he had no choice but to pull it over his head. Her hands were cool against the heated skin of his back, making him groan. She pulled them back around and quickly divested herself of her own shirt and tank top. He ran one fingertip over the swell above her bra, causing her to shiver.

In that moment, he thought back to her question earlier about what he was afraid of. Her laying there, so beautiful, yielding to him, was terrifying. And consuming. And those conflicting feelings tore through him until he didn't even want to think about which one would win out in the long run.

Bracing himself above her, he dragged his nose from the base of her throat to her belly button. The smell of her, light and fresh, turned his mouth greedy, over and under the lace barrier of her bra. Across her ribs and in the dip of her waist. She arched her back up to meet his movements, and bit down on one lip to stay quiet.

They rocked into each other, the sway of the mattress beneath them causing a friction between them that almost had him losing his mind. Not here, not like this. Jake rolled onto his back, sucking in steadying breaths. He looked over and saw Casey attempting to do the same.

She turned her head to look at him. "Do you not want-"

"Casey," he interrupted. "We're in a tent with my dog. There are a dozen other people around us, and the only thing separating us from them is a few thin layers of vinyl. You deserve better. You deserve *more* than this."

If there was some way that he could stare deeply enough at her that she could read the truth in what he was saying. Her brows tilted in. She saw something, he thought, but then her face smoothed out and she grinned slowly.

"Like champagne and rose petals and a fuzzy rug in front of a roaring fire?"

"Sure."

"That's so cheesy. But I appreciate you thinking of me." She traced the outline of his lips, something she'd done often in the past week. She moved her eyes up to his, and they were so serious, so guileless that his heart actually stuttered. "Jake, I-"

He cut her off again, this time with a kiss, ardent and hot. So maybe she was going to say she needed the latrine, but in her eyes he could *see* what she wanted to tell him. He couldn't hear it roll off her lips.

Just couldn't. He brushed his lips over her eyelids so he didn't have to see the disappointment that he knew would be shining there. He pulled the top sleeping bag over their bodies, and shifted so she could lay her head on his shoulder.

"We best get to sleep. Tomorrow's going to be a busy day."

She lightly kissed above his hammering heart. "Okay."

Tomorrow, it would better if they talked tomorrow.

20

CASEY ROLLED OVER, back protesting from the long night spent on the air mattress. She had only gotten about an hour of solid sleep after Jake whispered to her that he was going for a run before everyone got up. And it was her own fault. Jake never moved when he slept, but she had been so careful to not upset the precarious balance of the mattress as the slightest movement would send the whole surface rippling.

She laid there for hours, doing nothing more than slight drifting into sleep before a noise or gust of wind would cause her to swim back to wakefulness. And even when there hadn't been any noises, she would go over those last few minutes before Jake told her to go to sleep.

As much as she wished Jake had been the one to tell her about the deployment in the spring, that wasn't what really hurt her. Not after he'd explained it. He was so used to being alone, that even with her right in front of him, he couldn't see that she was precisely where she wanted to be. It wasn't personal to her, the way he held himself back, it was just the only way he knew. And it made her ache.

Last night, he'd done it again, and he *had* to know she realized it. He had physically blocked her from trying to show him, to tell him that he didn't need to live that way anymore. As sweet as it had been, those two small kisses on her eyelids, she felt the pang rip through her when she realized what he was doing. He was a tough nut, to be sure, and he was also disconcertingly good at reading her.

After how he'd been with the appearance of Steve, stepping up when she hadn't asked him to, giving her small, reassuring touches to fortify her throughout the night, it had been all she could do not to blurt out how she felt, literally biting down on her lip to stop the words from tumbling out.

It felt so cliche to think about how he made her heart race, because it felt more like a hammer to her ribs, like she might crack from the inside out if she didn't find an outlet for everything pulsing inside her. And how he made her skin tingle, because it was so much more staggering than a dinky little tingle. It was like saying the ripple on the surface of a pond was one step away from a tidal wave.

She sat up, reaching over to pull her sweatshirt out of her bag, feeling chilly for the first time since Jake had gone. While she was attempting to fix her sleep ravaged ponytail, she could hear the pounding of his feet and the pant of Remy's breathing outside the tent. The zipper snicked open slowly, like he was afraid of waking her.

"It's okay, I'm up," she called out. He ducked his head in, motioning for Remy to lay down outside the entrance of the tent. His chest still heaved from the run, and when he turned to pull a bottle of water from their small cooler, the line of sweat staining the back of his t-shirt made her smile. He'd asked her once earlier that week if she wanted to go for a run, and she had to explain to him that the only reason she went running was if someone was chasing her with a weapon.

He tipped the bottle back, taking long drags that had his adam's apple bobbing in his throat. She really, really wanted to drag her tongue along the whole surface. Sweat and everything. He'd probably taste like heaven. "Good run?"

He finally looked over at her, face flushed and damp. He nodded, still catching his breath. After a few more gulps of water, he sat down on the floor and leaned forward to grab the bottoms of his shoes, stretching out his muscles. "You sleep okay?"

She shrugged. "Not great."

"Cold?"

"No, you were right about the bags. I was more concerned about waking you up by moving around too much."

While he continued shifting his legs to stretch out different muscles, she ran her tongue along the bottom of her top teeth, thinking that this view was worth an early wake-up call any day. When she opened her mouth to tell him that, Stockton's voice boomed from somewhere outside their tent.

"Rise and shine, ladies and gentlemen. Breakfast at oh nine hundred and then we head out to the dunes."

Jake was quiet as he swapped his sweat drenched shirt for a new one, not turning his back while she slipped out of her pajama pants and into a clean pair of jeans. She looked over at him, noting the blank face, but he either didn't see her watching or he was choosing to ignore it. Neither sat comfortably in Casey's stomach, but she tamped it down and followed him out of the tent and into the sunny, fall morning.

Sitting down in the same chair from the night before, she sat down with an apple and granola bar from the food Jake had packed, feeling his continued silence next to her. He smiled when Ness started telling a story about something Stockton had done in his sleep the night before, and he answered Taylor when she oh-so-sweetly started asking him about possibly renting one of his units. Casey snorted into her granola bar and then covered it with a cough when they both turned to look at her. Yeah, she could just about imagine what Taylor wanted to do with Jake's unit.

VanderWall, what his first name was Casey had no idea, said that Steve didn't want to wake up for breakfast and would just get up in time to go to the dunes. Apparently the giant trailer belonged to Steve's Mom, who also owned the property. She'd overheard Steve telling Taylor and Candace that they were 'definitely more than welcome' to take the extra bed if they didn't feel like sleeping in their tent. Candace, who had been relatively quiet the entire night, raised one pierced eyebrow and gave Steve a look that roughly translated to *you've got to be shitting me.* Smart girl.

"You ever been out on the dunes?" Ness bumped into her shoulder, jolting Casey from unpleasant thoughts of how Steve had stared at her from across the fire the night before. She'd only caught his eyes once, but he hadn't looked away, twisting his lips in a way that was far too creepy to be considered a smile. She had quickly averted her eyes, but not before he gave her a quick wink. Suffice it to say, his presence was not being missed at breakfast. He could stay locked in that big ol' trailer as long as he wanted.

"Nope. Honestly, I don't even really know what 'riding the dunes' really is," Casey admitted.

"Oh honey, you're in for a treat. Hundreds and hundreds of trucks and four wheelers and dune buggies flying around, races popping up everywhere, climbing up and over every dune that you can see for miles." She reached a thin arm around Casey's shoulders, squeezing. "Lot of testosterone flowing. It's a thing of beauty. I swear, I get turned on just thinkin' about it."

Casey shook her head, smiling, thinking Ness reminded her a bit of Rachel. She balled up the wrapper from her granola bar, when Ness pointed at her hand.

"Those kind are great for care packages. For the guys."

"Yeah? I'll have to ask about all of that stuff, huh?"

"Oh girl, they get to know me pretty damn well at the post office by the time Chris gets home. I swear I almost asked one of them to be in the delivery room with me when we had our third."

Casey looked over at her, grinning. "You're not serious, are you?"

"Nah. My Mom was in there with me, took some pictures so we could send them to Chris."

"He wasn't there?" The thought of it made her shoulders droop. So much life missed, and Ness was joking about it.

"They were due home about a month later. Thankfully demobe didn't take as long as it sometimes can, so he didn't miss too much."

"Demobe?" Casey asked blankly.

"Demobilization," Jake said from the other side of her, having turned back to face them. "The process we have to go through once we get back stateside before we actually get back home."

Ness nudged her shoulder again. "You got a lot to learn, honey. I keep joking with the rest of our little club that we should make flashcards for the new girls. You'll know so many acronyms you'll think you were training for the FBI. Stick with me though; we'll get you through it, right Jake?"

Only Jake wasn't in his chair anymore. He was pushing his long legs past their tent, striding towards the small lake like the fires of hell were fast on his heels.

"What's his deal?"

Casey shook her head. "I have no idea. Do you think I should go after him?"

"You're asking me? I never wonder, honey, I just go. Partially because makeup sex with my husband is fricken' spectacular."

She let out a laugh that was short on humor, mind stumbling over the bits and pieces of the morning that might shed some light. She stood slowly, turning her uneaten apple in her hands. "Wish me luck then, I'm going in."

"Atta girl." Ness gave her a sympathetic smile and it bolstered Casey enough to take the first step.

She approached quietly, even though she knew he probably heard her long before she came to stand next to him. He looked over at her and then moved his eyes back to the water, tracking Remy as he sniffed his way around. The ground they were standing on, Jake with his arms crossed tightly over his chest and Casey with her hands loosely clasped behind her, was mostly grass. But the ground slowly shifted to small, gravelly rocks the closer it came to the water's edge. They were far enough away from the group that only a faint hum of conversation reached Casey's ears.

Casey pulled in a breath, knowing she'd have to speak first. She let it out silently, throwing up a little prayer that she wasn't about to botch this completely.

"Did you go camping a lot growing up?"

If he was surprised by her question, he didn't show it. He nodded his head twice and then cleared his throat.

"With my Dad, yeah."

He fell silent again and Casey chewed her lip, having never felt so...unbalanced.

"I know my brothers have said that their camping trips with our Dad are some of their best memories from growing up." He made a small sound in his throat, and she felt ridiculously thankful for that tiny little noise of acknowledgment. And then she felt ridiculous for being so relieved by it. "Is it something you'd want to do with your kids someday?"

This time he did glance sharply over at her, something flashing in his eyes before he erased it.

"No."

Okaaaay, how about I just offer to break my own fingers? Maybe we'd have more fun.

"Well, that's okay. Not all kids want to go camping anyway," she said lightly, then forced a small laugh. "Obviously, since it took almost thirty years to get me out here."

"I mean no, because I've never really planned on having kids."

Full stop.

Everything in her stopped for a moment. A really long, horrifying moment. She felt her mouth drop open and her hands fall to her side, one only barely holding on to the apple. "You don't want a family?"

He let out a sigh, moving his hands to his hips, looking anywhere but at her. He muttered something under his breath, but she couldn't make it out past the blood roaring in her ears.

"It's not because I don't like kids. Kids are fine. I just never saw that future for myself."

Something wilted inside Casey, just a little, and a shred of doubt sprouted in the space it left behind. She pushed some strength in her voice, something she felt sorely lacking in at the moment. But she squared her shoulders and turned towards him, practically daring him to look at her. His jaw clenched, but he stayed facing forward.

"Why not? Obviously a lot of people in the military get married and have families."

"Yeah. They do. But the divorce rate in the military is a lot higher than the national average. It's a hard life, Casey, one that I've never thought to subject someone to, let alone make children go through that kind of stress. Men miss entire pregnancies, first wedding anniversaries, first steps, first words, miss the signs that their wife is cheating on them because she's lonely and insecure after being left alone for a year. Aren't there when their Mom is diagnosed with fricken' *cancer*. And I won't even mention what happens when someone gets killed, what *that* does to the families, to have two uniforms show up on your doorstep some night with the worst news they'll ever get. It's not some romantic fairy tale to be in this life. I've seen all of that way too many times to think it's anything other than completely selfish to force someone to live through it."

The longer he spoke, the harder his voice got, and the doubt inside of her grew, insidious and choking. At least it *must* be choking, because she felt like she couldn't breathe. She tried to swallow and couldn't, feeling betrayed.

Not by him, not really, because he'd never promised her anything. She felt betrayed by herself, by her own stupid intuition. And that knowledge burned through her gut, followed swiftly by the frigid cold blast of embarrassment. She'd been so sure.

So incredibly, positively, adamantly, stupidly sure that this was it for her, and for him.

~

WHY WASN'T she saying anything?

Inside, Jake was squirming. She just stood there, staring at him the way he stared at the body of water that he couldn't even see in front of him anymore. Her chest barely moved, like she couldn't even force her body to pull in anything more than shallow little gulps of air. His run this morning hadn't cleared his head the way he thought it might, just turned his thoughts in circles and curves until he didn't know what he should do.

No, he knew now what he should have done. He should have kept his stupid asshole mouth shut until they got home. But hearing Ness talk to her about care packages and demobe shot all that panic back to the surface. He'd managed to keep it down all week, all fricken week. And here she was, tiptoeing around him like he was a bomb about to go off. And wasn't he? That little rant probably felt like explosions to her, one right after the other, effectively taking out every single thing she wanted.

I don't plan on getting married. Boom.

I don't plan on having kids. Boom.

There is no future with me. BOOM.

"You're right." Her voice was soft, but the words snapped his head over to look at her. Not a trace of anger filtered through her face. He almost wished it did, because it might be easier if she would get unreasonably angry with him. Maybe he could feel some shred of certainty that he was doing the right thing. He had to believe that now that he started down this road. "It's awful how much soldiers have to miss back home, and I'm sure it never gets any easier. But when you're with someone who's willing to make those sacrifices for their country, that's what *makes* a soldier, that's what makes someone like you and like Stockton into the honorable men you are. It's what would make someone...would make someone love you."

Her voice wobbled right at the end, and he couldn't take his eyes away.

"I didn't ask anyone to love me. And you and I have never talked about what would happen next."

Her face paled, but she nodded slowly. She looked down at where Remy had moved to sit next to him. He let out a soft whine, eyes flickering between Jake and Casey. She let out a slow breath and then stepped in front of him so that if he tried to look at the water again, he'd have no choice to look straight at her.

"I know you didn't. But you can't look me in the eye right now and tell me that you don't feel even a little of what I've felt this past week." She lifted one hand helplessly, letting it fall back against her leg. "We fit, Jake. For whatever reason, you and I fit."

"I knew better. I knew better than to cross that line with you." He stared down at the drying grass near Remy's paws when he spoke, because every word felt like rusty nails coming back up his throat, bitter, sharp and cold.

"Maybe that's true. But, you know what? You did cross the line. We both did. And you know what else? You're not disagreeing with me." She reached her hand up to cup his face, moving slowly like he was a cornered animal or something. "Please, Jake, just let me--"

He jerked his head back before she could touch him. If she touched him, he might end up on his knees in front of her. "Let you what? Try to force a relationship where I didn't ask for one?"

She reared back, like he'd slapped her.

"What?" The word was quietly spoken, but for the first time

since he started this suicide mission there was a spark of anger behind it. "Force you? I've never forced you. You kissed *me*, you asked *me* out, you shove your tongue down *my* throat at every chance. And am I delusional or were *you* not the one to invite me this weekend?"

Her anger felt like a freaking spike in his chest, right through the sternum. He clenched his jaw, looking briefly over his shoulder at everyone by the tents, who were blissfully out of earshot. Casey speared her hands into her ponytail, shaking her head.

"I don't even understand how we got here right now, Jake. You can't blame me for feeling a little blindsided."

"We just want different things, Casey. I knew it from the beginning and I knew we would end up here eventually, but I ignored every instinct that told me to leave you alone."

"You're *that* convinced that we wouldn't work?"

He nodded, and finally looked back at her. But when he saw the pity in her gaze his own anger surged.

"Don't look at me like that," he snapped.

"Like what?"

"Like I'm some abused little puppy you need to take home."

She snorted then. "You say that like I'd take home a puppy, abused or otherwise."

Unfortunately for her, he wasn't in the mood to joke anymore. "I know how this world works, how this life that I'm in works, Casey. You think it'll all play out perfectly, because everything in your life has."

She stiffened, drawing up. "Excuse me? You're punishing me because I've had a good life? Don't use my family against me, I don't care how mad you are right now."

"Why not? You've had such a damn picture perfect life; you can't fathom something not going your way, because it always does. That much has been crystal clear since that moment you walked through the door. Life is shit sometimes, Casey. Difference between you and me is that I've known it since I was eleven. You still haven't opened up your eyes wide enough to figure it out yet."

And he saw it, saw the barb strike and then stick. She dashed a hand under her eye, catching a tear before it fell. She turned away from him, and while he could breathe a little easier without her facing him, he hated himself so much in that moment.

"Yo." Stockton's voice reached him just before he felt a slap on his back. "We're ready to head out. Let's get this show on the road, Lieutenant Miller."

Apparently their body language didn't scream *we're in the middle of a fight, idiot* like he assumed it did, because Stockton seemed oblivious.

"I'll be there in a minute," he replied. Stockton ambled off, yelling off instructions about who was going to ride together. They stood in silence for a few more moments, every sniff that she pulled in screaming at him, making him want to hack his ears off so that he didn't have to hear it.

"I think I'm going to stay back from the dunes," she said in a thick voice. "You should go with them. I wouldn't mind a little quiet right now."

He closed his eyes. "I don't think that's a good idea. Maybe we should just pack up now."

"I can do some packing while you're gone. Please, just go."

"Fine." He rubbed the back of his neck, wanting to do just about anything except go riding on the dunes with a bunch of people who had no clue what he just did. That he'd just ripped the still-beating heart out of her chest and basically called her a naive twit.

It was a horrible idea to stick around any longer, but that's what she wanted. And he could give her that at least, some peace and quiet until they were forced to sit in a truck together for an hour and a half. "I'm leaving Remy here with you. And the truck in case you need it for any reason."

She didn't answer, just kept staring at the lake, arms wrapped around her middle. He turned to go when she called his name. Her eyes were reddened from the tears that tracked down her face.

"One thing I never would have pegged you for was a coward."

He'd said that to her once before, and the words stung coming back at him. And because she was right, he just stared back at her.

And like the coward he was, he broke the stare first and walked away.

21

CASEY FLIPPED OPEN the cover of the book she had brought along with her, hoping that she could drown herself in Liz's latest recommendation. But even the angst on the pages had nothing on what was currently cycling through her head. Her chest felt heavy and clogged from the last hour of fighting tears. She'd stayed out by the water until she heard the last truck file down the gravel road. Only Ness had ventured out to make sure she was okay. After an Oscar worthy performance where she convinced a very shrewd and suspicious Ness that it was just a PMS induced tiff with Jake, she'd done a little packing in the tent. Satisfied with her contribution considering she'd just been whacked over the head with the cliff's notes version of Jake's issues, she'd dragged her camping chair out by the lake, quite satisfied to wallow until everyone returned.

She heard Remy bark from where she made him get into the truck. It was definitely not the happiest sound she'd ever heard from him, but hey, just add him to the list of males who currently lived next door to her who didn't want to be around her. She twitched in her chair, determined not to feel guilty for putting him there. The temps were only in the mid-fifties and it wasn't too hot for him to be in cab of the truck. She'd left the windows open enough that he could stick his head out, for crying out loud, and she just could not handle him staring at her anymore. He looked so judgmental and rude, laying there with his head perched on giant paws, tracking every movement she made. She and the dog both knew whose side he would be on, and it was *not* Team Casey.

But he just kept on, and the guilt she felt propelled her out of the chair to go check on him. A branch snapped behind her, loud and unnatural. Goosebumps popped up along her arms, lifting hairs as they grew.

Please let it be Jake, please let it be Jake. Heck, please let it even be Taylor.

But when she turned, it most definitely was not Jake. Steve walked leisurely towards where she was frozen in place. She did not like this new development. At all.

"Looks like I really did win the lottery this weekend. Wasn't too fun watching you practically give soldier boy a lap dance last night, but I guess you get to make that up to me now." He spoke as slowly as he was moving, like anything faster or louder would scare her off. "You've teased me for years, and I'm done with playing your stupid, bitchy games."

She blinked, barely even paying attention to what was coming out of his mouth and tried to recall anything her brothers had ever taught her about self-defense. She'd never had to use it before, and she'd already made stupid move number one by not keeping her phone by her. No, technically stupid move number one in this case was putting Remy in the truck. So, so incredibly stupid. *But*, she thought with a shaky inhale, *I don't have to be stupid anymore.*

Keep him talking, try to distract him while you focus on what to do next.

Pay attention to your surroundings.

Look for anything you could possibly use as a weapon, no matter how insignificant it may seem. A pen, a nail file, dirt, almost anything can inflict damage if you use it the right way.

She could hear her brothers telling her what to do, as if they were standing right behind her.

"I'm sorry Steve, I didn't mean to tease you." She couldn't believe how even her voice was, because her entire body was shivering, like she was a wobbly house of cards and one stray breath would knock her over. "Why don't we go back by the tents and we can talk about it."

Back by her phone, and Remy. Her throat tightened hearing him bark in the truck, the sound frantic, not angry. She swallowed past the unexpected emotion.

Steve stopped a few feet away and cocked his head, eyes tracing over every inch of her. His eyes were off, more than usual. His pupils were tiny pinpricks, and he swayed briefly before steadying himself. She breathed through every raging instinct that told her to run and forced her body to stay still.

"No, think we'll stay right here."

Okay. There went Plan A. Her only options for a weapon out here were the chair she had been sitting in and her book. And unless she planned on paper-cutting him to death, the book wasn't really viable. At that thought, she choked on a bubble of hysterical laughter, somehow turning it into an innocuous sounding cough. They were a couple hundred feet away from the campsite and the safety of the truck. And since she had to get *past* him, the distance seemed about three times longer than what it actually was. Her heart trilled in her chest, making it difficult to breathe normally.

"Listen Steve, everyone should be back soon, so I really think we should head back to the tents. I wouldn't want Jake to worry if he can't find me." It was a reed thin bluff, she knew they could be gone for another couple hours, but she hoped that she sounded sincere enough he would back off.

His eyes narrowed to slits and he took another step towards her.

"Soldier boy isn't coming back quite yet, I think we're alone for a while."

The way he said alone, stretching the word, sent an ice pick down her spine. She took a deep breath and held it in while he walked one more step closer. She'd never wanted to inflict pain on someone so badly. That realization sobered her a bit, feeling the certainty of how much she would fight him. Her hands curled into themselves, and for just a second she wished for the cool metal of her Dad's shotgun.

"But don't you think Jake will notice you didn't go with everyone?" Her voice was stronger than before, and he stopped again, his brows pulling together on his forehead while he considered. Jake had to scare the crap out of him, and it bolstered her enough to keep from pleading. "You know he will. He'll come right back, and you and I both know that he wouldn't be happy if he knew you were scaring me. Because I think you're smarter than this. And I don't think you mean to be scaring me right now."

"Why would I be scaring you? I'm just coming to collect what you've been offering for so long. Flaunting yourself at work, flirting with every man that walks through the door." His voice trembled at the end, and she could see his control slipping as his eyes lost focus. He seemed to drift into a thought, and when he moved closer yet, she shifted her weight onto her left leg. Her fists tightened until she felt the sting of her nails pierce the flesh in her palm.

"Don't do this Steve," she said, feeling tears burn the back of her eyes. "Please, don't do this."

Her whispered plea made his chest puff up and he bared his teeth in a smile.

"I've always wanted to hear you beg," he growled, reaching towards her with a quickness she didn't expect. He wrapped his hands around her biceps, jerking her towards his chest, and she pulled her leg back and swung it forward, her knee connecting with soft flesh. He let out a strangled scream as he crumpled to one knee.

Not staying to make sure he stayed down, she flew towards the campground.

Trees blurred past as she screamed for help, not knowing or caring if anyone besides Remy was within hearing distance. The sounds coming out of her own throat were barely recognizable, hoarse and thick from desperation. Her lungs burned between the combination of the sprinting and cries for help, but she didn't slow. All she could hear was pounding feet, but she didn't know whether they were just hers. She made the curve through the two pine trees flanking the campsite and saw the back of Jake's truck, but the surge of relief she felt was short-lived.

In the seconds before she hit the ground, she was amazed at how much she noticed. His hand wrapping around her ponytail, the reflection of the sun sparking off the screen of her phone sitting on the opened tailgate of Jake's truck, and Remy barking inside the cab, body practically sideways as he tried to paw through the opened window. One of his front legs cleared the space, but since it was only striking air, he couldn't shift enough to get out. All of his movements seemed so fast, like he shouldn't be able to move at that pace.

Steve yanked his hand down, and she hit the ground flat with a sickening thud that forced the air out of her lungs in a loud *WHOOSH.* She struggled to pull in another breath, but her throat had completely closed up. Casey made a sound that was part groan and part whimper while Steve's shadow covered her. He placed his feet on either side of her hips and leaned down, resting his hands on his knees. Finally taking in a gulp of precious air, it was all she could do not to pass out. Her frantic pulse battered her eardrums, and black spots danced in the air around Steve's head. He was talking, calmly again, but she couldn't understand a word he was saying.

He dropped down then, straddling her hips and pinning her left hand into the hard ground with one knee. With a strange detachment, she wondered why he didn't do the same with her other hand. Oh, yeah. Her right hand was gripping the front of her long sleeve shirt, in an effort to...what? Stop him from ripping it off? He tried to pry her fist off her shirt, but even with two hands he couldn't. Her vision started to clear, and she whipped her head back and forth, screaming again, but he clamped one dirty hand over her mouth, muffling the sounds.

"*Shut up.* I can't think with you screaming like that." His cheeks were red and she watched a bead of sweat run down the side of his forehead, disappearing into the hair by his ears. Behind his hand, she kept screaming after taking in another breath through her nose. She tried to buck her body underneath his, planting her feet firmly against the ground and shoving upwards as hard as she could. He laughed, because it did nothing to move him. The laughter snapped her vision into focus.

She pulled her fingers from her shirt, striking at his face, aiming for his eyes but in her struggle, hit him across the cheek with her nails. His laughter stopped and she watched his other hand pull back across his heaving chest, and she knew he would hit her. She pulled her hand back, shoving at his heaving chest, sobbing behind his hand when she couldn't move him.

He uncovered her mouth just long enough to bring the back of his other hand down across her cheek, setting off explosions through her skull, little blasts of fireworks that ricocheted off of each other. They were red and black. She'd never seen black fireworks before, but she felt them moving through the bones of her face. She groaned and felt tears spring and fall unbidden. He grabbed her right hand, now limp after the dazing blow and pinned it underneath his other knee. She tried to curl it into the ground to gain some sort of traction, but all she managed to do was fill her fist with dirt. She could feel it, the cold grittiness biting into the skin underneath her fingernails.

She screwed her eyes shut, unwilling to watch if she had to endure, heard him pull down his zipper and then try rip open the top of her jeans. Unable to hear beyond her own incoherent pleas and prayers, she missed the slight pause in Steve's movements and the muffled curse that followed. Her eyes flew open when he pushed off his knees to scramble away from her. He let out a frantic shout when he tried to push up onto his feet but couldn't get his balance. What in the actual hell was going on?

All she saw vaulting over her was black, grey and tan. Remy latched onto Steve's arm knocking him easily back to the ground next to her. Casey scuttled backwards in the dirt, legs still too unsteady to bear her weight. Steve threw his head back and screamed as Remy clamped down harder. Remy shook his head, emitting some of the most terrifying sounds she'd ever heard. Blood ran down Steve's forearm, and she took a second to pull in a few deep breaths and savor the sight. Then she snapped back, unwilling to make another stupid mistake. She lurched to her feet, limping towards Jake's truck.

A high pitched yelp had her whipping around. Steve was trying to flip over, and had succeeded in getting his other arm out enough to punch Remy in the side. He pulled back his fist again and again, ramming it into the dog. Another yelp, but Remy didn't yield. Hands gripping the sides of her head, mind frantic wondering how long Remy could hold on, her eyes landed on a long, thick chunk of wood left near the remnants of last night's fire. Stockton had used it to stoke the flames. She gripped the jagged piece, hefting it by her side while she edged toward where the two bodies tangled on the dirt.

Neither of them paused while she stood there for a few agonizing seconds, waiting for an opening. Steve managed to get one foot on to the ground and pushed up enough that Remy's front paws dangled in the air. Casey gasped and staggered back.

No. Oh, no frickin way.

She planted her feet and pulled the stick back like a baseball bat. Remy yanked back down on Steve's arm. Steve's back was turned to Casey, so she swung her body around with every sore muscle singing, every ligament in tandem with what she needed to do, connecting solidly with the back of his head. He pitched forward and landed on the hard dirt, not moving, not even looking like he was breathing. The stick fell out of her hands and clattered to the ground. It sounded so loud now that the yelling and growling had stopped. Remy sniffed at Steve's head cautiously. She felt tremors start in her legs, adrenaline over-taking her body and she crumpled to the ground. Remy limped over, chest heaving, and plopped onto his haunches right next to her.

Feeling like it was the most natural thing in the world, she turned into Remy and wound her arms around his neck, burying her head into his wiry coat. The tears started in earnest then, and she dug her fingers into the loose skin around his shoulder blades, taking in giant, gulping breaths that smelled like dog and dirt and bonfire. Help. They still needed help. And her phone was still on the bed of the truck.

She tried to stand, but couldn't, sinking back down to her knees. Remy stood up, looking back at her. With a groan, she set her hand on his shoulder blades, using his solid weight to help lever herself up. She had to bend a bit to keep her hand on him, but it was enough that she kept her balance until they reached the truck. Swiping her phone off the black plastic lining, they both limped to the passenger side, where she wrenched the door open. She scooted over to the driver's side and Remy jumped in after her.

Saying a silent prayer of thanks that Jake had manual locks and windows, because she had no clue where he had left the keys, she secured both and tried to calm her shaking hands before attempting a call. As much as she wanted to call Jake first, she dialed 911. After explaining what happened, she gave direc-tions as best as she knew how, and the operator calmly told her to stay in the truck until the cops arrived. The steady, soothing voice of the dispatcher told Casey that there was a state trooper just a couple miles away and she would stay on the line until he got there.

Putting the phone on speaker, Casey went back to her home screen and saw the alerts. Three missed calls and two texts from Jake.

Just realized Steve bailed and stayed back, I'm going to grab someone's ride and come back just in case. Let me know when you get this.

Casey, I know you're mad at me, but please, call me when you get this. I took Stockton's truck and will be there in 15 minutes. Keep Remy by you.

She looked at the time on her phone and saw that he sent the last text seven minutes ago. It felt like it had been hours since she heard Steve walking up behind her. Remy leaned over as if sensing her train of thought and swiped his tongue up the side of her face. She sagged into him again, taking comfort from his solid weight.

"Don't think I'm gonna be okay with this licking thing tomorrow," her voice shook ridiculously as she said it. "This is a one day deal, you got it?"

As if he understood, he dipped his snout in agreement. Then he licked her again, soaking up salty tears with his rough tongue. She kept looking over her shoulder to make sure that Steve was still unconscious on the ground. Finally, *finally* the faint sound of sirens hit her ears and the sobs that she had managed to keep at bay completely overtook her. She dropped her head into her hands and felt sweet threads of relief push through her.

Remy shifted in the seat to watch where the cop car was pulling into the clearing. Despite how soothed she felt that help had finally arrived, it felt so impossible to swallow the cries still shivering through her body. As she was wiping the tears off her overheated cheeks, she saw the hackles on Remy's back start to rise.

A low growl started in his throat and got louder as he opened his mouth, his ears perking forward as the cop exited his vehicle and started towards the truck. His gun was drawn, but was pointed at Steve. His eyes, deep set in a wide face, darted between Steve and Casey inside the truck.

"Ma'am, are you alright in there?" His deep voice reached through the windshield and she felt herself relax further. Taking in her silent nod, he looked over at Steve. "Is he the one who attacked you?"

She liked this man that was pointing a loaded gun at Steve's head. Casey nodded again and put her arm around Remy, who was still directing his rumbling growl at the police officer. As she tried to smooth down the hair on his back, she crooned in his ear.

"It's okay, Remy, he's one of the good guys. It's okay."

His growling tapered off but he never took his eyes away from the officer. Almost forgetting she was there, Casey told the woman on the other end of the phone that help had arrived, and thanked her for staying on the line. The officer slowly approached Steve's body, still prone on the hard ground. He leaned down to check Steve's pulse and then holstered his weapon.

Pulling handcuffs from the belt around his waist, the officer put them around Steve's wrists behind his back. He stood back up and started walking back towards the truck. As he approached the driver's side where she sat, Remy immediately starting his warning again, leaning forward across Casey's lap and baring his teeth at the cop who smartly held his hands up and stepped back from the truck.

"Ma'am, I'm Officer MacMillan with the Michigan State Police. I don't want to upset your dog, but I'd like to check you over real quick if that's okay. There's an ambulance standing by not that far from here, but I want to be able to let them know the extent of your injuries when I give them okay to come back here."

She looked nervously back at Steve. The officer's face smoothed in understanding.

"If you want to wait for the female officer that's in the next car, I understand. But it *is* safe for you to come out now."

She could see the sincerity in his eyes. They were green, the same color as Jen's.

"Okay, I'll come out now." Casey turned to Remy who was still making his opinion on the subject known. Knowing it might not be the smartest thing to do to a growling dog, she put her hands on either side of his head and turned him until their eyes met.

"Shh Remy, I'm okay now. I'm okay." A couple more tears slipped out of the corner of her eyes when she said it, realizing fully just what he'd done for her. Holy crap, she was going to have to eat every bad thing she'd ever said about this dog. The growling stopped and he pulled his tongue up her face again, fully swiping across her thankfully closed mouth. "Ew. Okay, that's my limit."

She gave him the signal to stay, and turned back to the truck door. Her hand paused where it was wrapped tightly around the cool metal handle, and she took a deep breath before pulling it open. Casey carefully slid down off the seat until her feet hit the ground. The officer gently looked over the bruises on her face and arms before he explained that he was going to go call for the ambulances. She maintained her grip on the door as she watched him walk back to his car and speak into the radio.

Keeping her eyes trained on the police car, she almost didn't notice the truck that tore down the lane into the campsite.

Jake.

He was *only* fifteen minutes late.

The truck slammed into park, gears protesting at the rough treatment. Jake practically ripped the door off its hinges when he opened it. As relieved as she was that he was back, the wrath etched in his face made her shrink into the truck door.

"Where is he?" he bellowed, and a vein throbbed angrily in his neck. He hadn't even looked at the squad car. He'd barely looked at Casey. Officer MacMillan must have noticed her reaction to Jake and quickly stood up out of his seat, his hand resting on the grip of his pistol as he came around the front of the car.

"Sir, I'm going to have to ask you to stop right there." His voice was pure steel, and the compassion she had seen earlier was completely gone. Jake's head whipped around to look at him. His stance still radiated anger, but his eyes registered confusion.

"Me? I didn't do anything."

"What you're *doing* is scaring her," he gestured to Casey with the hand not by his gun.

Jake's shoulders sagged. "I didn't mean to."

"How did you know what happened if you weren't here?" MacMillan's hand had relaxed, but didn't stray far from his weapon. Jake sighed heavily, and finally looked over at her. His dark eyes had lost the hard edge of fury, and she could see something else in its place as their eyes held.

Regret. Guilt.

She could practically feel his gaze as he looked over her face. He clenched his jaw and turned back to MacMillan.

"I guessed, but didn't know for sure until I saw your car. Casey wanted to stay back to read while the rest of us went to the dunes. I didn't realize right away that Steve hadn't come. I was in the first group to leave, and I just assumed he came in a later vehicle. While we were waiting to get into the park, my friend received a text message implying that Steve hadn't come along. I don't know whether he stayed knowing that Casey was here too, or if that was a coincidence. She wasn't responding on her cell phone, so I decided to assume the worst."

He found her eyes again. His image started blurring and yup, the tears were starting all over again. She wrapped her arms tightly around herself, tucked her chin down into her chest and breathed slowly, methodically. Remy started whining in the truck now that Jake was here. Officer MacMillan asked Jake a few more questions, and seemingly satisfied with his answers, he looked towards her.

"The other squad car will be here any second. If she's up to it, we'll need to get her statement. The ambulances will be here shortly after, and I'd also like her to go to the hospital to get checked out. Plus we'll need to gather evidence for when she presses charges. Just try to keep your cool while you're talking to her okay? I think she could use a friend right now."

Jake nodded solemnly and slowly started towards her. She watched him, surprised at how nervous he seemed. He stopped about a foot away, and lifted his hand towards her face. She flinched, not really meaning to. She couldn't look away from him, not sure if she wanted him to touch her or not. He swallowed audibly and pulled his hand back to his side.

"Casey, I....I'm so," he looked down at the ground, and shook his head slowly. When he looked up again, his eyes were blazing. Not with anger though, and she felt relief at that. MacMillan was right, she needed comfort right now, not blind rage. "I'm so sorry I wasn't here."

She cleared her throat, and realized how sore it was from screaming. Muscles ached and bones throbbed that hadn't felt that way even five minutes ago. It seemed as though her body was just catching up.

"It's okay, Jake. You didn't know. I'm sorry I didn't listen to you."

Annoyance, and maybe a tinge of guilt, flashed through his eyes. "Don't apologize to me, Casey. I should have stayed." He hesitated, jamming his hands in his front pockets. "Did he..." He pulled in a breath and held it for a second while he searched her face. "Did he rape you?"

She heard the trepidation in his voice, and realized that he was just as scared as she had been. Well, maybe not *quite* as scared, but just the thought of Jake being afraid of anything made her want to comfort him. She took a small step forward, and slowly shook her head while she held his gaze.

"No, he didn't." The effect was immediate, his eyes closed briefly before he tilted his head up and stared into the sky for a few long seconds. When he brought his head back down, he looked past her shoulder at Steve's handcuffed form sprawled on the ground. His fists tightened, a rope of muscle popped in his neck and he went to move past her. Her hand shot forward before she could think about it, and she gripped his forearm. He peered down, eyes narrowing and brows bunching, looking stunned that she was stopping him. Then he dropped his gaze to her hand on his arm.

"Don't." She saw the struggle, how badly he wanted to ignore her and release some of his guilt and anger and frustration onto Steve in his helpless state. She understood all of it, really she did. But it wouldn't help her right now. "Please," she said more firmly.

He closed his eyes and nodded his head. His skin was so warm, but she still released her hold on his arm. He looked like he was about to reach for her when another squad car came into the clearing, followed by two ambulances. Their lights were flickering through the trees, but they didn't have their sirens on. The blinking red and blue reminded Casey of the fireworks she saw when Steve hit her, and she shuddered.

Jake shifted closer, looking down at her. "Are you cold?"

If only that were it. She tried to curl her lips into a reassuring smile, but knew she failed when it felt like a monumental task to lift even one side.

"No. I'm fine." She could tell he didn't believe her. He opened his mouth to say something when a surprisingly petite female officer walked over to them.

"Ms. Steadman? I'm Officer Spencer, and if it's okay with you, I'd like to take your statement while the paramedics check you out." She spoke with brisk efficiency, but there was an understanding in her dark eyes that made Casey feel at ease. Casey nodded and walked with her towards the waiting ambulance.

After Steve had been taken off to the hospital with Officer MacMillan and Spencer's partner, Jake parked himself next to his truck, close enough to hear without impeding the process. She insisted she didn't need to go to the hospital, and the paramedics agreed that besides the bruising, she seemed fine.

Officer Spencer was harder to convince. She asked Casey numerous times and in several different ways whether Steve had raped her.

"I said he didn't," Casey finally snapped. "Would you quit asking me?"

"I'm sorry," Spencer said, only softening a little. "You don't know how common it is that the victim doesn't tell us the full extent of what happened, hoping to spare themselves going through the rape kit at the hospital. I was pretty certain I believed you, but I wanted to make sure. For your sake."

"Trust me. If he did, I'd tell you. There is no way I'm letting him off the hook for anything."

Officer gave her an appraising look and a brisk nod, and Casey took it as approval. Casey answered questions about her history with Steve, feeling increasingly stupid for not making a bigger deal of his presence with Jake. That feeling only got worse when she told Officer Spencer about how insulted he'd been when she had turned him down at work.

"Sexual assault is often not about sex at all, Ms. Steadman. It's about power, control. It's a way for them to prove themselves. Seeing you here with someone else probably escalated his feelings towards you, or escalated his need to prove himself to you."

"So," she said, rubbing at her sore throat, "I should have seen this coming? That he might try something?"

"No." Her voice was firm, her eyes direct. "There is no way to expect that he would react that way. Because it's not the way a rational person responds to being turned down for a date. In the most simple terms, there's something not right in a person's head when they feel the need to do that to someone else."

She sniffed, gave a small shrug. "I still feel stupid, like I should have taken him more seriously."

"There is nothing wrong with not automatically seeing the worst in people. It's just that sometimes..."

Casey laughed humorlessly when Officer Spencer paused. "Life is shit sometimes. Right?"

"Unfortunately, yes."

Jake's head dropped, his eyes shut and his chin tucked into his chest. She felt hollow, no semblance of victory in throwing his own words back to him for the second time that day. She wanted to take it back, but instead bit her lip and continued answering questions for the report that would eventually be used to formally charge Steve.

They scraped underneath her fingernails for evidence after she told them that she scratched his face because he was covering her mouth. Hearing that, Jake rubbed a hand across his unshaven jaw and struggled to take even breaths. He hadn't moved from his spot, hadn't spoken since she started recounting what had happened. He had one arm through the open window, absently stroking Remy's head, who was still in the truck. When Casey hit the part in her story where Remy jumped in, quite literally, Jake's head snapped up.

"He did?" His voice was hoarse. She nodded, eyes filling for what felt like the hundredth time since she started telling them what happened. She couldn't begin to imagine what she looked like, but from the way he stared back at her, it wasn't good.

Officer Spencer interrupted then, asking how Steve was knocked out after Remy bit him. When Casey told her, Spencer grinned widely, and her serious face was completely transformed.

"You should be really proud of yourself, Ms. Steadman. Whoever taught you to swing a bat should be too."

Casey felt the closest thing to a genuine smile crawl across her face for the first time since breakfast.

"My brothers Michael and Caleb did. I was ten, the twins were eighteen, and Mom made me play summer softball. The boys bought me a pink bat, thinking I'd want to actually use it that way. We practiced how to swing until I had blisters on my hands. I hated *every* minute of it."

"Two brothers, huh? I bet they'll be pretty upset when they hear about this."

Casey cocked an eyebrow and shook her head. "No, I have four brothers. Four *older* brothers." Officer Spencer winced when she heard that. "And they will be certifiable when they hear about it. I'm not sure I even want to be around when they do."

Spencer regarded her thoughtfully. "I have brothers, I know how that goes. They're pretty protective of me, even though I'm older than them and carry a gun for a living. I'm sure you being the youngest makes it even worse, huh?"

Casey cut her eyes over to Jake, wondering how many other ways Officer Spencer could keep proving his points about her. "Yeah, they've always been there for me, even when I didn't want them to be."

"I'll tell you what, how about you and I go to your parent's house and we'll tell them together. If any of your brothers are there, fine. But if not, you ask your parents to tell them. That way they can get their mad out of the way before they see you. Sound good?"

When she didn't answer right away, Jake moved his eyes back to her. They were guarded, back to the brick-wall mode he was so ridiculously good at. His voice was even when he finally broke the silence stretching between them.

"I think that's a good idea. I'll pack up our stuff and take Remy to the vet to get his side checked out. Give him a steak for dinner."

Casey nodded once in agreement, dismissing her disappointment that he seemed fine with letting her leave without him. She thanked the paramedics and then took a few steps towards the truck. Jake looked wary at her approach, but moved to the side when Casey reached into the window to cup each side of Remy's head. She dug her fingers in behind his ginormous ears, and a low groan of approval moved up his throat. She smiled and leaned forward.

"Thank you," she whispered and then placed a small kiss on the top of his snout. After a final scratch under Remy's jaw, she grabbed her purse from the tent and followed Officer Spencer to her squad car.

"Sorry, but you've got to sit in the back," Spencer said and opened the back door for Casey. Before Casey sank into the backseat, she took one last look at Jake and saw him leaning into the truck with his forehead against Remy's. Her throat thickened, eyes that were already rubbed raw burned again. She swallowed it down as best she could, knowing that she had a lot more tears to shed before the day was done. Before turning on the car, Officer Spencer found a brush for Casey and passed it back through an opening in the grate separating them.

"Let's clean you up a bit before we see your parents, okay?"

Casey gave her a small smile as they started the long drive back.

22

CASEY HUNG the last shirt from her laundry basket, relieved to *finally* get things in order after having Dylan living under her roof for a week. Catching her reflection in the full length mirror she'd hung by the door in her bedroom, she skimmed her fingers over the faded yellow outline of the bruise on her cheek. Usually she covered it, whether she was leaving the house or not, but she finally felt like she could keep the concealer in the drawer.

The first morning after *it* had happened, she'd stared in the mirror and wiped one shaking finger across her cheekbone, smearing the flesh toned cream in a thick line. The second swipe was what shattered her.

Scrambling to find a brush so she didn't have to touch the bruise, she finally ripped the drawer from the tracks, overturning all of the contents onto the counter when she couldn't sift through the compacts and tubes and wands fast enough. Dylan found her on her knees, shoulders heaving and backbone sagging underneath the weight of her inability to tear the memories from her head. He'd rocked her where she sat, letting her purge until she felt like all of her bones had completely dissolved from the flow of salty liquid.

And as much as she loved him for sitting there with her silently, she desperately craved a different set of arms around her. A different type of comfort. One that she could inhale into her lungs and curl her body into.

Her phone rang from where it was charging in the kitchen, so she breathed out the memory and headed towards the noise. The ringing, trilling, musical chimes kind of made her want to rip her hair out because it felt like it hadn't stopped in the last week. Ever. The only thing she could figure is that her family must have a sign-up sheet.

3:00 PM- Dylan leaves house.

3:22 PM- Mom to call Casey.

"Hey Mom, what's up?"

"How'd your meeting go?"

Casey tilted her neck to the side, groaning a little when she got that satisfying little pop at the base of her skull.

"Fine. They're going to charge him with felony criminal sexual conduct, and the DA thinks he'll get eight to ten years since he had a prior on his record. I guess he would've been charged earlier if he hadn't been in the hospital. Court will probably be in the next couple days."

Her Mom's exhale was heavy through the phone. "That's good. I wish you would have let me or your father come with you."

"You guys didn't need to hear all that again. He just wanted to go over my statement and talk to me about the likelihood that Steve will take the plea bargain over going to trial, which he expects. Trial would be stupid for him since he was arrested on scene and they have evidence."

Casey didn't like telling it again either, but every day she felt a little stronger, every repetition of the words rendering them a little less powerful. The first three nights she woke in a cold sweat, never remembering what she'd been dreaming about, but the racing of heart told her exactly what, or who, was still chasing her. Dylan had showed up on her doorstep roughly three minutes after her parents had dropped her off that first day, duffel bag in hand and a resolute expression on his face.

The first few nights it had been nice knowing he was just out in the family room, sprawled on the couch, but after a week she was ready to start getting back to whatever her normal was. She had to know that she could sleep with no one in the next room, that she could flip the lock behind her and leave it unchecked for the rest of the night.

What this new normal looked like was still unknown, but it definitely didn't include Jake, that much was obvious. Not one sign of him all week. No calls, no texts, no tap from his side of the wall, some Morse code that she could interpret as 'I'm miserable without you'. If she hadn't heard the occasional rumble of his truck, she would have seriously considered that he'd stayed away from his own home for seven days just to avoid her. To be fair, she could have gone to him, but she didn't know what to say.

And what chafed more than anything was the way her family had been treating her since it happened. If she cut through the concerned hovering, the unceasing phone calls, the random stops and the weighted looks was the fact that they all fully expected her to crack. And they all wanted to be the one to put her together when it happened, because never had she needed to do it for herself.

"Honey, I'll listen to it a million times if it helps you," her Mom's voice wavered just a little and Casey sagged against the fridge, pounding her head backwards against the stainless steel.

"I know," she said. And she got it, really. Her family felt helpless and didn't really know what to do for her. Officer Spencer had given her the name of a counselor to talk to, and she'd gripped the card in her hand that morning, not quite able to punch in the numbers on her phone. She'd Googled some recovery stuff earlier and intended on leaving it at that. Maybe. "Honestly Mom, I think getting back to my routine will help.

Going back to work felt really good. I practically had to shove Dylan's car out into the street to get him to leave, but I *needed* to have my home back, you know?"

"Casey-"

"I *know*, Mom. I'm not saying I didn't appreciate him staying here, but you have to admit he was probably here as much to make himself feel better because he can't beat the ever-loving snot out of 'he who shall not be named'."

She let out a small laugh and Casey could hear her Dad rumbling something in the background. "You're probably right. And I'm proud of you, for wanting to get back on your feet, going back to work right away. Just make sure you're not pushing yourself."

"Yeah." She toyed with the drawstring of her gray fleece pants. "But maybe that's what I need to do. Push myself."

"Oh honey," she murmured. "This is about Jake, isn't it?"

"Is he right? You didn't say much when I told you about our fight."

Silence, and then the deep draw of breath. A sure sign Casey might not like this.

"He's not wrong, but he's not right either."

"Well, thanks for clearing that up."

"He's right that you've had a good life, a blessed life. You have a lot of people who love you and will be there for you no matter what. And other than losing your grandparents, death has not been something that you've had to deal with. It's different for him. Part of that was his choice, in becoming a soldier he knew it would be around him, but losing his parents, having no siblings, those things were out of his control. I'm sad for him that he doesn't have anyone, as are you. And while I don't think it's fair for him to punish you for the fact that you haven't experienced the same things as him, he's not wrong that you haven't had to see the uglier sides of the world like he has."

"So I am naive." She bit down on her lip, digging her teeth in to dull the prick of tears that sprang up.

"No." Her Mom's voice was firm. "Not naive. You have always been my optimist, always seeing the best in people. It's one of the things I love most about you."

"I sense a 'but' coming."

"*But*, we weren't as tough on you as we were on your brothers."

She walked in the family room, sinking into the couch and curling her legs under her, everything about the conversation making her feel tired and sad and exposed. "Okay, so I'm not naive, just spoiled and happily clueless about it." Her voice was sharper than she intended.

"Don't put words in my mouth, Casey Marie. No one said you were clueless." It was an odd relief to hear her Mom take on the flinty edge of annoyance. It made her feel less like she was made of glass.

Casey opened her mouth to reply, but heard a car door in the driveway. She stood up and looked out the front window, seeing the back end of Tate's black BMW. "Oh, for crying out loud."

"What is it?"

"Brother number three, here to check in. I'll call you back. Or actually, you'll probably call me as soon as he leaves because you guys must have some freaky eye-in-the-sky thing that notifies you the second I'm by myself. And don't even bother, because Rachel and Liz said they might stop by later. Love you."

She quickly hung up before her Mom could argue with her and she reached the door at the same time that Tate did. Somehow, she kept in the groan when she saw the brown leather duffel bag slung over his shoulder, dark and worn looking against his crisply pressed blue oxford shirt.

She sighed and moved to let him in. "Why is that every time I see a brother carrying one of those bags I get the distinct impression that my house is about to be invaded?" She expected him to laugh, or at least smile, but his lips were tight and his eyes tired looking. "What's wrong?"

He tossed his keys into the bowl on her kitchen counter and set his bag down, sitting heavily in one of her dining room chairs. "Sorry to barge in on you like this. Dylan told me you forced him to go back to his place, so I knew you'd have a couch free, and I don't really feel like staying at Mom and Dad's." He scrubbed a hand down his face and kept it over his mouth for a few seconds. He dropped it into his lap and watched her with an eyebrow raised. "Aren't you going to ask?"

She shrugged, taking in the weariness that hung on him. It had to be something with Natalie, she couldn't think of another reason he'd need a place to stay. "Last week I probably would have pried it out of you whether you wanted to tell me or not, but trust me, I'll be the last one to force you to talk about it."

He nodded, giving her a sad smile. "You doing okay?"

"I'm getting there. And while I *was* looking forward to having the place to myself, you're more than welcome to stay. I have a feeling you're a tidier roommate than Dylan is."

He laughed, ruffling her hair as he went to put his bag into her spare bedroom. Maybe, just maybe, she should consider actually putting a bed into it. "Thanks Tuck, you're the best."

"Yeah, tell me about it," she said, smoothing her hair back down and then sending a text to Rachel and Liz.

Tate is here to stay for a few days, but you're still welcome to come hang.

Her phone dinged back almost immediately from Rachel.

I'm already in comfies and have had three glasses of wine because my boss is demon spawn. Tell Tate he's not allowed to judge me if he's going to intrude on a girls night. Again.

She laughed, and the sound still felt rusty and unused. When Tate came back into the kitchen, she relayed the message to Tate.

Adopting a grave expression, he laid his hand over his heart. "I do solemnly swear, no judgment."

The girls arrived about an hour later, after she and Tate had finished eating dinner and she had managed not to completely recant her statement about not forcing him to talk about why he needed a place to stay. When she told him that, she didn't think he'd *actually* keep his mouth shut about it. She was pulling out some folded blankets for him when Liz and Rachel walked through the door.

"In case anyone is wondering, Liz wins the slowest driver of the year award." Rachel called out and immediately started rooting through Casey's fridge.

"It's called abiding by the speed limit, Red. You should try it sometime."

She scoffed, pulling out two already open bottles of wine in the door. "My car doesn't know how to go slow. And you started braking as soon as the light turned yellow, you almost caused a four car accident."

"Really?" Casey asked when she came into the kitchen.

"No, not really," Liz answered, and turned to give Casey a light squeeze. "How has your day been?"

"Good, met with the DA, had another random brother show up, but it was still better than hers apparently." They both watched while Rachel tipped one of the bottles completely upside down, emptying it into a large drinking glass. "You know, I do have wine glasses."

"Eh, this will save me a trip into the kitchen. Once I sit on that couch, I fully intend on not moving for the rest of the night. Where's the assassin of all things fun?"

Casey snorted and then clapped a hand over her mouth when Tate walked into the room. He'd changed into a faded t-shirt proclaiming his alma mater, Valparaiso, and some worn jeans. At least he looked amused, a welcome change from earlier.

"Really, Rachel, no thanks necessary for rescuing you in all your drunken glory. Not that I didn't enjoy the show, of course."

Rachel gave a haughty sniff and took a long sip of the wine, her eyes not moving from him. "You're violating my no judgment mandate. Doesn't that make you break out in hives to not follow the rules?"

"Only on weekdays."

"Funny. So, what's the deal? Somebody unclip your leash for the night?"

"Rachel," Casey whispered, smacking her on the arm.

The cup holding her wine sloshed forward but she righted it before anything spilled over. "Woah, easy Killer. I'm just asking. You Steadmans sure are a sensitive bunch."

Casey cut her gaze over to Tate, where he watched Rachel with narrowed, considering eyes. He pursed his lips and Casey held her breath. Holy mother of Mary she wanted to know so, so bad.

"So?" Rachel asked again, one eyebrow steeped high in challenge. He sat down in the chair closest to him, and then looked over at Casey, his face somber again.

"It's up to you, Case. If you want to know, I'll talk. But it might upset you, and I really don't want to add anything to what you're already dealing with."

"Tate, that's very sweet, but trust me, hearing someone else's drama sounds pretty good to me right now. And unless you plan on telling me that you just eloped, I don't think it'll ruin my night."

Rachel snorted into her cup, and Liz delicately cleared her throat.

"I broke up with Natalie."

"What?" Her head raced to wrap around that tidbit, and she *barely* resisted the urge to pump her fist in the air. "What happened?"

"She must have done something reeeeeally bad," Rachel said, eyes wide in her face.

"Are you okay?" Liz asked, sliding a hand over to Tate's arm.

He watched all three of them, his expression hovering somewhere between humor and disbelief. "I'm fine, thank you, Liz." He propped his elbows on the table and sank his head into his hands. All three of them just waited. And waited. And then waited some more.

Casey held her hands up. "Hello? What was it?"

He lifted his head and sighed. "I overheard her on the phone with her Mom."

"Okaaaay, and what'd she say?" Rachel prompted. "Use your *words*, Tate."

"She was talking about you, Casey. About what happened to you."

She swallowed. "Why do I get the feeling I don't want to hear this."

"Because you probably don't." He shook his head. "I almost wish I hadn't."

Rachel whirled into the kitchen, grabbed the other bottle of wine and set it in front of Tate with a thunk. "Here. Take a few swigs of this. Because if you need to drink in order to tell this story, then I will help you. I want to hear it."

"The short version?" He let out a short laugh, then shrugged and tipped the bottle back to his lips. He grimaced as he swallowed. "She told her Mom that you deserved what happened to you."

Casey's eyes pricked and everything stilled in the kitchen, the only sound was Liz's quick inhalation.

"Excuse me?" Rachel's voice was low, dangerous.

"Does that answer your question, Rachel? Because yes, it was really bad. And I can't forgive her." He folded his hands together in front of him on the table, staring at where his fingers gripped at each other. His broad shoulders slumped, and it lit a momentary spark of anger within Casey, seeing him so defeated by it. By Natalie.

"Wow." Casey rubbed a hand over her mouth, struggling to sift through her racing thoughts. "I knew she didn't like me, but...wow. That's, uh..." The first and most prevalent thought was that Natalie was a class A bitch. Second was mind-numbing relief that Tate actually left her. The third was just a low, persistent buzz underneath the other two, but she couldn't swat it away.

What if she's right?

Even thinking it once, letting it bolt to the forefront, was enough to make her clamp down on her lip to the point that she tasted blood. *What if she's right?*

"I'm sorry, Case." Tate's voice sounded so heavy.

She simply nodded, filtering through every encounter with Steve. The escalating creepiness, the way he stared, the anger and disbelief that she wouldn't go out with him. All of it screamed at her now, so glaringly obvious that something about him was off. And she missed it. She didn't, couldn't, or wouldn't see what was right in front of her.

Just like Jake. He'd never promised her anything, not even the tiniest hint of a promise, and she'd been blindsided by that too. The only difference was that she'd allowed Jake to bruise her somewhere that she couldn't hide it.

"I can't believe she said that," Liz said, rubbing her arms like she was cold.

"Gimme your keys, Liz." Rachel held out her hand.

Liz pulled her eyebrows together, looking over at Casey and Tate like they could explain it to her. Tate shrugged. Casey stared at some random point in her table, not answering, but kinda glad that none of them seemed to notice the nuclear bomb level melt-down happening inside of her.

"Why do you want them?" Liz asked.

Rachel gaped, hazel eyes all but spitting fire. "Why do you think? Tate can't hit her, because he's a guy, but I can. I can rip every shiny little hair out of her tiny little head. And I will. Glad-ly." She breathed through clenched teeth, snapping back at Tate when he predictably told her that wasn't going to happen. Their voices hummed around Casey, muffled by everything in her head.

What if she's right?

What then?

"Stop," she whispered, in no way slowing the volley between Rachel and Tate. Rachel was inches from his face, poking a finger in his chest. They flung words back and forth with barely a beat in between each one. Casey pushed a breath under her diaphragm and said it again, louder, stronger. "Stop. Both of you."

Liz sagged in relief, as always, hating the role of referee. Rachel crossed her arms and muttered an apology to Tate, who nodded.

"Tate, would you mind reading or something in my room? So I can have some girl time?" She bit down on the inside of her cheek to keep herself steady when pain flashed across his face.

"Are you mad at me, for telling you?" he asked, coming to stand in front of her.

"Of course not." She hugged him tightly, shaking her head into his chest, willing herself to hold it together. "You left her, because of me. How could I be mad at you?"

It was true, she wasn't mad at him. She was mad at Natalie, at Steve, at Jake. At herself.

He gave her a small smile, and tugged a piece of her hair. Before he disappeared down the hallway, he turned and gave Rachel one last assessing look, which was studiously ignored. When her door clicked shut, Casey sagged onto the arm of her couch.

"Well," Rachel said. "Leave it to Natalie to ruin a perfectly good evening where the worst thing we had to talk about was my job."

"Are you okay?" Liz asked, coming to sit next to her. "Geez, I have had to ask that way too much tonight."

Casey blinked rapidly, having a much harder time stemming the rising tide of tears now that Tate had left the room. One slipped through, then a second. She pressed a hand under her eye to stop the rest.

"Oh Casey," Liz breathed, wrapping slim arms around her.

"I didn't--" she hiccuped. "I didn't want him to see me do this. He'd never forgive himself."

"So what are we crying about, exactly?" Rachel asked, sitting on the coffee table so she could face them.

"We?" Casey sniffed back another tear. "*We* are not crying. I am crying. And seriously, I am so sick of it."

"Okay fine, what are *you* crying about exactly?"

"It's stupid."

Liz reached up and wiped another one that fell, speaking softly, firmly. "Nothing you feel right now is stupid, and not talking about it isn't going to help."

Just thinking it had sent her in a tailspin. It felt like speaking it out loud would give it even more power. She stood, brushing past Rachel's legs and then fell heavily into the couch cushions. Liz joined her, looking much more graceful than Casey as she sat. Casey bounced her legs, unable to ignore the concerned looks that her two friends aimed at her. She wanted to laugh it off, to give it an easy dismissal because it was just Natalie, the bitchiest bitch that ever drew breath. Simply cast it aside because of who said it.

Easy. She opened her mouth, then closed it again.

"Is it contagious tonight?" Rachel asked. "This whole not talking thing? It's us, Casey. Just tell us, quick, right now, just take a breath and spit it out."

Take a breath and spit it out. She held the air in her lungs for a second, looking at both of them, then let it out.

"What if she's right? What if Jake is right? It's like I'm having the most horrible mirror in the world strapped in front of my face and I can't pull it down no matter what I do." The words left her in a rush, no more than whisper, but her throat still felt raw.

For an indeterminable amount of time, they looked at her. It felt like hours, was probably only seconds.

Rachel set her glass down on the coffee table and gestured to

Liz like *I've got this one.* She scooted forward, perched on the edge
the mahogany table, knees touching Casey's. She rolled her lips
inward. Casey couldn't help but smile a little.

"Rachel Hennessy, speechless?"

"Cut me some slack, okay? This is one of those really big
friend moments that I don't want to completely screw up with my
big mouth."

Casey nodded, feeling a little unbalanced at seeing Rachel
like this. "Maybe if you did, I'd feel more normal right now."

"Seriously?" She looked dubious.

"Please," Casey said.

Liz groaned. "I don't know, I don't think Rachel unfiltered is
necessarily the best choice right now."

"I do. Everyone has been tiptoeing around me, all week. Even
right now, just having this discussion is driving me crazy because
normally you guys would never question how to talk to me. I feel
like I'm about to split out of my skin, so please, normal is good."

Rachel set her jaw. "Fantastic, because the first thing that
came into my head is that you just seriously pissed me off. I've
known you for over fifteen years, Casey, and I have no flippin'
clue who this girl is in front of me. You're going to look me in the
eye and ask us if Natalie is *right*? That you deserved to be
attacked? What kind of bullshit is that?"

Liz slapped a hand over her forehead. "Subtle, Rachel."

"Hey, if she wanted subtle, she should have asked you."

Casey felt the prickle of raised hairs at the back of her neck,
defensiveness sweeping through her. "Can you honestly blame
me for feeling a little unsure right now?"

"Unsure? No, I expect that. But you have straight up lost your
mind if you spend one second thinking her skinny ass is right.
She doesn't know you, she never has. You were *attacked*, Casey, by
someone who has multiple, big ol' screws loose in his head. What
about *that* makes you wonder if she's right?"

Casey slicked her tongue across the front of her teeth,

shrinking back in the couch. "I changed my mind. You do have a big mouth that ruins everything."

Rachel shrugged a shoulder, completely un-fazed. "Don't want to prove me wrong? Fine. I'll ask away then. Were you flashing him your cleavage? Flaunting a little leg? Begging him to hit you?"

"Of course not," she replied, tempered annoyance easily replacing the defensive feeling.

"And what did you do when he finally got to you?" Her voice was quieter now, face serious. Liz was perfectly still sitting next to her, the only movement between the three of them was Casey's fingers drumming on her leg.

"I--" she faltered, mind racing again, trying to figure out where Rachel was going with this. "I fought him."

"Because he didn't listen to you when you asked him to stop, right?"

"Obviously."

"You couldn't control what he did, so you made a choice to fight back."

She closed her eyes, smoothed her hands across the soft material of her pants. "Yes."

"You would never say that they deserved it, someone who went through what you just did. Because you understand that you and Steve both made choices that day. His put him in jail, and yours saved you. You see that, don't you?"

"Sometimes," she whispered.

"Natalie is an uppity bitch who needs her stilettos removed from her own ass, okay? You've never put any weight in what she said before, so why on earth would you start now?" Rachel asked.

Casey dug her fingers into her scalp, trying to keep from screaming. "Because in a matter of twenty four hours I went from laying in Jake's arms and doing everything I could to hold myself back from shouting that I was falling in love with him to being escorted into a police cruiser, my body and my heart completely bruised, and he wouldn't even look at me when I left. I was wrong about him, you guys, so wrong. And yeah, normally I could care less what someone like Natalie thinks about me. But if I was that wrong about Jake, so freaking blind about how he views me, what else did I not see?"

Rachel sighed, taking a slow sip of her wine. "So you're the baby of the family. Who cares? I'd wager a guess that if you polled a hundred families like yours, that youngest girl is gonna be a little spoiled. And Jake knew that before he ever went out with you. You were yourself with him, right?"

Casey huffed out a laugh, one that was just shy of sounding bitter. "More than I ever have been with any other guy. And look where it got me."

"I don't think that's really what he thinks of you," Liz interjected. "He felt something for you, it was so obvious. And a man like Jake wouldn't waste his time with somebody that he thought was frivolous. He would only do it because it meant something to him. *You* meant something to him."

Casey considered that, and the tiny sliver of hope that lit up felt an awful lot like panic. She shook her head. "I can't know that for sure. Jake is the definition of strong silent type, whatever he felt was locked down tighter than the flippin' White House. I just can't let myself wonder about that right now, it'll drive me insane."

Liz hummed, a small smile covering her face. "'If I could but know his heart, everything would become easy.'"

Rachel grinned. "Man, you made it almost two hours without throwing in an Austen quote. Could be a record, Blondie."

"Which one is that from?" Casey asked.

"Sense and Sensibility. You remind me a little bit of Marianne. She was so passionate, so desirous of love."

"Case, you're telling us you're in love with Jake, right?" Rachel asked.

She nodded, the lump growing in her throat again and she swallowed around it. "Yeah."

"So show him," Liz said, excitement making her blue eyes glow. "You can prove to everyone that you know how to fight for yourself, but show Jake that you're willing to fight for him too."

Another tear or two slipped out, happy and overwhelmed rather than desperate, and she made no move to wipe them away. Had he ever had anyone fight for him, for his happiness? He probably hadn't. And she wanted to, and would, as soon as she finished fighting for herself too.

She smiled at Rachel and Liz, it was watery and more than little wobbly. "You guys are really good at this."

"No shit, Sherlock," Rachel deadpanned. She leaned forward, scrubbing her hands together. "Now let's figure out how to get you your man."

23

JAKE TOOK one last sweep through the finished unit, running his hand along the granite countertop that reflected the under cabinet lighting he'd decided to install last minute. He'd ignored this unit until a few days ago. He needed the mindless release that could only be found in demolition, so he'd gotten an early start on the other two yet to be started units. Swinging a sledge hammer and ripping off trim that didn't actually need to be replaced had left him sweaty, spent and still just as defeated as he'd felt for the last two weeks. He felt like he didn't have the patience for the rest of the finish work in the unit that was closest to being rented. He knew he needed to get someone moved in, but that was just his head talking.

Everything else about him couldn't give two shits. All he could do, all he could think about, obsess about, beat himself up about, feel like ripping his skin off about was Casey. No matter what he'd seen in his life, any horrors in Iraq and Afghanistan couldn't replace the memory in his head of her face.

He'd never understood the phrase 'broken hearted' until he saw her huddled against the black of his truck, looking defeated, terrified and worst of all, unsure of him. Everything inside of him cracked and bled when he fully realized his part in what happened to her. And then her silence afterward had wrenched him wide open.

And most days he felt like he deserved it. But what he couldn't reconcile, no matter how much damage he did to walls and floors and counters, was how much he missed her. He'd pushed her away, so damned effectively, and now he was paying the price. Everything around him seemed hushed and lifeless without her. And the fact that he was thinking words like hushed and lifeless is how he knew how bad he had it.

It sucked.

Even Remy seemed depressed. Whining at the door after Jake had taken him along on a four mile run. Curling up on a sweatshirt on the floor that had last been worn by Casey. Jake knew it smelled like her, because when he found it stuck in between his sheets when he stripped them off the bed, he may have pulled in the faint smell of oranges when he pressed the soft cotton against his face. Immediately disgusted with the level of abject pathetic-ness he was capable of when it came to her, he'd chucked it on the floor, not quite ready to wash out its scent, and definitely not ready to bring it to her door. Obviously she didn't want to see him. And he couldn't blame her in the slightest. He still couldn't meet his own eyes in the bathroom mirror, because looking back at him was a man that felt so damn guilty about how he'd screwed it up with the first woman to really make him hope for more. With a woman that was so good, who deserved that *more* - more than anyone he'd ever met.

Dylan's car had been there for the first week, and a sleek sedan he'd seen parked at the Steadman's for the Labor Day picnic had been there for the week after. He didn't know who in her family it belonged to, but he couldn't decide between relief that she had someone there or overwhelming guilt that she felt the need to have someone with her every night. Guilt that he couldn't be that person.

Even though he wanted to be.

Even though he shouldn't.

Hell, he'd never felt more schizophrenic in his life than he had the last thirteen days.

He shook his head and focused on the last few touches in the unit that Casey had done sometime in the last two days. She must have used the spare key he gave her over a month ago, because when he walked in today, there were homey touches that he definitely would never have thought of, a tall woven vase filled with bright green grass in the corner of the dining room, colorful artwork hung on non-permanent hooks on the walls, and a few patterned chairs surrounding a low coffee table in the living room. Only a small plaque on a side table made any mention of the pieces being from Hearth and Home. She'd earned her rent discount, that was for sure, because the place looked much better than he'd anticipated.

It actually looked like a home. He skimmed a finger down the seam of one of the panels of wallpaper she'd hung, feeling a ridiculous tightening thinking about their first kiss. Everything she'd done within those walls had made it look comfortable and happy, inviting. Warm.

Frick. It was just like her.

Realizing that the placed looked perfect without him doing a thing, he locked the door behind him and stopped up short when he saw both Dylan and Tate standing in the driveway by Casey's back door. He pulled in a deep breath, and prepared himself for whatever they might throw at him. They turned at the same time to watch him approach. Tate gave him a small smile, but Dylan just crossed his arms in front of him and gave nothing away in his facial expression.

"Hey guys," he started, holding out his hand to Tate, knowing an ally when he saw one. Tate clasped his hand quickly, eyes darting over to Dylan when he didn't reciprocate Jake's greeting.

Dylan received an elbow in the side, and finally managed a grunt that might pass for a hello in civilized society.

But it wasn't a fist to the face, so he decided he could accept that.

"How's she doing?"

Dylan's eyes narrowed to slits, the exact same shade as Casey's, and it almost made Jake need to break eye contact, but he held her brother's gaze, even when he opened his mouth for his first jab. "Does that mean you actually give a shit?"

"Dylan," Tate said on a sigh. "Back off. This isn't easy on anyone."

Jake rubbed the back of his neck. "No, he has every right to ask. I'm not going to tell you anything that I should be saying to Casey first, but yes, I care. I just don't want to push her to talk to me if she's not ready."

The brothers looked at each other for a moment, then Dylan rolled his eyes and leaned back against his car, apparently conceding the round.

"She's getting better. Acted like she didn't need any help at first, but uh, she's really working hard to get herself back on track. Saw a counselor a couple times this week."

Jake nodded, trying to figure out if that made him feel better or worse. He knew enough about PTSD that a common response was to disconnect yourself from your support system, not wanting to talk about what happened to you, and seeing a counselor was a huge sign that she was taking this as seriously as she should.

Tate gave him a few details about what was happening with Steve's court case, and he breathed a sigh of relief knowing the guy would do a decent amount of jail time.

"She could've used you around, and it pisses me off that you weren't, Jake," Dylan finally spoke again once the other two had lapsed into a moment of silence.

"Believe me when I say there's nothing you can say that will make me feel worse."

"No?" he asked, eyebrows raised. "Might be fun for me to try though."

Tate scratched at his jaw, looking at the ground, but didn't say anything. Jake spread his hands out, facing Dylan fully. "Go ahead. Seriously. You want to take a swing at me, I'll let you have one. You want to chew my ass? Feel free."

Dylan shrugged a shoulder. "Well, if you're just gonna lay down and take it, it's not nearly as enjoyable."

Jake caught Tate trying not to smile, and it eased a little bit of tension.

"Look," Dylan said. "I know what you said to her before it happened."

"This the part where you try to break my jaw?" He might prefer that, actually.

"Dude, if you think I'm stupid enough to try and get into a fist fight with a former Army Ranger, then we'll have other problems besides my sister."

"I think you might be stupid enough," Tate interjected. "And I will not help you if it comes to that."

"Gee thanks," Dylan said dryly, then looked at Jake again, face hardening. "You want to know what part this is? This is the part where you tell us if you meant it, or if you just had a spectacular case of male PMS and don't know how to cop to it. We've seen her cry a lot in the last two weeks, and let's just say that shit-head behind bars hasn't been the only cause. Half the time I think you made her doubt herself more than he did. So *that's* what part this is, where you get to make me not want to break my knuckles on your pretty ass face."

Tate stayed silent, letting every barb fall out of Dylan's mouth uninhibited.

Jake set his hands on his hips, breathing out heavily, trying to tamp down the actual, visceral pain in his gut hearing the effect his panic-induced words had on her. He shook his head a few times and stared into a crack that threaded the driveway between where they stood facing each other. Literally and metaphorically they had a divide between them.

"As much as I want to tell you all the things that will give me the brother stamp of approval, I'm not a kiss ass. And I meant it earlier when I said I don't plan on saying things to you when I should be saying them to Casey first." Dylan opened his mouth to say something and Jake held up a hand to stop him. "I'll tell you this much, I wish to God I could take back what I said to her, and even more, I wish I'd never listened to her and let her stay behind. I may never forgive myself for that. But the fact is, I still think she's probably better off without me."

Jake's voice tapered off at the end of the sentence, and he mentally kicked his own ass to Lake Michigan and back at how telling that must be.

Not that he didn't want her, or miss her.

The silence stretched between them, and when Jake was about to start filling it with something, anything, Tate cleared his throat.

"I had just turned six when Casey was born, and I remember every single thing about that day. Dad called the house that morning to tell us, and Grandma let us crowd around the phone so we could hear him. His voice cracked when he said 'You have a sister, boys, and she's perfect'. I'd never seen my Dad cry, and I remember thinking that she must be a pretty big deal if she got him to do it." Jake smiled a little, thinking that Casey would probably love hearing that. "And holding her for the first time? She was so tiny. I knew I would do anything for her, to keep her safe, to keep her happy. And that's how all of us felt, from day one. And all of us, at some point, have failed her in that."

Ah, there it was. The requisite 'you shouldn't feel guilty' talk. He'd been there, done that, over and over and over in his head the past two weeks.

"Don't let me off the hook, Tate," he said gruffly. "I could've done something different."

"Hell yeah, you could've," Dylan added, clearly not ready to be in the forgiving brother mode just yet. His approach actually made Jake feel more comfortable. The threat of physical punishment made his muscles hum, maybe letting Dylan land a few punches would ease the guilt roiling through him.

But Tate gave his little brother a hard look, essentially telling him to shut the hell up, which Dylan surprisingly did. "I figured you'd seen enough bad in your life to know better than that, Jake."

Logic was a bitch. Especially when someone else slapped you with it. So many faces and moments and decisions, both in and out of war zones, flashed through his mind. And still, none of them pierced him the way Casey's face had, still the most beautiful thing he'd ever seen, dirty and disheveled and bruised. Jake looked up warily. "You're right. But I'm not gonna pretend that it's not different with her."

"Good," Tate said. "It should be different with her. She deserves that."

She did. And maybe Jake could let himself slip into a place where he deserved her back.

Dylan pushed off of Tate's car, slapping Jake on the shoulder. "I'm so thrilled that Tate could make this brotherly conversation as violence-free as possible, more for my sake than yours. But seriously, don't dick this up with my sister. I don't want to have to pretend threaten you again."

Jake laughed a little, especially because he and Dylan were matched in height, even though it looked like Jake had close to fifty pounds of muscle on him. But he bet that Dylan could fight dirty if necessary, and probably had on occasion.

Jake could still wipe the floor with him and then dispose of the body in about a hundred different ways, but he didn't think now was the moment to bring that up.

"Listen guys, I have drill this weekend, and I'd appreciate if I could hand Remy over to you now."

"You scared to face my little sister?" Dylan asked.

Jake blew out a breath, scraping a hand across his jaw. "I'll deny it if you ever told her, but yeah, I know I have to get this one right. Don't know if I'll quite be there in the next couple hours before I leave."

Tate nodded in approval. "I'll come with you and get him. I was hoping to talk to you about something else."

They said goodbye to Dylan, and then walked to Jake's door. "What'd you need to talk to me about?"

"A place to live actually. I'm wondering if you'd consider a six month lease on the unit you just finished."

Jake looked over in surprise, the unasked question written all over his face when Tate just sighed.

"I'll pay you an extra hundred a month for the shorter lease, and to not have to tell the story again. I want to buy a house, I'm just not ready to rush into anything right now."

Jake nodded, thinking it over while he bent over to greet Remy and start gathering the items he'd need for the weekend. One thing kept snagging on his thoughts as he went over the pros and cons. One tall, gorgeous, currently-not-speaking-to-him thing. "Does she know you're asking me?"

Tate grinned. "Oh man, you're totally scared of her. But yes, she does."

Jake made a noise in response. Tate leaned one hip against the kitchen counter.

"She really is doing well, Jake, I'm not just saying that to make you feel better."

"Believe me, I'm not under any impression that you'd say something just to make me feel better."

Tate laughed. "True. She asked me to help her make a budget a couple days ago. I tell you what, watching her count out her cash for her spending money for the next two weeks was as much entertainment as I've had in the last year."

Jake faced him, one brow raised. "She's going to operate cash only?"

"Oh yeah, she made me cut up all but one credit card for emergencies. I had to explain to her the difference between an actual emergency and a shoe emergency, which she didn't appreciate, but she's really serious about making some changes."

Jake sank back in a chair by his kitchen table, hands resting heavily on his knees while he processed that. "Wow."

"Pretty much. I'm proud of her. The last time I tried to talk to her about a budget, savings, and God forbid, a 401k, she told me she was on the Carrie Bradshaw investment plan, keeping all her money in her closet where she can see it. Man, it was the first time in my adult life I almost cried. And while I may not agree with your method of delivery, what you said to her lit a fire under ass in a really good way. None of us have ever been able to do it, I can tell you that much."

It stuck in Jake's throat a little bit, and he tried unsuccessfully to swallow past it, feeling like he was getting any sort of credit for positive changes she might be making. And not in a good way. It felt tight and uncomfortable, itching under his skin.

Tate rolled his eyes. "Just telling you that some good came out of it. No need to get all twitchy."

He stood and chucked the bag of dog food at Tate's chest, which he caught with an *oomph,* Jake just scowled and motioned for Remy to follow them out the door. "That any way to talk to your new landlord?"

Tate just laughed, but thanked him when Jake turned to go back home.

"I'll bring the paperwork by when I pick up Remy on Sunday. You think you'll be around?"

Okay, so it was a not so subtle way of asking if Casey would be there when he picked up his dog, and just thinking of facing her lit him up inside with a terrifying mix of anticipation, dread, and longing.

Tate smiled, seeing right through him. "I'm not sure. Tell you what? I'll give you my number, and if I'm not going to be here, I'll let you know."

Jake should just tell him to label his number as 'Chickenshit Miller'. He wasn't afraid of Casey, not really. But after these last two weeks, and the hell his mind and frick, his heart, had been through, he was definitely man enough to admit that he was completely and utterly afraid of what he might do when he finally saw her again.

24

SOMETIMES A WOMAN NEEDS to sit back and let her man fight his way back into her good graces, desperate and pleading and saying those three perfect, life changing words before she can say them herself. *And sometimes,* Casey mused, *you find yourself shivering on your man's front step waiting for him to get home because you don't want to give him a chance to run scared.*

And whether Jake knew it or not, he was still her man.

She never knew it was possible to completely change your outlook on your own life in such a short amount of time.

Sixteen days to be exact.

Working through what had happened to her with her counselor had been equal parts exhausting and liberating. At that moment, she understood the power in telling her story, telling how she fought back. She understood that making mature, future minded changes in your life didn't mean you were immature before.

And okay, it might take sixteen years to get the budget Tate had imposed on her to feel natural, but she'd stuck with it for five whole days so far without one slip-up.

When she had plotted all of this out, she hadn't factored in that it would be the first day to finally feel the icy grip of winter. Dull gray clouds stretched over every part of the sky, and even though there was no snow on the ground yet, the yellowing grass had crunched under feet, still hard from the frost the night before. She pulled her teal wool coat closer around her shoulders and buried her nose in the dark gray scarf she had looped around her neck. Her own hot breath warmed her cheeks even as the cold cement step beneath her seared through her jeans.

Oh sure, she could have waited inside until he pulled into the driveway. But, of the many things she could manage to do and still look graceful, sprinting across the front yard to barricade herself outside his door was not one of those things. Nope, she wanted the statement of her camped outside his door, waiting for his return.

Because she would. Wait for him.

She bounced her leg up and down, then checked the time on her phone again, wondering where the heck he was. He was usually home by now. She sucked in a breath through clenched teeth, hoping to soothe the anxious fluttering in her stomach. She heard a long, melancholy howl come from the general direction of her family room window and rolled her eyes. Remy acted like she committed high treason now if she didn't let him follow her every waking move. She grinned though, because he'd actually been her favorite house guest in the last couple weeks. He didn't hog the hot water like Dylan, didn't nitpick like a bored housewife over things she left strewn around her house like Tate.

The crunch of tire over loose gravel snapped her head up out of her scarf, and she swallowed down the sudden flurry of nerves that leapt up her throat. Suddenly she realized a potentially fatal flaw in her brilliant plan. Maybe not *fatal*. If he didn't see her sitting by his front door, he might park his truck and go straight to her place, ruining the entire visual impact she had so skillfully figured out. She bit down on her lip, watching the shiny black truck take the curve past the now skeletal branches of the lilac bushes.

"Please see me, please see me," she whispered under her breath. And then she saw it, the sudden jerk of his head towards her and the answering halt of the truck. She exhaled slowly and stood, wiping her perfectly clean hands together, then tucked them into her deep coat pockets. Jake took a few seconds in his truck, probably gathering his thoughts the same way that she was. He leaned down to get something off the passenger side floor and then pulled himself through the open door.

When he rounded the front of his truck, her heart did a decidedly ungraceful *thu-thump* when she saw him gripping a handful of bright pink tulips wrapped in generic green cellophane, looking bright and hopeful and completely incongruous with the rest of him. She kept staring at those tightly closed buds as he walked closer, then to the determined expression in his dark eyes, and every single word she had practiced dried up in her throat.

"Melinda got fired," she blurted out, then pinched her eyes shut in sheer mortification. He stopped a few feet away from where she still stood one step above him looking about as confused as she felt.

"Okay," he said slowly. Oh, just one syllable of his voice after so long felt like heaven. "What happened?"

Casey cleared her throat, aiming for delicate and lady like, but it ended up sounding horrifyingly loud in the silence around them. "I brought in the real estate agent that I had spoken to about my idea a couple weeks before she hijacked my binder. And umm, Tate worked his magic on my laptop, so I brought that in and showed Tom that the file had originated there. So Tom fired her and then gave me a raise. And I'm sure if I was a better person I would've felt horrible, but it was kinda awesome."

Jake rubbed the back of his neck with the hand not holding

the flowers, one side of his mouth almost lifting in a smile. "Good for you. I'm proud of you, Casey."

She bit down on her lip, attempting to cap every churning emotion that threatened to spill out at those words so casually spoken. "Really?"

He closed his eyes for a moment, then took another step closer to her. Moving closer? Good. Closing the eyes and not responding? Bad. Before he spoke, he looked down at the flowers, then back up at her. "Let's go inside, you must be cold."

Inviting her inside? Good.

She stepped to the side so he could unlock the door, and she walked inside in front of him when he gestured for her to do so. She quickly removed her coat and draped it over one of chairs, straightening the collar of her black off-the-shoulder sweater. She subtly inhaled the Jake-scented air around her while he flicked on a couple lights.

"Do you want to sit?"

"Are those flowers for me?" Oops. Her brain had sent the signal to say 'Why yes, I'd love to sit next to you on your functional, albeit boring, khaki colored couch'. Thankfully, his mouth curved up, and he nodded.

"Yeah. Stockton informed me that bringing a woman flowers is the best foundation for any conversation."

He'd talked to Stockton about her. For some reason, the thought of Jake confiding in a friend about their relationship made her heart squeeze as much as the flowers did.

She took the bouquet from him when he held it out, and relished the way his jaw clenched when their hands brushed in the process. If he felt even close to the charge that she did, she wasn't surprised. The little hairs on her arms all raised in tandem from that one teensy touch. She locked eyes with him, and felt the weight of it press down on her lungs, making it difficult to pull in a full breath.

"They're beautiful," she said, smiling at him. "Tulips are my favorite flower."

"I figured they might be."

"Yeah? Why's that?"

He leaned one shoulder up against the wall, crossing his arms over his chest. He looked at her with an intensity that was almost unsettling, and she squirmed a little, setting the tulips on the counter before she gripped the stems so hard that she snapped them. "You're not a cliche, so I didn't think it would be roses. And you're not simple, so daisies were out. I stood there staring at this cooler full of flowers, and when I saw those, they were you."

"Why?" she asked, voice ridiculously breathy. Maybe it was gauche to ask, but goodness gracious, a girl didn't hear things like this every day.

"Bright, elegant, beautiful, full of hope." Jake said the words easily, like he'd thought about it beforehand. He pushed off the wall, which made him seem closer, but he wasn't. She felt like she was shaking from the effort to stand still. "They're strong too. They can withstand a lot."

She felt a tear drop from her eye before she even realized she was crying. "And you think that's me?"

He stepped closer, using his thumb to brush the wetness from the top of her cheekbone. Her eyes wanted to flutter closed at the contact, but she forced them to stay open, not wanting to miss a second.

"I *know* that's you." He brought his other hand up and cupped the side of her face, then leaned his forehead against hers. She gripped each of his wrists, mainly because she couldn't *not* touch him, but also so she didn't actually fall over. "I'm sorry, Casey. For what I said, for how I said it, for leaving you there, for not coming back for you sooner, and for making you think for one second that you might be less than the incredible woman you are. I am so, so sorry. I feel like I don't even deserve to ask your forgiveness. But I'm going to, because I feel like crawling out of my skin without it. I've never met anyone in my life who deserves a good man more than you. You deserve so much more than I gave you a couple weeks ago, and I should have been here every single day since. I hate myself for thinking that I may have made any part of this worse for you."

She sniffed, and he wiped another errant tear, pulling his face back so he could look at her. The skin around his eyes looked lined, and he had dark circles where there were none before. The flowers and his heartfelt words had distracted her at first, but she saw the exhaustion now. It clung to him in the same way it had to her at first, and it made her want to soothe every inch of him. She smiled at him, trailing her hands from his wrists along his strong forearms to the crook of his elbows and back up again. His skin was warm and his hair was coarse and she relished the feel of both. "Of course I forgive you."

He exhaled heavily, but instead of pulling her in the way she expected him to, he stayed there, holding her face and not looking nearly as relieved as she hoped he would at her forgiveness.

"But I *hurt you*, Casey."

It wasn't a question. And she was glad for that, because she wouldn't have lied to him if it had been, so she simply nodded.

"You did. But, you made me see something that needed to be seen, Jake. I have learned more about myself in the last two weeks than in the previous twenty nine years combined. I still have things I need to work on, things that I can do better, but I don't know if I ever would have gotten started on any of this if it hadn't been for you."

He looked uncomfortable, and went to pull back, but she tightened her hands. "Oh no you don't, you got to make your little flower speech, now it's my turn."

He still dropped his hands, but she turned hers so that their fingers twined together. He stared down at where they were meshed together, then gave her a half smile. "When did you get so bossy?"

She smiled, then pulled him until they reached his couch, which, ugh, was just in desperate need of a few throw pillows. She said as much when she sat down, and his answering unamused stare made her want to do two things; laugh at him and then completely ravage him.

She did neither. "I need to apologize too."

His brows drew together. "For what?"

She traced one finger along the edging of the couch cushion and angled herself toward him more than she already was. "Just hear me out, because I practiced this." She took a deep breath and ignored the way he was trying not to smile. "I knew you probably carried some guilt from what happened to me, because you weren't there, and I didn't reach out to you. Jake, I didn't know what to say to *myself* to let go of the guilt that I felt over it, let alone you. And I never wanted you to shoulder that burden, because I certainly never blamed you. But I knew that if I went to you, for any reason, you would try to fix it. Fix me. And I needed to be able to fix myself. Does that make sense?"

He nodded, eyes tracking over every part of her face. Every single facial feature screamed at her that he'd wanted to interrupt her. That he wanted to argue with her for apologizing, but he hadn't. His intentional silence told her so much. That he would sit and listen as long as she needed him to.

So she talked. She talked about her counselor, she talked about her brothers staying with her, about her family hovering until she thought she might go postal, about her breakdown in the bathroom, about going back to work and how good it made her feel, about waking up that morning and finding Remy sprawled on her bed on top of her feet.

And with every word that came from her, she watched the subtle changes that played over his face. A tiny curve of his lips, a tightening at the hard edge of his jaw, the way his eyes would zero in on her mouth every so often. He took in everything she said, and that knowledge tilted her headfirst past any fear or doubt that she had.

"I'm so in love with you, Jake," she blurted, then clapped a hand over her eyes. The second blurt of the day. Boy, she was just rackin' em up, wasn't she? "Well, that came out differently than I had practiced, but I was actually working up to that, so if you could just-"

He set one finger over her mouth, stemming whatever was going to come out next. "Casey. Take your hand off your face. Please?"

She spread her fingers so she could peek through at him trying to gauge what his facial features would be able to tell her now. Between the slits, he looked a little fuzzy. She knew going into this that she was going to tell him. She also knew that he may not be in love with her. And for right now, she would be just fine if he didn't feel the need to have the words fall from his lips the way they seemed to do from hers. For now.

She slowly drew her hand away. His finger dragged down her mouth, parting her lips, then dipped beneath her chin to tilt her face up. Just that small movement had every nerve ending vibrating with unused tension. And just like that, she wanted to completely consume him. She'd start with those lips, firm and demanding like all the rest of him, and slowly work her way down until she knew what every inch of him tasted like.

He exerted just a hint of pressure where his finger still lingered, pulling her face closer to him until she had to shift her weight onto her knees. Only inches apart, he leaned the rest of the way and placed his lips underneath the curve of her jaw.

"I need you to do something for me." He didn't pull back, so his lips brushed against her overly sensitive skin with every word he spoke and she shivered, sliding her hands forward until they rested on his thighs that rested next to hers. "I haven't touched you in over two weeks, but if any part of this isn't okay with you, I need you to tell me and I'll stop."

Oh. Well hmm, let's think about that for about a half a second.

She pulled her head back and gripped the sides of his face, then sealed her mouth on top of his with a moan. Or maybe he moaned. She couldn't really tell because all the blood in her entire body whooshed through her head in a roar at the feel of him against her. His arms wound around her back, pushing into and around the ends of her hair, gripping her so tightly that she couldn't have pulled in a full breath if she wanted to. And she didn't.

Because if she had to die from oxygen deprivation, kissing Jake was a heckuva way to go.

For a moment, they pushed against each other, her trying to force him backwards and him doing the same. She broke apart from him, laughing breathlessly. He narrowed his eyes, which made her laugh even harder.

"You know, a man might have a problem if his woman laughs at him during a moment of passion."

She stopped laughing then, wondering if he realized what those words did to her. His woman. She traced her hand over the skin around his eyes, lightly lined from time in the sun, across his brow that wrinkled when he got that annoyed look on his face and over his lips that so rarely curved in a full smile. Yup. She loved him.

"And that same man may not be able to keep his hands to himself if that same woman keeps looking at him like that." His voice sounded husky and it made her smile.

"Well, I sure hope he doesn't."

He stood up, readjusted his jeans and cleared his throat, which made her giggle. He quirked an eyebrow, but held a hand out for her. She let him pull her up, and then pushed on her tiptoes to wind her arms around his neck and plant a hot, hard kiss on his mouth. He tightened his grip where it had landed on her hips, and worked his fingers just under the hem of her shirt, brushing the skin he found there.

Their path down the hallway to his bedroom proved remarkably difficult, considering they could barely keep their hands off of each other long enough to walk a straight line. Their clothes fell at various intervals along the way, and Casey had the vague impression that she may spontaneously combust into a gooey pile of lovesickness when Jake sat down on the bed and pulled her in between his legs. He pressed a kiss right above her belly button and looked up at her, his dark brown eyes practically glowing.

"Whatever you want, Casey, however you want it."

She doubted he even realized how perfect he was in that moment, letting her decide, letting her take control. It was why she had absolutely no problem pushing him backwards on the bed, and after one searing, searching kiss rolling them so that he pressed her down into his navy comforter. Arching up into him so that every part of her spine lifted off the bed, she felt wonderfully helpless when he pulled her hands from behind his neck so that they stretched above her.

Winding their fingers where he anchored them on the bed, he whispered into her ear how beautiful she was and how much he'd missed her, punctuating each word with a corresponding kiss or touch of his tongue against her neck and shoulders and lips. He bit down gently on her earlobe and she thought she might levitate off the mattress if not for his weight above her.

The throbbing cadence of her heart seemed to show up everywhere he touched her, to the point where she thought it must be stretched across every part of her skin. Because he was nothing if not thorough. The callouses on his hands pressed into her hips, across her breasts, along her waist, and with every pass of the roughened skin she felt her breath catch. She pressed her lips into the thick muscles of his shoulders, biting down more than once when the pressure he applied just crossed the threshold of being too hard. When they finally, finally came together, her breath left her lungs in a soft rush. With every rock of his hips she felt the slow, steady build spreading through her. And every cliche she'd ever read, the pinpricks of light behind her eyes, the detonation at her core, the explosion spreading to her fingers. All there.

Lots of pinpricks in lots of places besides behind her eyes and a really fricken big detonation that made her seriously question her ability to ever use her legs again. But even those things absolutely paled in comparison to the feeling that she got when Jake finally lifted his head from where he had buried it in her shoulder. He pressed a kiss to where her heart still thrashed with all the grace of a rabid bull.

"I love you too," he said simply.

She fought a smile. "You're just saying that because that was some really phenomenal sex."

His answering grin was unrepentant, a little smug and a whole lotta hot. His dimple popped out and she thought she may never leave his bed. "Phenomenal, huh?"

She nodded, pulling a stray piece of hair out of her mouth, how it got *there* was beyond her. "Life changing even."

"Life changing is good."

"Geez, are you just going to keep repeating everything I say?

He laughed and rolled to his back, dragging her with him so that she draped over his chest. She ran a finger under the defined line of his pectoral and then down along his side, smiling a little when he flinched away from the ticklish feeling. They laid like that until both of their hearts resumed their normal patterns.

"So," Casey started, almost hesitant to break the fantastic post-coital bubble going on, "you're okay to try this? Even though it's going to be hard when you leave?"

The heartbeat under her ear never faltered, just kept the rhythmic thumping while she waited for him to answer.

"We're not just going to try, Casey. We're gonna do it. And we'll get through it together."

Truly, she tried to bite down on the smile, but she just *couldn't*.

"I wish my parents could have met you," he said, dragging his hand up her back and settling it into the curve of her waist. She propped her chin on his chest so she could look at him. Despite the bittersweet statement, his face showed contentment, and she couldn't help but admire how good it looked on him.

"They totally would have loved me."

"They would have." She meant it to be funny, expecting him to smile at least, but his face was serious. "About a year before my Dad died, I remember overhearing my parents argue about something. I don't even remember what it was now. I asked him about it later, because I couldn't understand the concept of being angry at someone and still being able to love them. He told me that someday I'd meet a woman who probably wouldn't fit into any mold that I could imagine for myself, because the person who's most perfect for you won't just make you happy. They'll push you and challenge you, they'll keep you settled as much as they drive you crazy. But most of all, they'll make you the best version of yourself just by existing, just by being by your side." He closed his eyes and took a deep breath, tightening his arms as he let it out. "And honestly, until you, I didn't believe him that it could be like that. And I wish he could be here so I could tell him he was right."

Casey propped up on one elbow, giving him a soft kiss, lightly touching his tongue with hers before pulling back. She hoped Remy was set for the night at her place, because oh yeah, he wasn't going anywhere after that little speech. They were about to find out who was the stretchiest between the two of them. "You know, just when I think you can't say anything more perfect, you manage to surprise me."

"What can I say? I'm a wordsmith."

Shoulders shaking with laughter, she leaned down again to kiss him, completely unable to resist. "A *what*?"

"Wordsmith. Someone with a mastery of the English language."

"Ah," she said solemnly. "As long as you're my wordsmith, using that mastery only for me."

"All yours, trust me. You are all I can handle anyway."

She snuggled in to his side again, a smile stretching until she thought it might snap. "Perfect."

EPILOGUE

18 MONTHS LATER

SHE WAS GOING INSANE. Certifiably, padded room, strap her into a straight-jacket insane. The man was trying to kill her. Every parking space in the lot was full, American flags and yellow ribbons decorating most of the vehicles. She'd watched hundreds of families march inside with handmade signs and banners, all proclaiming their love for one of the soldiers returning. Maybe she was biased, but Ness's t-shirt had been her favorite. On the back, in blue and red letters was written 'You think Afghanistan was hot? Wait until we get home.'

But was Casey inside with everyone else watching the ceremony that would end with the beautiful chaos of hundreds of reuniting families?

Nope. Jake wanted her to wait outside. Because he decided that now was the moment that he would tap into the hidden wells of being overly dramatic that he had clearly not shown her until now. When he had called her from their demobilization in New Jersey, he said he didn't want to share that moment with anyone. He wanted just the two of them and clear, sunny American skies. Her Mom said it was romantic.

Blah, blah, blah. She just wanted her hands and lips on him

and her arms around him and even having to wait the extra minute it would take for him to run out of the gymnasium to find her seemed incredibly excessive.

Her hands tapped restlessly against her legs and then twined into the strings hanging from her cutoff jean shorts, pulling on the worn white strands. His deployment had been the longest eleven months of her life, waiting for him to come back to her. After forty seven handwritten letters, three hundred and thirty one emails, ten Skype chats (including one that ended with her modeling just her black boots, a few scraps of white lace and his extra set of dog tags), and eight monster care packages later, she was more than ready to have him back.

So was Remy. She'd been an acceptable substitute for Jake, stepping in for him in more ways than she cared to think about. And she didn't even want to get started on how she had started jogging just to keep Remy happy. Jogging. Yuck.

Okay, so her jog was really like a very fast walk. *But*, she still took him on a four mile loop at least three times a week. And on the plus side, she could probably bounce a quarter off her ass now. Hence the short denim shorts that were just a tad ambitious for the sixty-five degree April day.

She dropped her head back to stare up at the puffy white clouds that dotted the bright blue sky. Figuring that at least a minute had passed since she last looked, she flicked her eyes down to the Michael Kors watch Jake had bought her for Christmas. He'd been so adorably overwhelmed at the chaos of Christmas Eve at her parents' house. She breathed out heavily, even that memory not able to distract her for very long and slumped against the door of his truck. She still hated driving the big ol' thing, but he told her he absolutely refused to drive home in her 'tiny piece of Japanese metal'. Whatever.

In the moment of silence while she continued to wait, she whispered a prayer, thankful for Jake's safety and for the safe return of their entire company. It was just one of thousands of prayers that she'd said over the last year, but the knowledge that this time he was inside the brick walls just to her left made her eyes burn.

She quickly waved her hands in front of her face, that universal girl motion that somehow made the tears recede in order to save a face of carefully applied makeup.

The sharp pop of a metal door opening jerked her head up, snapping her spine off the black metal behind her.

Jake.

While the door swung shut behind him, she heard the roar of people in the gym. Shouts, laughter, all melding together in one giant chaotic noise of reunion. And maybe if she hadn't been looking at what she was looking at, she'd wish she could see it all unfold. But as it was, she wouldn't trade this for any view in the world.

Nothing, *nothing*, could be better than this.

He stopped just outside the closed door, looking about as amazingly, perfectly gorgeous as possible in his ACU's. Every alpha male fantasy she could have possibly conjured, just standing right in front of her. They smiled at the exact same time, and then he was in motion. His long legs pounded the last remaining feet to her, and she leapt into his outstretched arms. From where she had wrapped herself around his neck, she felt every ounce of relief that was expelled in the air that left his lungs in a rush. She pushed her nose into his neck, whimpered at the perfectness of his smell, and thought that her skin might actually be vibrating from how happy she was.

He pulled back, and she barely managed to release her grip to lean back and look at him.

"Hi," she said, grinning as he slowly set her back onto her feet. He cupped the sides of her face, then softly brushed his lips against hers. The tenderness wasn't what she expected after such a long separation, and she buried her face in his shoulder to try and regain control of her riotous emotions. He smoothed a hand down her hair and then gently tugged back on it until he could see her face again. He pinched his brows together, and dipped his head to kiss her again, then pulled back before their lips touched. Pfft, tease.

"What is it?" she asked, thinking he would have said something by now. He just shook his head, locking his eyes onto hers with such an intensity that it left her feeling dizzy. "Jake, are you okay?"

"I think you should marry me." After only hearing his deep voice through a computer or a phone for so long, the sound of the real thing was so potent that it actually took a second for the sentence to register. Then her jaw dropped and her hands fell to her sides.

"What?" she said weakly, feeling her heart slip into palpitations that echoed the what-the-frick-is-happening chant going through her skull. And then he sank down onto one knee in front of her and everything, her heart, her brain, it all stopped. Because nothing in her could do or see anything except him. He grabbed hold of one suddenly cold hand and stared up at her.

"I don't have a ring, because I honest to God did not plan to do this here, but Casey, if this last year and a half has shown me anything, it's that I love you so much and I cannot imagine going even one step further without knowing that for the rest of my life, you promise to be next to me. And even though the guys are barely afraid of me anymore because they said you pussified me, I don't care." He shook his head, grinning while she laughed through her shaky exhale. "You have made me so much better and so much happier than I ever thought possible. And you have given me a family, your family and I never thought I would have that again. You have given me everything, Casey. So please, I would be more honored than I could ever put into words if you would agree to be my wife." He kissed the knuckle of her ring finger, eyes never leaving her suddenly overflowing ones. "Will you marry me?"

She barely registered her "Yes." It came out on a sob, because she was so riveted by the sight of his broad shoulders sagging in relief and the way he leaned his head into her suddenly weak legs. Still, after almost two years of being with him, the sight of him like this yanked every ounce of breath from her lungs.

The sight of this handsome, strong, good-to-the-absolute-core man on his knees in front her still humbled her. Any dream she had growing up and finding the man she loved was nowhere even close to how the reality stacked up. She still didn't know what she'd done to be worthy of his love, but she sure wasn't going to question it, just keep loving him in the way that he so richly deserved.

She started to lean down to give him his long-overdue welcome home kiss, when he pulled back and stared at her shoes. Uh oh.

"Casey," he said in a warning tone. "Why are you wearing the American flag on your feet?"

She scoffed. "In case you didn't know, this is a pretty big occasion. It's not every day your soldier boyfriend slash fiancé comes home from almost a year in Afghanistan." And the four inch platform heels decorated in the good ol' stars and stripes were just the kind of patriotic gear she could get behind.

He unfolded from his perch on the ground, looking at her with a mix of mock consternation and blatant affection. "So, this is you doing your patriotic duty, huh?"

The heels boosted her height so that she only had to tilt her chin to kiss under his jaw, and she hummed in agreement. He clenched his fists where he held them around her waist, gripping the cotton of her white shirt, and she knew she had him. Finally, he leaned in and slanted a hard kiss over her mouth, claiming every inch of it the way she had been dying for him to do. She sighed into his mouth, every part of her body melting into him she was so heavy with happiness.

"Plus," she said, voice breathy when she pulled back. "I thought I could wear them for you. You know, *later*."

"Yeah?"

"Yeah."

"Well, God bless America."

She laughed and pressed another kiss to his lips. "Hold that thought soldier, you know my Mom has about fifty people and four tons of food waiting for you at their house. That party is the only reason she didn't throw a complete mutiny at the fact that you wanted it to just be me here today. You know we'll have to stay for at least a couple hours before any 'God bless America' happens."

He growled into her hair, sending little sparking vibrations down her spine. "I guess I can do that, considering your Mom sent some pretty kick ass care packages. She won the hearts of every guy in my unit with those homemade cookies. Stockton told me he might divorce Ness if it meant he could marry your Mom."

She drew back and arched a brow. "Are you saying her care packages were better than mine?"

He shook his head, dropping a kiss on her nose. "There is no right way for me to answer that question, so I respectfully plead the fifth."

Dang it. She and her Mom had an unofficial competition of who could send him better stuff. She figured she had it in the bag since she sent him a few tastefully risqué pictures. He grinned, seeing the way she pouted at his answer.

"See now, you stick that lip out there like that and we'll never make it to your parents. I'll share you for two hours and then you're mine for the rest of the night."

"Jake," she said on a sigh, then held out her hand for him and smiled when he took it, weaving their fingers together. "I'm yours forever. Now let's go home."

THE END

If you enjoyed *By Your Side*, check out the second book in the Three Little Words series, Light Me Up which features Rachel and Tate.

If you'd be so kind, please consider writing a review of this book on Amazon, Goodreads, Barnes & Noble, or iBooks. Indie authors depend on thoughtful and honest reviews to spread the word about their books. And if you finish your review, shoot me an email at ksorensenbooks@gmail.com with the link, and I'll send you a little goodie from *By Your Side*.

ACKNOWLEDGMENTS

Without the support of my husband, there is no way I could have done this. He patiently answered many "guy questions" that I probably should have known, allowed me to retreat to my laptop most nights without complaint, and talked about Jake and Casey more than he'd probably like to admit. He always believed that this was something I could do. That kind of support is rare, and I fully recognize how blessed I am to have it.

My parents, who instilled and nurtured my insatiable love of reading and raised me with the knowledge that they were proud of me no matter what I did.

To my sister Renee, and to Sarah, Keri and Rebekah for not laughing at me when I first told them I wanted to do this almost three years ago, I don't know if you guys know how much that meant to me.

Kristan Higgins, one of my absolute favorite authors, who took the time to write me a few kind words after my fan-girl email. Your response, so many months ago, is what rekindled the spark I needed to finish this. I hope to be as funny, generous, and kind with my readers as you are with yours. You gave me advice, and book recommendations, and honest feedback that was incredibly helpful. I can never repay you for all that you've done for me. Thank you so very much.

My very first beta reader, Danielle Stringer. Your offer to do this was so humbling and exciting and helpful. I'm glad we're stuck together as wives of those two crazy boys.

Jade Eby for formatting the crap out of this and making it all shiny and pretty. I can't wait to meet you in April.

Najla Qamber Designs for creating the absolute perfect cover. You're so freaking talented!

Leanne Jansen, MA, LLPC, for making sure Casey stayed consistent.

Major Ryan Senn of the Michigan National Guard (former Army Ranger and all around bad ass), for letting me pick his brain about the type of life Jake might lead.

Officer Dave Huizinga of the Grandville Police Department for reading that chapter so freaking long ago that was so horrible that I cringe thinking about it now. You marked the crap out of it in red, and it was so much better for it. Any errors in the above regards are mine alone.

Whitney Barbetti- Even though I didn't meet you until I was halfway through my second book, you more than earned a place in these acknowledgments. You did line edits for me when you have about a bajillion other things to do, and you have been somewhat of a fairy godmother to me throughout this process. I don't know what I'd do with your hand holding, your insane OCD when making teasers (NO ORPHANS OR WIDOWS), and your amazing, came-out-of-nowhere friendship. Your level of talent is incredibly inspiring to me, even though you hate plotting and that makes me sad. You're so baseballs.

Katrina Kirkpatrick- the best critique partner that has *ever* existed. You, my friend, were an answer to prayer. Your insight is invaluable to me. You make me laugh *every single day*, you understood me from day one and held me accountable to keep writing when the middle of this book (and pregnancy nausea and moving and having a second baby and raging self-doubt) threatened to derail me. I know without a shadow of a doubt that I would not have finished this book without you. THANK YOU. I can't wait to see you conquer the world with your beautiful writing this year.

And Katrina gets double thanks for introducing to me to my first group of 'author friends' in Brenda Rothert and Stephanie Reid (my second beta reader who made this book so much better with her incredibly detailed and thoughtful feedback). I truly have the best writing cheerleaders *ever*.

And last, but never, ever least...God; the Alpha, Omega and ultimate source of creativity. Thank You for every word and comma and period of this book and everything that might come after it. You've blessed me so incredibly in this life, any success I might have is just the cherry on top.

ABOUT THE AUTHOR

Karla Sorensen has been an avid reader her entire life, preferring stories with a happily-ever-after over just about any other kind. And considering she has an entire line item in her budget for books, she realized it might just be cheaper to write her own stories. She still keeps her toes in the world of health care marketing, where she made her living pre-babies. Now she stays home, writing and mommy-ing full time (this translates to almost every day being a 'pajama day' at the Sorensen household...don't judge). She lives in West Michigan with her husband, two exceptionally adorable sons, and big, shaggy rescue dog.

Find Karla online:
karlasorensen.com
ksorensenbooks@gmail.com

OTHER BOOKS BY KARLA SORENSEN

Washington Wolves

The Bombshell Effect (Luke and Allie's story)

Amazon

The Ex-Effect (Ava and Matthew's story)

Amazon

The Three Little Words Series

By Your Side

Amazon

Light Me Up

Amazon

Tell Them Lies

Amazon

The Bachelors of the Ridge Series

Dylan

Amazon

Garrett

Amazon

Cole

Amazon

Michael

Amazon

Tristan

Amazon

Standalone title

Hooked: A dark romantic comedy co-written with Whitney Barbetti

Amazon Universal Link

Stay up to date on Karla's upcoming releases!

Subscribe to her newsletter

BACHELORS OF THE RIDGE SERIES

Dylan

Garrett (book two) will release in the late fall/early winter of 2016, followed by Cole, Michael and then Tristan in 2017.

For exclusive teasers, content and giveaways, join Karla's Facebook reader group,
The Sorensen Sorority

Made in the USA
Monee, IL
17 April 2023

31982307R00194